W9-BYL-497

PRIVATE ALTARS

DISCARDED

184

PRIVATE

■

ALTARS

Katherine Mosby

RANDOM HOUSE • NEW YORK

MIDDLETOWN THRALL LIBRARY
11-19 DEPOT STREET
MIDDLETOWN, NY 10940
(914) 341-5454

Copyright © 1995 by Katherine Mosby

All rights reserved under International and Pan-American Copyright
Conventions.
Published in the United States by Random House, Inc., New York, and
simultaneously in Canada by Random House of Canada Limited,
Toronto.

Library of Congress Cataloging-in-Publication Data
Mosby, Katherine.
Private altars / Katherine Mosby. — 1st ed.
p.   cm.
ISBN 0-679-42896-8
I. Title.
PS3563.O88384P75   1995
813'.54—dc20   94-17412

Manufactured in the United States of America on acid-free paper.
98765432
First Edition

For Sterett

Is it, in Heav'n, a crime to love too well?
To bear too tender, or too firm a heart,
To act a lover's or a Roman's part?
Is there no bright reversion in the sky,
For those who greatly think, or bravely die?

—Alexander Pope, "Elegy to the Memory of
an Unfortunate Lady"

PRIVATE ALTARS

1

―■―

$\mathcal{T}$HERE HAD BEEN nothing portentous about that day in June, nothing which might have heralded what was to follow: no lunar eclipse, no unexplained lightning or shadows falling to the wrong side. Birds punctuated the sky, dipping and flaring their fanned wings in no way that augured anything out of the ordinary. There was, in fact, nothing remarkable about the day but the unrelenting heat adding gravity to air already weighted with the promise of rain.

But Addison had been warned. He was told things he didn't believe. They said the wisteria, which hung along the kitchen wall in plaits as thick as Rapunzel's braid, had bloomed twice the summer Vienna Daniels came to Winsville, bigger blossoms than the town had ever seen, purple as the flesh of mulberries, though she didn't know a blessed thing about gardening, and thought they were lilacs wrestling their way up to surround the attic window.

Then she painted the barn blue. She had walked into Henshaw's Hardware asking for paint the color of lapis lazuli. It took Henshaw five questions and four people to find out what lapis lazuli was—and then for a barn. And when her husband, Willard Daniels, refused to let the workmen paint the barn blue, she did it herself, or at least part of it, one whole side before she gave up painting on a ladder in a silk dress with her hair tied up in a patterned handkerchief like a kitchen maid.

She let the horse that Willard gave her but which she wouldn't ride follow her into town—before she stopped coming to town—where she bought it treats from Duffield's bakery. The horse would stand around, untethered, sighing through huge, flared nostrils, shifting its weight from foot to foot, until she finished her errands and collected the mail. Then it would shamble after her, in a lazy, bored way, never quite by her side, but never falling too far behind.

But more amazing still, Addison heard that she had tried to kill her husband, and that she spoke in tongues with the devil, and, when the moon was full, she bathed outdoors in a tin tub, drawing down the celestial luminosity to her skin. She was a socialist or a communist, Addison couldn't remember which, but the difference didn't amount to a boll weevil's bite anyhow, because neither one was a word you wanted on your back. She was a nigger-lover too, and she smoked cigarettes. They said that was what happened when you read too many books: it made your brain go soft, and Addison imagined this as the spongy texture of wood mushrooms or soggy crackers. She had thousands of books, they said.

Addison was awestruck. For almost a year before his move to Winsville, he had suspected his own soul was possessed by demons, which made it difficult for him to sleep at night, which filled his mouth with cusswords, made him restless and uneasy, bored by the sermons his mother and uncles preached from the back of a wagon to the unrepentant populace of towns within a ten-mile radius of their farm in Kentucky.

He had stopped reading the Bible altogether, except for the Song of Songs, which he read at night, thrilling himself in a way that he knew was heading him for a hell he would share with raging heathens. Moreover, he had recently been overcome by a passion for fiction. The same helpless way his cousin Nat, who had tapeworms, would eat in a compulsive fury to sate a hunger that was constant, he had read the four pulp novels he had stolen from the lending library over and over until the pages pulled out in his hand. The yellow edges of paper crumbled and disappeared as if he had absorbed them by osmosis, like the cadences of entire paragraphs that filled his head, inspiring him with possibilities more dazzling than any of those which had presented themselves in Alford, Kentucky.

And then there was Willa, Vienna Daniels' daughter, who, they said, could spit farther and run faster than any girl ought to. Willa did not seem to be fashioned from the same clay as the people Addison had known in Alford. Both Willa and Elliott embodied attributes Addison lacked and therefore admired to excess. They enjoyed a natural grace he knew he never would possess.

They did not seem to belong to the land in the same way he did: his large bones weighed him, with each lumbering footstep, to the earth. Willa especially seemed to hover with the energy of interrupted flight, like a human hummingbird, as if movement were her natural state, and stillness was produced only by great effort. Her features were fragile, and, like the finery of certain churches his mother called vainglorious, seemed to Addison all the more awesome for their impractical delicacy, so unlike the crudely hewn planes of his own face, whittled into recognizable humanity like the head of a walking stick. Willa's beauty was baffling and subtle: as evident as it was when her face was animated, so was it absent in repose, when her small, even features became indistinguishable from those of any number of pale and pretty girls.

The family called "the Daniels"—because no one was inclined to squander an extra syllable on a name already ending in s—elicited in Addison the need for language more extravagant than his meager vocabulary could muster. He could not later explain what exactly had made the first encounter with the Daniels seminal, but he would remember the way the light had dappled through the overhanging boughs of the plane trees, the shifting leaves stippling the path with that same kind of luminance he felt within him, exhilarating and elusive.

IT WAS THE fifth day of his first summer with his father. He had come from the Kentucky farm to which his mother had carried him as an infant when she left his father eleven years before. But when the cows came down with anthrax and his mother and uncle died, the family lost the farm.

Everything had been sold, even the dogs that had run through the dusty rooms following Addison, even his mother's toiletries, even his jackknife and St. Christopher medal. "It's too bad about the medal," his aunt had said, as she pressed her Bible into his hands. Then she had dabbed her handkerchief on her tongue and rubbed a smudge from his cheek. Clasping him awkwardly against her bulk one final time, she said, "You just remember this: our comedown was God's work and not Mr. Hoover's and you still have more than some who don't have another home to go to, so you keep your head up, hear?" Addison had then been handed over to the brakeman on a freight train who had agreed, as a favor to Aunt Gilly, to put Addison down in Winsville. His father, she had explained, could take care of him.

Thus it was that on the fifth day of his first summer with his father he had wandered on the Daniels property, which lay adjacent to his father's land, and had at one time included it. He knew enough to stay away from the great house, for even in those few days he had heard from the other children enough to know important things about The Heights: that it was a godless house, that there was a madwoman, that they didn't mix with townsfolk, and they bought their goods with hard cash.

He had also found out that they had more untilled land than anyone else in the county, which meant that they would have good hunting, a theory which was confirmed by the warnings to trespassers and poachers written in thick, hasty letters, illustrated by clumsy depictions of a skull and crossbones.

But Addison Aimes was eleven. He did not discern how childish the warnings were, how relatively low to the ground the signs were posted, or that they had been made out of bits of wood torn from produce crates, very much like the boxes his father used to ship apples, and consequently he was impressed. A sense of danger added considerably to the lure of wandering onto the Daniels' property, and moreover what he had heard made it impossible to stay away—not just what he had heard *about* The Heights, but what he heard *from* The Heights. In the evenings for example, there was, usually at about dusk, a carillon of calls: first, the even, three-beat intervals "*El*-li-ot," and then, later, out of the darkness, "Willa?" "Willa?" interrogative as the song of a thrush.

There were also the occasional shrieks of laughter the wind would carry, or the ethereal notes of piano music that he could hear sweeping out of their windows in a rush, with tatters of yellow curtains fluttering as if to follow, half out in the night air, twisting at the oversized French windows that were thrown open like a pair of arms unable to contain the fullness of such strange beauty.

And on his second night he had heard their gramophone

(no one he knew in Alford, Kentucky, had one) playing some kind of jazzy ragtime tune, raucous and wild as a roadhouse, redolent of the dangers his mother had tried to warn him about.

At first, his plan had been to poach from their property by stringing up traps in some of the wooded areas and if he had any luck, to sell the game in the colored part of town and use the money to buy himself another jackknife. But two things interfered with that plan.

One was the sense of guilt he was beginning to feel as his fascination with the Daniels grew, based on the disapproving awe with which the town of Winsville regarded them. To this local lore was added his father's own reticent admiration for Vienna Daniels, about whom Mr. Aimes would answer no questions nor countenance disrespect.

The other form of interference came from the Daniels children themselves. They must have noticed him on their land or perhaps he had left the rail down in one of the rotted stretches of fencing, where he entered. Maybe they spotted the footprints in the moist earth by the brook or saw where the ivy was crumpled where he had lain under a shade tree to listen to the profusion of birds calling brazenly in their untested sanctuary. Or maybe they had just read his mind or smelled his scent, the way Indians were said to do.

But they knew he'd been on their land and they knew where. On the fifth day of his first summer in Winsville he had taken his father's bicycle into town to do his errands. But before he returned to his father's house, to the prim austerity of a solitary old man, he had turned down the path that led onto the Daniels property. He had laid the bicycle on its side with the wheels still spinning and walked away from its whining buzz toward the laughter he heard coming from a thicket.

2

WILLA AND ELLIOTT had been preparing for this encounter for two days. It had been Elliott who had first noticed signs of an intruder when he went on his rounds to the nests. But it had been Willa who decided what they would do. Elliott had been so worried about possible harm to his animals that he considered sleeping in the barn, where the "orphans" lived: wounded animals he had found and brought home to heal; chicks that had fallen from a nest or been abandoned, strays, deformed or rejected specimens of wildlife that he named and loved.

There too, Elliott kept his personal library, consisting almost exclusively of books on the forms of fauna indigenous to the county: books on how to domesticate wildlife, books on the history of a particular species, or—the most dog-eared—the animal tales he read out loud to his menagerie, changing unhappy endings. He also kept a notebook in which he recorded, in code, his observations of nature and his progress in learning to speak the language of the birds.

Elliott's fear of poachers was not unjustified: the year before, a tramp had camped out on the west end of their property and had killed three pheasants, a wild turkey, and a brace of quail before Vienna had called one of the boys from the sheriff's office to come to The Heights and run the tramp out of town. Even then, her interests were not in preventing poaching; she had refused to press charges against the man, saying he was welcome to whatever he needed to fill an empty stomach, but he could not stay. He had been careless about the campfire, she said. He had left a site smoldering, and it was just luck that she had found it before the wind did.

The problem this time, though, was not one in which they could enlist Vienna as an ally. On the contrary, Vienna often encouraged them to let town children fish or swim in the creek or play their games in the fields; she pulled down the warning signs whenever she found them, which was rare, as she did not often venture into the remote corners they favored. Sister, too, chided them "not to make matters worse" with the town.

Sister's caveat, often issued, that "it was just not *natural—* children staying so much to themselves" would flutter to the surface of Vienna's consciousness, tormenting her like a piece of rubbish caught in the vortex of a wind which wound it round and round but was insufficient to carry it away. Then the familiar shame Vienna fought, in a struggle as invisible and constant as the pull of the tide, would well inside her and its heat would rise on her throat in mottled reds, and she would wonder if indeed she had communicated the disease of alienation to her children.

Sister had asked them to go over to Mr. Aimes's farm the day after Addison arrived, to welcome him with a date-nut cake, a gesture that used their sugar allowance for the week. So to the children Sister's views were clear. But Willa's views were more compelling: they ate the cake themselves while they discussed, at length, in the barn, the most effective methods to punish "the outrage that Addison had visited upon them," as Willa had put it, in language she borrowed from a religious pamphlet Miss Margayt had given her to discourage her from taking the Lord's name in vain.

The first idea that appealed to them was an ambush, but not knowing when the next "trespass" would occur, they would have to devote themselves to the tedium of keeping watch. Finally they evolved a plan: they would construct a booby trap that would catapult cow dung at Addison when he crossed the fence that divided his land and theirs.

Willa loved it. She clapped her sticky hands and whooped and threw straw up in the air and frightened the barn swallows roosting on a crossbeam above them. Elliott was more sober. He was often torn between the irresistible nature of Willa's enthusiasm and the anxiousness it so frequently occasioned in him: exploits seemed to be punished in degree proportional to the amount of excitement with which they had been created. And then, of course, he objected to her frightening his birds.

"But how?" he said, turning his face up earnestly toward the perch Willa had taken on a bale of hay. His glasses were badly smeared and he wiped his sleeve ineffectually across them. "That's your department," Willa said. "I mean, I can't figure *everything* out, you know." Elliott's face looked crestfallen. "But I have some ideas to start with," she added. "What we need is some kind of contraption to fling the cow pies . . . maybe a lever, maybe a way of hooking up a shovel like a seesaw," she said, as she ransacked the shed that was built into a corner of the barn, tossing down cutting shears, hoes, rusted clippers, and the broken handle of a broom.

"Don't make a mess," Elliott cautioned nervously, shifting his weight from foot to foot. Willa, who was now crouching over a box of assorted odds and ends, looked at him over her shoulder and squinted. "Stop *jiggling* or I won't let you in on this. Now I'm going to need the wagon and some yarn and a smoke if you can scrounge one for me off of Mackie."

"I thought you said this was *my* department," Elliott replied, as he turned to do her errands.

Willa was filling their dilapidated child's wagon with assorted tools when Elliott, who had gone to find the yarn, came running up to her. He said, panting as he caught his breath, that Sister wanted them both at the house and from the sounds of it they were in a heap of trouble and also they had better hide the wagon because if Vienna found it she would want to know what they were up to.

Addison was in one of their sycamores, straddling a limb with his body draped lazily around the branch, when he saw Elliott run by. He waited in the tree until dusk, hoping one of the Daniels would come back, or perhaps that he'd hear the piano again. Abruptly, the lulling sounds of the tree were pierced by an argument, though the words were indistinct. He could hear the sounds of doors slamming and something breaking, wailing and shouts and a few discernible curse words followed by dissonant chords on the piano, as if the keyboard was fighting too, shattering notes into sheer noise, then, from his father's farm, the dull report of a gun, and the echo, diminishing over distance. The combination of sounds made the hairs on Addison's arms freeze.

He slid down the tree and started to run home, stumbling on the uneven field, when he saw a thin figure with blond hair pulled back into a disheveled braid, wearing only a worn cotton nightgown through which he could see the outlines of a woman's slender body, the sharp jut of her hipbone, and a long length of leg moving beneath it. She was wandering out in the pasture where the horse grazed.

He knew without a moment's hesitation that she must be Vienna Daniels, Elliott and Willa's mother, the madwoman about whom he had heard so many strange stories. She was humming, hugging herself and hunching her shoulders forward. She turned and looked in his direction without seeing him, focusing on something at the horizon. Her face had the stamp of character intelligence sometimes bestows, and the look of ruined beauty.

Addison was so riveted by her presence that he backed straight into Mackie, a town boy of not more than seventeen who had recently been hired to tend to the property: repair some of the fencing, groom the horse, cut firewood, do odd jobs. Mackie was standing, almost hidden, in the shadow of a maple tree near the stable, one hand on his hip, the other cupping the tiny glow of a cigarette, watching. He winked at Addison and put his finger to his lips, jerking his head toward Vienna's back. Addison stood beside him for several minutes, watching the woman move erratically through the field toward the horse, which plodded affectionately up to her. She stood there barefoot, her arms around the horse's great neck, her face pressed into its dusty hide, clinging to it as if it were holding her up.

Addison could feel the heat from Mackie's body like a magnetic field that bound them together, insulated them in the shameful secret of someone else's pain. So he turned and ran through the woods that separated him from his father's farm, not caring that the underbrush scratched his bare legs, and that he would be covered with burrs and bruises by the time he got to his father's porch.

HIS FATHER WAS sitting in a wooden rocker, cleaning a woodcock, methodically ripping the feathers away from the stillwarm flesh. A breeze stirred the Indian grass and lifted the feathers that drifted to his feet, floating them in the air like milkweed, the soft down sifting in invisible currents like summer snow. Mr. Aimes looked up at his son and held his eye for almost a minute before he said, "What's bothering you? Your eyes are bugged out like a stomped tree frog."

"I just come from the other side of the pasture and I heard—"

"You heard a family sorting out their differences," his father cut in. "There's no news in that."

Addison tried again, wanting something from his father that he couldn't name but which would prove that he was kin, something which would identify him as the figure of those inflated fantasies that had nourished him through the lean years at his uncle's farm, changing each year to accommodate Addison's developing ideals.

"But *she* was out—the crazy woman."

Mr. Aimes's hands stopped tearing at the bird, but he didn't look up. "Vienna Daniels is not crazy, she's just different. Folks have no kind of tolerance for that. You'd be wise to learn to weigh the circumstance instead of judging the person."

Then Mr. Aimes shifted his weight and spat over the side of the porch railing as if to indicate that was all he had to say. Though he was determined to be a kind and instructive presence for his son, he was surprised by his own indifference to the boy.

The keen sense of loss he had felt years before, when his wife had taken Addison and twenty dollars in cash and left to devote herself to a religion that had claimed her with the suddenness and passion of a fever, had been gradually replaced with a pervasive disappointment by which he felt ennobled, and with which he held himself aloof from further pain. Then too, he had been shocked by how much Addison resembled his wife, while he found no trace of himself in his son. Images long since banished returned to him: he remembered the greasy breakfast plates uncleared on the table, the congealed food swarming with ants, wet baby clothes still sagging on the clothesline, the windows smeared with red lipstick crosses.

Inside, at the kitchen table, a place had been set for Addison. Hegemony, the girl who cooked and cleaned for Mr. Aimes, was sewing while she waited to prepare the woodcock Mr. Aimes was cleaning, her last task before she could begin the long walk home to the colored section of Winsville.

"What's shook you up so?" she asked, as she put down her sewing to brush his hair back behind his ears and pick a burr off his collar. She felt sorry for the funny-looking boy, all elbows and awkwardness, whose auntie had sent him to live in this dreary house with only Mr. Aimes for company, who spoke with such an awful twang that even some of the adults in Winsville had laughed, and who said *ma'am* to her, even though she was colored and worked for his father.

"Nuthing, ma'am," he had said, twisting away from the comfort she was offering with her outstretched arms, though he wanted it as badly as he feared that, if he accepted it, he might never pull himself back from the loss of his dogs, his mother, from the way the unfamiliar had engulfed him without warning.

"Don't fret yourself or you'll get a case of indigestion." Addison didn't answer.

"Then how about a glass of sweet milk?"

"No, ma'am, I don't drink milk no more."

"Then suit yourself. Dinner will be on soon enough," Hegemony said, picking up her sewing and whistling through the gap a missing tooth left in her mouth.

That night, after a silent supper with his father, Addison climbed the ladder to his bunk bed and lay on the lumpy mattress, looking at the knots in the wooden rafters, thinking about the Daniels. He had kept to himself the next day, wandering in the orchards of his father's apple farm and wondering, among other things, if the alleys between the trees were what his mother had meant when she had referred to "the straight and narrow" being the "apple of God's eye."

But on the fifth day of his first summer in Winsville, when Addison returned to the Daniels property he returned with the renewed interest of one who has made the necessary gesture of detachment before abandoning himself to a vice.

He could not have anticipated the way circumstance contrived against him; he did not know the punishment the Daniels children had had was on his behalf, because of a cake he would have found dry and gritty. So he could not have imagined the way Elliott and Willa had agreed, in the emotional inflation that follows and seems to compensate for certain kinds of abuses, that Addison Aimes was to be despised for ever after. He was to be, moreover, the focus and fulcrum of their desire for revenge in a blind discrimination that held him responsible not only for recent humiliations, but for all the indignities, real and imagined, petty and profound, of their current life.

Their vendetta focused them: they were filled with the pleasure of purpose, which inspired Elliott to create a catapult out of an old mousetrap Willa had found at the dump. The trajectory, however, even when the metal wing of a toy airplane was sacrificed to act as a lever, seesawing over a spool of thread, was not high enough to suit Willa. She spent hours squatting beside Elliott while they tried to develop a more effective "flinging-machine." Willa had decided, both because the mousetrap was too small and delicate to hoist cow dung through the air, and because it had occurred to her that the insult could be further refined, that the substance to assault Addison would have to be human.

Naturally, it fell to Elliott to provide even this: the ammunition. "Oh now don't be such a priss," Willa had cajoled, "I mean, you're the one who goes around collecting droppings and dingleberries all over the place."

"But that's different. That's scientific. I use books, guidebooks, and anyhow it's research."

"It's disgusting."

"It is not."

"Then what's the big deal? Huh? Just go, or else he'll come and we won't be ready and it'll be your fault for fussing."

Elliott did not say anything for a moment but he looked as if he were weighing his options and evaluating the logic of Willa's argument. Elliott, whose precocity had announced itself in full sentences when he was barely a year old, had shown from the start a temperamental inclination toward logic. Elliott liked inevitable conclusions; no matter how harsh or cold, they provided at least the comfort of something absolute, something definite. He pointed his elbow out in front of himself in order to examine a scab and pressed his lips together. He had not yet learned about sophistry.

"If it's no big deal, how come you don't do it yourself?"

"Simple. I don't have to *go* right now."

"Well, neither do I."

"Come on. It's easier for you to go than for me because you're a boy."

"That's only for pee-pee."

"No. It's for both."

"How do you know?"

"Elliott, I know lots of things that you don't know because I'm older. Now, for godsake, are you going to argue all day?"

Elliott walked a loose circle around the wagon, kicking up dirt with his toes. His hands were thrust into his pockets and his head bent down from the thin stem of his neck like a dandelion that has been picked and is beginning to wilt.

"O.K.," he said abruptly. He walked to an outcropping of rocks, luxuriantly overgrown with the lush leafage that springs up wherever the plow cannot reach, pulled down his overalls and squatted expectantly.

Willa crossed her arms on her chest and walked over to

coach him. His small face was concentrated with purpose and his lips were pursed tightly. His body, fragile and pale in the sun, seemed, as it sagged from his clasped knees, like an old man's. "That's it," Willa encouraged, as if he were embarking on a dangerous experiment.

"Willa," Elliott said quietly, "nothing's happening."

"You're not really trying."

"I *am* so."

"Well try harder," Willa insisted. "Make noise."

So, obediently, Elliott screwed himself into a little knot and squawked out some grunts. Willa started laughing.

"No, like this," she gasped, trying to demonstrate despite the hilarity which choked her. Elliott's bony frame started to shake with laughter too, until he was no longer able to keep the balance of his squat and tipped over. Willa shrieked with renewed delight, and collapsed beside him on the grass. Their mirth was contagious and complete. They clutched their sides. They threw clumps of grass at each other and managed to keep the hysterics going by emitting an appropriately scatological grunt or groan as soon as the laughter began to subside. Finally they lay on their backs, chests heaving, trying to catch their breath. Willa's hand idly pulled up blades of grass. Elliott turned onto his stomach and put his hand above his eyes; the sun was strong and his eyes were sensitive.

"Do you think we'll get arrested?" he asked. Willa twirled a blade of grass and thought for a minute.

"How will anyone know we did it?"

"Maybe they can tell about doodie; maybe it's like fingerprints."

Willa was silent. She was thinking about how Joseph, who worked at the train station carrying things, had been arrested for spitting at a white man. And that was only saliva. It had been pretty serious, though. He was taken to Bantanburg, where there was a courthouse and a bigger jail and a movie palace.

"Well, Elliott," she said, "I don't think we have any choice. We have to protect The Heights and your animals, don't forget, and the family name. And if we get caught, then we'll have to make a run for it and go someplace great, like New Orleans."

"But what about the animals?"

"We'll bring them with us."

She herself didn't much like Elliott's birds. She thought they were stupid, though she admired the way Elliott could imitate their calls, which were sometimes quite beautiful. His animals were even harder to love—a motley assortment of strays with scabs and bald spots or missing limbs or runny eyes—but he would never leave without them. Willa sprang to her feet and dusted herself off. "Stay here," she said as she started up toward the house.

When she returned she was struggling with a huge hamper filled with mayonnaise sandwiches and corn biscuits already hardened since breakfast, a thermos of cold coffee, a book and a cigarette, a pad of paper, a pencil, and a straw hat.

"Provisions," she said as she set the hamper down with a thud. "I'm going to make a list of the things we should pack up, just in case, while you eat these," she said, waving a hand over the sandwiches. She pulled out one for herself and propped the pad against her knees. "Here," she said, as she tossed Elliott the hat.

Elliott ambled over to the hamper.

"Does Fayette know you took these?"

"As a matter of fact, Fayette," she said, dragging the name out, "gave me permission *herself*."

"You didn't put on enough mayonnaise," Elliott commented, holding a sandwich in one hand and settling the straw hat on his head with the other.

"Just eat," Willa said, impatiently.

When she had finished her sandwich and Elliott had eaten his there were still two left.

"Elliott, finish those up."

"I can't. I'm full."

"That doesn't matter."

"I'm going back to practice now."

"You can practice the piano later. We have to prepare the mousetrap. And you have to keep eating until it comes out."

Elliott picked up a wilted sandwich and considered it carefully. He took another two bites. "This is giving me a stomachache."

"No it isn't. Just eat, for Christsake."

Elliott didn't respond, so Willa countered with a ploy she had watched Fayette use countless times: "C'mon, just one more bite. One more for me."

Elliott squeezed the remaining sandwich into a wad and threw it into the woods.

"I'm going to let a hungry animal eat it."

"Oh honestly, Elliott, you make me sick," Willa said, pulling the cigarette from behind her ear and rummaging in the hamper for matches.

"I'm going to tell on you, smoking. You heard what Fayette said about children smoking: 'white trash, white trash, white trash,' " Elliott repeated in a singsong voice, hopping away holding his right foot behind him.

"I'm not a child. I'm nine and a half years old. Marlene Overby is not thirteen and she's got a baby."

"The Overbys don't have cash, they is white trash, white trash, white trash," Elliott sang from several yards off.

"Just shut up!" Willa screamed, throwing her book at him.

Elliott darted off into the thicket and the book fell wide of him by several feet. Willa pushed her hair back behind her ears and replaced the cigarette in the hamper. She scrambled on all fours over to where the book had landed, then threw herself back into the shade under the tree and examined the book. Several of the pages had been creased, so she sat patiently unfolding each bent corner, muttering "stupid" quietly to herself before beginning to read.

3

———■———

*I*T WAS HER mother's book. Willa lay in the cool prickle of the grass and looked for a long time at her mother's signature in the front. The handwriting was elegant and precise, stark and angular like Vienna's high cheekbones and tapered fingers. The inscription read: New York, 1925. That was the last year of Vienna's other life, before she came to Winsville.

It amazed her to think of her mother having ever been other than she was now. Now that summer was upon them and their daily lessons with her were suspended, Vienna stayed in her nightgown in her attic room with her books and papers, emerging only for the tall glasses of bergamot tea and sweet crackers that sustained her through the day, or to give Elliott a piano lesson or help Willa with her Latin exercises. There were the occasional strange stories Vienna told with confusing urgency; like parables they were simple, but the stirring images often left Willa wistful and distracted, and she would remember later certain words or phrases that haunted her and seemed to contain the essence of her mother's singularity. It wasn't anything as easy to notice as Vienna's unique pronunciation, the way she shaped her words with a Northern breath, the staccato legacy of another origin. It had to do with the way she wove those words together so that they flew like sparks from a blacksmith's anvil, delicate flares from which she forged a message as strong as iron.

Sometimes Vienna would bring her silver brush-and-comb set down to the kitchen at breakfast time and arrange Willa's hair, but Vienna did not do up her own hair. Most days, she looked tired and sad. "Bedraggled" was what Sister called it. Aunt Augusta, who visited randomly, as if she were charged with the duty of surprise inspection, was always after Vienna to make more of an effort.

"You have to set an example. You have two small children who need you."

"They are getting along fine with things just as they are."

"Well how do you think it must be for them not to be able to have company? To hear talk in town about their mother being crazy?"

Aunt Augusta, whom Vienna refused to call Sister, the family nomenclature that had long since replaced her baptismal name, had a knack for making Vienna cry. Vienna, who could use her tongue with the quick grace of a rapier, never demonstrated her prowess in the duels Sister provoked. Vienna said it was because Sister was intellectually unarmed, but Willa didn't understand how that could be so if she got the last word. When Willa heard her mother's muffled tears, it would set her off like a trapped animal, thrashing through the house, kicking at doors and hollering, slamming the piano keys, raising a hellacious racket to drown out thought.

It outraged her more than she could hold in, more than Sister's disciplining for tantrums and ugly acts, which followed with sure certainty as days of deprivations and earfuls of biting words and, occasionally, the bristle end of a hairbrush. Willa didn't cry. No punishment yet inflicted had broken her stony resolve. Sister had once told Willa she was unnatural because of it. But then almost anything that didn't please Sister was deemed "unnatural."

Willa, though, would not understand for years why it bothered her so much more than Elliott's frequent tears, why it was different when Vienna cried, why the sobs seemed to come from the very marrow of her mother's bones with a kind of eloquence that was irrefutable.

Willa had her own notions about Vienna, ways of reconciling the vague and impractical oddities of her behavior with those that were sharp and shining and flew like a proud arrow through the prosaic quotidian of Winsville's tight heart.

Willa knew what the town children said, and she waited impatiently, angrily, for the day she never doubted would come, always on the after side of tomorrow, when she would see them damned. Then the Daniels would reclaim the elusive grail she had been taught to believe in by Sister through rumor and osmosis and pain, the lost legacy of greatness which would rid Willa for good of the secret shame that gnawed at her like hunger.

"It's a scandal the way you break their hearts. They sit outside your door and wait for you. If you are sick, then for heavensake go to a sanitarium and get well. Bad enough that they don't have a father."

Sister's words, which rose through the chimney flue to Willa's bedroom, were as bitter as the metal pail Willa had licked that winter, on a dare from Elliott, to see if her tongue would freeze stuck. It hadn't, but the taste stayed with her like the words, cold and scouring.

Willa had seen a photograph taken of Vienna before she came to Winsville. There were still times when she looked that beautiful, Willa thought. Times when she listened to Elliott play the piano and her head inclined toward him but her eyes were turned away, as if she were shy. When she smiled she was still lovely, and sometimes, reading aloud before bedtime, she would forget herself in the characters and her face would relax into a youthful radiance more captivating than the adventures being recounted.

Willa looked at the book and thought about how long it would take to read all of her mother's library. *"Promise me you'll read these,"* Vienna had whispered to Willa once, lifting her hand to indicate the stacks of books that lined her room. "They can save you."

The print was too small. "Whether I shall turn out to be the hero of my own life," she read. She put the book down and stretched. What a dumb way to start a book, as if everyone weren't automatically the hero of their own life. From the corner of her eye she saw Elliott. "Elliott!" she yelled. He looked up at her.

"Yeah?"

"You look baked. Where's your hat?"

"I don't know. It fell off."

"What are you doing?"

"I'm watching a cricket. I think his wing is torn. I tried to catch him."

"Well come here under this tree and out of the sun. You're getting red and puffy and Vienna will blame me."

"In a sec."

"*El*-liott."

"What?"

"Come here."

"Uh-huh. You come here. I've something to show you."

Willa let out an exaggerated sigh and stretched theatrically. "All right, ducky, but it better be good," she said, squinting as she came out into the bright sun.

"Over here," Elliott called back as he scampered in front, his glasses down to the tip of his nose and his head tilted back.

He stopped abruptly and held his arm out to prevent Willa from coming any closer. "I did it," he said with pride, beaming over the small turd that lay in the grass. He leaned over and fanned it extravagantly to wave off the fly that was settling on it. "What do you think?" he asked Willa, trying not to show how pleased he was with himself.

Willa picked up a twig and poked it. "Willa!" Elliott shouted with alarm. "What are you doing?"

"Just testing."

"Well, don't. You'll ruin it."

Willa narrowed her eyes and looked at her little brother.

"For godsake, you think this is going into a museum? It's only shit, you know."

"You're not supposed to swear, white trash."

Willa gave the turd a vicious thrust with a twig. "So there, smartie," she said with satisfaction.

"C'mon. *Cut it out.* We still have to get it to the mousetrap."

"The flinging-machine," Willa corrected, putting her hands on her hips.

"How do we get it there?"

"I have just the thing," Willa said, darting back to the tree. She returned holding open the book. "We'll just roll it into the center and use this as a tray."

"No, that's one of Mama's books," Elliott said sadly. He rarely used that appellation. The Daniels children were singular for their use of their mother's first name. Winsville assumed it was the application of a political idea of Vienna's, dangerous and foreign, but Sister alone knew the truth: that at the time her daughter learned to talk, Vienna had not felt she deserved to be called "Mother."

Willa was embarrassed by the word. She looked away, out at the sweep of field that rustled beyond them, waiting to be hayed, and nearer, at two grackles quarreling at the field's edge. This would be delicate.

"Vienna's never going to know. She's got so many besides. She's got at least fifteen others by this same fellow."

Willa's voice was soft and pleading. But she could see that it was not convincing him.

"We can't," Elliott said, firmly.

"Sure we can. Anyhow it's only two pages we'd ruin out of this whole *humongous* book." She flipped to the back to see how many pages there were, to bolster her argument. "Out of eight hundred—Jeez," she said, taken aback by the number, wondering why she hadn't picked a slimmer book to read.

"What is it?"

As Willa turned the book over to recall its title she realized her trump and knew just what was needed to break the tension:

"It's called *David Cacafield,*" Willa said, sucking in her cheeks to keep a straight face.

Elliott looked for himself and began to laugh his ridiculous, infectious laugh. He gave way with all the abandon of an eight-year-old enjoying his favorite kind of joke. He wrapped his arms around himself and his shoulders heaved in comic exaggeration. His eyes crinkled up and his glasses slid down his nose. Willa laughed too, but out of relief and the pleasure of victory.

Elliott sighed grandly and wiped his eyes and pushed his glasses back up and said, "O.K., but you do it."

As they walked back to the spot they had chosen as the most likely source of intrusion, Willa carried the open book out before her as if presenting a prize. She took small careful steps and kept her eyes fixed before her.

"You know, yours are darker than mine."

"What do you mean?"

"Well look at it. It's as dark as a sinner's soul."

"No it isn't," Elliott said defensively.

"It is so."

"Well everyone knows they're *supposed* to be black."

Willa didn't say anything. She was thinking about the word "supposed." She was thinking about what Miss Margayt had said about God's will: everything had a reason and a purpose. It would follow then that black things were supposed to be black. Willa thought about black things, idly making lists as was her custom: dogs' lips, ink, ants, Sunday shoes, ravens, cough syrup, the chalkboard, the iron skillet, nose hairs, men's umbrellas, licorice, preachers' coats. Though she read the Bible and could quote it better than Miss Margayt, Vienna didn't believe in God. It was one of the few subjects on which she was uniformly impassioned.

"Don't let them poison your mind," Vienna had said, holding Willa by the arm. When she let go there were hot red marks where her fingers had been.

Willa's attention was suddenly refocused. "Elliott," she called in a loud whisper. He was gamboling in front of her, humming.

"Huh?"

"Hush up."

Elliott stopped and cocked his head. The two of them stood still and listened. They could hear something but it was hard to make it out; the wind had swelled and filled the cluster of trees and the foliage of the thicket with the raspy sweeping of leaves. But behind that sound there was another, more precise, verging on the edge of recognition. Then it was obvious: it was the song of Mr. Aimes's bicycle, plaintive and yearning, desperate for oil and new springs, struggling with something snagged in the spokes.

Willa reached out and touched Elliott's shoulder. Her hand communicated the understanding that it was Addison weaving along the path to their land. Her other hand still balanced the open book, though somewhat shakily. Elliott's brow furrowed in earnestness as he motioned to her to follow him into the thicket. Willa could feel the thrill of excitement rushing in her veins and making it hard to suppress nervous laughter. As they thrashed through the underbrush to their hiding spot, they shushed each other noisily, trying not to let even the breath of a giggle escape. But Willa could see Elliott's shoulders shaking, and that alone was coercive. She let out a little snort and Elliott broke into a repressed hissing which lead to more sharp hushes. As they squatted and waited for Addison to approach the fence, their hearts pounded.

They could hear him skid to a stop and then they heard him lay the bicycle in the underbrush, the wheels still ticking, winding down, like a clock at the end of its spring. Addison's heart too was racing, and he held his breath. He had heard laughter from within the thicket. At last, he thought, he would meet them, the Daniels children, his new neighbors.

"Now," Willa said.

"Where is it?" Elliott whispered, panicking.

"Here," Willa said, thrusting the book, which still held the turd, into his hands.

"No—the machine!"

Willa looked around frantically, knowing the mousetrap and the balsa wing had to be near.

"Hurry up!" Elliott pleaded.

They could see him now, from where they crouched, and he was no more than thirty feet away.

"For godsake" Willa hissed at Elliott, "just throw it."

Elliott hesitated and Willa grabbed the book from him and as she yanked it up the two sides partially closed around their ammunition.

"Oh no, now look what you've done," Elliott said angrily.

"Never mind," Willa said, closing the book firmly and dropping it.

She jumped up out of the foliage and shouted with all her

might, "Hey you, Addison Aimes, I'll get you sooner or later and I hope it's sooner." Behind her she could hear Elliott rise from his squat and shout, "Me too!" And with that she began to pelt him with handfuls of earth.

Addison stood unmoving for several seconds in shock. Willa had sprung so unexpectedly from the thicket and had presented such a bizarre sight: she had stood up and shouted and thrown dirt up around her in clouds of rising dust. She had shouted his name and she had threatened him. She had stood with her skinny arms waving at him, throwing her snarled reddish-blond mat of hair back from her face like the streaming flame from a torch, with angry eyes and a delighted smile.

Willa's beauty was something for which Addison was unprepared, not only because she was so delicately featured, but because he had never before encountered passion expressed with such obvious pleasure; the spark and spunk of her angry dance transfixed him.

His first reaction, strangely, was to be flattered, even thrilled. Then he turned and ran to his father's bicycle, clods of grass and dirt falling behind him. As he ran he could feel the surge of panic and adrenaline choking him like tears. He was confused and upset: he was infatuated in a way that would change him like the sweep of a new season. He was almost at his house before he realized it had started to rain; the tapping at his back and shoulders was not pellets of dirt but heavy beads of water.

4

WHEN WILLARD DANIELS left her, Vienna took to bed.
She went to sleep for days—for weeks, it seemed. The help
came in and out, quiet and anxious at first, then less carefully:
dust coated the house with its dry, pale patina, filling cracks
and flecking the light with tiny motes, sparks of ethereal mica.
It was beautiful to watch, and Vienna observed it from her
bed with the resigned patience of one pinioned by depression.

But, like too much powder on an old woman's face, the
dust accentuated what it concealed: a state of disrepair. Food
was left out in the pantry to spoil. The imported sherry disappeared as well as the silver butter knives and Willard's cigars.
The cook let her young man come to the house, let him sit
in the living room and rub his cigarettes out on the wide board
floors that had not been waxed for several weeks.

Vienna could hear the voices below moving from room to
room, the suppressed gushes of laughter and the back door
slamming from time to time. She could hear her baby crying,
but she did not have the energy or the inclination to move.
She knew that Fayette would run up the stairs to tend to Willa.
Fayette was not like the others: she was fifteen and faithful.
From other rooms, she sang old, comforting songs from the
deep of her throat, while Vienna lay on her bed and wished

she were made of stone. Vienna concentrated on statuary: beautiful ruins, frozen moments, and broken monuments. Stillness was numbing, and she could feel herself becoming slow and heavy and solid.

There were occasional callers, prompted by curiosity as much as concern, but Vienna received no one. She was busy reviewing the mystery of her marriage detail by detail, unraveling the three years that had taken her from the classics department of a famous women's college, from a respected father in the North, to betrayal and a wrought-iron bed in Winsville.

Vienna listened to the wind and waited. Waiting was a state of mind that required no specific focus as its object. It was a way of suspending life, of immobilizing her emotions. She dozed and dreamed, but her thoughts returned to the very subjects or images she wanted to escape. Often she would cry out or roll to her other side as if to evade the pain.

She thought of Willard and her stomach clenched. She remembered those first mornings together: the way he would come into the bedroom in the thick of the light slanting in shafts across the waxed floorboards, cradling a bowl of sweet coffee in his hands. He would sit on the edge of the bed and put a hand, warm from carrying the coffee, on her forehead or cheek to wake her. Once he had kissed her and let the coffee he had sipped trickle into her mouth, slowly, like a mother bird feeding its young. She had loved him then with an aching that was as deep and profound as despair.

She remembered, too, the way he sang to her as he brushed her hair, proud of its shine and length, thrilling her scalp with his hands as if there were nothing in the world for him but her delight. Sometimes he had picked her up and slung her over his back like a sack of oats, though she would twist and kick, laughing until he couldn't hold her. Then he would fall onto the bed with her, into the sag in the center where now she lay alone. When he would roll onto his side, she would press herself against him, like wind trying to fill a wide unfurled sail.

She remembered the way he had of looking at her that rooted her in place, and had made her feel claimed. But she remembered too he was weak, and had done and said things that were lacerations that would not heal. He had struck her in the face with the back of his hand. He had turned to leave. From across the whitewashed kitchen, where the smell of apples, overripe and starting to rot, filled the room with the sweetness of decay, she had raised his gun and fired, not because she had wanted to kill him but because she had wanted to stop him, stop the words that stung like the spray of buckshot she released.

The chimney bricks were pocked, and blood had seeped through the French linen shirt she had ordered for him by mail, making speckles on the whitewash, random and delicate like the pattern on a bird's egg. She remembered him cursing and starting the car and driving over her flower beds and across the newly seeded lawn to the gravel road and out to where she could no longer hear the motor. She could not remember how long ago that had been.

She stretched her hands out to the side of the bed where the sheets were still cool and thought of Medea, who had given up everything: her title, her kingdom, her father, her people and, in the end, her soul, for an unworthy man who shook her from him like the dust of a difficult journey. She reflected on how well she had come to understand the classics since she left the classroom, to understand the nature of tragedy, the way in which one's undoing begins in some simple act or word which in itself means nothing.

IT WAS HARD for Vienna to return to a world without Willard; she no longer felt at home in the past she had left behind.

Indeed, it was difficult even to recall, much less re-create, a psychological landscape (since she had already accepted the logistics of physical exile) which precluded Willard. No matter how she retracted and withdrew, limiting herself to the land encompassed by the three hundred acres of The Heights, she was still in Winsville and Winsville was Daniels domain.

Everyone in Winsville knew the Daniels. The Daniels had been the richest family in Winsville for as long as anyone could remember: they lived outside of town in a house called The Heights, and they kept themselves apart. Daniels sons were sent North to school and the daughters were married off, went away, and seldom returned, except as the occasional unwanted widow or aging aunt, diseased and difficult, ignored and abandoned like the great house they would keep warm by ancient breath and blood, and which had been, for generations, suffering the decay which was, like other forms of decadence, a disease familiar to Southern gentility. Like animals responding to the migratory urges of their species, Daniels would return only to die, with their dust and their heirlooms.

Richer or more successful members of the family had moved to the cities, uncomfortable with the limitations of a small town that obstinately remained a small town, and perhaps, too, uncomfortable with a town that had watched them better themselves.

When the last of the Walker Daniels line died, in the Great War, the town had waited anxiously to see what would happen. Some said that The Heights would be sold, that the family would shed the house like a pelt that had grown bald or had simply been outgrown. Others shook their heads and said nothing, waiting patiently for another Daniels to appear.

And another Daniels did appear, the house having passed over to another branch of the family, after years of probate and litigation. Willard Daniels, then twenty-five, arrived one sweltering summer afternoon like a long-awaited answer full of pride and promise, driving down Center Street, honking the horn of the first automobile Winsville had seen with electric windshield wipers and two-beam headlights. Flashing his lights and waving at the same pace as the wipers, he greeted those he awoke on their porches with a hand gloved in gray leather.

Willard Daniels descended from the car like a matinee idol: he was stylish and tall and he carried himself like a public figure. He had easy, off-color jokes for the men who drank oily coffee or Coca-Colas at the hardware store. He remembered names and tipped his hat. He knew three variations of the Charleston and he taught them to the prettier girls of Winsville, finding them wherever he turned: behind the lunch counter of the drugstore, in the shabby town square, on the wooden bench near the depot, or on the porch of the post office. He was quick with a compliment too, and he listened with affected interest to large women talk about their health and unshaven men with dirty collars talk about the price of crops and how many hands high their favorite horse was. Willard organized a picnic at The Heights for the members of the county hunt club and he asked the town matrons for advice and favors. He appeared in the Episcopal church on Sundays, where he treated the congregation to his smooth, controlled tenor voice. In short, Willard Daniels seduced the town of Winsville in one summer.

Then Willard took his wide, bright smile away and when he returned he brought a bride with him: Vienna Daniels née Whitcomb, a bluestocking from New York, with two years of college, and dressing gowns from Paris, with the ability to play piano and speak languages, with blond hair and a white maid, with shoes and gloves for different times of day, with a marble bust of Quintilian, and four steamer trunks full of books— more books than in all the rest of Winsville.

Vienna Daniels was twenty, and accustomed to privileges. Rumors about the elopement, the rushed ceremony her father did not attend, about the fortune and friends she lost or left behind for Willard, were repeated in every kitchen and across every merchant's counter in Winsville that first week, adding considerably to the excitement her arrival generated. But it by no means guaranteed her a welcome.

Opinion divided about Vienna during her first weeks in Winsville. She had a kind of shy grace that impressed susceptible men; they were quick to help her down from the pony cart she drove to town, or to load the cart with her purchases, or to come to The Heights when there was a chore to be done. The women of Winsville, however, were less generously inclined. Vienna's very name elicited a xenophobia that set her apart as much as her learning and Northern ways, her fancy airs and her pride. And then too, as if that were not enough, there was her tongue.

Vienna was reserved but when she spoke it was with a candor that did not heed the banality of social convention. Moreover, she used uncommon words. She corrected guests when they misquoted or mispronounced or misguided conversation. She would let her eyes wander during small talk, and when they returned, often as not, they came to rest on the frayed cuffs or dirty nails or walleye of the speaker, whose voice would trail off to silence under her unabashed gaze.

Willard had reproached her furiously one evening after their guests has departed. "How could you stare at Biddy Markham like that? I would have thought you'd learned some manners up there at those fancy fine schools. Haven't you ever seen a harelip before? You made me downright ashamed."

"Biddy Markham knows better than the both of us about her harelip," Vienna returned patiently. "My looking at her didn't tell her what was on her face, it told her I wasn't afraid or surprised or repulsed by it. She was talking—for goodness sake, Willard, the polite thing to do, and what you would do instinctively with any other guest, was look at her. If you can't do that without feeling uncomfortable then you shouldn't ask her to the house."

But Willard went on; he was wound up with righteousness and it flew from him like an exploding cork.

"And what about Mr. Wiggins?"

"What about Mr. Wiggins?"

"You told him George Sand was a woman!"

"Well, she was. I can't help that."

"But you didn't have to be the one to enlighten him."

"His whole argument about women's suffrage owing its origin to a few free-thinking men was predicated on mistaken gender. Besides, she is far more famous for her life than for her letters. It is hard to imagine that it escaped his notice, if indeed he is expert on the subjects he claims, history being one of them."

"Vienna, you made a fool of him."

"He made a fool of himself. I was trying to help him trim his losses before he made it any worse. Biddy Markham wasn't about to let the subject go and he was bullying her, unfairly and wrongly because she is not well-read. I didn't, for example, disabuse him of the notion that Seneca was an Indian, even after all his patronizing remarks about Redskins and alcohol. Willard, he patted my hand and told me not to pay any heed to philosophy born in a bottle. All in all, I think I showed remarkable reserve: I don't mind that he is pompous or ignorant but he uses his little bit of learning like a weapon to hurt people."

"I am going to ask you only once to apologize for behaving in an unseemly manner in front of company and I hope you will spare me the embarrassment of future displays; they are neither ladylike nor becoming."

"I wear gloves on my hands when I leave the house," Vienna

replied, crisply inflecting her words, "but I will not wear a glove on my tongue when I am at home."

Willard had reduced Vienna to tears by the time he made his final pronouncement and shut the door. Willard was immune to the power of women's tears; they released him from any notion of accountability that he otherwise might have had. After years of his mother's manipulative and inebriated histrionics, he had come to feel, at the first sign of tears, nothing but resentment and a strong pull to be anywhere else.

Though Vienna never knew it, she had won a friend that night in the person of Biddy Markham, whose loyalty was as fierce as the expression permanently planted on her face. More than a decade later, Biddy Markham would leave her post behind the desk at the boardinghouse one sharp February morning without stopping to get her coat and run into the road to stand in the falling snow for a word with Willa. Biddy Markham had seen, through the steam-frosted bay window, Willa Daniels throwing snowballs at a bundle of town children outnumbering her, and, guessing the problem, Biddy had chosen her moment to speak. Scattering with her presence the knot of dark wool and felt coats more effectively than a well-aimed projectile, Biddy Markham swiftly picked her way to Willa in the erratic hopscotch of tamped snow and other people's footsteps she hoped would spare her unprotected shoes.

"Sugar, you look full into my ugly old face and mark my words. I only had but one meal with your mother, yet the whole time I was her company she looked at me straight and true without the least cringe or pity in her eyes. She looked at me like I was fine to look at. And do you know what? For that whole blessed evening I *felt* fine to look at. That may not seem like much to you, but it sure did to me. Wasn't no other person in this town ever gave that to me before."

Miss Markham bent her shivering frame over to meet Willa

face-to-face and put her numb hands on Willa's shoulders. "What do you think about that?" she asked.

Willa wiped her nose on a red woolen mitten and said, "She's just like that, but Miss Markham, you'll catch cold standing out here without a coat." Biddy Markham released Willa and tucked her hands into the pockets of the shapeless black cardigan that had become her trademark.

"Don't you worry about me," she said, pulling her lips into a gruesome smile. "I have that evening's glow inside to keep me warm. There have been other times a person's made me forget my face, but here's the difference: those were people who loved me, friends and family, and not many at that. To do that for a stranger I guess you have to be something special. So you remember this, being different doesn't make you special, but being special does make you different. I hope you'll join me in my prayer that Vienna Daniels never changes."

Miss Markham coughed into the handkerchief she kept tucked up a sleeve of her cardigan and which she had pulled out so theatrically that Willa half expected to see a frightened rabbit materialize, like at the Magic House in the carnival that stopped three days in Bantanburg the summer before. Then Biddy Markham turned and ran back to the boardinghouse, and, pausing on the threshold to stamp the snow from her shoes, she added, "You remember what I said, young lady, next time you feel like chunking a snowball."

"Yes, ma'am," Willa answered, and just before the door shut added "Thank you" so softly she was not sure Miss Markham had heard.

VIENNA MAY HAVE had other fans she didn't know about, but her detractors were hard to miss. Vienna didn't laugh at Winsville humor, and worse, she laughed at the things Winsville took seriously. She had given intimations of her ability to craft cutting remarks, though generally folks were careful not to give her occasion to demonstrate her verbal skills. They saved their slights for the safety of porch talk, never guessing that Vienna was, beneath what some took to be an intimidating façade, rather shy, and didn't make friends easily.

But the turning point in her socializing with Winsville women was the tea given by Mrs. Stepple, a pretty, matronly woman with a taste for unflattering hats and gossip. Margaret Stepple was popular despite her accomplishments as a snob, or perhaps because of them: she managed to work references to her "people" back in "Carolina" into most conversations over which she presided as self-appointed moderator. The prestige she derived from her husband's position as mayor was mitigated only by the fact that he was also the chemist who worked alternating shifts in the back room at the Rexall's drugstore on Center Street.

Mrs. Stepple had gone to a finishing school in North Carolina and took great pride in knowing how to do things "smartly": she served iced tea in the champagne flutes she had ordered specially from an importer in New Orleans and put a sprig of fresh mint in each glass as a decorative flourish, and she cut her tomato sandwiches, which were made with mayonnaise and not butter, into small, even triangles. She had been the first hostess in Winsville to offer men "cocktails" before dinner and she added seltzer from bottles as blue as barber's astringent to the cherry juice she served to women.

Mrs. Stepple insisted that her husband wear his jacket through supper, even on the nights in August when the heat hung so heavy in the house that conversation was choked and only the occasional crack of heat lightning outside penetrated the smothering stillness which seemed to suck the nutrients from the air and wilted even Mrs. Stepple's reliable appetite.

"Margaret, for the life of me, I don't see why we need to keep up appearances," Mr. Stepple would pant, lifting his napkin to wipe the tears of sweat which ran down from the crown of his nearly bald pate, in rivulets neatly divided by the few remaining strands of hair combed forward to cover as much of his head as possible.

"Everett, you're the *mayor*," Mrs. Stepple would invariably reply, in a dialogue almost as old as their marriage, "and folks around here depend upon you to set an example."

Margaret Stepple liked to think that the "niceties" by which they distinguished themselves and on which her reputation, in particular, rested, were the cohesive force which bound the town together safely, ensuring that the decorum for which she stood, like a ship's weathered but noble figurehead, was maintained and chaos and petty crime were kept, if not entirely beyond the town limits, at least from the Stepples' door.

Vienna's arrival in town had excited and agitated Mrs. Stepple in equal measure, for on the one hand she was thrilled to have, *finally*, someone in town with enough social prominence for Mrs. Stepple to gain by association, rather than to suffer the diminishment she felt at having always to bend, albeit with indulgent patience, to those she bettered.

The tales circulating about Vienna's background were as numerous as the variations of splendor Winsville's population could imagine, and comprised, therefore, a handful of familiar themes, like the pulp novels of romance that informed them, diverse enough in detail to differ but all bearing the stamp of an author of limited range.

The biography endorsed by Mrs. Stepple featured a father who had made a name for himself as a diplomat, traveling extensively abroad with a foreign wife of near-royal lineage, whose early death prompted him to move to New York, forsaking his former life among dignitaries to make an unspeakable fortune on the stock market, while his only child was raised in luxury by an impeccable staff of servants, whose livery Mrs. Stepple accorded the lavish pomp of footmen she had seen in a nineteenth-century illustrated "Cinderella."

It was over Mrs. Stepple's weekly quilting bee that she embroidered this version of the story, carefully coloring the parts which most pleased her yearnings for grandeur, even if they were to be sated only by the happenstance of proximity, the way an unremarkable dress could be redeemed by the opulent distraction of a fashionable accessory, and a carefully chosen wine could impart distinction to an otherwise bland meal.

Miss Margayt, whose stitches had twice been criticized, questioned the near-royal lineage of Vienna's mother, wanting to know from what crown she descended, and Mrs. Stepple, stung as if it were her own family in "Carolina" that was being scrutinized, had snapped out, "Of course she must have had a fancy birth. Do you suppose a man like that would have married a common Kraut?"

Miss Margayt was about to hazard the idea that the city for which Vienna was named was not located in Germany, the country which had claimed so many of Mrs. Stepple's clan in the Great War and for which Mrs. Stepple reserved a righteous venom. While this would improve still further Vienna's stature in Mrs. Stepple's eyes, Miss Margayt knew that her position in the quilting bee was tenuous, that some of the ladies found her religious discussions to be tedious, and rather than risk another reprimand, she chose instead to keep her tongue and turn her attentions to the somber patch of cotton she had been allotted. But for all of Mrs. Stepple's greedy pleasure in the expectation of importance, shared or vicarious, which would accrue to her through Vienna, for she never doubted that Vienna would recognize in her the kinship of refinement, she was reluctant to relinquish to Vienna the social scepter which she had held for so long.

In the face of this dilemma, she found her self-confidence eroding with each new discussion of Vienna she herself instigated. And like the child who will scratch a rash raw in the vain effort to find relief, she felt the source of her discomfort spread, and the desperate need to scratch it out, deepen. The insecurities which had tormented her in her youth now returned more virulently. Having lain in remission for years, their powers had multiplied and swelled in dormancy only to more fully devastate her now.

And as in her unhappy teens, as the least accomplished and attractive of three sisters, the focus and emblem of her misery was the small, slightly raised mole on her right cheekbone, from which grew two long, blunt hairs. Although the blemish was prominent in Mrs. Stepple's view, it often went unnoticed by others on first meeting her. As a young woman, Mrs. Stepple had tortured herself by plucking and trimming the hairs, sending for cures and ointments, salves and removers from every disreputable charlatan in the market. It was whispered uncharitably, when her engagement was announced to Mr. Stepple, that only his position as a chemist had entitled him to marry into "her people."

After having learned to enjoy, at long last, the luxury of sitting before her vanity and contemplating an image which, after one or two generous sweeps of a powder brush, pleased her (her face having grown fuller from the respect of neighbors and having softened to accept their deference), it seemed a debilitating defeat to find, under the reappraisal Vienna's arrival had catalyzed, that the mole dominated her face more stridently now than it had before crow's-feet had formed, pointing like insistent arrows at the disfigurement just beyond their reach.

In her preparations for the tea she was to give in Vienna's honor, Mrs. Stepple exacted from her servants an attention to detail that had her maid and her maid's sister, who was called in for the day, in tears in the pantry by noon. Otherwise insignificant choices—whether to put the seeded mustard on the tea tray in a china dish or to anoint individually the cucumber sandwiches, whether the pink "Lady's Blush" roses, which filled her silver punch bowl, looked better on the upright pianola or on the side table by the yellow curtains, and whether she should wear her pink crepe dress with the green satin piping or the navy linen with lace trim, which was cooler but less formal—took on the gravity with which a condemned man might weight the methods of execution.

By midmorning it was clear that the day was growing unexpectedly hot and when Everett Stepple returned to the house shortly after lunch to change into a fresh shirt, as his wife had taught him to do, he had suggested, in passing, that lemonade might be more welcome to the ladies. Mrs. Stepple, who was upstairs at her vanity, applying to her mole an additional layer of La Doré's flesh-colored complexion powder, which claimed on the tin to use "the genuine juice of lily bulbs to invigorate the skin and reduce unwanted growths," responded to her husband's earnest advice by slamming shut her bedroom door.

But Vienna was innocently unsuspecting of the backstage hysterics. Her own preoccupations were centered exclusively on calculating how long she must stay at the tea which took her from a novel she was loath to leave and whether it would be possible to get back to The Heights in time for a radio broadcast of Fauré's Requiem, which was being conducted by a musician Vienna had met in New York two years prior and who had impressed her enormously at the time.

Vienna didn't notice the mole at first. There had been such a lot of new names to forget and then Mrs. Stepple had been chattering continuously, filling the room with exclamations and interrupting herself like a startled sparrow. And before Vienna had finished the first cup of tea, which had been overbrewed to the point of bitterness, she had already determined that the conversation to be had around Mrs. Stepple's tea table was aggressively dull. It was as remote from her interests as the hieroglyphs spewed from the endless coiling tongue of a ticker-tape machine. She felt always slightly behind, as if she were translating and a particular word or phrase would detain her. Mrs. Stepple had dammed the flow of discourse at the subject of the weather and now the other women, like tributaries trickling into the swell, eagerly contributed their complacencies.

"A couple nuther days like this and we'll wilt right up like corncob dolls," Mrs. Stepple had persisted, expanding now into figurative language. The powder on her upper lip was matted with moisture and she was wishing she had chosen to wear her linen dress. Vienna was reflecting on the colloquial inversion "couple nuther," wondering if, were it uncoupled from the Southern drawl, it would still irritate her, when Mrs. Stepple continued, flourishing her handkerchief at her brow, "Yes, indeed, if this continues, after that last spell of hot we had, the wells will give out and we'll be fighting for water like Jews over silver. They might even have to stop the roadwork!"

Vienna looked at her hostess abruptly, as if suddenly remembering a burner left lit or a bath she had drawn absentmindedly, and amid the tittering tribute to Mrs. Stepple's humor, she quietly completed her first full sentence. "Thank you, Mrs. Stepple, for the tea, but I really must get back now."

Vienna was twenty, and though she was getting too old to rely on the polite, self-effacing etiquette that served her so well in her father's drawing room, she had not acquired the moderation of a social modality with which to replace it, having grown, of necessity, more comfortable with her solitary pursuits than the often lonely and frequently tiring demands of company. Efforts to treat conversation like badminton, in which the subject was skillfully volleyed with an athletic vigor, satisfying stretches sailing the subject whizzing back with a spin or unexpected lift had the effect of fatiguing her companions, and when Vienna didn't make an effort, her remarks ventured quickly from the cropped enclosure of polite predictability, and at best, made people uncomfortable.

She was, moreover, unfamiliar with the distinctions of hierarchy in a society in which most families had hanging laundry and wandering chickens behind the house. Her eyes had not yet learned to sort the various shades of gray in the monochrome of tawdriness with which she viewed all of Winsville, like a visitor to an exotic culture who finds all the natives equally uncivilized and does not know if the tribal chief is the one in the most or the fewest feathers.

Vienna rose and stood to extend her hand to Mrs. Stepple, who still held the teapot poised to serve seconds. As Vienna stood there, and Mrs. Stepple continued to clutch the teapot, frozen in the posture of shock, with only her eyes betraying the wild panic of a woman who stands before her blazing house holding a jar of pickles or basket of laundry she has unaccountably carried with her, Vienna calmly regarded her mole.

That final reproach, for Mrs. Stepple would always think of it that way, spurred her into motion. She set the teapot down and despite Vienna's urging everyone to stay seated, followed her to the door with a last burst of words, the ill-fitting locutions of departure woven uncomfortably and repetitively together as if there were some final phrase to be found which would smooth away the awkwardness of the rebuff she felt and find another avenue to the retreating dream of privilege and power that Vienna had embodied.

But it was never found and Vienna left—with the cucumber sandwiches untouched, the tomato sandwiches still piled artfully, overlapped like tumbled dominoes, the arrangement of cheese squares undisturbed in their regimental rows, forming a greasy sheen of sweat, a hardness darkening the edges. Mrs. Stepple returned to survey the room with astonished eyes. Her lace handkerchief danced around her face like a moth fanning delicately at a bruised melon. The other women were embarrassed. "Did you evers" and "upon my souls" and "well I nevers" filled the overfurnished room like the nervous coughs that circulate in church during a sermon about wantonness.

But if the women understood anything, it was their own vulnerability to the thoughtless whims of a girl half their age with twice their money and so they were quick to suppose a malice that did not exist. They could not imagine it was indifference, not malice, that determined how little Vienna wanted to be even a guest, never mind a celebrity, among the gawking manipulative women who kept her from her bridegroom and her books.

That first gaffe established a chill from which Vienna could not recover herself; all further attempts to befriend Mrs. Stepple were received with a suspicion that found fault with each foray, until Vienna could not help but recognize the hostility that gleamed under the thin veneer of hospitality. After that, Vienna gradually withdrew from Winsville "society" and Winsville, on the whole, was relieved to let her recede from a position of prominence. Everyone, that is, except Willard, who watched Vienna, without intention or effort, turn Winsville against her as quickly as he had won it over. By Christmas, though the town remained polite, obsequious even, Vienna Daniels could count only one friend, and that was Miss Alisha Felix, the schoolteacher, who was several years older than Vienna, unmarried and likely to remain so.

5

 (decorative rule)

*I*F WINSVILLE IGNORED her that first fall, Vienna hardly noticed; she was busy. She filled the ruled accounting ledger Willard gave her with hexameter and cross-hatched sketches. She had projects: no sooner did she look at something than it needed work. She moved through the house rearranging, fixing, changing. The bedrooms smelled of mildew and windows had been painted shut. The grandfather clock wouldn't chime and the dining-room chandelier was draped in dust and missing crystal pendants. The front stairs had a broken tread and several of the balusters were loose. As for the kitchen, well, it was simply unmanageable. Appended to the house by a narrow passage, it had a dirt floor in which bricks had been set in a herringbone pattern zigzagging away from the large black hearthstone. Over time, the bricks had worn into the earth unevenly and now the floor rose and dipped like the gently swelling surface of a sea. Not only did the warp of the floor make the kitchen hard to work in, but the low ebbs accumulated crumbs and cooking dirt which a broom only swept deeper into the earthen seams. Attempts to wash the floor produced a thin film of muddy water that left the brickwork no cleaner when it dried and encouraged fungal growth to sprout between the bricks, accentuating with its green tracery the jagged element of the design.

Having the rustic romance of a conservatory in the kitchen might have appealed to Vienna if she did not already long for the immaculate kitchen of her father's house, not so much for its tesselated floor, scrubbed and scoured and swept into a gleaming tribute to hygiene, but because she missed the delicacy of its offerings. Vienna had already dismissed two cooks, but she remained staunchly optimistic about finding someone who could do more than fry and smother, some-one whose idea of flavor was not inextricably linked to pork fat or molasses. A gardener had been engaged to transform the balding lawn into a deep carpet of resodded green and a variety of bulbs and bushes had been ordered. Plans for a gazebo spread across the dining-room table. Catalogues of seeds and fruit trees were stacked on the sideboard. Swatches of fabrics were pinned to sofas and seat cushions and curtains, and linens shrouded such furniture as had been pronounced unacceptable.

By the enormous energy Vienna poured into transforming The Heights, Willard measured the extent of her disappoint-ment. Every chair that was lugged into the hall to be stored was a reproach. The bric-a-brac packed into boxes embarrassed him. Though most of it was awful, it was his; it had come with the house and was what he had offered Vienna when he brought her to Winsville as his bride. But that same determina-tion, the industriousness that now focused her energy, was partly why he had married her. Whether it was that he had hoped it would, by example or contagion, propel him into a more purposeful life, or that he expected, merely by association and proximity, to feel his need for activity satisfied, he found the gulf between them widened rather than reduced by this difference.

She pushed him to attend to the needs of the property. One of the barns was rotted beyond repair and would need to be taken down before it collapsed. Parcels of land that had lain fallow too long would have to be reclaimed and fertilized for farming. The pastures needed new fences and one of the wells had gone dry.

Willard tried. He liked to go to Bantanburg to the auctions. He bought machinery they didn't need and traded horses he should have kept. Willard talked to hired hands and foremen, enjoying their deference and company while Vienna pored over the unruled paper that covered her desk. When she was not at work on her poem—an epic meant to imitate Virgil in structure, Dante in scope, and Pope in tone, an ambition she announced shyly but without irony—she consulted almanacs, made lists, and translated obscure sources on farming and husbandry: monastic monographs, medieval harvest poems, and her chief reference, her handbook and guide, Virgil's *Georgics*, line by painstaking line.

Their land was as lush as a politician's promise, rolling out from under the house in gentle waves that undulated to the stone wall dividing the vast lawn from the first pasture. Willard liked it as it was: wild and uncultivated, yielding nothing more than an open view and enough hay for the horses. He had plans, of course, but they were intended for other people's property. With the exception of the ninety acres of The Heights that were being leased to a neighboring farmer by an arrangement that preceded Willard's authority and over which there was already an easement dispute, Willard's land was free of sweat and the smell of manure. It made him feel rich.

But the truth was otherwise. Without the dowry Vienna had sacrificed, the Daniels were land poor. The capital Willard had come into when he inherited the house was being spent with the same heady spontaneity which had initially charmed and won Vienna when she was still subject to her father's somber rule, living in a huge and humorless house in which decorum, like an immutable law as ineluctable as gravity, determined the substance of her days, reverberating invisibly within the tasteful walls, silent as the servants.

One morning Willard found Vienna out on the lawn with a spade, digging holes in the ground in what looked like a random pattern.

"Vee, what in heaven's name are you doing there?" he called from the bottom of the porch steps.

"I'm testing the soil," she called back.

"What are you testing it for?"

"To determine if it is heavy or light."

"*What?*"

"So we'll know what crops will flourish. It is all explained in the book I've been translating. Don't you remember my telling you about it? The hexameter, the allusions to Callimachus and Hesiod? It's a gold mine of literary influences as well as the very practical advice we need to make a go of this," she said, waving her arm over the land.

Willard stared at her.

"You mean that Latin thing?"

"Oh Willard, can't you ever be more precise? It's a didactic poem. And yes, the *Georgics* was written in Latin, and thank heaven for that, because my Greek is slipping." Her tone was breezy and cheerful.

"Christ almighty, Vienna," Willard shouted, "you've been bending in the sun too long. It's too damn hot to fry your brain with such obsolete nonsense. I'm not having any dead poet fertilize my fields."

Not long after that, Willard consulted Dr. Barstow. He mentioned quite casually, of course, lest he be the agent of scandal, his concern. Dr. Barstow had laughed. "She's not crazy, Willard. She's educated. Sometimes it's just hard to tell the difference."

And Willard too, had laughed, relishing the relief of confession. But that was before he found her standing in the first field past the hazel grove with her arms outstretched, still as a statue, waiting with the patience of a plant for birds to alight on her.

He watched her in terror for a full fifteen minutes, hoping she would, like a sleepwalker awaking, return to the familiar safety of behavior he recognized as sane.

WILLARD CONTINUED TO attend dinners and meetings, spending his evenings in town, accepting invitations, in spite of Vienna's polite notes, the diplomatic evasions she penned in brown ink. "Such a melancholy color, like a sparrow's back: it's the perfect color for regret."

And there were times when, still bright from the admiration of married women and blushing daughters, the backslapping congratulatory tones he elicited from well-fed farmers, he would take the shortcut across the fields to Vienna. In the recklessness of the dark and the heat of unaged whiskey, he would ride through the cut corn rows calling her name until he was aching and out of breath and he could see the lights of the house, rising with the land like a beacon.

Vienna never heard him, though, never knew there were moments when her memory was more pressing than the danger of the horse's hoof finding a rut or rock or groundhog's burrow, waiting like a mine to break the bones or back of the horse and rider. "Take the motorcar," she would suggest, "it's so much less affected."

But his urgency was filled with anger as well as longing. He yearned for the smiles other men bestow like a toast, at the end of an evening when one is helping a handsome woman with her coat. Instead, he accepted the sympathetic nods of men whose wives were reputed to be difficult.

He missed too, the long walks back from town with his arm linked through hers and her head leaning softly on his shoulder as they teased the evening over, those times when Vienna would come to life in the night air like a hothouse triumph, animated and playful after the strain of indifferent conversation, finding the phrase or image so exact that Willard would be struck, days later, remembering it. The smell of her hair and the crisp scrape of gravel, comforting as the sound of pecans being shelled, were pleasures that were simple and immediate.

When he returned, the horse would be damp with sweat and Willard's dress shirt would be flecked with foam from its mouth, an emblem of exertion and excitement Willard wore proudly, like a schoolboy reveling in the ennobling stains of a playing field's battle. He would dismount and walk the wheezing horse the last stretch toward the glow of the house to let the animal cool, the reins looped over his arm and his arm looped over the horse's back, patting the broad neck, muttering to the twitching ears the kindnesses he had meant to save for Vienna.

There were nights when he lingered in the barn, after the tack had been hung on the wall, and a currycomb had brushed the dust and sweat from the horse's coat, after Willard had watched it slurp water from a pail, and had scattered fresh straw in its stall, nights when he returned long after the groom had gone to sleep in the room attached to the barn. Then he would stop at the pump and wash his hands before heading for the house. Sometimes he would pause at the unshuttered windows, closed against insects, and look in. And there she would be, in the sitting room, candles burning and a fire even on the warmest nights, reading, with a dictionary beside her. There she would be, sitting straight as a stalk, the blush of fire on her hair, in her cheek, waiting for him.

Then defeat would flood him, the notion of his marriage, like the bride before him, eluding him, always on the other side of simplicity, the way he could press his cheek against the cool of the glass pane, and feel in his gut the invisible barriers that divided him from the happiness he had expected.

He remembered, too, the mornings when it was easy, when he would be drawn back to the bedroom to marvel at Vienna, furled in sleep, tangled in the bedclothes where he had lain and which still held his body's heat. Those moments, the light fanning across the planked oak floor, the desultory breeze shuffling Vienna's hair across the blanched linen like scattered wheat, the low calls of mourning doves on mysterious whirring wings, making what Vienna called an "avian purr," all of it sifting into the room through the window lace, such moments were like gifts strewn before him, waiting to be claimed.

But remembering them only made him harsher, coming in from the porch without wiping the stable muck from his boots, bitter and sarcastic in his dress shirt and his father's cuff links, his loneliness wrapped tightly around him, insulating and abrasive as a cape of hemp.

"Another edifying evening with Great Minds?" he had once sneered at her from the darkness of the unlit hallway, leaning only his head into view. "Yes," she had said simply, looking up at him and folding a finger into her book to mark her page, "and you?"

ULYSSA WAS THE name of Vienna's horse—the horse that some said had cost the marriage. The horse was Arabian, the only one of its kind in the county and the symbol to Winsville of

Vienna's peculiarity. At first it had been a great joke to them that Vienna should have the most expensive horse for ten miles square but never ride, that she should train the horse to come when she whistled and that they should take walks together, side by side along the dusty road or across the Daniels land.

But with time the jokes became more bitter. A fancy horse would have been enough to swallow—a show jumper or a track racer, something the town could take pride in, bet on, share vicariously as they had done with Dorian, the gray that Willard rode with such enviable recklessness, jumping ditches or boxwood on a dare, bringing notoriety to the town along with eager breeders who spent money and spat with equal ease. But there were boys elsewhere in the county pulling plows on farms where the mule had died and money was too thin to afford another, and there was no pleasure to be gleaned from waste.

One afternoon Willard had returned from an auction outside Bantanburg, immensely proud and intoxicated by his own extravagance. His cheeks were flushed and he almost looked sheepish. He had burst into her study where she was bent over her Greek lesson and he had picked her up and carried her, squirming in protest, out to the pasture behind the barn. "Don't look, O.K., now look," he had said as he set her down beside the thoroughbred.

Then Willard had stood back, lit a cigar, and beamed. Vienna approached tentatively. She gave the horse a few pats and the horse turned its muzzle toward her and stared expectantly.

"She's beautiful, Willard."

"She's yours."

"But what will I do with her?"

"You'll ride her, of course."

Vienna fingered a strand from her chignon that had fallen loose but stopped herself from putting it in her mouth as she sometimes did in private.

"No, Willard. I told you all about that."

"We can worry about it later, when she's less green. For now, think of her as a pet."

"I'll have to find her the right name."

"Anything you like. We'll have a plaque put up in her stall. I'm going to put her in the box next to Dorian."

"No."

"No what?"

"Not next to Dorian. He'll frighten her."

Willard laughed and his confident tenor swelled and broke like a cresting wave. He kissed the top of her hair. His horse was known for being temperamental, and it increased the satisfaction he derived from having mastered the animal, making Dorian more valuable to him than a horse would be with similar attributes but a more even disposition. Even Ray, the stablehand, who had an uncanny way with horses, refused to groom Dorian.

Willard envisioned himself instructing Vienna to ride. That was something he could teach her and he longed for the role of mentor. Afterward, it would become something they could do together, but at which he would always be better. A vision of connubial satisfaction flooded him.

But within a matter of months he had grown to hate the horse, and the derision it begot. It seemed he could hardly purchase a cigar without someone making a crack, and the jokes he suffered with a forced smile were demeaning. Henshaw had suggested that next time the carnival came to town, Willard should buy himself a carousel horse and see if he could get his wife on that.

For a long time after Winsville had accepted the sight of

Ulyssa as a familiar curiosity, no more inspiring of comment than Mr. Joe's idiot son, or Miss Margayt's talking bird that said "Amen" and "Praise the Lord," Willard continued to think that the smiles he received in town were references to the unfortunate purchase of the horse, rather than simply a welcome.

6

------■------

𝒯T WAS LIKE a fire, they said, the way that friendship caught. Alisha Felix and Vienna acted as if they'd never known company before, carrying on like children, full of secrets and inseparable. Alisha Felix wasn't from Jackson County, but Winsville would have forgiven that, if it weren't for the way she and Vienna took up and made no time for anything that wasn't theirs.

It started with an exchange of books. A simple act of sharing interests and objects, most people reckoned, but by the third volume, Alisha Felix was all but living at The Heights, coming down from Redley Road as soon as the bell released her from the classroom, bringing small presents like tokens of courtship. As Miss Margayt told the ladies at the bake sale: "There is nothing simple about it. The way they get together, I don't care what those books are about, is just plain delirious, like a couple of drunks on a talking streak."

Miss Felix had been a librarian in Maryland for several years before she started teaching, before she arrived in Winsville, cheerful and disorganized as a traveling show, with a large broken suitcase wrapped in twine, two banged-up crates, and a yellow ladderback chair, in which she sat, slowly eating an apple and taking in the view from the train stop until the boy she had given a coin to returned with Mr. Stepple, who took off lunch to drive her up to Redley Road.

Though Alisha Felix did not have the formal education that Vienna had, she had even more raw curiosity and had made of her opportunities an advantage that distinguished her from the ladies of the bake sale as much as her brightly colored clothing or her loud, loose laugh, extravagant as the blooming burst of a peony. Next to laughing, she liked to sing, and she would howl out show tunes and folksongs for her own pleasure, inventing lyrics or altering the melody as it suited her, troubling little over her lack of talent or training.

"What do I care if I miss a note or my voice isn't pretty? It makes me feel full and happy," she told Vienna, who was shy about singing, and had noticed that when she joined her voice to Willard's, he always stopped singing, sometimes as abruptly as a door slammed shut.

"Come on, let's sing my version of 'Maybel's got her eye on you,' " Alisha urged, undissuadable. "This damn house is dying for it."

When Alisha began booming out the first verse and picking up objects from around the living room and using them like dance-hall props, Vienna laughed, and by the end of the second verse she sang, growing more tuneless as she laughed harder and lost her breath and Alisha shouted "Louder!" between the verses until neither of them could finish. Gasping like fish, they flopped onto the down-filled sofa in contortions of hilarity, and Alisha said, "Stop or I'll pee right here on your grandmother's cushion."

"Willard's grandmother's cousin's cushion," Vienna coughed out, and that started them off again so that Alisha could hardly get out, "Oh, in that case I guess it's all right." And on they went, wisecracking and singing until it was time for Alisha to leave.

Soon after that, they started to exchange clothing, accessories mostly, since they weren't the same size—Alisha being shorter and fuller figured than Vienna. But shawls and scarves, earrings and gloves, perfume and hats became interchangeable.

When Willard went out of town, Alisha would stay in one of the unused bedrooms that had previously stored the uglier furniture or broken chairs Vienna didn't care to have fixed. After Alisha had tried all the different beds, and complained that she was starting to feel like Goldilocks, they settled on the room across the hall from the master bedroom, where they could talk at night with the doors open.

They made curtains from a lace bedspread and painted the wainscot dark green because Vienna said "green is the color of heaven" and Alisha said "anything is better than what it is now, the sickly color of old-lady skin, all pasty gray and peeling off."

They smoked cigarettes together in front of the parlor fire and drank chicory coffee. They read a Bernard Shaw play out loud and dressed up like Oscar Wilde and ate cinnamon toast for dinner. They made guest lists of dinner parties for the dead, haggling over whether Rabelais and Lawrence Sterne would get on, if Boccaccio would steal the silver or be boorish at the table and who would talk to Jane Austen. They drank sherry from the cordial glasses and once made papier-mâché masks late at night on the kitchen floor.

"Pick the most frightening person you can think of, here in Winsville," Alisha said. They worked in opposite corners of the kitchen, guarding their projects from view, and murmuring to themselves over a particular effect or complaining when the paper was too wet, until, finally, they were ready to leave the masks to dry.

That morning Vienna didn't mind that breakfast was late and didn't notice that the help was staying out of sight. Alisha was telling her dream, which seemed to Vienna as rambling and incoherent as many of the episodes in Alisha's life that she told without wonder, casually, like someone reciting in a language they don't understand, a messenger for whom the meaning is not meant.

They carried their teacups and saucers with them as they walked down to the maple grove, spilling most of the contents along the way. Never had the outlines of the world looked so crisp and focused: the trees, the broken fence, the wasps' nest and overturned wheelbarrow, all of it looked radiant and warm. They lay in the damp grass and listened to the whirr and ticking of insects like overwound timepieces spurring the season on.

"Tell me more about Ray Campbell," Vienna asked.

"Ray? What more is there to tell? He was a mean son of a bitch but he was funny. He sure could make me laugh when he didn't make me cry."

Vienna still blushed when Alisha used coarse language, but it thrilled her and she admired Alisha's boldness. It represented the freedom and hard edge that separated her from Vienna.

"Teach me to curse right," Vienna interrupted.

"What do you mean? You're the one with the vocabulary; don't pretend you don't know those words," Alisha replied defensively. She knew that she did not have the refinement Vienna took for granted and sometimes it made her testy.

"Sure I know the words, but I don't know how to use them comfortably, like a man would, to give a story bite and back-bone, or like you do. It sounds so"—Vienna groped a moment for the right word—"so confident and ready for whatever the world has got."

"Confident!" Alisha brightened. "It's just coarse, you little fool," she said, throwing a handful of grass at Vienna. "But I'll teach you, hell, I'm a teacher after all."

Vienna brushed the grass off of her lap and pulled a blade

from her hair and smiled at Alisha. "You were saying, before I interrupted you, what a son of a bitch Ray was. Go on, I'll be quiet."

"Well all right then, he was also a con man but I didn't care. I couldn't help myself. He was good-looking in an ugly sort of way. If you were to see a photograph of him, you'd see features that didn't add up, a big nose and small eyes and a cleft chin. But in person, he could charm the hat off your head. He'd start by making you laugh and being crazy and telling you a mouthful of nonsense that you'd know was just words but damn, if they weren't just the right words."

"Naturally—he was a con man."

"No. That wasn't it. It was almost like a gift, the way that man could talk. It was like poetry, without the prissy or sentimental part. It was carnal and soulful and exhilarating, as if he were talking with his hands in an improper way."

Alisha stopped for a moment. Her eyes were moist and her voice was a little unsteady. "I'll tell you another thing too. That bastard was an astonishing lover."

Vienna wanted to ask what made him different from the others, but Alisha was standing up, stretching her arms and brushing off her skirt.

"It's damp here from the dew and I'm getting a crick in my back. Let's go back to the house. I could do with a long soak in Willard's tub."

Vienna picked up the teacups and looked at her friend. Willard didn't like Alisha, she thought. He had asked Vienna not to wear her clothing, saying that the colors were too garish and had the sheen of cheap fabric. He said Alisha had all the subtlety of a cigar-store Indian. But now, as Vienna regarded Alisha standing in the sun, multicolored as a Gypsy quilt, she said, "You look magnificent, like a cathedral." Alisha laughed and shook her head and started walking. "No, I mean it, just then, with the sun at your back, you looked like a stained-glass window, a blaze of glory."

"You'd better watch out," Alisha called out giddily as she broke into a run, "or you'll get religion, like Miss Margayt."

Vienna ran past her, swift and straight, taking the hill without breaking pace and yelling in the wind of her own speed, "Miss Margayt's just in it for the wine, I want the Word."

Alisha had slowed to a walk when she realized she would be outrun and she cupped her hand around her mouth and answered, "No, you want the *dirty* words." Vienna waited at the top of the hill for Alisha, with her arms spread and her head tilted up at the dizzying sun, feeling the world spin beneath her. "Yes, I want those too. I want all of it, for *my* church, right here, with the blessings of these trees and my noble, foul-mouthed friend, for ever and ever amen."

"Bless you," Alisha said as she reached Vienna and slipped her arm around her. "And it truly is a blessing: You know the individual voices of these trees better than a blind man, and more than that, I believe you actually understand them—all those shudders and sighs and creaking confessions, all that solitude." Alisha turned to her friend and smiled grandly. "Look there, those branches are bowing just for you."

WHEN THEY FINALLY finished the masks, and the paint had dried, it was dark again.

"Let's each take a candle and meet up in the dining room with our masks on in five minutes," Vienna said, restless as a child on her birthday. Then she ran upstairs to the attic and churned through a trunk of old clothes for a particularly hideous hat she had once seen there. The clothes gave off a disturbing odor as she rummaged through them, but she continued until she found the crumpled hat, sporting a spray of feathers in the front that were now bent and balding and covered with dust.

She shook the dust from the hat with a few quick snaps of her wrist and put it on, fussing in front of an age-speckled mirror to fit the mask under the hat brim so that she could see through the eyeholes. Then she took off her shoes and walked downstairs, placing her feet so the worn planks would not creak. Her heart was pounding in her ears and a nervous giggle caught somewhere low in her throat.

The house was still. "Alisha," she said softly. There was no answer and a sudden fear enveloped her, more disorienting than the darkness. She bumped into a chair in the black yawn of the hallway; the sound it made seemed absurdly loud and unfamiliar and she was beginning to feel foolish and alone. She tiptoed to the threshold of the dining room. "Alisha, come out. I'm scaring myself," she said.

"Alisha?" she whispered, lighting her candle to scan the shadows, but even after adjusting to the swollen depths of the lightless room, she could not make out any comforting shapes. Vienna sat at the head of the table and listened to the house breathe its almost imperceptible sigh of wood expanding or settling, ticking behind walls and under floorboards like an old dog dreaming. Somewhere a fly scuffed against a window-pane, tiny and insistent, its fury irregular and insignificant, absorbed into the quiet night. Sound too, had its palette, the myriad minutiae, blending like an auditory equivalent of black, into the meaningless blur of silence.

The tallow ran down her hand and she let it harden as she waited in the suffocating closeness of the shuttered room. Vienna felt, not the wax cooling into the cast of an opaque teardrop, but some delicate nuance of happiness stiffen within her like a damaged limb she had learned to use too late, atrophying in the absence of her friend.

WHEN ALISHA SUDDENLY shouted "Surprise!" and sprang up from behind the Aubusson screen, Vienna burst into heavy, hollow sobs.

"Honey, don't cry," Alisha said. "Please, now stop."

Alisha's voice was comforting and womanly as she put her hand on Vienna's, but inwardly she was annoyed, partly because she was made uncomfortable by the revelation of weakness, so often demanding a compensatory strength from her that she resented neediness in others, as if it diminished her own limited resources, and partly because she felt the sour reproach of her own guilt. She had not meant to hide—it had started as part of the game—but in watching Vienna she had suddenly felt herself stumbling upon something private, and in an instant the world they shared had shifted, making it too awkward to acknowledge her friend's presence. So she had waited, hoping Vienna would leave the room and let her escape to make a more graceful entrance, but each minute that trapped her behind the musty screen only made the situation worse.

She was painfully reminded of a couple in Baltimore whose friendship she had sought. They had responded by inviting her to dinner. Alisha remembered everything about that evening, each detail building slowly as a fugue: the rustle of Mrs. Tuck's silk slip, crisp as tissue paper under a blue dinner dress, the cut-crystal wineglasses, one of which was slightly chipped, candlesticks like miniature Corinthian columns, the steam rising off the roast lamb fragrant with rosemary and cloves, the conversation that held them at the table past midnight, filling her with the surging rush of ideas perfectly put, exploding in a hundred directions at once. She recalled the oversized book of European woodcuts bound in Italian leather that the three of them had leafed through while Mr. Tuck smoked his cigar, a cat in heat filling the garden with angry throaty calls, and the smell of talcum when Mrs. Tuck kissed her cheek and said goodnight.

It had been the longest time she had held on to heaven and felt its grace, a full six hours without a moment's lapse, as much, perhaps, as all the other flashes throughout her life put together because this was consecutive, cumulative, and what had preceded seemed like the random flares of matches struck in darkness, sustained for no longer and illuminating no more, compared to the bonfire of this beatitude which she took home and fell asleep with.

How many variations of thank-you notes had she not composed, not one of which seemed sufficient and all of which ended in the fireplace, where they burned into curled ashen whispers, delicate dust that sometimes held a ghostly watermark? An occasional word would remain unsinged, having floated on a current of heat to a corner the flames could not blacken, a lone surviving proof that her penmanship was poor.

Finally, she ran out of good paper. By then, wearied by guilt and disappointed effort, she felt that she could not afford to compromise on the quality of fiber and finish that would carry her inarticulate admiration. The store which supplied her with the original box of note cards had replaced them with a more expensive and heavier laid paper she could not afford. Alisha became fixated on finding another shop that carried the cream cards with a rosebud watermark, but because of her schedule her search was confined to the weekends.

She dreaded the chance encounter which might bring her face-to-face with the Tucks before they received her note, and therefore she sedulously avoided the streets and stores they were likely to frequent, going so far as to work in the basement bindery for the fortnight following the dinner instead of behind the library desk. Then a day came when she realized that too much time had lapsed, that her note would be encumbered if not vitiated by the delay, that her explanations would seem paltry, awkward, and artificial. She remembered the unavoidable embarrassment that had made it easier in the end to sacrifice the friendship than bear the burden of her failure, which had become irrational, spreading self-reproach like an infected wound.

Looking down at Vienna, Alisha knew intuitively that if she were to try to explain she would succeed only in exacerbating the indiscretion, that concretizing it in speech would be a further violation, spreading the stain she wished to remove and perhaps destroying the whole delicate fabric of their friendship. But Vienna asked for no explanation or apology, merely took Alisha's hand and pressed it gently. "Let's go to the pantry and see what's there—you must be hungry by now. We had barely two bites for dinner," she said, taking her mask off.

Relief rushed through Alisha, as heady as the new cider and cold chicken, the salted ham and fried potatoes that Fayette had wrapped in wax paper—filling and tasty, but the food had nothing to do with the yearning that made Alisha talk now, hardly stopping to swallow, interrupting herself in her greed and gratitude for Vienna's approbation.

"Slow down there, Miss Felix, you'll make me dizzy with so many unfinished sentences, and hand me the saltcellar, please."

"Here," said Alisha, handing over the salt with a flourish, "now listen up, because this part of the story will put hair on your chest." Vienna watched with a mixture of pride and astonishment that dulled her own desire for food, the gusto and showmanship of Alisha's appetite, comparing the odd grace of her friend's almost seamless ingestion with the irritating habit Willard had of lifting his fork out before him and then lurching suddenly toward the food as if to intercept it on its perilous journey to his mouth.

"There was no real way to figure it; as long as Big T. was around to make life heavy, Little T. was O.K., I mean he could tell a joke or spin a story out of Indian grass and air, and he'd get between me and the belt when Big T. had soaked up too much rye, and there were other things too; he taught me how to fish and shoot, and I bet I could still shoot the buffalo out of a nickel if you gave me a rifle on a still day, but then when Big T. died—I already told you *that* grisly piece of the past—Little T. started to change.

"He was petty and overbearing, like Big T. on a drunk, but the thing of it was Little T. didn't drink. And then he took up with a tarty type named Helen, but boys called her Melon, since she was a big bovine girl, with a pair of udders. She didn't have much in the way of aptitude but she had a fine gift for bossing and a real mean mouth, vindictive and shrill as a jaybird.

"So there she was, exercising her jaw and nothing else, and he'd just take it, but for the rest of the world it was like he was getting even. It got so that just seeing him approach would sour your stomach, and this was the boy whose smile was supposed to be a sign the angels hadn't forgotten us in Rising Pine, Alabama. Swear to God, that's what folks said. I don't know if I can even remember which way his smile went, it's been that long.

"Anyhow, when the dog died, and I still think he had a hand in that too, there was no reason to stay so I went. On the back of a load of lumber, and I don't want to talk about the splinters, I started my journey and that was ten years ago this spring, and I've seen five states since then, but you know, I still don't feel like I've found home."

Vienna sighed and, folding her napkin with military precision into a small square, said, "I know. I never felt, in all those years in my father's house, as if I were 'home,' though certainly that was where my heart was, or rather, those who had any claim to it."

"I'll bet it was plush, though," Alisha interjected.

"Yes, it was beautiful, like a marble statue that you admire from a distance but never want to touch. But then, shortly before I met Willard, my father made inquiries into houses on the Hudson that could be let for the season. This was partially for my benefit, I suppose, because he imagined that the quiet of the country would have a salutary effect on my shyness.

"It was arranged that we would be shown two houses, and then on a lark, we were shown a third, which had long been vacant and was in great need of repair. The gentleman with the keys was very apologetic, not at all sure it would do. The owner, he said, had been trying to sell the house, but he was certain it could be let on very favorable terms—just the wrong thing to say to my father, who hates haggling and regards a bargain as beneath him. He disdains any form of discount because if a thing is not expensive he never feels he has got his money's worth. It was already late afternoon and I think my father had by then tired of the whole proposition.

"The façade of the house was not distinguished, but once I entered the front hall, I felt, as I had in those odd dreams from which you wake disoriented and sad, as if I had come home. The proportions of the windows, the afternoon light filling the rooms like furniture, such graceful lines—familiar and pleasing, as if I'd designed it myself. Have you ever thought that there were forms of happiness waiting for us to appropriate them by sheer recognition?

"My love for that house was immediate, uncalculated, and all the more poignant because I understood then that I had also been waiting. As I walked through those rooms and felt myself relaxing into the breadth of their dimensions, I hoped someone would find me as I found that house: a place of repose for his heart."

"So what happened, I mean with the house?" Alisha asked.

"Oh," Vienna said casually, "my father didn't take it. There were broken windows and water stains, the wallpaper was peeling in the parlor. He found it squalid, and was so put out by the experience he took us to Europe at the month's end."

"Didn't you tell him? Didn't you try to explain?"

Vienna shook her head. "What would have been the use? Either you understood or you didn't."

"But you, who put such stock in words . . ."

"For ideas, yes, but this was love," Vienna said softly.

"Love is an idea," Alisha persisted.

Vienna turned her head abruptly and her pupils contracted as she faced the light. "Yes, but I didn't know that then."

IT WASN'T UNTIL the following morning that they got around to the masks again. "We missed our moment. They won't look as good in daylight," Alisha reflected over breakfast on the porch. Vienna stretched and replied through a yawn, "I don't know what it is about your accent that allows it to escape my censure, especially at this early hour."

"Honey, I started out with an accent so slow and lazy I guess it just couldn't keep up with my peregrinations." Alisha laughed. "And don't forget I spent a good amount of time in the North."

"Maryland," Vienna said authoritatively, waving a piece of buttered toast in a dismissive gesture, "is *not* the North."

"Well at least I've crossed the Mason-Dixon line. Now stop stalling and show me that mask or we'll still be sitting here like rejects from Mardi Gras when Willard gets home."

Vienna reached beneath the table and pulled out the papier-mâché face that had already begun to warp. "Ta Ta Ta Da," she said, making a trumpet sound with her lips.

"Mrs. Stepple?" Alisha's voice was thin and incredulous. "Damn, I never would have thought of her; that's very sly of you. You are subtle like a fox, my dear."

"Alisha! It was a joke . . . there is nothing wrong with Mrs. Stepple except that she wears too much pink and she's a natural soporific."

"You are wrong there. Sanctimony is dangerous and her brand, mixed with ignorance and goodly intentions, is a treacherous combination."

"I only picked her, Alisha, because I couldn't think of anyone I was really afraid of in Winsville. It was meant to make you laugh. Besides," Vienna continued, languidly reaching for Alisha's battered sun hat to wave away a large fly, "I thought Miss Margayt's face would be too challenging for such a crude medium."

Alisha whistled and threw back her head, combing her curls with her fingers. Overhead a turkey vulture dipped in the air like a kite responding to an unsteady hand, but by the time Alisha pointed, it was out of view. A woodpecker rattled invisibly from a distance and chimney swifts, anxious in the eaves, burst from the ivied wall and darted back with the fretful celerity of a dark fan being flung open and then clacked shut.

"Don't let this peaceable kingdom fool you. I don't know if it's because you're young or prideful, honey, but you had best learn to pick your steps with care down here. This town, hell, any town, is like a sleeping lion that you try not to wake, but if you do, sister, I hope you'll know how to chuck its chin and stroke its stinky mane. Not afraid! I'm plenty afraid, and if I'm an outsider in these parts, then you might as well be from the golden moon. I don't know how Willard puts up with your myopic bravery. It's not worth a pail of hogslop to a hound."

"Miss Felix, if you are going to continue preaching I'll get you a crate to stand on and a tin can to collect nickels."

Alisha leaned forward and snatched her straw hat off Vienna's head. "Are you listening to me?" she asked.

"Yes, ma'am, and I do wish you wouldn't be so tiresome. You're beginning to sound like a superstitious old mammy, full of doom and dogma and last night's bathtub gin."

Alisha chuckled and lit a cigarette, looking around her as if to spot eavesdroppers, and said, "Well just don't tell the darkies; I'd hate for any of your help to think I was edging in on their domain. Anyways, I've said my piece."

"Well good. Now you can show me your mask."

Vienna reached for the cigarette Alisha held, not because she enjoyed smoking but because her friend did, and it was another way to participate in Alisha's pleasure.

"Nooo, I don't think so. I have a better idea besides. C'mon, we'll go to Old Duda's shack. It's behind the quarry and I wouldn't mind a swim before it gets too cold."

"I'm not traveling halfway to Bantanburg to see some crazy woman's tar-paper hovel and you *have* to show me your mask."

Vienna looked under the table and then leaned over to Alisha, who was smiling, still shaking her head no. Vienna started patting Alisha's clothing while Alisha swatted her away, with "that tickles and it's not out here."

"You're a fiendish cheat—I'm not moving until you at least tell me who it was."

"Watch yourself, there's a bee sharing your breakfast," Alisha warned.

Vienna calmly picked up the jam jar and screwed the lid on, trapping the bee inside, continuing her protest. "I can be just as stubborn as you."

"Here, hand it over to me, I'll take care of it," Alisha said, reaching for the jar. She lifted out the mired bee and a lump of raspberry jam on her teaspoon and said, "Yep, I'll bet you can be stony as a wall but where's the fun in that?" and then she tossed the sticky mess over the rail into a clump of boxwood. Looking up at Vienna as she handed her back the teaspoon, she went on, "I'll tell you what: if you come with me now, where I want to go, I promise I'll show you the mask later. I'll *give* you the mask, how's that?"

"That's the most pathetic bribe, really," Vienna returned, rising from the table and walking to the end of the porch, where she stood with her back to Alisha, looking beyond the hayfield, in which a cluster of bent backs labored around a haystack, industrious as ants. Her gaze swept past their indistinct efforts blurred in the rippling heat of Indian summer, out to the rows of cut corn that combed the last field in view, bending off to meet at the horizon like an exercise in perspective, and she said, "I was hoping you could do better than that."

"If we take the horses, it would be about half an hour."

"We're not taking the horses and I have to be here when Willard gets back, which will be any minute."

"And I have papers to grade before tomorrow. So we'll take the bicycles. But it will take longer, an hour at the least."

Vienna reached for her gold watchcase, which hung from a long delicate chain around her neck, and having pulled it from her modest bosom, where it rested on hot days like a cool hand on her heart, snapped the engraved lid open and then clicked it closed, she pronounced with pleasure: "Impossible."

7
---■---

OLD DUDA'S SHACK was a precariously slanting jumble of planks that had never seen a coat of paint and wore the uneven stains of weather and rot, propped up on one side by a rusting metal pole at a forty-five-degree angle and by a low-hanging tree branch on which a corner of the roof's eaves rested. The uneven boards, set badly to begin with and warped by rain, left cracks in the walls that had been filled with wadded newspaper and then tarred over, leaving shiny black gashes that contributed to the wounded look of the place. It was set in a small clearing, but rich and ruthless greenery encroached on what little open land there was, threatening to overtake the small yard and decaying cabin, casting hungry shadows over the edges of the clearing, yearning to lick the corner in which crouched, stoically, Old Duda's shack.

The apparent disregard for order or upkeep had been prefigured by the random disintegrating refuse that dotted the woods like the remains of a domestic battle, increasing in frequency as Alisha and Vienna approached the clearing, signaling, even before they heard the laughter and broken bits of song, not just a human presence but one that had lost interest in the world's regard.

"Son," said Alisha Felix, without a trace of humor in her voice, "you're too young to go pointing your doodle at me. Unhand yourself this instant, you hear? Go on, get your britches and quit eyeballing me," reprimanding the nearest and only stationary one of a half-dozen, half-dressed colored children that littered the overgrown yard, scrambling among the broken crates, rusted bedsprings, dented cans, and indeterminate debris that filled the clearing, whooping with delight as a few scrawny chickens pecking at the rubbish scattered before them.

The tiny boy dropped his hand to his side obediently and instead, scratched a flaky patch of skin on his side, but his fledgling erection still sprouted from between his bowed legs. The smell from an ancient outhouse defined the clearing like an invisible fence, and Vienna said, "Let's go."

Alisha slapped a mosquito into a bloody smear on her neck. "Damn it, we didn't come through half a mile of dust and brambles just to turn back." Alisha had not been able to find the footpath, so they had had to make their way through the underbrush, snagging their clothing on briars and collecting burrs, their ankles streaked with burning scratches and their stockings ruined. The children had stopped their play and now stood wide-eyed, frozen in place.

"But the bicycles . . ."

"Those bicycles will be fine where we left them. No one can see them from the road—that's what's important."

Alisha stepped forward from the protecting shade of a sycamore and pointed at the oldest child, a thin girl of no more than eight. "Hey, you there in the red shirt, you know where we can find Old Duda?"

The little girl limped forward, exposing a large runny sore that encased her swollen knee and spread halfway down her shin. "Who be wantin t'know?" she answered warily.

"Dear Lord," Vienna gasped, seeing the leg wound. "Let me talk to her," she said firmly as she stepped in front of Alisha and picked her way over a tree root that burst from the ground like a stiffened tentacle, undulating in and out of earth in its black, buckling reach for the house.

"Don't be afraid, child—I have something for you," Vienna coaxed in a creamy voice as she advanced, scavenging in her small purse. She pulled out a silver card case and a butter candy and extended her hand from a slight distance, the way you might feed a skittish colt a carrot, careful not to approach too close. She gave the girl the sweet first, saying, "This is for you," and then while the girl fingered the candy with a mixture of greed and suspicion, she handed her a calling card, saying, "and this is for Old Duda." The girl pulled at her plaits as if deliberating, then speedily unwrapped the paper covering the candy and popped it into her mouth, while her brothers and sisters looked on jealously. Then she turned, and holding the card high in the air with one hand as if to keep it out of reach of the others, she hobbled quickly toward the sagging shack shouting something about big ladies.

Immediately the remaining children surrounded them, reaching out their small grimy hands in silent entreaty, with one exception—the shank-sprung three-year-old waddled over to the discarded candy wrapper and began to lick it with oblivious determination. "Scat, go on, scat," was Alisha's futile attempt to disband them, and then turning to Vienna, she said, "That was a fool thing to do, now they all want some and will be pestering us till Christmas." Alisha was put out not only because Vienna had succeeded where she had failed, but because it set a bad example. One didn't reward a sassy-mouthed colored child and that was that, she thought. Alisha added impatiently, "You don't know the first thing about how to be in these situations, giving out a calling card, sweet Jesus, just look at the place! And you sashay in with la-de-da manners where—" but she was interrupted by a corncob that came sailing toward them, scattering the children like swallows.

"Git away from mah bidness," Old Duda was shrieking hoarsely at the children, throwing corncobs at them as they ducked away laughing, darting behind trees. Old Duda herself looked not unlike a dried corncob. She was diminutive and ancient and as she shuffled over to them she muttered angrily at the children.

"Which one Miz Vienna?" she asked, squinting her face into a small raisin, her mouth, empty of almost all its teeth, puckered into a tight knot.

Vienna put out her hand and said, "Pleased to meet you." Old Duda held Vienna's hand clasped in her own, nodding and smiling with her last five stained teeth. Old Duda's hands were rough as bark and tiny, like a raccoon's, and Vienna wanted to extricate her own hand from the fierce grip of the old woman but didn't dare offend her.

"Y'all here fo' some cress?" Duda asked, finally dropping Vienna's hand.

"Watercress," Alisha whispered.

"Oh no, thank you. My friend, Miss Felix," Vienna replied, pulling Alisha into the conversation by putting her arm around her, "would like," and then, puzzled, because she was not really certain what it was Alisha wanted after all, said, "she would like to tell you herself the purpose of our call."

Old Duda was plainly disappointed. She chewed her gums and shook her head while Alisha explained that she was there for a fortune reading and a cure for headache.

Old Duda turned her head and spat behind her. "O.K., bud I git mah monies firs' and she come too," she said, jerking her head in Vienna's direction.

Vienna demurred, even after she had been offered a free

fortune reading and smiling at Alisha and then at Old Duda, she said, "Perhaps another day, but for the moment I think I shall wait here and enjoy"—she paused—"the lovely"—she paused again, scanning the setting rapidly—"afternoon." Old Duda nodded in approval and shouted something incomprehensible to the girl in red who lingered by the door to the shack, working the sweet vigorously in her mouth. A chair was produced and after much commotion and direction, Vienna was settled in the chair down by the creek that flowed slowly some fifty feet behind the shack.

It was there that the watercress grew in abundance. Vienna picked a sprig and chewed a leaf, clearing her head from the stifling smell of the outhouse, which she felt still clung to her though she was well away from its waft. The sun sifted through the dense foliage, casting spotlights of isolated attention: on the wide end of a mossy log, the churn of water folding over the sharp edge of a rock, and the iridescent sheen of a grackle's feather fallen in a clump of wild mint. Vienna walked to the water and rinsed her hands, letting it numb her wrists and grip her heart with its shocking thrill of cold clarity. She was tempted to take off her shoes and stockings and wade, but she knew she was being watched by the children, whose presence she felt as surely as the birds knew that behind the sweltering dazzle of sun was the press of season's shift, as yet invisible in the leaves.

She felt unhappy about her inequity in dispensing the candy, knowing that pennies for such treats were uncommon to those upturned palms and that small injustices of that sort were more likely to be hard felt than the larger ones to which they had had to become inured. She reached into her small purse again and this time pulled out the coins that had collected at the bottom, two nickels and six pennies, and tossed them into the shallowest part of the creek where they glinted, the coppers especially, like treasure rather than charity.

An amazing sense of calm filled her as she sank back in the chair. Her dress was ruined: the hem was torn in two places and badly soiled, two covered buttons were missing, and the lace on her sleeves was snagged. Vienna started to laugh. From the leafy blue shadows she heard her laughter echo back from the children. She leaned over to pick the burrs from her stockings, humming quietly to herself with contentment. The leaves overhead rustled suddenly, and there was a dull thud to her right. From the corner of her eye, she saw it and shrieked. Out of nowhere the children materialized in a swell of sound and movement, thrashing with sticks and branches, screaming and weaving and shouting at each other, and there, in the center of their frenzied dance, was the large black snake that had fallen from the tree.

One of the boys was trying to move it with a stick, twisting and jumping as if the stick was electrifying him, but it was too thin and bent flimsily against the snake's coiled weight. Another boy, reeling out from behind, whipped at the snake with a leafy branch, and the two girls dodged in and out between the boys, tossing rocks and shouting instructions, none of which were being obeyed. The snake started to wrap around one of the sticks prodding at it; someone dropped the stick, and Vienna, who had been trying to catch the bowlegged toddler before he got knocked over in the fracas, shouted furiously, "Run, goddamnit!" and everyone jumped back as the snake hissed and sprang and their ears were dulled by the sudden report of a shotgun.

Alisha stood fifteen feet behind them, pointing the barrel of Old Duda's shotgun at the ground as she emptied the chamber with shaking hands. Tears sprang from her eyes and she broke into incoherent sobs. Old Duda shuffled up behind her and put her arm around her and Alisha wept. "You done fine, baby, n'one hurt. N'one hurt but Mistah Snake," Old Duda said quietly, patting Alisha's back with her tiny hands.

The children were already pressed into a huddle to examine the splattered remains of the snake, laughing and prodding again with their sticks, flicking the meat at one another and shrieking in high spirits.

"Here," Old Duda said to Vienna, handing her a faded bandanna from around her neck, "you git some col' water on dis fo' our frien'."

WHEN THE TWO of them left, Old Duda and the children had stood grouped as if for a portrait, solemnly clustered together, waving and calling until Vienna and Alisha had disappeared from view. They had been shown the footpath, so the retreat was swift and Vienna led, holding in her hand Alisha's brown bottle of headache cure. Alisha held the wet bandanna clenched in her fist; she had stopped crying but she was still shaken and walked in silence until they were at the road, retrieving the bicycles.

"You were tremendous back there. I was immensely proud of you," Vienna said, finally.

"There's nothing to be proud of. I didn't know how wide the shell would open and y'all were so damn close and moving all the time, I took a crazy chance, and it's just luck that I didn't kill one of those children. From the way everyone was carrying on, we thought there was something really dangerous. I was afraid it might be . . . I don't even know what I thought it might be, but a black snake's not poisonous. Worse you'd get is a nasty bite, but it won't kill you if you did. Anyways, if those damn kids hadn't been attacking it, the damn thing would have probably slunk off quietly; they don't mess with trouble if they can help it."

Vienna felt chastened and deflated: too many emotions had played upon her and she was exhausted. She handed Alisha the medicine bottle and began bicycling. "We have a box of tablets at The Heights. If that's what you needed, you had only to ask."

"I don't doubt Old Duda's recipe is just as good. She knows herbs better than a witch. That's how she got free, you know, on account of her curing a Payson boy of fever after the doctors gave him up. She puts it about a year before the Emancipation Proclamation, which goes to show how old she is. I figure just to have lived that long in this county is credentials enough for me.

"Colored folk have come to her ever since, not for serious sickness, mind you, but for aches and pains. Whites too, for that matter, the ones that can't afford Dr. Barstow because he only takes cash money, or those who would just as soon not have the world know what ails them."

"And which are you?" Vienna asked.

Alisha's spirits were lifting; they had crested the hardest hill on the road back to Winsville and she was already anticipating a vanilla soda from Henshaw's refrigerated machine, which chilled the bottles till you could hardly hold them.

"You ought to know me better than to think I could fit into an easy category," she replied, smiling. "And you know what Duda said is causing these headaches?"

"Too much excitement?"

"An allergy. She says I should stay away from dogwood, cinnamon, and the color blue."

That made them both laugh until a hiccup fit punctuated Alisha's boisterous hilarity and made her stop pedaling and as she leaned over the handlebars and held her nose, she looked at her distorted reflection in the metal.

"I need," she hiccupped soberly, arching her eyebrows, "some lip rouge."

"You need to hold your breath longer and count bald men."

"This is the last one. I can feel it."

Vienna stood by her bicycle and kicked a rock with the toe of her shoe. The light had changed and the heat was lifting like dust, rising from the dry road as if the afternoon was pulling back its force, sucking the starlings up from the field in the vortex of its retreat, leaving behind the sweet smell of rain on the way.

"Maybe Old Duda's medicine will double for a hiccup cure," Vienna suggested.

Alisha smiled and shook her head. "She knows what she's doing. You should have seen the insides of her place. It was tidy as a parched bone. She has to keep the outside looking like a wreck that nobody would want, or somebody might want it.

"I'll bet she doesn't pay anything for it now but what it takes to keep it standing, but, you know, if she smartened up that yard with a picket fence and flowers, it wouldn't sit right with some around here. There'd be more than a couple families making trouble just for the pleasure of it. I guess that's why she didn't want me coming in at first, being as she didn't know us. But she said she thought on it, and best as she could remember, when trouble comes it doesn't announce itself with a calling card."

Vienna laughed as she gathered up her dress to get back on the bicycle. "After all your fussing."

"Yeah," Alisha said sheepishly, "I've never been a lady, in the grand sense, so I don't always know the right way of doing things. But I've developed a nose for knowing the wrong way of going about a thing and I can usually keep shut of that. Say, it's going to rain," she added, her nose sniffing the wind like a pointer. "If we pedal hard we can probably make it to the filling station before it breaks."

They started pumping in earnest, no longer talking, looking

at the farmhouses as only milestones to move toward or away from in their race against the darkening air. An occasional leaf would fly up and whirl against a leg or into the spokes of their wheels. The crowns of the trees deepened their color, heaving wind unevenly through the full branches.

When the first splats hit the road they were large, random stains on the dry earth, dark as tobacco spit. Then heat lightning cracked behind them and Alisha said, "Count." They held their breath, counting, and at four by Alisha's count and five by Vienna's, the thunder rolled over them as if brushing the trees and loosening the rain that came spilling down as branches dipped beneath its weight.

"Let's stop a spell under those twining trees till we see which way the storm is moving," Alisha shouted, because now the rain was a thick veil obscuring the reaches of their view as it flattened perspective into a loud, dense blur, dark as smoke.

"Yes, but leave the bicycle, *leave the bicycle*," Vienna shouted back, throwing her own bicycle into the thick grass banking the road next to the split-rail fence that enclosed a grazing meadow. They ran yelping and stumbling, their wet clothes clinging against them like climbing vines trying to hold them back. Then in the muddy and meek protection of the low boughs, they laughed as they wrung out their hair and hems.

"Looks like we had all the luck today," Alisha said, trying to press herself against the tree trunk.

"Yes, it's been marvelous," Vienna agreed, hearing no irony through the steady drumming, "I can't say when I've felt so clean," she said, and then, looking down at the dark splotches of mud that streaked upward from her encrusted shoes, she smiled at the strange truth of it.

"I think it will blow over in another handful of minutes."

"Oh, I'm in no hurry," Vienna assured her, watching a

yellow mongrel appear out of the haze of road they had run from, and come anxiously to their warmth, bringing with him the rank stink of wet pelt.

"What brand of insult is this, coming on all fours to foul what little air we've got that's not wet?" Alisha asked the dog, tenderness pushing through her harsh words, while the dog nosed at her knees.

"Settle him downwind if you can," Vienna said, sliding her back against the tree until she was in a squat. She was suddenly queasy and ravenous and calm all at once. They should have packed a picnic, she thought, though it was only a small regret, hardly taking hold in her mind, which was still racing from the momentum of the day, like the wheels of the bicycle when she abandoned it.

Alisha sat hugging her knees and pulled the dog down beside her. The boughs left large gaps in the protection they provided and the water funneled through the breaks or down the bend of a branch like sturdy channels flowing from a spout. Staring at the water guttering through the tree, she remembered the outdoor shower she had used in the summer months of her girlhood and felt her old unsettled ache.

"There's no point to this after all. We should try to get to the next farm and get dry."

Vienna nodded. "My legs are shaking a little. Give me two minutes and I'll be ready."

"Don't you dare get sick on me," Alisha joked, but her voice was dry and tight. The afternoon had defeated her. She had meant it to go differently and it was with reluctance and anger that she yielded to its twisting deviations from her vision. Now she was just tired by it and felt heavy with sadness, as if she were responsible for having failed to pull from the day its bright promise.

Vienna rose and pushed back a spray of leaves that hung near her face. The rain was beginning to slacken; she listened to its pitch rise, as the air, which had felt taut beneath the weight of the downpour, relaxed to receive a looser rhythm of distinct drops. She wanted to stand beneath the boughs of the generous old tree until the last drop's imperceptible fall had been absorbed by the darkened ground and the leaves shaped the moist air into the hushed syllables that spoke to her. Most of all, she wanted to talk about the remarkable day that her friend had wrought from a morning as ordinary as a housefly, the way she felt herself expand to let it fill her, and now the quiet fullness that was hers, beneath the fatigue of muscles and the dull call of her stomach, something she would not forget and which she had not hoped for in the long months she had been a stranger in Winsville.

The light was deepening from behind the hunched shadow of mountain that pointed toward Bantenburg, burnishing the damp air. Vienna could smell in it the rusty tang of moss and the musk of wet earth, the patina of ripeness fermenting in a late fall. She breathed deeply to let her words rise slowly, waiting for them to well into the solidity of a sentence.

"Do you suppose," Alisha asked her abruptly, "your father figured Willard was after your money?"

Vienna was stunned by the suddenness of the question and instantly started walking, letting the question goad her into movement. As she distanced herself from the moment's awkwardness she considered her response, and turned to Alisha, who kept pace at her side, waiting.

"No. I don't think that was why my father opposed Willard. That interpretation would be too insulting to me. You see, his objections came from too high an estimation of my worth: my father could not have imagined the emotional bankruptcy or blindness which would have placed a higher value on his pocketbook than on his progeny. It was simply that he didn't feel Willard was fine enough to deserve his daughter, regardless of her income." Vienna's voice was so matter-of-fact, so devoid of inflection or inflation in its unembarrassed response that Alisha might have thought she was hearing the calm recitation of a recipe for cornbread. The clumsiness of her question came to her swiftly, robbing her of any satisfaction in Vienna's honest offering.

As they picked up their bicycles and walked beside them on the muddy road, they were silent. Alisha wanted to say, "He was right, your father was right," not because she wanted to hurt Vienna, but because once again Vienna had chosen not to be hurt by her, and in understanding this, she embraced Mr. Whitcomb's lofty elevation of Vienna, who walked with bedraggled dignity next to her, ready to deflect with courage and kindness her own tactless jibes.

"I know what you're thinking," Vienna said, breaking their silence.

"No. Yes, maybe you do, but not all the way. I was thinking you are lucky to have had such a father, regardless of his income."

"And I'm thinking that without my father or my income, I am still lucky, for having found you."

Alisha smiled and turned her head away, and turning, she caught sight of a buggy coming up the hill behind them. She stopped walking and poured herself into a vigorous wave, using both hands to signal the farmer, whose face was still too far off to see clearly.

"We're saved!" she called out gaily, breaking into a booming version of "Show Me the Way to Go Home."

DURING THE RIDE back to The Heights, Vienna was silent, looking over occasionally to study the farmer, his oversized hands working the reins to the mule team, the skin freckled with liver spots like the speckled spread of tarnish on unpolished silver, and the raised blue veins that crossed and forked like a map of the difficult backroads he had traveled to get no further than a clean Sunday shirt, new rubber wheels for his buggy, and two mules he was more proud of than he was of his feckless children.

When he put them down at the open-gated entrance of the drive to The Heights and handed down the bicycles, Vienna tried to offer him two crumpled bills, stained a jaundiced yellow from the lining of her purse where the dye had run. Lifting his hat to reveal a tawny brush of hair, he merely nodded and, mumbling to the mules, rolled off.

Alisha leaned the bicycle against the gate and said, "I'm going too. I'll come by to get my things later."

"Don't be absurd, Willard can run you back to Redley Road in the car."

"No, I don't feel like asking a favor of Willard Daniels just now. I imagine he's already out of the mood for my face. You go on in and take yourself a hot bath and have a good feed and let me get back home."

Vienna stood for a moment without moving, feeling twice dismissed, holding her bicycle in one hand and the wadded bills in the other, considering what Alisha had said, as if only now had she remembered her husband. "Alisha," she called, and Alisha, who was already turning to leave, answered, "What, honey?"

"If Willard asks, don't let him know we ate in the kitchen. Of course it doesn't matter but that's just the sort of thing that he bothers about."

Alisha laughed and shook her head. "It don't take much to put him in a quiver, but I won't breathe a word, that's a promise."

Vienna turned too, and started up the drive, leaving both of the bicycles to be picked up by someone else later. The gravel was still polished and dark from the rain as she followed its path up to the waiting house.

8

━━■━━

WILLARD DANIELS HAD been drinking bootleg bourbon on the front porch for almost three hours, having settled the decanter beside him on the small Queen Anne tea table he had brought outside and placed to the right of the oak rocker he had chosen as his station for the afternoon. Beside the large weathered porch furniture, the polished cherrywood looked dainty, almost prim, and certainly out of place, like an over-dressed matron among field hands, ostentatiously delicate, its pie-crust edge as gratuitous as a lace ruffle.

Spread across Willard's lap were the month's accumulation of bills, none of which was urgent enough to be paid, but all of which added to the burdensome weight that kept him planted in the rocker. He was angry, but his anger had yet to find its direction; it swept in random review over the people and events of his tenure at The Heights, dowsing for a source, the wellspring from which his troubles emanated.

Willard Daniels was a young man accustomed to life's easy bounty; even as a child he was aware that he had been favored with his father's height, even teeth, and effortless charm, his mother's dark eyes, full mouth, and straight hair, while his older sister, Augusta, had drawn from the two an unfortunate medley of genes that produced skin blemishes, thin lips, a helmet of stiff, frizzled hair as intractable as barbed wire, a quick temper, and a meager sense of humor discernible only to the long initiated.

He had been the much-hoped-for son, and the final child, a fast favorite in a family that took no pains to disguise its appreciation for an heir and lacked the capaciousness to include more than one in the nucleus of its doting regard. Being raised under the steady blaze of a reverence that excluded any rivals, Willard had naturally grown to assume that the larger world would welcome him in magnified reflections of the admiration he had hitherto generated by being nothing more than himself, and for a while, at least, it had.

He therefore had the tendency to take setbacks hard and suffer frustration in a less gentlemanly style than might have been expected. When an investment went bad or a horse went lame, when his watch broke or the weather turned, Willard took it as a personal affront. And recently he had been feeling much persecuted, victimized by the unaccountable way things had started going wrong. It wasn't just that he had overspent on the renovations of The Heights. The money had disappeared in repairs to the plumbing and outbuildings, in replacing gas fixtures with electricity, and patching the roof: nothing that had added noticeably to the appearance of the house itself.

He had succeeded in making The Heights functional but not formal. Under the unsparing glare of electric lights, the generations of neglect were made acutely visible. All the floors needed to be sanded and stained. There wasn't a room in the house that couldn't use fresh paint or paper. The window drapes were sallowed with age and the shutters sagged on their hinges. One of the porch columns was rotting and the furniture was a downright depressing collection of odds and ends. Most of the furnishings were battered Victoriana, heavy and dark, a few items of Rococo Revival as elaborate as mausoleum decoration, a handful of bentwood and unraveling wicker chairs, a smattering of austere Federal pieces and, in the dining room, six lyre-back side chairs of French provenance, but over the years most things of value or beauty had been steadily removed: sold at auction to finance repairs or the cost of lingering illnesses.

It didn't make sense to have left Morgana, North Carolina, where he had had such a promising start, to come to a town like Winsville for anything less than to conquer it, with all the attendant trimmings and spoils. But having come, it would be hard to return to Morgana defeated by a backward farm town in which he was armed with advantages unhoped for by most men who make their mark and their money and move on.

For Willard, Winsville was an opportunity waiting for someone to come along and sharpen his teeth on. The land was rich and the taxes were low and it was within striking distance of Washington. It was, in Willard's estimation, only a lack of ambition or imagination or plain education that kept farmers planting tobacco to the ruination of the soil. Willard poured himself another drink and cursed the tenant farmer who had secured a lease to work ninety acres of The Heights from a nitwit lawyer who was handling the estate before Willard arrived. Moreover, this jackass was already beginning to implement the very ideas Willard considered his own, the private resource that he had yet to draw upon, and worse still, John Aimes was spewing at the mouth about it down at Henshaw's Hardware, chewing off those sun-leathered ears that had nothing better to do than listen up about crop rotation and insecticide and aerial dusting and shipping to the cities.

Willard took a long sip and considered the sky; spring had arrived early, though he expected there would probably be a cold snap just after the dogwood opened. Soon the front lawn would become a battlefield between him and the groundhogs that were ruining the work he had hired two gardeners to do: make the entrance and porch view manicured magnificence. The squirrels had dug up many of the initial plantings until Mrs. Stepple had stopped by and advised scattering mothballs among the new bulbs.

"If *she* knows to do that, why in creation don't my lawn boys know to do that?" Willard had fumed to Dr. Barstow, the next visitor to make his way to The Heights. It was too maddening: Willard had already spent one afternoon in a quiet fury much like this one, trying, from a chair on the porch, to rid his property of squirrels with a .22. He had succeeded in terrifying the help, riddling an ancient elm with bullet holes, killing one squirrel, and putting a congregation of crows to flight. Willard sighed and put his feet up on the rail. Dusk was his favorite time of day and he was irritated that he could not enjoy it properly. He usually felt better once he had found someone or something to blame, and when he heard Vienna singing upstairs, he understood suddenly that Miss Alisha Felix was responsible for more than a rimption of his troubles.

If *she* were not around, Vienna would have settled down, would have made her peace with Winsville and taken her place among the good women who worshiped God on Sundays in pretty, frivolously trimmed hats and somber dresses, and devoted the rest of the week to their husbands and homes. Thinking this, Willard drew comfort into a private place as deep within him as the marrow of his bones, where he had felt the corrosion of doubt.

There were times, though he tried to swallow back the notion, when he felt his marriage tearing off out of control like a horse with the bit in its teeth, carrying him in a direction-less flight in which he was helpless to do anything more than struggle to stay seated. If the problem had been merely equestrian, he could have waited to see if it would run itself out or he could have jumped off with good odds of a hurt no worse than a small ache. With his marriage, though, both choices seemed too dangerous to consider. Day by day, the distance between himself and the easy peace he had planned to find seemed to lengthen until his imagination could no longer bridge the gulf, and he found his mind moving to easier targets, the distractions which brought immediate relief and fed his inclination for pleasures that he no longer associated with Vienna.

He had met Vienna in a world in which she had been prized, and the very fact that he stood so small a chance of gaining that prize had fired his desire for it. But now, like an exotic artifact from another land, removed from the culture that deemed it precious, Vienna lacked the one thing Willard needed to sustain his admiration: a consensus. Despite the adulation on which he had been raised, he had never trusted his choice alone to guide him, and because he lacked the confidence to lead opinion, he was doomed to follow it. It was not surprising that he felt the stunned futility of a man who returns from a perilous journey to find his treasure regarded with the quiet embarrassment due the fool who spent so much for a dusty shard of pottery when he could have bought a whole shiny new vase without very much of a walk.

But what galled him more than his own waning love was the suspicion that Vienna's love was also wanting. He could have borne with practiced patience the attentions of a wife whose charms he no longer favored, but the idea of a learned indifference to his own considerable appeal was insufferable.

As he fumed over the indignity of such a situation, he considered Vienna's recent news. Pregnancy was one of those special dispensations, like a brain tumor or questionable bloodlines, which could explain almost any oddity. There was a fleeting relief in the thought, but Willard did not linger on it. His reaction to the pregnancy was complex, and generally he preferred not to think about it. Whatever mitigating compensations it might offer, it also demanded compromises with which Willard was not entirely comfortable. So he returned to the problem of Alisha Felix with the predictability of a tongue worrying a painful tooth.

When Vienna stepped out onto the porch, still slim and pale as a birch, calling her husband to the table, Willard felt himself succumb to the afternoon, to the gathering force of glancing questions, distilled corn mash, and chafed pride. The anger he contained like a door swollen shut in its frame suddenly sprung to release a rush of blackness.

"Alisha Felix is a cheap piece of trouble," he began.

"Miss Felix is my friend."

"You've hit the problem spang on its head. Call her a friend, but she is nothing more than an undertow pulling you out to the dark waters she inhabits because there is nowhere else for her to go."

"Willard, this is whiskey talk. Please stop or you'll take it too far."

"Too far! She's the one's gone too far. You never go anywhere with her you don't return from looking like you've been lynched. No, from now on she can spelunk for hell with someone else."

"Keep your voice down," Vienna pleaded softly. "Only once were we caught in the weather, but it was months ago in the fall, and besides you can't fault Alisha for that. We've had a few outings and a bit of fun. You won't begrudge me that, I hope, and I don't see how it justifies such a lather."

"Fun!" Willard snorted. "Was it fun spending four days in bed with legs a leper would be ashamed to own, and half the house brewing snakeroot tincture and camomile poultice and God knows what else for your poison ivy?"

"That was unfortunate, but certainly not Alisha's fault. Blame me if you must. Those were my legs, after all, that so repelled you," Vienna said, with the cutting chill of dry ice in her voice.

"Your legs are not the issue and don't change the subject. You're lucky to be alive, traipsing behind that woman. Only an idiot would choose to swim in a quarry full of snapping turtles and water moccasins. A farmer's boy was wrapped in a Medusa's snarl of the damn things when they pulled him out of there dead."

"That's an apocryphal tale and you know it. Plenty of people swim there without incident, and I count myself among them."

"There's more than enough running water around here for decent folks to drown in if that's your aim. Leave that waterhole to the coloreds that don't have sense enough to stay away," Willard hissed, attempting to modulate his voice. He rocked furiously in his chair, his knuckles a luminous white grip on the armrests.

"I thank you for your concern about my welfare and I will not swim in the quarry again, if that will make you happy."

"Much obliged," Willard returned sarcastically, his hand lifting an invisible hat. "But it will take a little more than that to make me happy."

"What did you have in mind?" Vienna asked, turning her head away, her eyes squinting at the horizon.

"Oh, the list is long, but you could begin by shedding that miserable blight upon this house by the name of Felix."

"That," Vienna said firmly, her lips tightening involuntarily, "is not an option. Try another."

"I *have* tried and tried and tried, and now it's your turn, Mrs. Daniels, to try."

"Very well, Willard," Vienna said slowly, sighing and shutting her eyes, "I will see Miss Felix only under the shelter of this roof, where I am relatively safe from disfigurement, censure, inclemency, and vipers—the water kind, I mean."

Vienna waited for a moment after she finished speaking for her heart to stop pounding and then she turned, walked to the door and, pulling it open, added, "Your supper is waiting, if you can swallow your bile first."

Willard hoisted himself heavily from the rocker and was immediately struck by the thickening effects of his drinking. His feet felt unusually large and clumsy and his body carried his weight like shifting ballast. He straightened himself with effort, which made his head swim momentarily, as if he were falling, and he recognized a feeling that so often visited him in dreams, waking him upright in bed with his hands outstretched to stop himself. When the disorienting spin of gravity subsided, he felt clear enough to want the last word, so he balanced himself on the worn threshold across which he had lightly carried Vienna eight months before into the giddy promise of mutual nurture and unbound expectation. Directing his words like sharp darts aimed at his wife's retreating form, as if she bore away with her the possible fulfillment of that dream, he said, "Alisha Felix has terrible posture and her clothes are an assault on the eye. Tell her to molt some of those fiercer colors."

Vienna's voice drifted softly down to him from the second-floor landing, light as snow falling in an empty field, her words dissolving in the dry air between them: " *If thine eye offend thee, pluck it out.*' It's a much simpler solution, don't you think, than enforcing a dress code?"

9

———■———

*A*LISHA FELIX ENJOYED a certain notoriety for being the only regular visitor to The Heights. The privilege of Vienna's confidences translated into an extra button or a length of ribbon at the notions shop, a Sunday gazette held for her until after two at the sundries counter of the general store, and an invitation (declined) to Mrs. Stepple's sewing circle. It ensured a friendly hello at Henshaw's Hardware and prompt service at the bakery.

Everyone expected Alisha to provide the link, the leak through which Vienna's seclusion could be parlayed into a sustaining source of gossip, the process of transformation which turned Daniels chaff into Winsville's hominy without the effort or awkwardness of direct discourse. Everyone knew that Vienna was pregnant, that Willard's business trips had become increasingly frequent and of greater duration, but they could only guess as to whether this was dictated by necessity or inclination, in response to problems pecuniary or domestic.

But Alisha was nobody's fool: she knew full well that by satisfying her audience she would lose her hold over them and so she maintained a calculated distance from disclosure, conveying by inference just enough flavor to season their speculation, relying on a hint or pause to suggest the words that she withheld. She relished her position as pontiff, bridging Winsville and The Heights, and she savored the power endowed by the obliquity in which she traded almost as much as the actual secrets she shared with no one.

She alone knew what the rest of the town only imagined in late-night dyspeptic conjecture: that Vienna's indifference or inability to entertain deprived Willard of the audience and admiration he required to be content in a town the size of Winsville, and that he sought it elsewhere. She knew that Willard's relationship with Vienna was frequently congenial but rarely carnal, that the connubial expectations of both were at best confused, and that the advent of Vienna's pregnancy had introduced an element of chance on which the delicate equation teetered.

Alisha Felix was aware of what Winsville was not: that Willard was deeply in debt, that he had drained his resources on failed speculations and was selling properties he held elsewhere in a desperate attempt to remain solvent and sanguine, and that he found the notion of paternity an unwelcome burden save for the birth of a boy, which would provide sufficient interest on the investment of tiresome responsibility to make the proposition viable.

Alisha could calibrate to the exact decimal the degree to which the South weighed on Vienna, though Willard refused to accept that West Virginia even *was* Southern, and how in response Vienna was growing quirky and withdrawn almost apace with her burgeoning belly. Alisha, who knew the rate at which Vienna's regrets multiplied as intimately as the times table that covered a wall of her schoolroom, could quickly calculate the sum of how many letters to Vienna's father had been returned with the request "Let us wait a full year before breaking silence or bread together" written on the back of the unopened envelope.

And only Alisha felt the change—a change in which Alisha found herself at the center, enjoying a calm much like the strange stillness said to be found at the heart of a tornado. Maybe it began with Vienna's pregnancy, which increasingly limited the range of their outings until Vienna was content with the confinement of The Heights. Or maybe it began with the restriction Willard placed on their friendship, which had the perverse effect of throwing him into greater contact with Alisha than either of them wanted.

Or, perhaps, it began with a story Vienna told Alisha when they were lying together in the hammock between two chestnut trees. Alisha asked Vienna if there were anything she would have done differently in her life if she had had the chance. Vienna adjusted the plush pillow beneath her head and said thoughtfully, "When I was seventeen, my father and I returned from Italy via England. My mother had a girlhood friend with whom we stayed for a weekend in Hampshire, in a very old house famous for its gardens. I don't remember much about my mother's friend, except that she was large and kind and she spoke so softly that everyone had to lean over the dinner table to hear her.

"What I do remember vividly is the old woman, a relative of some kind, who lived in the east wing, over the library. She was ailing and took all her meals upstairs, in her bedroom; we were never introduced. One day, though, I found her in the library, sitting at an elaborate rosewood writing desk, looking for something in one of the many pigeonholes and drawers. She smelled of jasmine and ambergris, sweet and exotic and old. She was tremendously old. Her hands trembled.

"She smiled at me and motioned me over by patting the footstool in front of her. As I approached I could see her eyes were clouded and that it was hard for her to appraise me with only the slash of light from where the damask curtains gapped. She seated me in front of her and took my hand. She told me that when she was my age or thereabouts she had fallen in love with an Italian count. He had a waxed mustache and dimples, and he said the cleverest things in broken English. She became determined to marry him and when he asked for her hand, her family had agreed, with one proviso: that she learn to speak fluent Italian before she wed. Then the old woman laughed in a way that made it hard to know if I should also laugh. Her voice had a crackling quality, like leaves crumbling, and much as the situation made me uncomfortable, there was something very appealing about her. She still held my hand between her own and for some reason that made me feel warm and sleepy: her skin was flecked with age and soft and loose like a ripe cheese and its touch comforted me. 'Of course,' the old lady said in a dramatic whisper, 'when I spoke his language I understood that he was not the man I imagined, and I married Lord Brenwaithe instead.' Then she laughed again and walked slowly across the room. She paused at the door and wagged her index finger at me before she left the library.

"I don't say that I oughtn't to have married Willard, but I certainly should have learned more about *this* before I did," Vienna said, flicking her wrist in a gesture broad enough to include the house and land and state. "It would have made this year so much easier," she concluded calmly, giving the hammock a gentle sway by extending her foot over the side and lazily pushing away from the ground.

Many things occurred to Alisha in the unfolding of that tale, but none was more dangerous than the realization that she shared with Willard something Vienna never would: the commonality of being born in the South, bred under the broad shadow of the Civil War that cast its umbrage over two generations, to steep its children's children in the legacy and lore of loss. The very things about Willard that were foreign to Vienna were familiar to her, and suddenly she recognized her advantage. She understood Willard.

Not that she didn't sympathize with Vienna's complaints about the way Willard would meticulously clean his nails with a silver penknife and wipe the blade on whatever was handy, be it a linen napkin or lace antimacassar, or agree that his petulance was childish and his stories were repetitive, and his way of jiggling his knees so that the dinner table shook was annoying, but in Alisha's experience men had done a lot worse than that without the virtues of a good name, good looks, and a general disposition to please. Besides, she now had another side of the story with which to balance these shortcomings, namely Willard's catalogue of petty grievances, like the fact that Vienna indiscriminately sipped from the nearest glass, regardless of whether or not it was her own, or that she hiccupped loudly and without shame and thought nothing of greeting visitors with ink stains on her hands and was unfailingly firm with everyone but the servants.

Alisha was also dismayed by the paucity of knowledge on which Vienna had based her decision to marry, ephemera of no more substance than a hunch. Vienna cited only the most fragile expressions of intuition and nuance, such as the way Willard had first kissed her—not the quality of the kiss, but the very fact that he had taken it, unlike the others who had always asked permission, and doing so, had forfeited the moment of privilege. Alisha had great respect for Vienna's abilities as a scholar; her erudition was extreme and her intellect could be intimidating, yet she had eloped with a man about whose life she knew less than the pork she chose for her table, having no qualms about interrogating the butcher with the ruthlessness of a journalist researching a scandal.

When confronted with the insubstantiality of these claims, Vienna had only laughed and quoted from Ecclesiastes, "In much wisdom is much grief: and he that increaseth knowledge increaseth sorrow."

Vienna's sporting acceptance of a situation she would neither renounce nor praise was maddening to Alisha; try as she would, she received only more ironic invocations of Scripture, which increased Alisha's discomfort because she had never been quite able to determine Vienna's idiosyncratic relationship to her faith. Therefore, when Vienna responded to her wheedling with "I gave my heart to know wisdom, and to know madness and folly: I perceived this also is vexation of spirit," Alisha was unable to decipher the core of what she inferred was undoubtedly a jest at her expense.

Clearly it was some form of mockery, coming from a woman who had recently dismissed the Episcopal minister from Bantanburg, an imposing man with a booming voice and an elaborate network of delicate red veins making his nose look like complicated circuitry, who had come collecting for the Easter pageant, with her blithe remark, "No thank you, we're buying no indulgences today." To find the same woman who had sampled services in every faith to evaluate the musicality of the organist and choir before choosing the congregation into which her baby would be christened now barricading herself behind the impregnable sanctity of Scripture was a maneuver Alisha admired and hated for its tactical efficiency.

Ever so slowly, Alisha turned her attention to Willard as Vienna turned her attention to the child growing inside her, Alisha's tenderness activated by the childish simplicity of what Willard seemed to need and his poignant inability to attain it. Moreover, Alisha was a woman who knew herself primarily through those who had loved her, and that Vienna didn't seem to require a man to act as her reflecting glass prompted in Alisha a comparison by which she felt herself diminished.

If she noticed anything, Vienna was relieved at the reduction in tension between her husband and her friend. Now that the three of them were spending more time together, Vienna was pleased by the truce she took to be a tribute to their concern for her. She encouraged a friendship between them that allowed her to withdraw when she felt fatigued by the fatuous preoccupations of her pregnancy.

If Willard flirted with her friend, it amused her; Vienna was comforted by the notion that Alisha's easy wit and extensive curiosity were no longer exercised for her satisfaction alone, and she was proud of Alisha as she watched her husband discover in her friend the qualities she had found so appealing. Seeing Alisha through the incipient admiration of her husband renewed and confirmed Vienna's own estimation of her. When Alisha laughed at Willard's jokes, it relieved Vienna of the obligation to do so, and while Vienna was surprised to find Alisha's sense of humor catholic enough to embrace the obvious and puerile, it was nonetheless an unexpected but welcome bonus.

For the first time since she came to Winsville, Vienna relaxed and took her days with the long strides and easy gait of someone content with herself. The extra weight looked well on her, and as she told Alisha, finally she had bosoms worth notice. Before Willard, she had not thought more about her body than that it got her where she wanted to go; she had been told by schoolmates that she had an enviable frame for clothes to hang from, that she could wear the new fashions with the lean length required for the fabric to drape properly, but that she wore clothes well merely meant to Vienna that she needed to spend less time and attention selecting them.

It was only after a stray remark of Willard's that Vienna first considered her body objectively. He had once said, while she sat on his lap, that she was not built for comfort. When she asked him what he meant, he had explained that her angularity cut like a flint, and women were intended to have protective padding, like a well-designed bicycle seat. The remark had wounded her and for a time she had clung to it, despite a conflicting worldliness that acknowledged men who preferred a slimmer ideal. Willard had added to the injury by later suggesting that she could do with a more current hairstyle—the beauty shop in Bantanburg had women lining up for permanent waves, and he would be glad to drop her off one afternoon. It had been a shock to hear him recant the nearly fulsome praise he had lavished on her long hair, and the elegant intricacies of the knots and coils she wore during their brief courtship. But that was before she noticed inconsistencies of her own—some of the very attributes with which Willard had won her affection had become the same ones that now challenged it, so it became easier for her to accept the unfavorable discrepancy of a taste altered than a taste unalterable. But even those considerations now seemed remote in the well-being Vienna enjoyed.

Exactly when she became apprehensive would be difficult to determine: there were so many distracting factors following Willa's birth, among which Willa herself was perhaps the most compelling. Her birth involved an unusually drawn-out delivery because, heedless of the advice repeated at hourly intervals by the attending physician at the Bantanburg hospital, Vienna refused to have a cesarean section. Then Willa did not nurse properly for several weeks, adding to the general hysteria into which the house had been thrown by her arrival. And on top of all this, Vienna had her father's death to contend with.

Willard's trips had been something Vienna took little notice of, not only because she had become accustomed to their frequency but because in his absence she could attend to the infant without feeling that she was juggling her limited energy between two equally demanding claims and, more important, without having to apologize for the baby's incessant squalling or field tactless questions regarding her own competence as a mother.

As to Alisha, it had seemed entirely natural, if not predictable that their friendship should suffer some temporary diminishment under the despotic reign of an infant, but the impediment was not one that Vienna felt would have long-lasting implications. In a matter of months, Willa made the transition to a regular feeding schedule and slept through the night. Fayette was becoming increasingly comfortable handling the baby and sharing the responsibilities, which were ultimately more satisfying to her than unvaried cleaning and cooking.

It was only when Vienna's life finally settled back into a familiar routine, when she returned to her translations and the ongoing struggle with her epic poem, that she realized the domestic landscape was different. It was not clear to her until summer, when Alisha was released into the luxury and wallow of vacation time, and by then she found herself in the pull of forces that had been gathering momentum during the long year in which she had been preoccupied with parenthood. Vienna emerged from her myopia unprepared for what she confronted, like a dreamer awaking to find herself precariously perched on a roof.

Vienna had looked forward to the summer, with its abundant opportunities for the outings she had craved during the months she had been housebound by Willa and by raw weather, remembering the previous year's adventures with a yearning that seemed almost physical. There were new tires on the bicycles and she had collected ideas for projects and excursions with the assiduous care of a curator.

But Alisha was strangely unmoved by suggestions that would have elicited profane approval the year before, resembling in motive and method the exploits that had been the cornerstone of their friendship. Her visits to The Heights corresponded with predictable regularity to Willard's presence as unerringly as they had once coincided with his absence. Willard was becoming sloppy, almost cavalier about his evening forays. He returned home in a haze of dime-store scent: obvious compositions of vanilla and rose attar that hung as heavily on clothes and hair as cigar smoke. Drunken and loud, he was liable to wake the baby to a shattering wail, which in turn set him off in a competing ill-tempered roar.

Of course Vienna tried to confront the situation, but Willard maneuvered away from answers with such ease that Vienna found herself longing for a direct response, even if it were mendacious. When Vienna turned to her friend for comfort, she found her friend was not there, was oddly occupied with lesson plans and replacing chalkboards or distributing free samples of dental cream sent by the Colgate company to promote healthier hygiene and introduce its product to the backwoods of Jackson County.

But Alisha Felix was there the night Willard sold off ninety of his best acres to John Aimes, the night Vienna exploded in accusations and Alisha defended Willard, that last night at The Heights before access to The Heights was closed to her. That was the night Vienna smashed every one of the Limoges dishes that served twenty-four and had never been used, their trip from New York a mover's nightmare, individually wrapped in white tissue paper and stacked between balls of newspaper in a wooden trunk, and when at last they lay in shards down to the last demitasse, Vienna started in on the willowware.

Alisha was there that night when Willard announced his departure, when he asked her to go with him, not because he loved her, which he did not, but because he had been drinking and he was angry, but leaving alone seemed hard. She had said yes, not because she loved him, which she did, but because she could feel the heat of his face burning his cheeks to a red glow, and she mistook anger for passion, and because she loved Vienna even more and wanted to know what it was like to be her, who was beautiful, who played piano and spoke languages, was too fine for Winsville but didn't leave. Alisha had always known she would leave, and this was as good a chance as any.

Alisha was there when Willard left without her, though she waited in the barn half the night, in the dust and hay and damp, knowing he would not come for her. She heard the reverberating shot, not knowing who held the gun or who held up their hand against it, wishing that she could have put herself between them in a different way even if it had meant absorbing the blast in her double heart, duplicitous and devoted.

Alisha Felix left the barn in time to see Willard pull the car away, and Vienna's shape waver at the window before closing a curtain on Alisha's tenure in Winsville, the two-year stay that ended as abruptly as it began, with Alisha at the station waiting for the first train, with a large broken suitcase bound up in twine, two battered crates, and a yellow ladderback chair.

JOHN AIMES KNEW that night that he was paying twice the going price for the Daniels property, and handed the check over gladly, not because he expected to make a significant return on the land but because he had watched Willard in the neighboring towns and hoped that, flush with new funds, Willard would seize the opportunity to flee his many debts and disillusionments and put Winsville behind him. Aimes had been observing, with the trained eyes of a veteran, the trajectory of domestic discord pieced together from the flimsy clues he gleaned by following Willard to the late-night cafés, roadhouses, and social clubs. He had waited patiently in shadowed corners of dingy rooms for confirmation of the bitter ferment of unproductive fights and failed reconciliations, compromises and conditions exacted in anger and abandoned with haste, leaving both parties feeling wronged and empty, inviting into the vacuum the balm of meaningless but flattering flirtations.

Aimes was a patient man, and it seemed at last as if his patience would be rewarded. He bore Willard no ill will, but if there was anything in his power he could do to hasten his young neighbor's inevitable departure, he would do it without remorse—in fact, he would do it with the grim kindness of a man putting down an injured horse. The money he gave Willard that night, his entire savings, was calculated to work as efficiently and quickly as a well-placed bullet.

When he heard the shot, he thought for a moment he had made a mistake, had underestimated the depths of Willard's despair, or worse, of Vienna's stoic strength, and he ran to The Heights across land that had just become his own, through the wooded shortcut and past the outbuildings, preparing himself for either eventuality. He girded himself to comfort the wife of a suicide or to take the blame for murder, imagining himself saving Vienna from the sin by which she freed herself to reward him with a love he would then have earned, confident that the deed he held to the ninety acres and the alcohol level in Willard's blood would make credible the plea of self-defense. He knew the local lawyer, Mr. Woodruff, could testify to the irrational emotion Willard had evinced on the subject of those acres, so that seller's remorse and wild threats would surprise no jury, if it ever came to that.

By the time John Aimes reached the blue barn, he was equally exhilarated by the fantasy he had evolved and the rush of adrenaline that pounded in his heart, and as he stopped behind the barn to catch his breath he noticed the slight tumescence, the first palpable sign of desires stirring in him in longer than he cared to calculate. It was with dismay complicated by ambivalence that he saw Willard run to the car, alive and whole and hell-bent on his exit.

For the first time since he heard the shot, Aimes considered another alternative, one too brutal and tragic to accept as the end of the hope he had nursed through white nights bent over books of etiquette and long hours tending Daniels land, watching calluses build on his hands and heels under the chafe of daily friction as slowly and surely as it eroded the affection of his young neighbors. That the trajectory of betterment he had followed like a shooting star across his neat fields could end with Vienna's being taken from him instead of being given to him was an unthinkable twist in the gift fate had bestowed when it landed him on Willard's property.

But there she was, at the window, turning away from him with unseeing eyes. It would be months before John Aimes understood the irony of his mistake, how unwittingly he had ensured Vienna's unattainability, and insulated Willard beyond the reproach of proximity.

WHEN VIENNA ROSE from her bed, it was with the bewilderment of one returning from the wilderness. It had been nearly seven weeks, and the doctor had been called in when she could no longer keep food down. Fayette herself had gone to fetch him, carrying Willa on her hip down the gravel road and on into town. To compensate for being barefoot, she had worn a blue felt cloche that was by far the most fashionable thing she owned and made her look older than her fifteen years. All the way to the back door of the doctor's office, she had rehearsed the one-sentence summary she had pared down until it was as lean as she was. "Come, Dr. Barstow," Fayette had announced, "Miss Vienna is having herself a breakdown."

He was the same doctor, Vienna learned, who had dressed Willard's wound. Quite casually, as he unpacked his leather satchel at the foot of her bed, he mentioned treating an accident in which a gun had misfired: "There was a single graze on the shoulder, and the slightest powder burn. The skin near the collarbone might be discolored. Buckshot wounds aren't usually *discreet*. Very lucky, all in all."

Fayette crouched outside Vienna's door, frightened and protective, listening to the doctor's harsh cigarette voice. She heard him admiring the Hepplewhite chest of drawers, the Oriental runner, and the Italian pen-and-ink drawings. He looked into Vienna's ears and asked her if she had ever been to Florence. He tapped her back and talked wistfully about Giotto. He depressed her tongue with a flat piece of metal as he rhapsodized about the quattrocento, the hill towns, the frescoes.

Vienna's cheeks flooded with color, as if the doctor's praise found its way to her like water finding its level, as if the recognition of her spirit, as identified by the things she loved, was itself the palliative which restored to her not only health but the desire for health. She found herself animated, wanting to interrupt, to question and compare. The lethargy lifted. Ideas welled up, pooling into sentences. It was as if another language were being spoken, one she recognized as her mother tongue.

Dr. Barstow sat by her side a long time, smoking Chesterfields—long enough to imbue the quilt on which he sat with the heavy acrid smell which clung to him and which he had made his own, like a shadow he had adopted, visible in the stains on his fingers and teeth. The blue smoke flooded into the long rays that striped the room, mapping the currents of air, the density of light, in slow, dissolving swirls.

Vienna talked. She talked about the quality of the sun on the hayricks and likened it to the way in which the Siennese used gilt; she talked about the pinks of the Fra Angelico angels and the gleam of bronze reliefs. She talked about the architecture of ascension, the way in which the height of the cathedrals, the elongation of the perspective created by tapered columns, lead the eyes upward toward the heavens and the afterlife, whereas the small, homelike buildings of the Baptist churches root one here on earth, in the scale of the domestic, the here and now as familiar as the kitchen.

When she finally paused, her mouth was dry and she was hungry. She looked into the doctor's bloodshot eyes and saw that they were unfocused; she concluded his thoughts were elsewhere. Vienna was suddenly embarrassed and tired. He too, looked tired. He coughed into a discolored handkerchief and stood up. "It's been a pleasure," he said, taking her hand in his, "and you should feel better soon, when the morning sickness passes."

10

─ ■ ─

*V*IENNA LOOKED OUT at the green haze of budding trees
and at the fields patchworked with random fecundity. Spring
was late and she was feeling bloated and heavy; it was her
eighth month in the pregnancy that had announced itself with
the irony of an afterthought weeks after the dissolution of her
marriage, like a final sally, a Pyrrhic victory, though whose
she could not yet say.

From the kitchen came the limping cadence of Fayette
thwacking ants with a flyswatter, a loud strike followed by the
hoarse drag of the mesh as the dead were wiped off the surfaces
on which they fell. Ants, Vienna thought, are the manifesta-
tion of sorrow: the unwelcome truths we want to ignore or
kill—the tragic festering in Arcadia, in microcosm but in mul-
titudes. She looked up, suddenly jolted out of her reverie. She
could hear shouts carried by the wind coming from the back
end of the property, where the scrub and overgrowth blossomed
into a scraggly wood.

She had discovered early on how the wind, if the conditions
were right, could carry a snatch of a conversation, an exchange
or a name, the high end of a laugh or just the contour of a
voice. She had been unnerved by this at first; it seemed as if

the elements were conspiring to force town life upon her regardless of her inclination, making her an eavesdropper, as rude as the wind was ruthless. But what she heard now chilled her to the bone, though she could not have said why exactly, except that she could hear, as if distilled from the words that were lost, a kind of anger she had only recently come to know, drunken and dangerous. And then she heard, clear as if it came from across the porch, the word *nigger* ring out like a slap, stunning and blunt.

She walked quickly into the kitchen, looking for Fayette, but Fayette was now down by the shed, hanging up Willa's clothes. Vienna could see her through the cracked kitchen window. The line was so slack that all the bloomers and lace frocks would eventually slide down to meet in a wet mess in the middle. How many times have I told her to tighten the line first? she thought with irritation.

"Don't bother with that now," Vienna called through the screen door. "Willa has a fever. I want you to take her in to Dr. Barstow. If he isn't in his office, I want you to wait until he gets back. Do you understand?"

Fayette looked at her quizzically. "I just put her down for a nap not thirty minutes ago and she seemed fine, though I—"

Vienna interrupted her sharply, repeating, "Do you understand?" Fayette nodded awkwardly. Her long narrow frame gave her the elongated elegance of a mannerist sculpture, but when she was nervous or confused her movements were exaggerated—she became more like a marionette than a Modigliani.

"I'll take a blanket, case we should sit a while," she said, not knowing what was wrong, fearful of leaving Vienna alone with her sudden moods and deep unhappiness but afraid to refuse, not understanding why Vienna wanted her and Willa away, at the only other place she considered safe in Winsville.

She started up the path to the house, through the crabgrass and the clover, looking down at where her footsteps had flattened the green like a carpet worn thin. Then she heard, coming from the woods, the sounds of thrashing in the undergrowth, as if someone were clearing a path. When she heard the cursing, she broke into a run.

Fayette first went to the linen cabinet and grabbed a patchwork quilt that Vienna had commissioned from one of the local women but had never used, then she picked Willa up from her baby bed and hoisted her onto a hip like a sack of groceries, holding the quilt between them as padding against the edge of her bone.

Fayette held her head at an angle, as she did when she set about something with purpose, and went down the front stairs, running her free hand along the cool sleek neck of the banister. When she reached the foyer she could feel the afternoon lifting, the first hint of evening in the air, and she felt a chill rise from her skin, making her walk quickly and evenly so as not to wake Willa, who nestled against her, sodden with sleep. She looked back once, before the bend in the road, and saw Vienna's pregnant profile walking up the hill toward the horse pasture. Fayette shook her head and clucked to herself and spat through the gap in her teeth for the comfort of habit.

Dr. Barstow drove out toward The Heights as soon as he heard the rumor. He passed Fayette on the road and cursed to himself. His hands were too shaky to light a cigarette so he chewed at his lower lip and pushed the car into fourth gear. He had packed a pistol under the linen bandages in his medical bag. The car shuddered and ticked, skidding slightly on the unpaved road, before Barstow turned down the overgrown path that ran back to Mr. Aimes's orchard. The car sprayed mud and stones to either side, cutting a wild path in the damp ground as it veered to avoid the larger rocks and ruts. Dr. Barstow wanted a drink badly.

He pulled the car up to the house and called out "John" several times. There was no answer. The wind was rising and leaves scuttled in whirling currents. He listened carefully, but the wind was absorbing into its rush the sounds of the angry men he was trying to track. He gave one final shout of "John Aimes!" letting the final vowel trail off in the gravel of his strained voice. He scratched out a quick note on his prescription pad and poked it under the kitchen door, then got back in the car. He drove up to The Heights, a light sweat moistening his neck.

He parked prominently in front of the house and walked up the porch steps. Dr. Barstow knocked on the door as he opened it, knowing already that no one was home. He went into the kitchen and put his black bag on the wooden table next to a bowl of fruit rotting to a sticky brown. He unpacked some equipment from the bag and put the kettle on. Then he poured himself a drink from a battered flask he had also packed in his kit and walked out to the sitting room. There were sheets over the furniture, so he returned to the kitchen and sat at the kitchen table, drinking bourbon from a mason jar he found in the sink.

When the door banged open behind him, he spilled bourbon on his shirt as he swung around. "Jeezuus, John. Hellofaway to come up behind a person! I thought you might be . . ."

"Where is she?" John Aimes interrupted.

"Damned if I know," Barstow said, dabbing with a handkerchief at the stain on his shirt.

"What about the hired girl and the baby?"

"I passed them on my way up. She must have figured it out and sent them on to town."

"Christ almighty," Aimes muttered, kicking at the heavy

oak table with the toe of his worn field boot. "Easy there," Dr. Barstow snapped, putting a hand out to still the glass and fruit bowl, which quivered from the impact.

"How'd you know?" Aimes asked, looking vulnerable and boyish despite fatigued eyes and heavy silver stubble shadowing his jaw. Although the two men were not friends, there was between them a mutual respect that made their interaction easier.

"Heard it from a whore. I knew something was up when there were no men out back of the Lazy Swan or on Henshaw's porch. So who have they got?" Dr. Barstow asked. It occurred to him with a twinge of regret that John Aimes, for all his prim integrity and his earnest industriousness, would have made a good friend, had not social bounderies separated the farmer from the gentleman. Aimes was largely uneducated, but the appeal of his company, such as Dr. Barstow gleaned in the intimacy of their exchange, was precisely that Aimes was not a man who required conversation. It suddenly struck Barstow that while he was very social, he didn't much enjoy the company of others, and that Aimes, on the other hand, was unapologetically withdrawn, but not because of any bitterness toward his fellow man.

"Dunno exactly," Aimes answered, pushing his grizzled hair from his sun-creased forehead. "One of the new boys from the mill, I think. But how'd you know they'd come here?"

"Just a hunch. It's an obvious choice: a couple hundred acres of obscurity with no one around but women—one pregnant, one colored, and one a baby."

"The wind was carrying like a telephone before the weather shifted and the storm started coming in. I heard the motorcars and then the shouting. Damn it all, I'm going up to the north end, I guess. You coming with me?" Aimes asked impatiently, his wiry body already straining toward the door.

"No, I'm staying right here. She'll need me for an alibi and maybe more besides. But take this with you," Dr. Barstow said, pulling the handgun out from under the bandages.

"Keep it." John Aimes laughed, touched. "I got my shotgun outside." He lurched through the door, letting the screen slam behind him.

Dr. Barstow picked up the jar and took another swig, a pained ironic smile curling his lips as if he had just swallowed turpentine. John Aimes. Who'd have ever guessed his valentine? Dr. Barstow rolled a cigarette and smoked it slowly, killing time, taking in the revelation with the gray-blue spiral of smoke.

HE HAD GONE through all his smokes and several fingers of bourbon and was dozing, lulled by the light spattering of rain against the kitchen window, when he heard the shots. Three in a row and then one and then two more. The last two sounded closer than the others.

He sprang out of his chair and went to the window. Looking out through the irregularities in the glass pane, he rolled up his shirtsleeves in tight, even folds and then started unwinding the bandages. He took several white enamel bowls from the cabinets and assembled them on the table, filling some with the water he had kept at a low boil. After he had sterilized a scalpel he rolled up his trouser leg and nicked his calf. His hands worked steadily and his lips were pinched. He wiped blood on the bandages and dipped them into the water, tinging it bright red. Then he applied a styptic to the wound and put a plaster on it. When he was done, he rolled down his pants leg and stood up, surveying the debris he had arranged on the table. It looked convincing. As an afterthought, he rolled his left sleeve down, dipped it in the bloody water and let the stain travel up his sleeve past the cuff before rolling it back up again.

The door creaked and she stood there panting and trembling. "I'm chilled," she said.

He stood for a moment staring. She was wearing Willard's clothes and her hair was swept up under a hunting cap. When Vienna had resumed an ambulatory life in the weeks after Willard left her, one of the first things she had done was dress a scarecrow in her husband's clothes. It had been a jarring sight, visible from the road and subject to much speculation in the town. That had been six months ago, but now, the way the clothing hung limply from her lean extremities and pulled tight across her swollen belly, the way blond strands of hair escaped the loose hold of the cap, it seemed poignantly familiar, as if she had become that effigy of loss or anger.

Then Dr. Barstow noticed the dark stain on Vienna's trousers. She looked down, following his gaze, and felt the wet fabric. Her face contracted in humiliation.

"You didn't pass water, you broke it," Dr. Barstow said calmly. "Get upstairs quickly. Wash and put on a nightdress. And if you hear anyone come into the house, start screaming. Make it sound like pain, not fright."

She nodded, looking down at her leg again. Then she saw the table. "What's been going on here. It looks like . . ."

"It looks like it's been a difficult afternoon," Dr. Barstow interrupted. "This," he said proudly, pointing his finger at the bloody array, "is premature labor. Very mature premature labor."

Vienna looked nonplussed.

"I've been here for hours," he said, "and so have you, so hide those clothes while you're at it."

Vienna stopped at the table long enough to lift the jar to her nose and pass it back and forth. "You have been drinking," she said as she slipped by, carefully holding herself so as not to brush against him as she passed.

Dr. Barstow smiled to himself and shook his head. He could hear the storm suddenly break and rain start thudding heavily on the roof. The room darkened and thunder cracked and rolled in long unraveling coils. It seemed strangely cozy in the empty room, the richness of the weather surrounding the house.

A few minutes later there was a scraping of boots at the door and John Aimes staggered in, wet, muddied, and frightened.

"You didn't get hit, did you?" Dr. Barstow asked. "I heard the gunplay. It doesn't take that many bullets to kill one Negro."

"Two of those were mine. She fired in the air to break the party up. I aimed in the air to add shots from another direction so as they would know there was more than one and get confused. Otherwise they might have closed in on her."

"Where was she doing this from?" Dr. Barstow asked, handing Aimes his flask.

"I couldn't tell for sure. I think she was up in one of the trees in a deer watch."

Dr. Barstow whistled, thinking of how dangerous the rickety perches were; the wood rotted after a season or two and the construction was usually makeshift and hasty.

"So they scattered?"

"Yep."

"What about the colored boy?"

"He tore off as soon as she fired the shots. Don't know how far he'll get, though. His hands were tied behind him and you need hands to get through the brush. It gets pretty thick back in there."

"The weather will save his ass now," Dr. Barstow said, dismissively. "They're not going to chase him through this storm."

"She O.K.?" Aimes gulped, jerking his head toward the display on the table he only now noticed.

"I think so, since that there is my blood, but I'm about to go up and find out. I'd like it a whole lot better if she tried to kill herself in more conventional ways."

"What the hell does that mean?" Aimes snapped.

"Just a bad joke." Dr. Barstow shrugged. "You should go on home now. You might have visitors, you know."

"You don't need any help?"

Dr. Barstow picked up his black leather bag and paused for a moment, considering. "Yes, check the barn before you go."

"What for?"

"She couldn't have gotten there and back as fast as she did on foot."

"She don't ride. Everyone in Winsville knows that."

"There's always a first time," Dr. Barstow said, smiling.

DR. BARSTOW WASHED his hands at the kitchen sink, wiped them dry with a dish towel, and held them out in front of him to see if they were steady. Then he pressed them into the small of his back and stretched into a painful arch. His back ached and his throat was raw from the number of cigarettes he had consumed in the last few hours, and he prayed that this delivery would be easy, since he was far from fresh.

"James, come out here a sec," John Aimes called to him.

Dr. Barstow cracked the screen door open and looked out at the rain which had just become heavier and slanting. John Aimes was waving to him from the barn. "I'll be right there," he called back.

Aimes ran halfway back to the house to meet him. As they ran together to the barn, Aimes talked excitedly, oblivious of the downpour.

"You were right. The horse is hot under the chest and its coat is sweaty. There is a stain on the shoulder which I just don't get."

"Blood?"

"Yeah, a little, but mostly just wet."

"Did you clean it off?"

"Not yet. I wanted you to see it," John Aimes said, pulling back the barn door, solicitous as a student. His voice wavered with a giddy excitement unusual to his deadpan, practical demeanor. "The damnedest thing is I don't see any sign of a saddle. Even if she used a blanket or a pad underneath, there would be an outline on the coat, and the saddles are all dry. I checked them. There's dust on all of them. I don't think they've been used since Willard left."

Dr. Barstow smiled again as he ran his hand over the horse's right shoulder.

"I don't get it," Mr. Aimes said, shaking his head.

"Amazing. She did it bareback," Dr. Barstow said quietly. "No wonder she broke her water. Clean the horse off and put it back in its stall. No one would ever believe it. She's airtight. The rain will wash away any tracks."

John Aimes swallowed uncomfortably. "I found the gun too. It's over there," he said, gesturing with his arm.

"Well clean it and put it on the rack. I'd better get back to the house; she'll be contracting soon." Dr. Barstow cracked his knuckles.

"I hope the baby's still alive," Aimes said, staring at the damp stain on the horse's coat.

"If it's anything like its mother it should pull through."

"Well, if you need me, holler," Aimes said, as he shifted his weight from one foot to the other, reluctant to detain Dr. Barstow further, but wanting to forestall the conclusion that ended with him alone in the house he had not, in four years, made a home.

"Uh-huh," Barstow said, turning back toward The Heights, enjoying his momentary advantage in having access to Vienna in a way that was vital and intimate and excluded John Aimes, though he knew that she would have preferred to squat in a ditch rather than admit a need for him.

WITHIN TWO WEEKS of Elliott's birth, Sister arrived. She descended from the 12:40 train wearing a shapeless brown dress, a traveling hat, and a look of grim determination. She had in her hand a much-creased telegram, which had been sent to her anonymously three days before, and which she consulted nervously, folding and unfolding the paper clumsily, for she had never learned to be dexterous with cotton gloves on.

Her face was as sturdy and as plain as the trunk she brought with her from Morgana, so it occasioned some surprise when she introduced herself at the station as Augusta Daniels, sister to Willard Daniels, and inquired about transportation to take her to The Heights.

The town was frankly disappointed. Willard had never mentioned a sister, and if he had, no one would have imagined a dumpy older woman as devoid of charm and style as Willard was blessed. Nevertheless, there she was. And there she was prepared to stay, with her brother's wife, at The Heights, until she had discharged her duty, or satisfied her curiosity, or until her brother's return, which was to say, indefinitely. "My brother inherited the house. It seems I've inherited the family," she said to Mr. Aimes, who was giving her a ride to The Heights.

"You sound a little tired from your journey," he said, after a long silence.

"Do I?" Sister answered, in a way that ended their exchange as firmly as a slap.

11

■

ELLIOTT WANTED TO know, when he was still small enough to be kissed firmly on the forehead without suffering the rigor mortis of indignation, why colored people didn't cast white shadows, since white folks' shadows were black. Shadows fascinated him and seemed as clearly magical as anything Aladdin's lamp had ever produced. His own shadow could delight him into shrill shrieks of pleasure just by dodging from view when he turned, or by stretching out like rubber against the side of the barn.

Fayette said she didn't know much about how shadows worked; there was probably a law against it, she had grumbled, since laws don't like coloreds having anything white a'tal. "You ask Vienna, sugar, I'm busy and she'll be able to tell you right."

"Elliott," Vienna welcomed him from her desk, smiling and pushing away the pile of foolscap which was her epic poem, the solitary endeavor that shaped the better part of her day and was, like Penelope's weaving, under constant revision, so that its progress was as slow and stately as the growth of a tree, to be measured against decades. She scooped him up into her bony lap. "What brings you inside?" Both of her children had demonstrated a preference for the outdoors from the first wobbling steps that had led them out of the house with the unerring fixity of a compass. In fine weather, Vienna expected to see them return only for lessons or lemonade. Elliott squirmed into a more comfortable position and settled himself. "I need to know about shadows," he began, looking up into Vienna's face. Vienna nodded seriously as he posed his query and repeated Fayette's speculations on the subject.

"Hmmm, that's complicated," she said, removing from his wandering fingers her favorite fountain pen, which had already stained one of his palms blue. "Do you want to know about the laws of nature or the nature of laws?" Vienna asked him.

Elliott laughed. He loved reversals—they had some of that same magic of shadows. "Science or myth?" she offered.

"Tell me the myth!" he shouted exuberantly, grabbing her finger in his hand. Vienna smiled. "Do you remember the stories of Ovid?" she asked. "Sure I do," Elliott answered. They were among his favorites, having to do with animals and birds and transformations, like Aesop but longer and more complicated.

"I ask because you have often been frustrated at his endings." This was also true. Elliott objected to the bitter injustices that were left unrighted and had shed tears of outrage into his pillow for the fates of Philomela and Arachne. Sister had campaigned against such stories, saying they were too violent and perverse for small children, but Vienna maintained that they were no worse than the tales of the Brothers Grimm.

The children had settled the matter themselves when Fayette had caught them trying to bury Sister's substitute text, A Posy of Stories for Budding Hearts, behind the blue barn. In their defense they had said they were tired of "Little Sue" and "Gentle James" but hadn't wanted to hurt Sister's feelings. It was a crime for which they had not been punished, though

Sister had left them two days early, with the understanding that they would not receive Christmas presents from her that year.

Elliott rotated a glass paperweight in his hands and admitted this was so, but insisted that was no reason not to go on. "Very well," Vienna said, replacing the paperweight on the desk at some distance from Elliott, "Shadows were the resident angels—"

Elliott interrupted, "What do you mean, resident?"

"Internal, living inside, *residing* within."

"Like a genie?"

"Exactly."

"Go on," Elliott prompted.

"It is this genie's job to help man be whole."

"I don't get it," Elliott said flatly.

"Everyone has some little piece of themselves missing. That is what keeps them from being gods, and in their struggle to find or make up for the missing piece, they sometimes make their worst mistakes. So they were given an angel to help them cope."

Elliott nodded. "Then what?"

"These angels, or genies if you like, know about darkness and night and can live in the deep of men's souls, and speak to us in dreams."

"Uh-huh, but what about the shadows?" Elliott prompted.

"We're coming to that. There was once a fellow—"

"Did he have a camel?"

"Yes he did. He sat up nights beside his camel and stared at the stars until he couldn't content himself with just enjoying their light."

"Uh-oh," Elliott murmured, recognizing the shape of trouble on the way.

Vienna absentmindedly picked a fleck of straw from Elliott's hair as she talked. "The fellow thought if he could get rid of the darkness inside him, he could shine as brightly as those stars. Of course, he was being vain and foolish. Everyone knows stars need darkness to shine. But he tried everything he could think of to get rid of his dark angel, but the angel stayed, trying to protect him."

"How come he didn't want to be protected?" Elliott asked, probing the interior of his nostril meditatively. Vienna peeled Elliott's hand from his face and placed her ivory-handled paper knife in his paw to distract him from his self-mining. "Whether it was because he wanted the brightness badly enough not to care what he sacrificed for it or because he flattered himself that having it, he wouldn't need anything else, we will never know. But finally, after thirty days without sleep, the man succeeded in forcing the genie out. In a panic, the angel did a desperate thing: he appeared in the daylight. It was against the rules to become visible, so the angel appeared to the man as a shadow, the blackened reflection of himself. It was a bold thing for the angel to do—and it was an act of devotion and love. He followed his man closely and never left him, trying always to catch his eye. Instead, he drew the attention of the very gods who gave him to the man. And you can believe that they were furious with the man's arrogance in wanting to be like the stars and furious with his ingratitude for trying to shed the gift of the angel."

"You bet they were!" exclaimed Elliott, fully identifying with the gods.

"But they were also touched by the faithfulness of the angel and his love for the foolish man. They thought long and hard about what to do, and this is what they decided: the gods punished the man by giving him what he wanted. They let him have a little dazzle of starlight. But he paid dearly— with it came a blinding vanity that would prevent him from recognizing himself among men, and would separate him forever from his angel."

Elliott poked Vienna with the blunt point of the paper knife—"You mean he had to stay biggety for all time?"

"Yes," Vienna sighed. "That is exactly what I mean. All he could see was his own pale light, not half as bright as a firefly."

"What about his genie?"

"Oh, the angels were never allowed back in men after that. But still they follow us faithfully, as our shadows, reminders of our mysterious selves, and sometimes they sneak back inside when we are asleep, but mostly we don't listen."

"That's very sad," said Elliott.

"Yes," Vienna agreed, "it is."

"That was a really dumb trade."

"Well, it could have been worse," Vienna said tenderly, looking at Elliott's pallor, hair that lit up in sunlight as white as a tungsten bulb. "It only means we have to remember we're all the same underneath, that everyone under the sun casts a black shadow."

"Yeah, but it's that guy's fault."

"Elliott, baby, he was no different from anyone else for having a foolish streak or some greed or wanting things that were wrong for him. That is as common to all of us as our having a shadow. Only most people are a little luckier than that poor fellow and they don't get what they want and, if they're wise, they later realize they have been spared or else they go through life cursing the kindness of fate."

Elliott was silent for a moment as he scratched a mosquito bite on his calf. He had an instinctive warmth reserved for any kind of runt or underdog or scapegoat, but contemplating this last reversal of Vienna's, in which the villain had become the victim in one quick breath, confused Elliott. He didn't bother to untangle it. "So who is there to blame?" he asked.

"Maybe no one. Maybe the story isn't really about blame but shame," Vienna answered, reflecting Elliott's broad smile, for this was the kind of twist he could embrace unconditionally. It turned, after all, on a rhyme, which was satisfying in so many ways.

"How do you mean?" he asked, squirming down from her lap and bending attentively over an untied shoe to practice a relatively new operation.

"I mean maybe it is our shame over what's missing in us that makes us sometimes want things we should know better than to want, and maybe it's shame again that makes us cling to those mistakes and makes it hard to admit to the world when we have been wrong. And shame that makes us turn away from the self our shadow shows us," Vienna said, sensing the shift in Elliott's attention, suddenly wanting to pull him back to her for another embrace but knowing the moment for that was past and now he would only squirm away.

"I love what my shadow shows me and I knew shadows were good," Elliott announced proudly, finishing a lopsided double knot and straightening himself up.

"Of course you did, baby, anyone who can't appreciate the sweetness of the shade they offer is a sorry person indeed."

"My shadow looks like this," Elliott said, stretching himself as long as he could and reaching his arms to their fullest extension over his head, "and like this," he added, hopping suddenly to the side in a half-crouch, "and this," he said, striking increasingly silly poses and giggling as he whirled around the room in a dance that completely absorbed him until he suddenly turned and dashed out the door.

Vienna stared at her desk for a long time wondering about what she had said and what, if anything, Elliott had understood of its adumbrated meaning. It was only later in the afternoon, when she stood by the window to close the shutters, that she saw him standing in the yard using her silver hand mirror to see behind him, choreographing Willa and Fayette—who stood like bored chess pieces on the lawn, moving lazily to the directions he issued with the animated gestures of a conductor—into a configuration in which all their shadows merged and mingled on the unkempt grass.

12

———■———

$\mathcal{J}$T WOULD BE hard to say when Vienna stopped fighting
her solitude, when she came to see it as a calling, like saint-
hood, for which one is selected by forces that can be neither
named nor avoided. She began to think of herself as cloistered,
her life resembling a nun's in that it was a sacrifice, a personal
devotion for which she had been prepared since childhood in
the name of a great cause, armed only with her inner resources.
But it was a source of unmitigated pain to Vienna that she
did not know what that cause was. Some days, she felt it was
near, that moment of epiphany, when putting down a book
or pulling up a weed, she would learn what she was suffering
for. But always it eluded her. Like the right word that lingers
just beyond the tongue, it beckoned from the farther reaches
of her brain but would not be mouthed.

Some days, when it was far, so out of reach that the very
notion of meaning was bankrupt and alien, she could do nothing but watch the wind and wish that she could cry. Those
were days when it was impossible to work on the poem Willard
had found such a risible endeavor, her twelve-book ambition,
homage to the *Aeneid* and frame for a cycle of seasons. Even
her translations, a practice like the scales she played until her

fingers were warm, seemed hollow ritual on those days when walking past the barns and across the field to the weeping beech or the sycamores was exercise only, devoid of comfort. It was then that she would think of herself as a Penelope without suitors, a woman without the promised return, without the definition or shape to her life that waiting confers. Therefore it didn't matter if the men she knew were confronting dangers that impeded or promoted their goals, making headlines or headway, suffering setbacks or just suffering: none of it had to do with her.

Vienna didn't often think of Willard; when she did, it was usually kindly, even tenderly. That was the luxury afforded by knowing he would not return; she could remember the way his shoulders shrugged as he laughed, and the smell of his skin, earthy and familiar as wet grass, or the slightly salty taste of his brow when she kissed it. She recalled how he performed meaningless, everyday acts—opening an umbrella, hailing a cab, or stepping out of a car—with none of the awkwardness common to most men. She thought of his animal grace, his astonishing style, and the way he moved with seamless confidence, knowing that the air would part for him like an invisible throng through which he made his way with pleasure.

Vienna smiled at the memory of his boyish impetuosity, the delight he took in physical risks, and the way he would walk into a room and sweep her into a waltz. When she thought of him detail by detail, she could resurrect his charm, taking a part at a time to represent the whole. In this way, she came to feel grateful to him for having left. He had done a difficult and noble thing for her—whether he meant to or not didn't matter—because in the end his departure allowed her to give her children something she could not have given them if he had stayed: her love for their father.

His absence became an act of generosity far more meaningful than the tithing that came with the house, the monthly check forwarded from his bank account to her bank account through the attorneys at Baintree and Slake, who had their main office in Bantanburg but kept a small office in Winsville, not much larger than a sitting room with nothing in it but a desk, three leather chairs, a calendar, an electric fan, and Mr. James Joseph Woodruff III.

Mr. Woodruff had been aspiring for ten years to be promoted to the Bantanburg office and so he performed his duties with excessive care, living in terror lest he make a mistake that might cost him his coveted place in the front room, where two clerks shuffled across the kingwood parquet fetching papers or copying them for Mr. Baintree or Mr. Slake. A long case clock chimed the hours, and tea was served from a gleaming silver urn every afternoon at four. It was to attain that august company that Mr. Woodruff had first read law some twenty years before, when he had made it his ambition to become a gentleman and keep his hands and shirt clean.

Vienna Daniels made him extremely nervous. In her presence he was likely to knock over his water glass or splay the nib of his fountain pen, spattering ink on the documents he was presenting to her. His stutter, which was on most occasions mild, exacerbated to the point that Vienna would finish his sentences for him or supply her own, to which he would nod in affirmation or negation. His hands grew damp days in advance of a scheduled appointment and shook so noticeably during their meetings that he could not hold his papers without their rattling noisily. Vienna had hypothesized that he drank during the long hours between business. She had put the allegation in a letter to the austere and eminent Mr. Baintree following an unsuccessful encounter in which Mr. Woodruff had been so jarred by a question she had put to him that he had forgotten to inform her that the title of The Heights had been put in her name, which meant that she was responsible for the taxes. Since then he had gone to such ridiculous lengths to demonstrate his sobriety to her whenever they met that Vienna had only become confirmed in her theory about his perpetual inebriation.

Now that the quarterly dividends from Willard's stocks were being transferred to Vienna's bank, Mr. Woodruff had fewer occasions to meet with her and could return to the beloved pastime with which he beguiled the uneventful days manning the Winsville office: namely, reading up on English maritime law. Mr. Woodruff was a secret Anglophile, and he sometimes wondered guiltily if his being detained so long in Winsville wasn't a punishment visited upon him for his revering English civilization above the civilization best represented by his peerless employers. But try as he would to balance the admiration that was his to bestow, the English always came out ahead, if for no other reason than that their system of justice had the good sense to retain the venerable tradition of wigs. That, to a bald bachelor, was enough to tip the scales.

Mr. Woodruff had not seen Willard for so many years and had, in the interim, absorbed so many references to him from Vienna phrased in the past tense, that the lawyer had for a long time thought of Willard as deceased as opposed to departed. His one memorable interaction with Willard, over a contract he had written entitling a local farmer named Aimes to lease Willard's land, had occasioned such vitriol and invective on Mr. Daniels' part that Mr. Woodruff had been comforted by the notion that there was now one less client who could threaten his long-awaited position at the main office.

It was because of this long-standing misapprehension that Mr. Woodruff had committed a most unfortunate blunder, and one which he felt sure had doomed him to more years in Winsville. He had been under his desk, searching for the finial to a new desk lamp that had fallen from his fingers when he tried to polish it on his sleeve. As he was attempting to retrieve the finial from the dark of the cramped cubbyhole in which he habitually hid his large feet and a volume of *The Black Book of Admiralty*, the door opened. When he heard Vienna Daniels' distinctive voice calling his name he had panicked.

His imagination was circumscribed by the ignoble confinement in which he had been found: he could not envision a dignified way to crawl out from the small space into which he had wedged his entire body. So he had stayed put, holding his breath, hoping she would leave. But she didn't. After an interminable minute or two, she said, "Mr. Woodruff, please come out of there. I don't have time for games, and I can see your shoes." He had been so flustered by the time he managed to squeeze out from under the desk that he had handed her the finial and asked her for no apparent reason if she had any plans to marry. "I am married! That is the whole point," she had informed him, before turning and leaving, her business unbroached and the finial still in her hand, sniffing the air for a telltale smell as she strode briskly out the door.

To Vienna, that *was* the whole point. When she thought of herself, it was in precisely that way: married, not to Willard as much as to the idea of Willard as an acceptable spouse, even if it meant telling her children extraordinary tales to explain his absence, tales in which Vienna reworked truths about Willard, his daring, agility, and ambition, into enterprises of exotic exploration in which he filled the vacuum left by Peary, Shackleton, Scott, Stanley, and Burton singlehandedly in his efforts to find not *terra nova* but *opulentia nova*, braving adventures more dazzling and wondrous than those that delayed Odysseus.

That Vienna was lying to her children about their father's whereabouts or occupation never occurred to her. The stories she told contained an essential probity in that they correctly represented the salient features of the situation—that Willard was alive, that Willard was away, and that Willard was unable to return. Beyond those truths, it didn't seem significant to Vienna if she embellished or distorted the particulars. She was merely interpreting the truth and rendering it poetic—lyrical, palatable, and instructive. In this, she considered herself to be honoring Aristotle's dictum that it is not the function of the poet to relate what has happened but what might happen, to prefer what ought to be to what is. She followed his injunction to reveal universal truths rather than specifics. Because she was narrating on what he called the higher poetic level rather than on the lower historical one, she could inform her subject with the whimsy of imagination; it afforded her the opportunity to make their father known to her children by elevating him to the epic mode, in which, through fear and pity for his travails, they could come to understand and love him.

To this application of Aristotelian poetics Vienna added Horace, embracing his idea that the aim of the poet is to inform or delight or both. *"Educare et delectare"* was written in bold purple letters on a stiff piece of cardboard and tacked to the wall near her desk. As a result, her children knew about dog teams and ice caps, the danger of "white-outs," in which light refracting on blowing snow causes the horizon to disappear, the delicate charm of "whispering stars," the crackling sound of a breath's moisture crystallizing in the freezing air. They knew about baleen whales and elephant seals and the brown skua bird. Elliott could draw a map of Antarctica without confusing the Weddell Sea and the Ross Sea. Willa and Elliott knew that the Amazon was the second longest river in the world and that it had over five hundred tributaries. When they drew pictures of the jungles, they used every crayon in the box. They could tell you about piranhas and rubber plants and Brazil nuts, and best of all, cannibals. Elliott was in love with the doe-eyed llamas of Peru and Willa wanted a kangaroo to carry her favorite dolls around, like a walking toy chest. Elliott thought that Australia should get a special medal for having the best animals: the koala bear, wombat, kangaroo, platypus, flying opossum, and wallaby couldn't have delighted him more if he had invented them himself. Shortly after Elliott became interested in camels, his father's adventures ranged into the desert lands of Arabia and were largely inspired by T. E. Lawrence's *Seven Pillars of Wisdom*.

Sacrificing her freedom to remarry by remaining faithful to the fantasy she invented for her children did not seem a hardship to Vienna. The men who populated her restricted world were not contending for her heart and had certainly not commanded her notice beyond the peripheral orbit in which they rotated around her; their lives interested Vienna not an iota.

Without the inclination to remarry, divorce offered no advantage and conclusively pronounced a failure that society was reluctant to accept. Vienna had met a divorcée once, in New York, in 1925, the year of the solar eclipse, the last full year she shared with her father. The divorcée had sat with Vienna in the library of the Renwicks' country house and they had talked about the Scopes Trial together. Vienna remembered the divorcée had seemed grateful for the conversation, and had offered Vienna a nip of bootleg liquor from an exquisite enamel flask she kept in her purse. The divorcée left later in the afternoon, but remained the subject of much conversation and not a little ridicule throughout the rest of the weekend. Vienna had felt sorry for her and remembered her pale, plump hands nervously toying with a silk tassel on one of the pillows on the sofa.

It was not until Gray Saunder came to see the weeping beech

that Vienna realized she was lonely. There was, suddenly, a void in her life that neither her children, her books, nor her trees could fill. And that it should be brought to her attention by a tall, gangly botanist visiting from England surprised her more than the discovery he precipitated.

Grayson Stepwill Saunder was twenty-four, two years younger than Vienna, and on holiday from a doctoral thesis at Oxford. His arms and legs were long and thin and when he sat in the Morris chair in the music room he looked, as Willa, with a five-year-old's insight, had aptly noted, like a praying mantis. The attenuation of his limbs seemed to defy the logistics of supporting or transporting his body. Even his hair was thin. It was fair, and hung limply over a high pale brow like wilted ribbon grass—or tamped rushes, depending on the weather. He had a lopsided smile that showed tiny, child-sized teeth, and a dry sense of humor. He said that irony was a necessary asset to one who devoted his days to plants; without it, one could miss the subtle jokes.

It was entirely a fluke that he happened through Winsville. After three weeks in Boston, Gray Saunder had taken a train south to visit friends in Washington. Two weeks into his stay, an illness in his hosts' family had called them away, leaving him to his own devices with the house and car at his disposal. That was when Gray decided to explore the Shenandoah Valley, stopping at a few of the Civil War battle sites he remembered from his early schooldays with an impassioned history professor, whose principal tool of pedagogy was enforced memorization. He got lost repeatedly on poorly marked back roads because he would be distracted from his goal by roadside specimens of wildflowers or weeds that led him from asphalt onto rutty dirt lanes.

He forgot his map at one of the many stops he made to examine trees or ask amused locals by what name a sprig he held out to them was known, or how long a particular flower bloomed. In his pearl-gray flannels and crisp white shirt, silk tie, and straw hat, he commanded their attention. His accent and appearance combined to elicit smiles and offers of spring water or coffee or fried pie. Always he left his new friends with the same question: "What do you recommend I see in these parts?" The answers he received mostly featured natural landmarks, a cave or waterfall, mountain view or tree cleft by lightning, though occasionally a prize pig or cow was suggested, and once, a newborn limbless kitten.

In his efforts to find Antietam he crossed into Maryland and then into West Virginia before succumbing to car trouble outside of Bantanburg. It was there that he heard about the weeping beech from the mechanic's wife, a beleaguered woman originally from Winsville, with children clinging to every available part of her. Her face was worn like eroded stone and her mouth was tight with worry, but her eyes softened when she said, "It's a right wonder, prettiest thing going in Winsville aside from the blue neon sign they've got down at the filling station. The house ain't half bad neither, if you don't mind the Daniels."

Her husband added, "They don't have a dog and Mrs. Daniels don't bite so I 'spect you'll do fine. President Hoover didn't leave her much to bark about 'cept that there tree and a big ole house she cain't hardly afford to patch, but she's got a heap a pride just the same."

The wife gave Gray a knowing look and put in a final advisory: "She talks funny too, from speaking with the dead."

"Eula Ann, you mean speaking dead languages, sugar, that's not the same thing as hoodoo." Eula Ann kept her mouth puckered and her eyebrows raised and her eyes trained on Gray as if to override the correction.

After a long night on a sagging metal cot at the Dew Sleep Inn on the outskirts of Bantanburg, Grayson Saunder decided to redeem the detour with a stop at The Heights before he left the area. His college at Oxford was graced with a weeping beech within its formal enclosed garden; it formed the centerpiece of an otherwise cloying display of horticultural virtuosity, and he had often taken refuge from the rich abundance of competing colors and scents under its boughs.

Eula Ann was right, the weeping beech was a marvelous thing to behold and after a greasy breakfast, Gray set off in quest of The Heights, calculating that he would probably not get far enough south to see an avenue of live oaks and cheerfully accepting a more familiar but closer substitute.

When Vienna came to the door, there Gray stood, his hat in one hand, a volume of Yeats's poems clutched in the other, beaming his skewed smile at her. After a moment in which the two regarded each other, he said "Excuse me, madam, but my Baedeker guide to the hamlets and hollows of the West Virginia panhandle"—he waved the book without revealing its title—"indicates an arboreal delight uncommon to these parts, and I was hoping, um, I was embolden by the proverb: 'Fortes fortuna adiuvat.' "* The Latin was not meant to test the veracity of Eula Ann's account, but, accepting its authority, to provide a passport into the extraterritoriality of an embassy to the ancient world, in which Mrs. Daniels represented the linguistic attaché to the classics.

Without a pause or a blink, Vienna answered, "Faber est quisque fortunae suae."† Grayson Saunder laughed with unexpected delight at her quickness and bowed slightly, sweeping his hat behind him in mock chivalry and sallied in return, "Then let my will suffice!" Vienna curtsied, and smiling back at him, opened wide the door to The Heights. And there, after returning the car to his friends in Washington some days later with a profusion of apologies, excuses, and a large basket of

* Fortune favors the brave.
† Every man makes his own fortune.

expensive flowers, he stayed, until a week into the first term of his final school year.

"Would you mind terribly if I introduced you to our maid as family? We so rarely have visitors . . ." Vienna asked at the end of that first day, when it was understood that he was staying on, though neither of them had mentioned it.

"I would be honored," Grayson Saunder answered. By the following afternoon, when Fayette walked over to Mr. Aimes's house to return a flour sifter she had borrowed from Hegemony until their own, broken by Willa's dramatic recreation of a blizzard for the benefit of her indulged doll, Miss Nostril, could be replaced, Fayette told Hegemony, "He's family all right, he just as downright odd as she is, and plumb crazy over trees, too!"

13

---

*I*N GRAY, VIENNA found her complement: it occurred to her as they played chess together one evening, Gray using Mr. Woodruff's finial to replace a missing pawn. Elliott was cavorting at their feet with a captured knight, his favorite piece because it was represented by a horse; occasionally he would interrupt their game with the neighing that was integral to his own. Just before he checkmated her king, Gray asked Vienna if she happened to remember Aristophanes' speech in the *Symposium*. She remembered it well—she had just then been thinking of it—the proposition that love began with a race of people who were self-sufficient until Zeus cut them in two, like a walnut cracked apart, leaving the halves to seek each other out, recognizing their missing part only by the love which drew them to and identified their mate. She nodded yes to him and he nodded back and then he took her queen.

It wasn't just that Gray felt the immanent spirit of trees move him as readily as branches bowed to wind, or that he shared her love for a canon of literature usually left to the delectation of silverfish, or that his imagination was as agile and febrile as a dancing flame. It wasn't even the amusing quirks that marked his behavior as eccentric which made her fall in love with him. It was much simpler: it was that with him she felt understood and accepted.

To him she had confided the onerous guilt she felt at her father's sudden death, the heart failure which precluded their reconciliation and that seemed by its very name no mere accident but a metaphor by which she was indicted in his death, compounded by the news arriving at the same time as her daughter, whose difficult, two-day labor prevented Vienna from seeing her father buried. And all this pain was only exacerbated by her father's unanticipated generosity but lack of amnesty, as evinced by his final will, in which he left all his wealth to her, but not one token or souvenir. After a year and a half of probate, after Willard, who had raged so bitterly about her father's financial inclemency, had left, the inheritance arrived like a death-row reprieve, offering her overwhelming choices she could barely contain, like rich foods that sicken a stomach shrunken by malnutrition. That was four months before the stock market crashed and snatched from her the promise of anything beyond a modest subsistence.

Gray heard this and other confessions: the shame she felt at mourning her friend Alisha's absence more than her husband's, the indifference with which she had regarded Willa during her depression, the troubling dreams she sometimes had that haunted her for days, and the petty promptings of a stubborn pride that turned her from the clumsy overtures of kindness initiated by neighbors like Mr. Aimes. Vienna bemoaned her inability to recall the voice of the English nanny who had raised her after her mother's riding accident, a fall that had reduced Mrs. Whitcomb to an insentient victim of a long and undignified death, which had frightened Vienna and made it hard for her not to recoil from the sight of the wasted woman in whom she no longer recognized her mother.

All this Gray heard without flinching or withdrawing the

steady regard in which he made his admiration known, his pale-green eyes attentive as a surgeon's, ready to administer a soothing word or the absolution of his hand tenderly lifting a fallen lock of hair from her forehead or pressing her hand against the warmth of his cheek.

Elliott adored him, clamored endlessly for piggyback rides and stories and snatches of Scottish lullabies; he told Gray his best jokes, over and over again and followed him around the house like an irrepressible puppy. Willa was more reserved at first, almost wary, until at last she surrendered herself to the delights of shameless flirtation. After resisting the entrancing pull of his ghost stories and the tales of Walla Land, she had been won over by his tricks—not the embarrassingly dumb kind of thing that Sophronius Moody the general store clerk did, like pulling coins out of her nose, but making from a sheet of Christmas wrap a delicate crane or swan or swallow. That would have been treasure enough, but he had gone further, stringing them from a peeled branch of hickory so that they hung above her desk, floating overhead in slow, endless circles.

Even Fayette, after posing for Gray's photograph album, for which she had uncharacteristically primped and preened, straightening her eyebrows with a licked finger, pinching her cheeks and plumping the bow on her battered hat before standing absolutely rigid with her eyes open wide as if she had been electrocuted to ensure that she didn't blink, started fussing over Mr. Saunder just as if he had been visiting royalty. For the rest of the house, Gray Saunder's presence was a diverting pleasure, an unforeseen, welcome treat that they took in stride, like the serendipitous landing of a swallowtail butterfly on one's forearm or the discovery of an unbroken robin's egg or arrowhead. For Vienna, it was as confusing and troubling as it was thrilling.

When Gray would climb the stairs at six for his evening bath, a forty-minute affair to which he would bring provisions for every possible contingency: chocolate creams or ginger-snaps, a volume of poetry (he had only once dropped a book into the tub and after three days' drying in the sun it remained permanently puffed, bulging out of its binding like a plump man in a ill-fitting suit), a glass of sherry, a vial of sandalwood oil, and a Turkish cigarette, Vienna would invariably follow.

For the duration of his bath, she would sit on the foot of her bed, intoxicated by the rich scent of the amber oil wafting across the hall as it dispersed in the steaming water. She listened to him splash and hum, reciting lines of poems which caught his fancy and could be improved only by resounding off the tile walls. He usually ended his ablutions with a booming bit of Gilbert and Sullivan or "Rule, Britannia," although once she heard "God Save the Queen" delivered in an irreverent falsetto. All the while, Vienna sat on her bed imagining him naked, dizzy with desire and shame, absentmindedly twisting the wedding ring on her finger until it chafed. And when he emerged, slightly pink and smelling of talcum beneath an impossibly starched fresh shirt and rumpled linen suit he would smile at her innocently and offer her his arm to descend to dinner. At night, she twisted sleeplessly in damp sheets, knowing he was only a few footsteps away, in the bedroom Alisha used to occupy.

It got so that even as Gray was explaining to her the differences between broadleaf hardwoods, the simple or compound leaves, showing her the opposition of maple leaves on a branch and contrasting it with the alternating ones of elms and oaks, or pointing out how the palmate lobes on a sweetgum contrasted with the toothed leaves of poplars and birches, all Vienna could think about was his flesh as he leaned near her to show the leaves. The heat of his skin burned into her mind and dazed her: she saw sunspots; she couldn't concentrate, and asked the same question twice or forgot a train of thought midsentence. She was delirious, off-balance, and subject to sudden palpitations that gripped her heart and made her hands tremble. Her appetite doubled. She was dying: she made a will. The idea of death brought equal measures of fear and comfort not unlike the effects of standing too near Gray Saunder. Finally, she admitted to herself she was in love.

Gray seemed oblivious to her distress. Throughout June he worked diligently in the mornings behind the house at a trestle table he had dragged up from the basement, drawing wispy renderings of weeds and pods, grasses and roots, annotating the pages with notes scripted in an ornate hand, as if his words, reflecting their subject, had sprouted lavish tendrils that curled competitively toward the margins. In the afternoons, he would embark on a project that usually included the children. By the month's end, he had taught Willa to swim, fabricated a float for Elliott out of a tire with a twined-rope seat, built a tree house without putting a single nail in the ancient apple tree he had selected for his site, and instituted a weekly croquet tournament, having made a special trip to Washington for the purchase of an authentic set of mallets, wickets, and balls after it became clear that, despite his best efforts, no one at The Heights could fathom the rules of cricket.

Fayette proved to be exceptionally gifted at these games, and but for the frequency with which she forfeited a turn to make the cucumber-and-watercress sandwiches Gray ate almost continuously until dinner, she would have been declared the house champion. In her stead, the prize of molasses chews or a paper glider or homemade kite with tinsel trimmings went to Willa for most improvement or to Elliott for stamina and showmanship in the face of insuperable odds (he had trouble wielding the mallet, which was nearly as tall as he was) or to Vienna for grace of form. But after the final game of the season, the clay trophy, asymmetrical as its maker's smile, was presented to Fayette, along with a blue cloth sash covered with good-conduct stars that she wore proudly over her shoulder until it started to shed, leaving a winking trail of fallen gold glimmer on the floor behind her.

On the Fourth of July, Willa and Elliott went into Winsville early in the afternoon to watch the men set up fireworks and the women's committee hang swags of bunting on a teetery dais on which Mr. Stepple would stand to give a speech before the festivities began—a barbecue in front of the volunteer fire station, a raffle, a pie-eating contest, and a performance by the Bantanburg High School band. The fireworks would signal the finale to the celebration that had been weeks in the planning, during which Mrs. Stepple had alienated almost all of the women on her decoration committee by the bossiness of her ministrations and the relative extravagance of the project, which demanded not inconsiderable donations from a town badly hurt by the Depression.

Left to join the revelry later in the day, Vienna and Gray wandered over the property, enjoying the luxury of a quiet interrupted only by the occasional burst of desultory conversation. "Did you ever meet Willard's mother?" Gray asked, continuing a discussion they had abandoned to contemplate the chilling waters of the creek.

"Indeed I did. Willard brought me down for the inspection immediately after the wedding, before we came to Winsville."

"Well?"

"At the risk of being too kind, let us say she was an unmitigated horror of untempered ignorance, sugarcoated barbs, and intoxicated self-absorption."

"That bad?" Gray laughed, poking his walking stick into the water as they crossed over the bridge made by two planks laid across a shallow.

"Worse still." Vienna smiled, for it felt good to finally voice the judgment she had so long refrained from admitting even to herself, partly out of loyalty to Willard and partly for fear of it contaminating her view of him, sullying him by association, too intimate to be ignored and too fundamental to address.

"Do tell," Gray urged, his eyes sparkling and his tone conspiratorial.

"She positively *oozed* over him, calling him sugarplum and pumpkin and darling and handsome and almost smothering him in cooing embraces and compliments, many on the theme of how fine his physique was, and what a dashing cut of man he had become. She actually blew him kisses from her chaise longue when he left the room, while at me she directed her shrapnel of verbal slights."

Gray made a face and Vienna continued, in an imitation Southern drawl, "You're so much *thinner* than I imagined; his other loves were always so full-bodied. But he's right, of course, it's better that one's wife not be *too* voluptuous. But I really don't see what all the fuss was—getting married like a pair of escaped convicts. *Our* family has always married at St. Timothy's and I can't help but think poor Willard would have preferred it. But what do I know, I'm just a silly old woman, about to die. What an *interesting* outfit! Is that what people are wearing up in New York? What a nice hat. It is *so* hard to wear a hat well. Now tell me all about yourself. You must be all tuckered out after a trip like that. Willard *used* to be so careful with his money. How much did those tickets cost, and the hotel? Don't tell me—my heart is probably not strong enough to bear his extravagance. He doesn't have endless money, you know. Not like those boys in the North that you are probably used to. I do hope you'll join me in a little drinkie-drink before dinner. I've invited Lily Maywell from down the street. Such a *lovely* girl, always so smartly put together. Of course, most anything *would* show her figure to advantage. She's one of Willard's oldest friends. They were *so* close, just inseparable. I'm sure she's positively *dying* to see him again. We have missed him so. I just hope I live long enough to see him again since this is such a short stay."

Gray's elongated frame was bent by hilarity and when he finally stood straight, sighing, and wiping the tears budding at the corners of his eyes, he asked, "What did Willard do in the face of this?"

"Nothing. He wavered between amusement and indifference at what he took to be witty mischief," Vienna answered, twisting the stem of a wild daisy with a vigor that betrayed greater emotion than she voiced.

"And what did you do?"

"What *could* I do . . ." Vienna said, momentarily wistful, letting the depetaled flower fall. But quickly returning to a flirtatious mirth, a sly smile flickered across her lips as she continued, "but remember Shelley's Ozymandias and despair: 'Of that colossal wreck, boundless and bare . . .' "

"At least the old dowager is ill, that's some compensation."

"Not at all, she is a dragon of good health, despite her rigorous imbibing and general indolence. She'll outlive us both!"

Gray took the straw hat from his head and started filling it with the occasional leaf or sprig that he might later press. "Do you ever hear from her?" he asked.

"Only once, shortly after Willard left; I received a five-page letter outlining, in rather hysterical language, the shame I had brought upon the Daniels name, at least that was the main argument: there were many digressions and asides, all in character, however. She's an accomplished monologuist with limited themes."

"And no word from the man himself?"

"Not that I haven't written," Vienna replied, smiling broadly.

"Right. From the outback and frozen tundra . . . it's quite brilliant, you know, sending the letters to those poor foreign postmasters or consul clerks to mail back. Now that you're finished with them, I imagine the Daniels clan must miss you awfully, you were such a focusing force for them. They're probably undone by your silence."

Vienna stopped walking, waved away a dragonfly, and turned to look back at Gray. The crisp white shirt in which he had started, starched to stand by itself, now relaxed into the loose slouch of his linen jacket, draping his torso in folds that hung from the shelf of his collarbone, billowing down to the cinch of his belt. As he paused over a spray of milkweed, his limp shirt seemed invested with the nobility of a Roman toga. The only aspect of him that retained any semblance of formality was the clip of his English accent. Vienna smiled again, and cupping her hand over her brow to shield her eyes from the glare, answered, "I'm not entirely rid of them. There *is* a sister who comes around on her own initiative, just to make sure I'm paying my dues."

"How jolly. What's her name?"

"Sister."

"No—that's too Gothic. You're inventing now."

Vienna laughed. "I promise it's true. She does have a name, Augusta, but no one calls her by it. Except me. She's much older. I'd feel sorry for her if she wasn't so impossible. She's not like the mother at all. Just the opposite, in fact. No frilly boudoir or feathered fans for her. She's terribly no-nonsense. It's a little frightening, actually. But I do think she genuinely cares for the children, she just doesn't understand them."

"I had an Aunt Augusta, once, when I was very small."

"I don't believe you were ever very small."

"Well I was, and my Aunt Augusta was even smaller," Gray went on, developing another tale of the Stepwill Saunder legend. By the time he had finished the narrative of Uncle Harry, tiny Aunt Augusta's brother, who had made a name for himself in India and returned to England with a secret curry recipe known only to the Stepwills, they had arrived at the weeping beech.

"COME," GRAY SAID, taking Vienna by the hand and leading her under the drapery of the hanging boughs, "I have something to show you." Vienna blinked for a moment, adjusting to the deep shade of the enclosure formed by the green curtain of drooping boughs lit only by the filtered light piercing random gaps in the foliage, pooling in uneven patterns on the dark earth.

Her pupils widened to take in the oilcloth and the feed pail converted to an ice bucket, from which the distinctive shape of a champagne bottle rose. "French champagne!" Vienna gasped, "where did you find it? I haven't had even a taste for years."

"I must say it took almost as much research as my thesis," Gray said proudly.

"To celebrate the Declaration of Independence?" Vienna asked incredulously.

"No," Gray said quietly, his back turned toward her as he worked the cork up into a foaming burst. Spilling the champagne into a glass and handing it to Vienna, he said, "To celebrate a declaration of dependence. I hold this truth to be self-evident, that all women are not created equal, and I surrender myself, utterly and abjectly, to the divine Mrs. Daniels, may she have mercy on my spirit and none on my flesh."

He chinked his glass against hers and gulped a long swallow.

Vienna stared at him, speechless. Then she lifted the glass and tilted its contents down her throat without tasting it, coughing in the last gulp and holding her glass out for more. He filled the glass halfway, letting the froth surge over the rim and cascade onto her hand. After two more swallows, of a more restrained nature, Vienna sputtered out, "I'm married."

"I'm desperate," Gray responded evenly, spreading the oilcloth out as if for a picnic.

"I don't know what to do," Vienna said, nervously twirling the glass in her hand, her eyes lowered to avoid Gray's.

"Sit here," he said, patting the space beside him on the oilcloth with one hand and reaching for her glass with the other.

Vienna obeyed, folding her knees beneath her like a camel collapsing after an arduous trip. Then, taking her temples in his hands, Grayson Stepwill Saunder began to cover her face with shy kisses, grazing her brow and cheekbone, edging along the hairline and down to an ear, where he whispered, "It's most unkind of you to leave me hanging like this. Vienna, I'm dying for you minute by minute. Let me . . ."

He worked his murmuring lips back from her neck to her mouth and then he stopped talking. He moved her down with his kiss and clung to her like a man drowning, releasing only one hand at a time to graze her hip, her thigh, her shoulder, and breasts, searching her body in a greed confused by the wealth of opportunity. Only when he realized she was meeting his kisses with her own did he relax enough to pull back his head and look at her. "Christ, Vienna, you're so beautiful," he said. The warmth of his words on her neck was making her tremble and she held his waist against her, pulling him back with a breathless, "Don't bother about the buttons."

"I have to warn you," Gray said, smiling over her, "I've read Ovid's *Art of Love*."

"So have I." Vienna laughed, fumbling with his pants.

"And *The Art of Courtly Love*, by Capellanus."

"Mmm, so I see."

Gray began kissing her again, pushing himself against the scald of her exposed flesh, pressing limb against limb, inhaling in moans the smell of her skin with its faded trace of frangipani. He could feel her breath in his pulse drawing him into her undulations until finally they sighed together and were still. With an involuntary quiver, Vienna held him as the rippling throb dissipated, like widening circles spreading across water; then, having caught their breath, they burst out laughing.

Lying together in an entangled sprawl, Gray bent an arm under his head and looked up at the interstices of light punctuating their blue-green canopy and said with evident satisfaction in his voice, "*Venia necessitati datur,*"* and Vienna replied, "*Exceptis excipiendis.*"† Then finishing the last of the champagne, they played a verbal game they had invented and refined on their long walks together. The trick was finding the connection between the two items paired and then coming up with a third that fit the category, which could be as simple as things that are squalid, or as subtle as things that disappear when you touch them.

"Fireworks and pomegranates?" Gray asked.

"A hand throwing confetti," Vienna answered, after carefully considering the link. Then it was her turn and she offered, "A spider's web and pine needles?" "Oh," he answered, grasping at once the notion of delicacy, "Easy: the sound of snow." He thought for a moment and then asked, "The tapering sound of a flute and a young bamboo shoot?"

Vienna burst out laughing: "Grayson Saunder, the most sublime example of attenuation," she said, rising on an elbow

---

* Indulgence is granted to necessity.
† The proper exceptions having been made.

to kiss his stomach, then, resting her head there with an ear on his navel, she studied his phallus, which lay in a wrinkled curl, gnarled as the root of a tree, and smiling to herself, she fell into the enfolding comfort of slumber.

When she awoke, it was time for them to pack up the accoutrements of seduction and head back to the house, change clothes, and join the others in Winsville. From that day on, until Gray left for England, they were lovers, furtively stealing kisses, pressing hands or passing notes with valorous discretion in the house, but never making love there; always that act was consecrated elsewhere, in one of the barns or under the weeping beech, in the creaking tree house, or in the used 1928 Chevrolet that Vienna bought in the summer of 1931 and had used exactly six times in the year that she had owned it.

By the time they found Fayette and the children in the dense crowd that packed Center Street, Willa had already won a miserable-looking goldfish in an open mason jar filled with grayish water, but she had given it to Elliott, who clutched it proudly to his chest, slopping the water on his shirt when the unruly crowd jostled him. Gray picked Elliott up and put him on his shoulders and consigned the goldfish to the care of Fayette, who was more than happy to trade responsibilities. "Please point out Mrs. Stepple," Gray asked Vienna, who obliged him with an introduction.

"An English cousin?" Margaret Stepple repeated with surprise, "I thought your mother was Venetian."

"No, English," Vienna corrected her, adding, "I was named Vienna because that is where I was conceived."

Mrs. Stepple feigned a modest embarrassment at the notion and then tittering as she pumped Gray's hand, exclaimed, "A kissing cousin, no doubt, I can almost see a resemblance!"

Walking away from the meeting, Gray murmured to Vienna, "You were right indeed, she has a very shallow root system," and of Mr. Woodruff, who was spotted retreating swiftly down a back street next to a blonde with heavily painted saurian eyes and peroxide topiary, "Ah, yes, the damaged winter crown attempting to cross-pollinate with fuller foliage," and of Sophronius Moody he commented, "Oh dear, such a bulbous trunk, poor thing—beyond mere pruning now." Thus, wandering through the crowd, Vienna and Gray catalogued a botanical equivalent to a bestiary that illuminated essential characteristics of the more prominent personae of Winsville.

The fireworks, when they were finally lit, were a disappointment to the Daniels. Elliott had long since fallen asleep, exhausted by anticipation. Willa felt gypped because three of the ten displays were duds; Fayette had gone to view the spectacle from the collection of Hoover carts congregated just beyond town where the Negro population sat and picnicked, and Gray and Vienna were too distracted by their own conflagration to be much impressed by the two-bit pyrotechnics.

But the rest of Winsville considered the celebration a huge success; it was often recalled with admiration during the following years, although no attempts to repeat it were made. Winsville reckoned with anemic morale by sitting tight and waiting for the New Deal to give them something more substantial than a few fizzling bursts of spinning colored light.

14

$\mathcal{I}$N AUGUST, WITH his departure already a month overdue, Gray began his campaign to win from Vienna the promise of a shared future. He had tried several variations of proposals meant to transcend the complication of her already being married. He offered to marry her if she would divorce Willard. He offered to marry her even if she didn't divorce Willard. He offered to bring her family to England to live with him in sin. He offered to return to Winsville after completing his doctorate to live with her in sin. But Vienna was reluctant to let him commit himself to a compromised union.

"Think of your own future, without the entanglement I would bring to it. And think of your family. Surely they aspire for your wife more than a divorced American with two children, two years your elder." Her voice in these discussions wavered between the forced sternness she adopted when she chided her children and the urgent pleading of withheld tears.

"First," Gray countered, with the patience of a stone, "I can only hope to assuage the caprice of my own heart and wouldn't presume to interpret the longings of my parents any more than I would dare interrupt the formidable silence of Buddha beneath the Bodhi Tree. Second, no one would hold against you an accident of youth, a brief alliance with a bounder, and third, two years does not signify."

"Willard wasn't a bounder," Vienna answered, testily retreating to the equivocation of small differences, the vanity of detail. "He didn't beat me, and he didn't gamble away the food on our table, and after all, I am the one who fired at him. Imagine if that ever came out! Think of the sensational headlines, the scandal with which you would be connected."

"That was nearly four years ago—besides, no one knows about it, no charge was ever made. It would be nothing more than vicious rumor at best."

"Exactly my point. I couldn't couple your name with that kind of ignominy."

"I only wish you had hit your mark. If you were Willard's widow we could be done with this dreary discussion," Gray parried, countering her solemnity with staunch good humor, slipping into the ironic mode to add buoyancy to his native tongue-in-cheek. He knew the importance of one party maintaining a disengaged stance lest the discussion escalate into an argument: the emotions fueling these exchanges were too volatile to risk igniting.

"Don't say that, Gray. Willard wasn't a bad man, just the *wrong* man, and if I had actually hurt him I would never have recovered from it. It's bad enough living with what I did do."

"I won't quibble over the distinction: being the wrong man for you would be burden enough to bring out the bad in any man. So then why stay wedded to such a benighted soul?"

"Out of consideration for you. Our life would begin with a stain, a handicap, and I've seen how easily love is damaged without any impediments at all."

Sometimes, in exasperation, Gray would run his hands through his hair until it stood in frantic dishevelment, and though the gesture seemed to calm him, his appearance suggested otherwise, and Vienna understood the heartfelt despair his body expressed even when his voice was carefully modulated. "Do you think I care what people say? Do you doubt I love you more than the sanction of society? Can't you see you will ruin me more surely if you sacrifice yourself to save me?"

Round and round the discussions went. Sometimes Gray tried to cajole or tease her into an acceptance, telling her that although he didn't have "endless money like the boys she knew up North," he could take her and the children to Walla Land, where they could live a palatial existence among the indifferent natives. Or he would threaten desperate acts, like giving himself up as the Lindbergh kidnapper, or sillier solutions, like abducting the weeping beech and holding it hostage despite the ludicrous number of camouflaged bedsheets required to hide something that large. Sometimes he would wait until well into a tryst, when she was weak with longing and breathless beneath his caresses, and then he would have her repeat the affirmation of her love, the promise of forever that he extracted between kisses, only to be accused of cheating later, when they clung together in the last drowsy moments before propriety returned them to their separate beds, when Vienna would claim, from within the comfort of his arms, that agreements made under duress of desire were not binding.

When Gray finally decided to leave in early September, after sending a series of earnest, reassuring, but mendacious telegrams to his family and the Oxford don who supervised his studies, it was with the understanding that Vienna would begin divorce proceedings as soon as she was able to locate Willard.

Fayette had prepared a send-off to rival a Roman banquet; for two days she had been cooking and baking, filling the pantry with oatmeal cookies, blackberry pie, lemon cake, apple crisp, fried pork chops, baked honey ham, stewed carrots, cabbage salad, potato strings, baked butternut squash, shredded beets, buttermilk biscuits, cheese biscuits, and buttered parsnips. Several times, Vienna had gently cautioned her about the abundance of food relative to the number of mouths, but Fayette was undaunted.

"What Mr. Gray needs is to eat this whole corny-copia. Man's so thin he could hide behind a straw, and what he don't eat tonight I'll pack in a hamper so as he'll have foods on the voyage. I for one don't care to see him disappear sideways behind the next toothpick he takes up."

Vienna stopped interfering: she understood that Fayette didn't care to see him disappear, period, and the kitchen frenzy was her way of containing the loss. It was there that Fayette had mediated the sadness of the miscarriages that followed her marriage, translating her tragedy into treats for the children "she already had," and transforming herself from an angular adolescent into a woman whose form sorrow had softened. To the Daniels children, the departure had less reality. Elliott had drawn a menagerie of crayoned animals to accompany Gray on the crossing and Willa made a ribbon bracelet for Gray on which, in crooked stitches, she had sewn the legend, "Of all colors Gray is best."

Gray had been very moved by the gifts and gestures his departure occasioned, but none pleased him as much as Vienna's. At their last secret meeting, she had removed her wedding ring and handed it to him without a word. In its place, Gray had put on her finger a gold signet ring of his own design, ordered from Tiffany and Company in New York, on which was engraved a tree in full foliage, its trunk encircled by a pair of arms whose hands clasped in front center, like the buckle of a belt. The ring was so long delayed that he had despaired of its arriving in time for him to show her the inscription that ran around the flat interior of the band, enclosing her finger with the words EVER WORSHIPPING MY PATRON SAINT OF TREES—GSS.

Vienna cried. It was, she said, the most beautiful thing she owned and the most precious. She wished she had something equally special to give Gray, but he said, "You do, you have, but if you don't stop crying now I'll join you and then we will both be adrift in the baleful brine, and I am not much of a sailor." He licked the tears from her eyes, saying, "Shhh."

They had agreed to part at the house. Neither of them wanted to test their skill at a restrained farewell in public, so it had been arranged that Hezekial Moody, Sophronius's younger, slimmer brother, would take Gray with him when he drove to Walker's Junction to deliver a large order of sweet feed. From there, Gray could take the fast train to Baltimore, with an afternoon connection to New York. The *Lavinia*, on which he had booked passage, was sailing the following noon.

Zeke honked his horn in front of The Heights at 10:00 A.M. sharp, helped throw luggage in the back of the truck on top of the sacks of feed, and after one or two cursory remarks about the fine weather, honked his horn again with the efficient air of a bus driver signaling departure, and drove off, spraying dust and gravel in his wake so that the assembled household could hardly see Gray's face turned back to smile at them as he receded down the drive.

JUST BEFORE ONE that afternoon, two cars pulled up in front of the house, disgorging Mr. Stepple and Sophronius Moody from one vehicle and from the other, a stranger to Vienna, Hal Farney from Walker's Junction, an officer of the law. Mr. Stepple didn't say anything; he just looked down at the ground or lifted a hand to pat Sophronius's massive shoulder that quivered as he cried almost silently, sounding only the sharp inhalations of breath that punctuated his grief.

Mr. Farney took Vienna's arm and began apologizing. "It was an accident. Jim Hollin never shud a had such a load on that truck. They weren't but two miles out of the junction going up the hill—it's a pretty steep incline, behind Jim's truck they were when the logs started to fall off. Says he could hear it happening so he hit the brake, worse thing he could do, and his load just dumped down behind him. I'm very sorry, ma'am. We've got the whole road closed down to Whitley's field."

Vienna just stared at him, so he continued, helplessly repeating himself. "I'm awful sorry, ma'am, about your cousin and Mr. Moody. It was a terrible accident all right. Jim ought never have tried to take that big a load like that. We've got him down at the station now. Ma'am? You understand what I'm saying, the two gentlemen were killed. Their truck was crushed up like a—"

"That's enough," Mr. Stepple interrupted, "I think Mrs. Daniels might want to sit down. Here, help her up those steps," he directed, pulling Sophronius behind him and parking him on the porch with a large clean handkerchief and the instruction, "Give your nose a blow, son, that's right, pull yourself together some. It's gonna be O.K."

Inside the cool of the front hallway, Mr. Farney wiped his brow, and sat wearily in one of the chairs against the wainscoting. Vienna sat on the bottom step of the front stairs and Mr. Stepple stood between them like an anxious translator, uncomfortable with the language of loss. "We need to know who to notify, who are his next of kin."

Pale to begin with, the color in Vienna's face was gone; contrasted against the cobalt blue of her crepe dress, she looked corpselike herself. But for the pallor, her face didn't betray so much as a twitch of emotion. It was her hands that couldn't hold back until the men left. As she wrote out the particulars, they were shaking so badly that she clenched the left one in a tight fist while her right one rendered her distinctive writing unrecognizable in the palsied characters swarming across the piece of foolscap. When she handed the paper to Mr. Farney, she looked up at him expectantly, as if this were only the first step in a long process.

"You don't need to identify the body, Sophronius already verified them both. It's shook him up pretty bad—there's no need for you to see . . ."

Once again, Mr. Stepple intercepted. "It was merciful quick, that much was clear. Hal, I don't think there's anything more to do here. I suggest we leave Mrs. Daniels in peace and try to get instructions from his parents in London now about the, uh, body. I'll run Sophronius home and you can call me later."

Vienna reached out and touched Mr. Farney's arm as he was leaving. "You said it was logs, what kind?" Mr. Farney paused at the door, taken aback at the peculiarity of her only question.

"Pine trees actually, Jim was taking them to the mill."

The two men exchanged a nervous glance as they shut the door on Vienna, who was repeating the word *evergreens* to herself, rolling it on her tongue, as though it had acquired weight and texture: sad as a secret and soft as a moan.

THAT NIGHT VIENNA set fire to the weeping beech. Mr. Aimes saw the smoke from his front porch and ran out to the field with a stack of horsehair blankets under his arm. He pulled Vienna away from the bonfire she had constructed at the base of the trunk, and threw the blankets over the smoldering remains of a pile of clothes she was burning. The fire was surprisingly easy to put out, or rather the tree had been harder to burn than she had imagined, because of the densely draped boughs which shielded it from wind. The trunk was slightly singed and a few of the boughs would need pruning, but not much damage had been done. "Live wood don't burn," John Aimes said in his terse way, tamping out the last sparks. "Leastways not without a lot more kerosene and wind than you've got here." Then, picking through the scorched clothing, he asked her, "Whatever did you do that for, burning up your pretty dresses? I heard about what happened to your cousin, but this won't help none."

"I guess I can do what I want with my things, John Aimes," Vienna said quietly.

"Yep, that you can. With your things, these dresses and the like, though many folks hereabouts would be proud to wear what you don't want, seems a darn shame to waste it. But that tree ain't yours anymore'n the sky is yours. It's a thing of God, Mrs. Daniels, as clearly marked as anything I know."

"Yes, I know," Vienna said. "You see"—her voice broke— "I am the patron saint of trees," she said in a hoarse whisper. "I was trying to save it," she wept, her words drawn through the distortions of pain. Mr. Aimes shook his head and asked, "From what?"

"From what?" Vienna repeated incredulously, spinning around to aim her words at him. "From the world! From the world!" she cried, a hysterical intonation to her voice.

Mr. Aimes spoke to her as he would to a child rendered docile by the exertions of a tantrum, using her elbow as a tiller to steer her back to The Heights. "You're just broken up with grief, that's all," he said, reassuring himself as he tried to comfort her. "Hearts in pain don't reason well, that's a fact. The shock and such's like to make a person do whatever wild thing comes to mind. You'll be yourself again after a little sleep. Didn't those boys give you some apple brandy with the news? That's what you need—a slug of something bracing, whiskey, whatever, it don't matter much. That'd buck you right up, you hear?"

AFTER THAT, VIENNA reclaimed her solitude with the devotion of a penitent. There were a few changes, but nothing Winsville would especially notice. From that day on, Vienna wore only gray—lavender gray, dove gray, silver gray and sage gray, pale pearl grays and dark charcoal grays, but always she wore gray. She chose a few simple patterns that were comfortable and Fayette repeated the dresses again and again on the Singer sewing machine Vienna had given her as an extravagant wedding present when Fayette had married Grant, turning out a wardrobe that became Vienna's uniform, the emblem of an order of one. Vienna never mentioned divorce to Mr. Woodruff or tried to locate Willard, but the letters stopped: when the children asked about their father, ready for the next installment, she said in a voice emptied by honesty, "I don't know where he is," or "No, there has been no letter." After a while, they stopped asking.

15

———■———

*E*VERYTHING REMINDED VIENNA of Gray: the kite Willa
flew with expertise, its tinsel signals flashing from the sky in
a code Vienna never cracked but never doubted was rife with
meaning, or those species of the green world Gray had drawn
or painted in such delicate tints, the tunes her son hummed
or the calls of certain birds, the ones Gray said he liked best
because they introduced themselves by name—whippoorwills,
bobwhites, phoebes, and killdeer—birds so plentiful to her
land they filled the air with its primary vocabulary, all of which
could be reduced to one message: Gray.

Then there was his letter, arriving two days after his death,
resurrecting his voice on a white postcard in unexpected words
spoken from the grave, a gesture made in whimsy the day he
went to the post office to send cables, taking on weight and
shape by the turn of events that mediated his missive, the large
letters blossoming in black ink:

LITTERAE SCRIPTAE MANENT
ET EIUS AMOR QUOQUE

which she read again and again like a prayer fluttering up from ash: *the written word remains and his love also.*

ZEKE'S FUNERAL WAS held on a Wednesday in the Methodist church at the west end of Center street. Vienna sat in the front pew, squeezed in between Sophronius and his mother, surrounded by Moodys. They placed her among them because she was, like them, a surviving relative of the great tragedy, as it was referred to, and because, while Gray might be mentioned in the service, there would no other memorial for him. Because he had once told Vienna he liked the idea of becoming gray literally, and reuniting with the plant world immediately, to enjoy what he said would be his "salad days," he had been cremated, his ashes returned to England.

"Just goes to show what kind of people she comes from that wouldn't give that boy a decent burial," Miss Margayt had hissed to Mrs. Stepple only to be overheard and reprimanded by Dr. Barstow who said, "Seems understandable enough to want to bring him home. That's where charity begins, they say."

The church had an unusual turnout. The pews were packed and folding chairs had been set up in the back. Zeke had been a good friend to the local farmers, letting credit build longer than was probably wise, and accepting barter payments when he could. It was a tribute to his popularity that so many leathered faces turned up midweek during harvesttime. The minister made a lame joke about how good it was to see so many Baptists in his church, a remark that Mrs. Stepple considered in very poor taste under the circumstances, though most people laughed, and were relieved to do so.

The service was long and the church was stifling. Handheld fans flapped languidly in a futile attempt to stir the air. The effluvia of wilting bouquets disseminated a sickening sweetness, overpowering as the death it bespoke. Clumps of flowers were crowded on the altar; they covered the casket, and overflowed the steps down to the center aisle. There was only one arrangement that included Gray's name with Zeke's on the ribbon edged in black and that was the one Vienna brought, a modest collection of cornflowers, the only blue among masses of white and red and yellow. Vienna's flowers were almost entirely overshadowed by a large cross of white carnations with the banner that read, "Good-bye Zeke from Henshaw's Hardware—We Care."

It was there in the Methodist church that Vienna had her epiphany, the private illumination sparked by two words that chanced to hit her ear at just the right angle of inflection to be transformed by her imagination. The minister was droning on about everlasting life and the mysterious ways of the Lord, interweaving a mention of the dead or bereaved like the well-timed chord struck on an organ, an oratory cue calculated to wake the sleeping and to renew the tears of the insomnious.

During one such summons, Vienna could have sworn she heard, as the gentlemen chosen to abide with angels were named, "Gray Saunder" become, on the sententious tongue of the drawling clergyman, "grace yonder." Grace yonder is what she heard, though context and logic refuted her ears. It was as though the heat and tears and floral essence mixed with the pain and patience and faith that filled the room, and a strange alchemy occurred. Words and wonder met, and Vienna understood in that moment the idea of heaven reified, as surely as if she had seen a dove fly from the minister's mouth; from the hocus-pocus of the podium the transcendent had occurred, filling her with the fleeting presence of her lost lover: the sandalwood scent of his skin, the lifting sense of loss and tingling light, the swarm of distant stars, and then the eclipse.

She came to on the grass in front of the church. Dr. Barstow was leaning over her, his hand on her wrist and his eyes on his pocket watch. Someone else stood behind her head, but Vienna couldn't see to whom it was Dr. Barstow said, "She's all right, it was just the heat. No, I won't need those smelling salts. You go on back inside now and add your voice to that pretty hymn."

Dr. Barstow kept her lying on her back for a full five minutes, refusing to let her sit up, though she begged, mortified lest the congregation find her lying in their way. Dr. Barstow fanned her with his black hat, waving it gently by her head and looking away, as if he was embarrassed or bored.

"What happened? Did I do anything foolish?" she asked him. He turned his head and looked down at her, his hand suddenly stilled. "No. You fainted from the heat. You fell in a demure little heap with your skirts about you, if that's your concern."

"It isn't," Vienna said, her color rising. Dr. Barstow laughed. "Good, that's better. All signs of life are back, even ire."

"Did I say anything, or make noise?"

"Nope. Full decorum there too. You made the tiniest cry, like a hinge yawning, that's all. No one would have noticed at all if you hadn't slid to the floor. The minister should thank you for adding something memorable to a very familiar formula."

"Dr. Barstow, did you hear him talk about grace, grace yonder?" Vienna asked, closing her eyes rather than squinting up into the sun. Even with her lids closed, the sun repeated itself in blinding spots that swarmed against the black.

"Maybe. To tell the truth, I don't pay too much attention."

"Then why bother going?" Vienna asked curtly, although she was herself a proclaimed agnostic.

Dr. Barstow considered her question and then laughed. "I

guess because it helps me heal these people if they see me in church."

"That is rather cynical," Vienna said, continuing the conversational feistiness that compensated for the helplessness of her position. Tilting her head up, she opened her eyes to see his expression. Dr. Barstow quickly squatted beside her so that she could make eye contact more comfortably. "On the contrary," he said, "I am relying to some extent on the power of their own faith to augment the sometimes meager capacity of science to serve them. What helps them helps me. If I didn't believe it helped, that would be cynical."

After Dr. Barstow had taken her pulse a second time, he suggested that she try standing, cautioning her to rise very slowly, which she did, accepting his outstretched hand as she steadied herself to examine her gray organdy dress, gauzy and silvered as a web, looking for the insult of grass stains on the ethereal fabric.

"Do you want me to take you home?" Dr. Barstow asked in his ever-weary voice, as if the world was too much with him, anchoring him with burdensome pedestrian concerns, like an Atlas of the mundane.

"Thank you," Vienna said, eager to disappear while the town was still contained in the church, gathered together in a single purpose, complete and complex as a finished jigsaw puzzle, before they spilled out into the odd jumble of ill-fitting personalities. "I would appreciate it, if you don't mind."

"Not at all, my duties end well before interment," Dr. Barstow replied. "Let's go then."

"HE HAS A hole for a heart and his love's leaked out," is what Winsville said about Dr. Barstow. He visited roadhouse whores, but a lot of men did that. What galled Winsville was that Dr. Barstow seemed to prefer them to the decent young women who had set their sights on him, women whom an old bachelor thin of hair and thick of waist should have been proud to catch. In his youth he had been vain about his looks, average as they were, but in aging he had let himself go, seeming to flaunt the slightly debauched air he had acquired.

As he sat beside Vienna in the car, he indeed looked very much like a man with a hole for a heart. His eyes squinted at the road and his face was pale beneath the hasty shave he had given himself that morning. He drove in the silence of acute concentration. He was, in fact, trying to find a way to tell Vienna that he knew, that he understood, that he had been called to set the broken arm of a mechanic's child and the child's mother, formerly of Winsville, had mentioned with an ironic laugh that she had sent a stranger on to The Heights to see what he could see.

It had been a chilling moment for Dr. Barstow, not because he had ever believed that Grayson Saunder was Vienna's cousin—he had suspected from the start that there was some dissembling. Barstow had assumed Gray was an old friend from an earlier incarnation, someone who had known Vienna Whitcomb in the fierce glory from which she had been demoted like an angel smote. Drawn by chance and curiosity to the area, he had rediscovered her, and circumstance had combined with inclination to permit an extended stay.

For Vienna to have taken into her home a stranger with nothing more to recommend him than the stray remark of a mechanic's wife and sheer dumb luck forced Dr. Barstow to the inevitable conclusion that Grayson Saunder was her lover, that her indifference to remarriage was not due to an irreproachable virtue or higher moral stature, but a damning reflection on the men she'd met in Winsville. It was the realization of a moment, but it had taken more than two months of rotgut rye and wasted women to accept, as if the enlargement of his liver was necessary or compensatory for the shrinking of his heart. This, not because James Barstow had ever thought he had much chance with Vienna, but because he had comforted himself with the idea that no one else had either.

The ride to The Heights was quick, the mile and a half sped by before he found the right words and when Vienna shut the door and leaned into the passenger's window to thank him, he merely nodded and drove away. Retreating in silence, he took solace in the rusty eloquence of his dilapidated automobile as it shuddered and sighed.

He was waved down as he passed the graveyard by Biddy Markham, who was in the road brandishing her soggy handkerchief like a flag of truce. Biddy ran over to the passenger door and leaned in as Vienna had done minutes before. "Hey," she said, "can I catch a lift back to town? The day's heat and the Moodys' hysterics have taken it right out of me. I feel about as useful and spirited as this wet rag," she said, raising the handkerchief like an exclamation point.

"Hop in," Dr. Barstow said. Years ago, when he was setting up his practice in Winsville, he had suggested to Biddy an operation that could minimize the disfigurement of her harelip. After much consideration she had declined, and now, knowing her face as well as he did, he was glad of it. Seated beside him, Biddy apologized. "Sorry to turn you into a taxi, James. I just couldn't stay and I didn't want to walk back with the others."

"Is it your arthritis again?"

"Oh no, that's just fine, thanks and amen. No, it was the sharp remarks some of the ladies were making about Vienna that finished me off."

"Such as?"

"General unkindness about her fainting, putting it down to a way to take attention from Zeke, or a sorry excuse to leave, and the like. And on and on about her showing up in gray for the funeral. You know, if she had worn sackcloth and ashes they still would have found fault, and she was just as bereaved as the rest of them."

"Or more so," Dr. Barstow said.

"Or more so," Biddy concurred, wanting to be agreeable and to champion what she took to be a dig at the hypocrisy of certain mourners who only days before would tell you soon as breathe about what a fool Zeke Moody was, that his brother had a fat body, but he had a fat brain and was bound to be out of business by the day's end.

"Well, I guess there's something to be said for sorrow, though I don't quite know what it is," Biddy said as she got out of the car. "I was fond of Zeke, and I imagine Vienna's cousin must have been a fine young man too."

"I would bet on it," Dr. Barstow agreed as he waved good-bye to Biddy, grateful to be alone and remembering out of the recesses of his long-forgotten education a couplet of Shakespeare's, a sonnet he couldn't place but would spend the night searching for, the poem he had once recited to a drowsy auditorium, the source and completion of the words he had found so readily in the car, as though they had been branded on his memory: "That I an accessory needs must be/ To that sweet thief which sourly robs from me."

WINSVILLE BECAME ACCUSTOMED to seeing, as they passed down the road, Vienna perched in the limb of a tree, pruning damaged branches or paring away the jagged bark struck in a recent storm, patiently smoothing the exposed wound before sealing it with her own mixture of fungicide and pitch, or midway up a rickety ladder plugging a hollow in a tree trunk with layers of sawdust and bitumen. They noticed the braced limbs, the linen bandages wrapped around the trunks of certain trees, which signified her presence as certainly as the dark plasters she smeared over the initials boys carved into the living wood.

Mrs. Stepple, to her credit, recognized the growing competence with which Vienna cared for trees, not just the ones on her own property, but those lining the road into town, and the trees which bordered the small square in front of the post office. Two years after her tending, the dogwood and locust flowered so profusely and prodigiously that people from Bantanburg and Walker's Junction began to make Winsville their destination for Sunday drives, and Amos's Blue Star Luncheonette started to have a thriving weekend business. The Overby children showed up in a tatterdemalion cluster with a folding card table, from which they hawked their mother's basket weaving, cedar sachets, potpourri, and clover honey, and the town was so relieved to see some signs of industry from the Overby clan that nobody did anything about the occasional complaints from out-of-towners about being shortchanged or sassed.

It was Margaret Stepple, in fact, who put together the petition to have Winsville pay Vienna a small stipend for her work, a petition that failed because Margaret could only get eight signatures—her own, her husband's, Biddy Markham's, John Aimes's, James Barstow's, Sophronius Moody's, and the illegible scribble of the Snead sisters, a pair of nearly invisible spinsters who roomed in Biddy Markham's boardinghouse, sedulously avoiding notice except at church, where they held up the collection basket to dig out fifteen cents change on a quarter's donation, examining the pennies and nickels to find the shiniest and least-worn coinage available.

Of the political or economic repercussions of her work, Vienna was oblivious. She read up diligently on her subject, acquiring an impressive library devoted to tree maintenance, surgery, fungus and disease, grafting, root care and insect damage, practicing the application of new methods and the adaptation of old ones, watching with satisfaction as the crowns of trees filled in bald gaps, as new leaves pushed out in spring unblemished by cankers or deformities.

She staked saplings, checking the ties with maternal concern to be sure there was no chafing, mulched young trees and fed the roots of venerable old ones, many of which she judged to be older than Winsville itself. Though she was busiest in autumn, she worked year round, humming in self-absorbed concentration. Depending on the season, her laced-up rubber boots, cream-colored linen duster, and battered, wide-brimmed straw hat were the only sartorial concessions she made to an otherwise unvaried habiliment of dainty gray dresses.

She dismissed the occasional praise which came her way like the random leaves that fluttered into the wide pockets of her duster as she toiled. The care she provided was not intended to prompt comment or promote concern. She neither proselytized nor proscribed in the name of her avocation, though she recognized often as not the names represented by the recurring initials brutally gouged into the oldest and most beautiful of Winsville's trees. It had, as far as she was concerned, nothing to do with anyone else, and it was something for which, had Mrs. Stepple's petition succeeded, she would never have accepted payment.

It was through her husbandry of the trees that she atoned for the damage (bark singed in an irregular shape) she had inflicted on the weeping beech, the pride of all her charges, and it was through their care that she came to love her land with a fierce, adventitious loyalty that precluded the possibility of ever leaving it. This was an attitude Vienna would have never imagined herself embracing years before, when she first beheld The Heights in the company of Dory, her Irish lady's maid from New York, who had burst into tears of disapproval upon viewing the rustic terrain and rural Federal architecture aspiring to the grandeur of English manors Dory felt were more befitting and to which she returned less than a fortnight later, taking with her a cameo brooch and a paisley shawl, presumably in lieu of her final salary and as recompense for the hardship she had suffered in her brief exposure to the South.

Gray had once jokingly suggested to Vienna that The Heights secede from Winsville, and if necessary, from West Virginia. Now she found the trees had become for her the link that bound her to the earth from which they sprang and in which their roots were deeply buried. Regardless of the ideological differences dividing her from the prevailing powers, she would never abdicate the minor position of service she held. And there was another reason, too: a woman singularly unschooled in the handicraft arts that occupied the restless hands of so many of her contemporaries, the needlework, knitting, hooking, and quilting in which other women found refuge from the world of words, Vienna had discovered a manual diversion that complemented her unending efforts to finish her manuscript.

In this way she had achieved an odd balance to her life, one in which the secular and cerebral intertwined with the physical and spiritual like the crossed branches of pleached fruit trees. She modeled herself on the trees she knew and loved, imitating the genius of nature that allowed them to be solidly grounded by soil and gravity while yet crowning the sky, embracing earth and heaven simultaneously.

"So WRITE IT down," Vienna said as she bent to pick up twigs that the storm had blown down from the elms. "If you write your idea down, it will become a treatise."

"What's that?" Elliott asked, bending over too so he could see her eyes.

"It is an important document in which you say everything people should know about a subject."

"How do you spell it?"

"T-R-E-A-T-I-S-E."

"O.K.," Elliott said, pushing his glasses up on his nose. "I can do that." He stood waiting for her to say something more. Vienna straightened up, gathering the twigs in her arms like a bouquet of cut flowers and scanning the lawn for the next tree she would work on. She was no longer aware of Elliott, and he felt her absence, her attention lifting from the ground they shared, like a breeze rising, scattering the starlings into the air, leaving the brown grass empty.

Elliott went back into the house and sharpened his pencil vigorously, diminishing it by almost an inch until he had created a point sharp enough to proceed with the surgical accuracy required to convey his thoughts. He flipped forward to a clean page in his notebook and wrote:

Treaty on Birds

The thing that everyone should know about birds is that they are always asking questions, which is why they are calling out and then sometimes you hear another bird answering. That also explains why they look so confused most of the time and are always looking around with their heads. Some of the things they wonder about just have to do with birds but some of the questions are interesting to people too, like where does the wind go when it blows or why is the grass wet in the morning. To be continued.

Then he went off to find Willa. She was sitting cross-legged on the kitchen floor, one suspender of her overall sagging down on her arm. Her hair was bunched up messily on her head and held by an elastic, as it always was when she experimented, because once, during their attempt to distill the light from lightning bugs, she had accidentally burned her bangs. She hadn't been hurt—but the kitchen had been filled with a foul smell that had attracted Vienna's attention, and her censure. Elliott watched Willa surrounding a broken line of ants with a barricade of burning kitchen matches.

"What are you doing to them?" Elliott asked, squinting through his glasses.

"I'm having a festival of fire."

"You're going to go to hell."

"And you're going to heaven, but no one you like's gonna be there."

"How come you say that?"

"Remember what Miss Margayt said about it being easier to get a fat man through a needle's eye than a camel into heaven?"

"What does that mean?"

"I don't know, but no one you like is going to be there." Elliott, who had resumed work on a drawing he had begun that morning, paused in his crayoning to consider.

"Why can't fat people get into heaven again?" he asked, still confused. Willa sighed as if it were obvious, and shrugged her suspender back onto her shoulder.

"Because fat people take up more space than everyone else and if God is everywhere then there is less room for God where fat people are. They squeeze him out, so they are godless."

"Oh." Elliott nodded, returning to his coloring. If the picture came out well he would use it as an illustration for his *Treaty on Birds*. He looked over at Willa's project and said, "You're just burning those ants into little crisps."

"No, Elliott, I'm testing their *moral fiber*. They do it in the church. Vienna told me about it. I'm conducting a holy inquisition."

"They don't do it at *our* church," Elliott said, pulling up his left knicker to monitor the progress of a scab.

"They don't do anything interesting at our church, just nag, nag, nag, like Sister. I don't know why you still bother to go; you could stay with me and Vienna and have pancakes all morning."

"I like the music, and they let me do all the good solos."

"Well, this was a bust." Willa sighed, stretching her arms over her head. "Not a single one of them passed the test of enlightenment."

Elliott pushed his chair away from the table and positioned it nearer to the pyre of matchsticks. From this vantage he could see how dirty Willa's feet were and reflexively he checked his own, which were nearly as bad. Then he put his elbow on his knee and his chin in his hand and in a dreamy voice he asked, "Willa, you know what I don't get? The Holy Ghost! How come he doesn't come out at Halloween and show himself? People would like that."

Elliott smiled just thinking of it. His own costumes were makeshift assemblages that never inspired fear, except for the one time he had worn a papier-mâché mask he had found in the back of an armoire, wrapped in newspaper. The mask was of a handsome man's face, but the expression was frozen, and there was something very disturbing about the effect—worse than if it had just been outright ghoulish. But the mask had disintegrated before Elliott had an opportunity to show it off to the household.

Willa, having considered the question of the Holy Ghost, formulated her definitive answer: "Because, Elliott, he's only a second-rate goblin. He saves the scary stuff till after you're dead and can't tell about it."

Elliott shook his head. The mysteries of birds were so much more accessible to his imagination than the enigma of religion. Willa came over to the table and bit into one of Elliott's crayons. "Do you suppose you could pinch a lump of frankincense for me next Sunday? I think that's what's missing from my experiment," she said thoughtfully.

16

■

*W*ILLA HAD A mean streak a mile wide according to Sister, who was always going on about it, which only made it worse. But Vienna understood, and therefore forgave what she could not condone. Children need love most when they least deserve it, she had rationalized when she discussed with Sister the incident involving Buba, the little Negro boy who would accompany Etta when she came on Saturdays to The Heights to do the "particulars": chores like ironing and waxing, polishing the silver, tasks which Fayette never found time to do during the week.

Buba was a few years younger than Elliott, but because he had had an accident at the age of two, he could not talk. It was an especially gruesome story: on his second birthday his gifts had included a stick of peppermint candy, which he had in his mouth when he wandered out onto the decayed back porch and fell through some rotting timber.

The fall was no more than six feet, but he hit his chin, and the force of the impact clamped his jaw shut, severing an inch of his tongue. He was taken to the nearest doctor, a veterinarian who treated coloreds on the side. No attempt was made to reconnect the severed section of Buba's tongue, though Etta had carried it in a rag filled with the ice she had bought to make ice cream for his birthday. Buba had been bleeding profusely and the doctor was concerned only with suturing the stump so the bleeding would stop. Beyond that they would need to go to Bantanburg.

Buba was probably as bright as any other child from the town, but because his attempts at communication had been reduced to repetitions of slobbery "*b*"noises, because he could not control his salivation and wore a dirty bib around his neck, it came to be assumed that he was simple. No attempt had been made to educate him; he tagged along behind Etta, the oldest sister in an enormous family, who would tether him, like an affectionate mongrel, in the yard of the house in which she was working.

"Don't get involved in their business," Sister had said when Vienna objected. Sister often punctuated her comments by crossing her arms or putting her hands at her waist and thrusting her hips forward in a way that emphasized her ungainliness. Her large bones and the gracelessness of her movements combined with the unflattering boxy styles and drab colors she wore to give the impression she was carrying more bulk than she actually had. Willa thought of Sister as "lumpy," like an old sofa with shot springs, but to Vienna there was something contentious about the way Sister used her heft. But while Sister's posturing succeeded in offending Vienna, it failed to intimidate her.

"Augusta, I can't have *human beings* tied up on my property. I don't care if this *is* the South."

This was just the kind of remark that made Sister sweat with anger. She bristled at references to Vienna's ownership of her family's property and she hated slights to the South, especially from Northerners, which is what Vienna would be until her dying day.

"Then mind him yourself, while the rest of us work," Sister snapped back. Vienna, in turn, was wounded by Sister's staunch disregard of intellectual pursuits, the "work" Vienna did, up in the attic study. She pulled back, as if cringing beneath a blow. Hunching her shoulders forward, she wrapped her arms around herself in a characteristic gesture of retreat and began to hum, for insulation, as she wandered away.

Her father had warned her, years before: *You will regret this caprice. You are impulsive and inexperienced. You think what is different is charming. That is a luxury you can only preserve from a distance. You will not fit in, and thank God, for they are not civilized in the South. They seem to be, but like snake-oil salesmen it's nothing but sweet talk and two-bit charm. Their notions of chivalry and honor are no better than petrified wood—good for nothing; try to hold it and you have a fistful of dust. You will be unhappy and ruined, and in that you will have your only real connection to the South.*

For days, Vienna hummed. She hardly ate. She stayed in her faded nightgown and thought. But before the next Saturday arrived, with little Buba in tow, she had a solution. Willa and Elliott were to take him with them to the barn, where he could play untethered without danger of wandering off or hurting himself. Both children had scowled and protested. "He might hurt the animals," Elliott had whined. "He'll be in the way," Willa complained. The Daniels children were solitary by circumstance and nature. They never mixed with other children except at the yearly town fair games, choir practice, or occasional birthday parties, which they attended reluctantly, taken at Sister's insistence, who then stood with the other adults watching them with nervous ambition.

But Vienna had been undissuadable, and Sister had added the caveat, "Stop that whining or you'll turn into mosquitoes, and Lord knows we have enough already." So, the following

Saturday, Willa had led Buba by the hand, squeezing it a little too hard, down to the second barn, the more rotted of the two, in which Elliott kept his animals. Elliott trailed a few feet behind, his chin tucked into his chest, eyeglasses askew, looking solemn.

When they reached the barn, Willa pointed to a pile of hay and said, "Sit." Buba sat, hunching over his knees, looking terrified. Then turning to Elliott, whose upper lip wore a magenta Fu-Manchu mustache of dried grape juice, she said, "Well, have a good time. I'm going to the brook," punctuating it with a tongue thrust.

"*Wil*-la," Elliott whimpered, "you can't!"

"Just watch," she said gleefully, turning and skipping into a run with her arms out like wings as she sped down the incline toward the brook.

Elliott looked over at Buba embarrassedly and then up at the rafters, where in one corner barn swallows had nested, and in another a wounded pigeon huddled. "Well, I guess I'll feed the birds now," he mumbled awkwardly. He got up and went over to a broken bureau that had been abandoned there, permanently retired to the service of the children's games, and pulled open the bottom drawer where he kept his supplies. He had a misshapen metal measuring cup, several battered books, a notepad, a box of crayons, and a bag of birdseed. He measured out some feed and then started calling, soft and exact, his mouth filling with rushing trills.

Buba watched in amazement, drool hanging thickly off his lower lip. "Watch out, now," Elliott cautioned as a fledgling barn owl darted down, knocking the tin cup out of his hand and scattering the feed, "sometimes they poop on you." Then the roosting pigeons swooped down in a fury of feathers, fighting for the seed, squawking away the injured one whenever it tried to come near.

"Oh, don't be so rude," Elliott admonished his birds, offering the injured pigeon a perch on a stick and lifting him above the ruckus to the top of the bureau, where he could be given a bread ball that was brown with kneading, and had a bit of blue corduroy lint stuck to it. A bluejay tried brashly to fly up, shrieking aggressively, but Elliott waved him away.

Buba's eyes were wide and unblinking. He watched in amazement as Elliott coaxed a limping baby raccoon out of a makeshift shelter in an apple crate. "Be careful not to frighten him. He's still jumpy and liable to bite, but he'll be ready to leave soon," Elliott warned, burrowing down into his pocket for another wadded-up piece of bread. "He doesn't have a name yet, but I'm thinking of calling him Achilles, because of his paw," he went on in his rapid, slightly raspy patter. "Here, d'you want to feed him?" Elliott asked softly, holding the peanut-butter breadball out encouragingly toward Buba. Buba did not respond.

"That's O.K.," Elliott said kindly, "Willa won't either."

Next Elliott climbed up into the hay and returned with a scrawny-looking kitten. "This is Cataline. They tried to drown her. I found the gunnysack with the whole litter, but the others were dead. She was pretty badly scratched up by them all trying to get out. I don't think one of her eyes works too well now."

Elliott stood for a moment, holding the cat against his chest, stroking her head and waiting for a response. He let out a deep quivering sigh. He had been sighing like that since he was a baby. Vienna had said of him, "He may be only a baby but he has an old soul." Buba stared up at Elliott and made one of his gargly sputtering noises.

Elliott handed the kitten over to Buba, who held it clumsily against his bib. "Just stay here a sec, I'm going to call in Murphy," Elliott said. He walked over to the door and whistled a code of trills. He repeated it several times and finally picked up a bent spoon and clanged it against an empty water pail. There was a rustling in the underbrush and a nearly bald dog clambered out into the open and loped, swaying, toward Elliott.

"Murphy's going to just sit here at the door where the birds won't fuss about him. I have to put some oil on his burns."

Elliott dug back down in the drawer and produced a tin of Italian olive oil, the very tin that Sister had accused Etta of stealing two weeks before. Buba remembered it clearly. The whole way home, two miles, Etta had cursed and spat. She had asked him, rhetorically, at different intervals in the long walk back to town, "What kind of crazy trick's in her head? Accusing me over some greasy oil that don't even taste right? I ought to quit is what I ought to do."

Sister's relationship to the hired help was predicated on suspicion. She always asked for shopping receipts, which Fayette found insulting because she was honest, and Etta found insulting because she was not. Vienna's attitude had been that if Etta was pilfering it was insignificant and should be considered a perquisite for years of punctuality and hard work. But Sister found that kind of leniency as appalling as the inflated wages Vienna insisted on paying.

Buba stared at the tin as if it contained some kind of magic potion, having both the power to hurt and to heal, for as he worked Elliott explained in his earnest, patient way how the dog had been burned, how some boys had found him down by the tracks and thrown gasoline on him and set him on fire, how Miss Queenie from the post office heard the howling and saw him running which just made it worse and threw a mail bag over him which was how he survived at all, though he lost most of his fur and the animal doctor said it might never grow back but he needed to be oiled and sure enough, it was helping, for some of the skin was pretty raw but now—here Elliott interrupted his breathless narrative to point—it was getting dark and leathery and looked more like a hide.

"He might whimper a bit," Elliott said, "but he knows it's good for him. At first we had to make a special formula out of golden seal, thyme, nasturtium, and garlic to prevent infection; it smelled pretty bad. Then you combine chickweed, camomile, marigold, and comfrey for the burns, but now this is all we need."

Buba put the kitten down in the hay and came over to the door to watch intently. Elliott worked carefully, his forehead wrinkled in concentration as he massaged the olive oil over the dog, muttering reassurances in a low whisper. Buba held out his hand to hold the tin for Elliott and tried to imitate Elliott's gentle monologue.

When Elliott finished, he looked over at Buba. "Here, gimme your hand," he commanded, and put it in front of Murphy's face to be licked. "He knows his friends this way," Elliott said, warming to the idea of a protégé.

"Aywaht," Buba said with difficulty.

"Huh?"

"Aywaht," Buba repeated, smiling and pointing to Elliott.

"Yes, exactly. I'm Elliott." Elliott beamed. "I'm going to teach you everything I know. You can help me. You can be my assistant."

Buba smiled, letting a long thread of saliva escape as he made a burbly sound of pleasure.

"O.K., now we can go to the nests and check on the babies, but you can't touch; they're too little and we have human smell on us." Elliott thought to himself that Buba had a particularly strong human smell, but he didn't say anything about it. He was too elated by Buba's unquestioning admiration.

So it began. Saturdays passed and Elliott's ability to decode Buba's wet sputterings increased until their communication became a comfortable alternation of terse and loquacious responses. Elliott came to know almost intuitively what Buba was trying to say with his slurpy syllables and Buba would listen contentedly to Elliott ramble on, expounding his theories about animals and what they said to each other, translating back and forth among his gallery of friends.

Moreover, Elliott had undertaken to teach Buba a language he could master. If he did not have enough tongue to speak fluently to humans, he could, nonetheless, learn to imitate in the back of his throat the watery whistles of certain birds, and as the weeks went by Buba became so adept at this that he would lie for hours on the bank of the brook, carrying on dialogues with birds he came to know and distinguish by their subtle and distinctive inflections, which identified them as clearly as their markings. Meanwhile Elliott would check on the nests, counting eggs and describing in his notebook new birds for which he had no names other than those he invented for himself, and then taught to Buba.

But one Saturday, after breakfast, Willa wanted Elliott to come with her on an expedition to the dump, for she had heard in Henshaw's Hardware that Pinky Evans, the railroad clerk, had died, and what personal belongings he had that had not been sold by Mrs. Cornish, who rented him a room, were going to be added to the rubbish pile. "There's bound to be good stuff there, since he traveled all over the place on sleeping cars and collected all sorts of things that would be good to have," Willa had urged.

"Naw, I don't think so," Elliott said, furrowing his brow. "Mrs. Cornish is sure to have picked it over pretty good. Anyhow, I've got other things to do."

"Oh yeah, like what, fr'instance?"

"Just things," Elliott answered, a guilty smile crinkling the corners of his mouth.

Willa wasn't looking at Elliott, though, as she gnawed at

the cuticle of her thumb, her feet swung up on the kitchen table and crossed at the ankle. "Well, d'you mind telling me what's so very important that you can't come?"

"Willa, let me be, will you? Buba and I are going to look for turtle eggs."

Willa's hand dropped from her mouth as she stared at her little brother incredulously.

"*Buba?* You mean you're not coming to the dump because of Buba? That is so stupid! We can leave him in the barn. Sister doesn't care, and Vienna will never know. He's not going to *say* anything, you know."

"I don't want to leave him in the barn. We're going to look for turtle eggs, like I told you."

Willa stood up abruptly, snapping her hand in the air to discharge the pain of the last pull on her cuticle that had just drawn a bead of blood. "But I'm telling you, you don't have to," she said, loud with exasperation.

"I know. I want to," Elliott said meekly, overly intent on reading the words printed on the molasses tin, avoiding Willa's eyes.

"You mean you'd rather go with Buba, Bububububa?"

Elliott had been at the point of suggesting that they bring Buba with them, since he didn't want to risk missing the good finds and because he had never gone against Willa before, but she had been mean about Buba, so he steeled himself and said, "Yes, I'd rather go with Buba."

Willa flushed up to her hairline, revealing her redhead's heritage. Elliott had always gone foraging with her. He had always wanted to do what she was doing. "Tagalong," she had called him. Now she realized what a mistake she had made, leaving him with Buba for so many Saturdays while she had gone off on her own.

"Suit yourself, stinko. I don't care abububuout what you

- 186 -

do anyhow," she said before she slammed out the kitchen door.

She went down to the dump fuming and kicking stones, though Sister had told her only the day before that she wasn't to ruin her shoes like that, and it wasn't ladylike besides. But by the time she found Mr. Evans' personal effects she had forgiven Elliott. A pile of picture postcards in a rusted tea tin had gone a long way toward assuaging her anger and there was a large broken wooden trunk which she needed help in hauling back.

Willa started to head home with the tea tin under her arm when she nearly tripped over a perambulator lying on its side under the corner of a sodden and shredded mattress. She stopped to pull it out and stand it up. The canopy was torn and one side of the carriage was deeply dented, but it would be a perfect bed for one of Elliott's animals. She broke into a run. By the time she got to the barn she was sweaty and panting. "Elliott," she called excitedly, but there was no answer. She climbed up to the hayloft and saw his notebooks lying open. Next to them was a pad of ruled paper on which Elliott had drawn some of the symbols he used in his notebooks, organized by headings in his neat Palmer script. Under Elliott's symbols were large clumsy imitations in crayon. Willa's face hardened and her hand closed into a fist. "Goddamn him, goddamn him," she shouted, kicking the notebook down to the lower level. "He's teaching Buba his secret code, the idiot broomhead."

Willa was shaking as she climbed down the ladder, and she was fighting back tears, which came to her so rarely. It was incomprehensible. Elliott had never taught her the symbols, though she had never much cared before. This represented a betrayal of which she would never have imagined him capable.

Jealous and wounded, she ran from the barn and went to

look for him. It was late in the afternoon before she found them, for she had given up once, and gone back to the house to eat. But seeing Etta in the kitchen ironing had only renewed her anger, and when Sister had asked what she was doing inside by herself on such a fine day, Willa had felt her shame again. "Leave me be, can't you," she had snapped.

"Won't you," Sister corrected, with her usual martyred patience, *tsk*ing to herself at Willa's rumpled shirt, mussed hair, and cheeks scalded red from exertion. Sister didn't believe a body should move rapidly, much less in the heat.

"What a mouth that girl has," Etta had remarked to Sister.

"It *is* a disappointment and a trial, frankly, but I have to choose my battles with her or we would be at war all day," Sister explained after Willa had left the room.

BUBA AND ELLIOTT were on the other side of the railroad tracks that ran through a corner of the Daniels property. The ground was marshy where earth had been displaced to bank the track. Willa came up out of the swamp grass, mud up to her knees, and asked Elliott, "What do you think you're doing?"

"I'm giving Buba here a turtle egg that he can hatch and then have for a pet," Elliott said, opening his palm to reveal his prize. "It took us forever to find it," he said proudly, gesturing to include Buba, who stood beside him grinning. "Murphy found it actually, but he was so excited we were afraid he would eat it and so we had to send him home."

"Well you're coming with me now to the dump," Willa said, taking Elliott by the arm. Elliott shook her off.

"Let go, Willa, this is delicate, and Buba still has to get it home."

"I don't give a damn about Buba or his stupid egg," she said, grabbing it out of Elliott's hand.

"Give it back," Elliott shouted, trying to get it from her, but she held it over her head, switching it back and forth between her hands, twisting away from him. "Willa," Elliott shrieked, "I hate you, give it back."

The words stung her.

"Oh yeah? Oh yeah, you sneaky b.m. pellet? Well, I hate you and your goddamn egg and most of all I hate Buba," she shouted, throwing the egg square at Buba's chest. "Go away, you horrid little nigger," she yelled.

Buba let out a wounded cry. The sound was chilling, and it hung in their ears after he had disappeared, yelping, into the brush. Elliott threw himself on Willa and started slugging. They tumbled to the ground, where they tussled until Elliott managed to pin down one of Willa's arms. She bit him in the shoulder and he pulled back crying, his glasses broken and his face swollen and blotchy.

"I'm telling. This time you're going to get it," he panted, scrambling to his feet.

"I don't care," Willa answered, pushing her hair from her face defiantly and wiping her nose with her arm.

"You're just plain mean and I hate you and I hope Sister gives it to you good," Elliott said, picking up his glasses and trying to bend one of the earpieces back until it broke off in his hand. He started sobbing, and holding the glasses on his nose with his finger he started back to the house.

"Tattletale," Willa shouted after him. "Go ahead, see if I care."

But she did care. That was the terrible part about it all. She started to follow him but stopped. What was the point in going home? She went instead to the weeping beech and hid beneath its drapery. She sat for a long time under its pendulous shelter reliving the incident by the tracks, waiting for her heart to stop pounding. She had only said *nigger* because it was the most powerful word in her arsenal, one that frightened even her with its palpable malice. When it had grown dark and she could no longer tolerate the mosquitoes, she got up and brushed herself off and made little *x*'s with her fingernails on the bites to stop them from itching before taking the long route home, going back by the road.

She had only been walking for about ten minutes when Clem Morgan, the new sheriff, drove by her and stopped his car. He cranked his neck out the window and called, "Willa Daniels, that you?" He was twenty-six and good-looking: he carried a Bakelite comb in his pocket, next to his whistle, and he was the kind of man who flirted just as easily with little girls as big ones.

Willa crouched quickly by the side of the road.

"Willa, get in the car. I'm taking you home," he said, starting to get out of the car.

"Are you arresting me?" she called from the darkness.

"I will if you don't come here right now," Clem called back.

Willa came sheepishly toward the car. "You going up to The Heights?"

"Yep."

"O.K. but I'm dirty. I'll muss up your seat," she said quietly.

"That don't make no difference." Clem laughed. "We've had a heap worse'n you in here," he said, opening the door for her. "Your kind of dirt washes off," he added, winking at her.

Willa pulled herself away from him and slumped by the passenger door. She didn't even try to look at his tooled leather holster or the heavy black gun it held. He chewed his gum in silence, without offering her a stick, though she would have refused it on principle. Still, she thought, he ought to offer if he's going to chew so loudly.

As they drove up the gravel to the house, Willa could see

a crowd had gathered on the porch. There were men holding dogs on leashes with one hand and smoking cigarettes with the other, cluttering the lawn with their bulky bodies. Some of them held torches. It almost looked like a party, but there were no paper lanterns and no music.

Clem got out of the car and shouted, "I got me the prize before the treasure hunt even began!" There was clapping and whistling from the crowd as Clem pulled Willa out of the car and held her arm up, like a hunter posing with his prey. "What's going on?" she asked warily, trying to pull her arm down, uncomfortable with the attention.

"I'll tell you what's going on," Sister said, breathless from having run all the way down the drive. "Frankly, I would wring your neck right now if the deputy sheriff weren't standing by to stop me. What's going on indeed!" Sister grabbed Willa roughly by the back of the neck and pushed her forward through the throng. As she was hustled into the house she saw Vienna in the parlor talking to Dr. Barstow. "Is Vienna O.K.?" she asked, since Vienna usually stayed in her study whenever Dr. Barstow came to the house.

"Buba is still missing, and now it's dark and if he doesn't turn up soon you're not going to be O.K., do you hear me?" Sister pushed Willa into the bathroom and shut the door behind them. "Get into the tub and wash yourself. Elliott's hysterical and having asthma. We had to call Dr. Barstow and Mr. Aimes has organized a search party and Etta is beside herself and as far as I can tell this is all your doing."

Sister left Willa alone in the bathroom and went back out to the men on the lawn. Willa could hear the buzzing of voices outside and Clem's distinctive laugh. She had undressed and was standing naked beside the bathtub, waiting for the water to cool, when the door cracked open and Etta poked her head in.

"Willa, honey, you all right? You ain't hurt or nuthin'?"

Willa shook her head and looked away.

"Can I come in then?"

"Well," Willa said slowly, as if she weren't sure whether the reservation should be on her or Etta's side. "I'm not wearing anything."

"Don't mind me, I've seen enough nine-year-olds not to notice another."

"Ten," Willa corrected, though she was still a month shy.

"Uh-huh, and ten-year-olds too. Go 'head and clean yourself up and don't mind me." Etta closed the door behind her and Willa stepped gingerly into the steaming water.

"Willa, baby, I gotta talk to you, see, and find out where's Buba at, 'cause they don't want to be bothering about a colored boy."

"I didn't mean it, really, Etta," Willa started, but she stopped when she heard Vienna on the stairs, her voice pinched in anger, saying, "Just get him out of my house or I will do it myself!" Then Sister's voice responded with authority, "This is no time to get high and mighty with the law and you might remember that the rest of us live here too."

Vienna threw the door to the bathroom open and told Etta in a hush to go downstairs and go home as if everything was normal. Sister crowded in behind Vienna and explained that Mr. Aimes was still going to go out searching after everyone left.

"And you," Sister said to Willa, shaking her finger angrily, "don't leave this room until I get back."

Willa could hear Sister and Vienna squabbling outside the bathroom door, so she got out of the tub and stood with her ear to the keyhole, listening closely, since they had lowered their voices. Then she heard Dr. Barstow's scratchy deep cigarette voice and Sister excusing herself.

"I warned you before," Dr. Barstow said, "what was it, nine years ago?"

"Eight. He was eight in April," Vienna answered. Behind the door, Willa strained to hear what they were saying in hushed voices about Elliott. Her stomach tensed and she forgot that she was cold, wet, and without a towel.

Vienna winced at the memory. After Elliott's birth, she had argued and insisted and finally she had begged, but Dr. Barstow had gone ahead and filled in the certificate of birth as the afternoon of April first, though in reality it had been early morning of the second. April Fool's Day was what he had written. "What is wrong with everyone in this town? You can't tamper with the truth like that," she had said with what little voice she had left. "I won't have my son be made a fool by you and your fear of Winsville's lawless trash."

Dr. Barstow had been unshakable. "Based on the circumstance of his premature birth, I don't think your son is the one who is a fool," he had said. For a long while after that she had not spoken to him, though whenever he had come to the house, summoned by the help, or by Sister, he had not failed to end the visit with the words, "And please give my regards to Vienna."

She had held it against him, too, that he would not accept payment for that visit, or any subsequent visit. Always the money was returned with a note saying, "I'd rather have your thanks." Vienna herself was never ill enough to require his services, and when he became convinced that Vienna stayed well just to keep him away, he made no effort to assuage her anger. He had laughed when Sister tried once to apologize for what she found an uncomfortable and embarrassing situation. "I don't mind being the reason she's fit. That's my job as her doctor," he had said. In truth, he was relieved. He had long ago come to terms with his limitations, and he knew that he could not cure what ailed her if it were to manifest itself in illness.

"Very well, eight years ago," Dr. Barstow continued.

"But this is different," Vienna whispered, her neck flushing slightly as her voice took on a note of urgency.

"No, it's only a different sheriff, and Clem's probably a little testier, since he's not from around these parts and never knew Winsville when the Daniels ran the town. He's young and still has to prove himself. Don't volunteer for trouble. You're not a big favorite with the mayor's wife either, and John Aimes and I won't always be able to bail you out."

"John Aimes is a joke," Vienna said dismissively.

Dr. Barstow smiled. He had seen how awkward John was around Vienna and was amused by it.

"Nonetheless he's offering his help."

"I never asked for his help or yours. I can think and act for myself."

"That's an expensive privilege. It may cost you in ways you are not prepared to pay, Mrs. Daniels. You might consider acting for others occasionally."

Vienna's voice grew hard. "That's exactly the point. I am acting for others, others who can't act for themselves because of the backward . . ."

Dr. Barstow cut her off. "Don't make a cause out of this child. You have your own children to worry about."

But here Vienna interrupted him. "I have to live with myself."

"Your children have to live with the town."

"Your concern, Dr. Barstow, is misplaced. Buba is still . . ."

"Don't use Buba as a pawn in your battle to change the world. You'll only make matters more difficult for his family and for yours. For God's sake, just go downstairs and thank Clem. He found Willa, after all. Send his men away and wait until they have gone before anyone goes out for Buba.

Discretion, Mrs. Daniels, is the better part of valor and in fact, the only viable way to be valiant around here."

Vienna was boiling. "Is that the best you can do—trot out a weary cliché to hide behind?"

"I dare say it's not nearly as tired a cliché as the righteous endangering the innocent."

"That was unworthy of you," Vienna said softly, and her austere features were momentarily illuminated by a fragility foreign to her face. She looked crestfallen. Dr. Barstow looked down, struggling to find the right words searing within him. His attention was drawn to a puddle of water forming near his right shoe, where the slant of the floor tapered off. "There seems to be a leak here," he said, the moment lost now, as it so often was, and the yet unformulated rush of self-expression subsided back into the depths of mundane existence, the domain he had learned to find safe, familiar, and even cozy in the comfort of routine.

Vienna looked down and then over to the door.

"Willa Daniels, how dare you eavesdrop like a common criminal!" There was a slappering of wet feet and a splash that convinced Vienna that Willa was no longer by the door.

"How much do you think she heard?" Vienna asked, starting down the stairs.

"Enough for me to owe you an apology for speaking as I did," Dr. Barstow said stiffly, his voice sounding flat to his ear.

"Oh, please," Vienna said curtly. "I won't accept an apology from you until you accept payment from me."

"Pride goeth before a fall."

"Dr. Barstow, I fell the day I came to The Heights."

"Well I'll be there when you land," he countered, with a tenderness that embarrassed him and for which he compensated by pushing past her and walking hurriedly to his car, in which a few men already sat waiting for a ride back to town.

17

---■---

ILLA SAT IN the tub, letting the water grow cold, waiting for Sister to return, waiting for punishment or news. She was hungry and her hands were wrinkling, but the house was silent. The water in the bath was brown and had things floating in it.

She scooped up a blade of grass and stuck it to the side of the tub above the waterline. The scab on her knee had grown soggy and stung, but she didn't have the heart to pick at it. Nor did she dare get out. She was thinking about what Dr. Barstow had said to Vienna. Willa didn't like him: he had messy eyebrows and sour breath that had a stale smell like old pennies and he was always serious. There were deep lines in his forehead like the cracks that scar the ground during a drought.

Willa thought too of the dump, all her prizes lost because of Elliott's obstinance and betrayal. And she thought of Buba's howl, and what she had said, and felt the shame rise up in her like the bitterness of medicine that can't be swallowed away. She wondered if Elliott had told that part. She sat there for so long she lost track of time. It seemed like hours before she heard voices again.

"I'll get him," Vienna was saying as she passed the bathroom door.

"No, he can't go, Vienna, he's sick," Sister insisted from the landing.

"I'll go," Willa shouted from the bathroom.

"Oh Lord, how long have you been sitting there?" Sister asked, opening the bathroom door.

"Since you said."

"For all mercy sake, you must be withered right up and cold to boot. Wash your teeth, get into your nightclothes, and go to bed. You're not going anywhere but upstairs, this instant. Don't you have any sense at all, sitting there like a toad on a log? Do you have any idea what time it is?" Sister said, trying not to be harsh, because she liked to think of herself as fair, but Willa never let her get as close as Elliott did. Therefore Willa was relegated to a less balanced distribution of Sister's moods, mostly catching her exasperation.

"I'm hungry."

"Mr. Aimes is sending for his Hegemony since Fayette is at her sister's tonight. When she gets here, she can fix you a cold supper. So then don't wash your teeth yet."

"I can get supper myself," Willa sulked. It irked her to be scolded for doing what she was told, especially as it had taken some effort.

"I don't want you here alone, so you will please show Hegemony where everything is in the kitchen and mind your manners."

As Willa emerged from the bathroom in her nightgown, she saw Elliott in the hall, being bundled into a jacket.

"Hey, where's he going?" she called out. Sister, Elliott, and Mr. Aimes all turned to look up the stairs at her, but no one said anything.

"Why's everyone acting so funny?"

"Put on your slippers," was all Sister said as she closed the front door behind them.

OUTSIDE, ELLIOTT BLINKED in the darkness. His glasses had been temporarily fixed with a safety pin to hold the broken earpiece, but they fit even more loosely now and slid down his nose when he moved his head. There was a tangy-sweet smell of applewood smoke lacing the still night air and the last gardenia blooms lent their pale perfume to the shadows that crossed the lawn like a phantom trellis.

"Where are we going?"

"Keep your voice down, baby. We have to find Buba, and we need you to show us exactly where you last saw him. Mr. Aimes already went out once with a search party but they couldn't find a beacon in this darkness, much less a colored boy, and so the others went home. Everyone's more interested in dinner now." Sister sighed, as if she herself could be included in that group. She pushed her hands deep into the pockets of the man's canvas work jacket that she wore over her brown housedress.

"How come you don't want Willa to know?" Elliott asked, pushing his glasses up again.

Mr. Aimes caught Sister's eye. "Just in case anyone comes to the house asking questions, hon, we don't want them to know our business," she said.

"Like who?"

"Oh well, just anyone. Someone who might have had too much to drink at the roadhouse. It's Saturday night and there are always a few fellows looking for a little trouble if they don't have a date."

"But why would they come to The Heights?"

Mr. Aimes stopped to light another lantern, which he

handed to Elliott. "Can you hold that steady?" he asked gently, squatting before Elliott.

"Yes, sir, but why would they come to the house?"

Sister sighed and said, "Elliott, don't ask so many questions. Concentrate on one thing at a time. We want to get Buba home as quickly as possible."

Elliott fell silent and walked ahead of Sister and Mr. Aimes, wondering whether he should get Murphy to help them find Buba. He had never trained Murphy to follow a scent, but his confidence in Murphy's tracking abilities was unbounded. He thought proudly of how Murphy had found the turtle egg and then remembered his anger.

"What's gonna happen to Willa?" Elliott asked, suddenly turning around and lifting his lantern to see Sister, whose unrushed pace had left her several yards behind.

"What's that, hon?"

"What did you do to Willa?"

"Don't you worry about Willa. She'll have her reckoning yet, and don't get too far ahead. Stop a bit by the barn and catch your breath. We'll meet up with you there," Sister said, turning back to her conversation with Mr. Aimes.

"You know what they call her in town," he was saying in a pinched voice.

"She doesn't go to town anymore," Sister replied, adjusting the black felt hat she had crushed on her head out of force of habit before leaving the house.

"But you know what they say?" Aimes urged.

"They say a lot of things, John, and I do my best not to mind that kind of talk," Sister continued, frustrating Aimes with a perverse reluctance to gossip at anyone else's initiative, even if, as was now the case, her exact sentiments were voiced.

"Folks say she's a nigger-lover," Aimes said, swallowing hard and taking a long stride ahead of Sister.

Sister stopped and sighed dramatically. "I can't say I know why you would repeat such a thing to me, as if I don't have enough already on my plate to swallow." The modulations of martyrdom were Sister's own slightly defensive version of flirtation, though she would never have recognized it as such.

"Because it's dangerous talk in these parts. You can't just ignore it and Etta's brother has everyone riled up with that new car of his—getting ahead of himself and attracting the wrong kind of attention." Aimes's concern remained steadfast; the worry in his voice was for Vienna alone, and, realizing this, Sister lifted her lantern to observe that in profile his chin was weak and he had hair in his ears.

"And just what do you suggest I do?" Sister asked, irritably. "I can't control Vienna. I'm not my brother's keeper."

"No, but you mind his house and family."

Sister joked unexpectedly, "Does that makes me the house-keeper?"

"You know I didn't mean that. It is just that someone's got to—"

Sister interrupted, her old fractiousness returning, "I appreciate your concern, but there is nothing I can do more than I am already doing. I'm sure you are aware that I am not entirely welcome here, in my own family's house." Her voice fluttered slightly, as it did when she indulged her notions of being undervalued, a theme she returned to almost as often as her pronouncements of what was "not right." "And while I don't condone my brother's behavior—clearly, I don't, I am here after all because I am ashamed of his having abandoned his wife, because that is what it amounts to, this 'venture' of his which has kept him in Texas this whole time—just an easy pretext really, with a Mexican floozie and the vain hope of getting rich and throwing it in our faces, and I know this firsthand, mind you, because I went there myself and I saw what I saw and I was frankly appalled, but that doesn't make it any easier coming here and trying to do right by these children. I'm not saying he was right, but I will say I have done what I can, though no one knows as well as I do how unnatural my sister-in-law's life is and how I suffer for it, I really do." Sister concluded her unbroken catalogue of injury and injustice with the breathless triumph of an auctioneer hammering down a sale and then dabbed at her nose with a handkerchief, as if to remind Aimes of her femininity.

Mr. Aimes closed his mouth and swallowed. There was nothing more to say, and he was sorry he had tried at all, a feeling he so often had after approaching Sister. She had a way of turning the simplest things into a long harangue with herself at the center, fighting off recrimination.

"Well, here's the barn. I guess we should get going now," he said, taking refuge in the practical, as he had done so often before. A fence to fix, a gun to clean, a broken latch, a dry well, or an ax handle to sand—those were reliable ways to move through the parts of the day that were not already given over to work. John Aimes believed in doing. It had been his salvation, though he suspected that it was a shallow one and did not hold it against Vienna that she might sit for hours on end doing nothing more than listening to the wide-throated gramophone wail Italian opera. In fact, he admired her all the more for it, and for her ability to delight in her own company and to eat an entire box of chocolates without shame. And, thinking of her, he pulled his socks up and retucked his shirt, which glowed luminously white against the dark night.

ELLIOTT WAITED BESIDE the barn, looking up at the night sky. God was up there watching him back, and watching Buba too and Mr. Moody, who was kindly: he always sneaked Elliot a fireball or licorice shoestring or jawbreaker whenever he came into his store. It seemed very unfair, Elliott thought, looking up at the wavering light from the stars, that Sophronius Moody was not going to be allowed into heaven. Mr. Moody was addicted to Nehi sodas and drank at least ten a day. He was so fat he had to order his clothing specially from Washington. He sweated a lot; there were always beads of perspiration on his upper lip even in winter, even when he wasn't moving.

Willa wouldn't take the fireballs because they were often sticky, especially if Mr. Moody held them in his hand too long before pretending to pull them from her ear. But Elliott always took them, even if they were sticky, not because he especially wanted the candy—about sweets Willa was generally more venal than Elliott—but because he liked Mr. Moody for having peppermint breath and being jolly and laughing at his own jokes until he was red in the face. Elliott felt sorry for him; in the midst of his merriment he looked as if he were about to die and Sister said he was dim. Mr. Moody had white in the corners of his mouth. Sister said it was a symptom of a soul sickness, but Willa insisted, privately, it was rabies.

"That's the sure sign. Foaming at the mouth! White flecks just like he's got. It's not his fault but it's dis-*gust*ing and it means he could go crazy just like that," she had said, snapping her fingers in Elliott's face. "I wouldn't take any more fireballs from him if I was you."

It didn't seem fair. Elliott sighed one of his deep sighs, trying to catch his breath and somehow force it down into the tightness of his chest, and then he picked up the lantern he had been given. He was tired and he wanted to go home, but he knew he couldn't. He had to lead Mr. Aimes and the others back to Buba. It made him feel important and scared the way he had been gotten out of bed after Clem had left. He pushed his glasses back up on his nose, wondering if he would get

another pair or if he would have to make do with the broken
ones. Two moths were fluttering at the glass panes of his
lantern and he tried to shoo them away with his hand. They
would die if he let them get to the flame. He'd seen them do
it a hundred times. It was part of the mystery that was making
him miserable. It seemed to him the only decent thing was
for God to make Mr. Moody get thinner. He had mentioned
it once or twice in his prayers, but every time he checked Mr.
Moody was just as fat or fatter. He had tried to talk about it
with Vienna during his piano lesson, which was the only time
Elliott could count on Vienna's complete attention. She had
said not to worry about God. "This is it, right here, right now.
The Chopin nocturne that you just played on the piano is
heaven and the fields and trees that heard it are heaven. It's
not a future tense you have to whisper about. It's the present
progressive."

When he had told Willa about a present heaven she was
standing on her bed in her nightgown trying to stick a picture
to the wall.

"You got it wrong, Elliott. What she meant was that you
got lots of presents in heaven. Everyone knows that." Willa
wouldn't say more because the picture of the Taj Mahal she
had ripped from a magazine wasn't staying up and it frustrated
her.

The next time he had talked with Willa about God was
worse. She had wanted a monkey for her birthday, and had
prayed regularly for three weeks before. She was very angry
when she got a pink dress with a scratchy stiff petticoat sewn
into the skirt to make it puff out. When Sister said it was fit
for a little princess, Willa said only sissies wore pink. After
that, she told Elliott she wasn't sure there was a God after all.
She wrote Him three letters to complain and never got an
answer.

"Did you stamp them?" Elliott asked solemnly.

"Of course I did! I used Vienna's airmail stamps."

Elliott had let it drop for a while, but then that very afternoon he had had a startling breakthrough which he had wanted to share with Willa, only she had been so horrid about the egg he wasn't sure he would ever tell her. But it was irresistible and overwhelming: he had discovered positive proof of God! The thought of it made him start coughing again.

Somewhere to his left he heard the whistling wings of a woodcock in flight, followed by a quick, pinging "*tok*" from his right, reminiscent of a northern raven. He looked over at the black mass of the woods, a shadow with density, and smiled at the profusion of fireflies. He had never seen so many. Thousands of lightning bugs sparked irregularly among the trees, casting a magical sheen on the hulking shape of the woods. Their sparkling reminded him of fairy tales, and calmed him. They were like miniature winks of stars, he thought, glancing up to compare. No, starlight was stronger, steadier, more jewellike, a pattern without movement, but shimmering before him was the kind of dazzle, the certain, sudden, unpredictable flashes that reminded him of the giddy joy of running down the cement sidewalks in Bantanburg with his eyes on the ground, trying to step on all the diamond mica the sun would discover for him as he ran.

He suddenly felt almost dizzy with happiness. It suffused his body and gathered with bursting pressure in his chest, knotted his throat, and made his knees weak. He heard a nighthawk and then, farther away, a Henslow's sparrow. They were waiting for him behind the magical scrim of fireflies, with Buba and God. Vienna had a theory about bees and now it turned out she was right. She had said they were wise, and, ever since, Elliott had listened to them, trying to understand their minute messages. That afternoon he and Buba had had an encounter with a bee, but Buba was not of the temperament to stay still and listen. Buba swiped at the bee when it buzzed too near his shirt and Elliott had been obliged to knock it to the ground with his notepad, warning Buba not to make a bee angry or he would have no choice but to kill it. He had squatted over the bee with the pad poised, ready to attack it again. The bee lay on its back between two blades of grass. Its legs rotated around each other while it buzzed and vibrated on the ground. Then the bee folded its legs in a prayer position and was still.

"Buba, look at this. It's dead now. You can look," Elliott urged, because Buba was still keeping a cautious distance. Elliott waved him over authoritatively. "C'mere," he said, and Buba joined him in a reluctant squat.

"See its little hands? It's praying, Buba. That means there *must* be a God if even bees pray when they die!" Buba didn't seem to appreciate the profound importance of this, but Elliott's excitement was undampened. After all, they had never discussed God before and Buba could be one of those heathens Miss Margayt was always going on about before choir practice. They were, he remembered, often "black heathens," so it was logical that Buba was not excited. Willa would be, though. She would whistle and clap her hands and dance and find a way for them to get famous.

ELLIOTT'S THOUGHTS WERE interrupted by the heavy plodding tread of Sister and Mr. Aimes. Vienna had chosen a different route, which she covered alone, insisting she could move faster that way and they could double the area of the search. The woods Elliott knew by heart in daylight were strangely transformed at night, and familiar landmarks distorted by shadow took on the appearance of menacing grotesques. In spite of his fear, there was something compelling about the dark faces his imagination superimposed on a twisted tree limb or tangle of climbing ivy, as arresting as the pictures of gargoyles he had found in one of Vienna's books.

They moved slowly through the brush, stumbling around impediments that materialized suddenly from the opaque gloom. Mr. Aimes muttered irritably about the miser-thin slice of moon, and Sister bemoaned with her usual frankness the ordeal she suffered dutifully, if not silently: the enshrouding mist of bugs and the hidden potential of every root to reveal itself to be a camouflaged snake, waiting for her next footfall to strike. At some point, Mr. Aimes put Elliott on his shoulders, and though Elliott was fatigued by the long tramp, he wasn't sure it was preferable to ride hunching under the overhang of certain boughs, his contortion expressing itself in cramps and aches he didn't dare mention, for fear of competing with Sister's monologue of distress.

They crossed paths twice with Vienna, and the second time Sister demanded that they rest a spell and reconsider the plan; it was after eleven and Sister's sense of commitment was as sorely frayed as her thick but sensitive ankles. In a small clearing the group gathered around the three lanterns and shared a thermos of hot chocolate and a handful of gingersnaps, the supplementary repast Vienna had stuffed into one of the pockets of her duster.

Elliott ignored the discouraged conversation of the adults to listen to the modulating *hoo* of a barred owl, sounding vaguely like unkind laughter, and nearer, the whining quaver of a screech owl. Then he heard the soft crescendo of an ovenbird and reflected sadly that the cry was one of Buba's favorites. He looked away from the direction of its call, distracted by a chuck-will's-widow and the nasal voice of a goatsucker. "Listen," he said, "there's a nighthawk somewhere over there," but his companions continued their discussion, paying no heed to the opportunities for birding the expedition offered.

A lull in the discussion followed the consumption of Vienna's meager provisions as the adults silently procrastinated resuming their task. Mr. Aimes alerted the crouching women to the nighthawk Elliott had already identified, causing him to scowl in the darkness, but the closer calls of a mockingbird and a whippoorwill gave Elliott a momentary chance to outshine Mr. Aimes, and while Sister was completing a banal thought on the plaintive song of the whippoorwill, Elliott suddenly stood up.

"What is it?" Vienna asked.

"A blue-winged warbler," Elliott answered, as he moved attentively in its direction.

"Please, Elliott," Sister admonished, "we don't have time for this, and stay within the circle of light or we'll lose you too." But Elliott had already stumbled noisily into foliage and was gone. Vienna sprang up and grabbed a lantern, following quickly behind the rustle and snap of Elliott's footsteps. The other two reluctantly clambered off in pursuit rather than be left behind.

Elliott stood breathless beneath a cluster of trees, alert as a bird dog, listening. It came again, the song of the ovenbird and then, in quick succession, the blue-winged warbler. Elliott tugged on Vienna's sleeve and whispered excitedly, "It's Buba, I know it for sure. Those birds don't call at night."

Vienna cupped a hand to her mouth and called, "Buba, Buba, where are you?" but only silence and the whippoorwill called back. "Is that him?" she asked Elliott.

"No, that's a bird. Buba can't do that one yet."

Vienna called again but there was no sound except from Sister, who thrashed up to them, muttering something to Mr. Aimes. Vienna's heart sank at this second defeat. She patted

Elliott's head and said gently, "Maybe you were mistaken; it's easy to get confused when hope and fear are competing for your attention."

Then Elliott gave a long series of whistles, warbling notes he had to insert his dirty fingers into his mouth to make. There was only silence and the random rustle of leaves. Elliott snapped his fingers a few times, biting his lip in thought and then he smiled; he tipped his head back and let out his best imitation of Murphy's victory howl followed by their code call: the harsh cluck of the iridescent grackle.

Overhead there was a creak and a flurry of leaves rained down with the wet word, "Ahwhot?"

"It's me and my mother and Mr. Aimes and Sister. C'mon down, we were worried sick about you." The leaves parted and Buba's face peered down into the lantern's rim of light.

"Come on, son, put your leg here," Mr. Aimes encouraged. "Don't use that ladder. It's liable to break or give you a nasty splinter. I should have taken down that old deerwatch years ago, I've certainly meant to a thousand times. Might look like a tree house, but it can't be trusted. That's right now, swing your other leg over."

When Mr. Aimes set Buba safely on the ground Vienna knelt down before him and clutched him in a tight embrace, saying, "It's all over now, you can relax, that's right, hush now, hush. Calm your worried heart," and Buba put his arms around her and blubbered into her shoulder. He had lost his bib and his shirtfront was damp. Vienna lifted him up carefully against her as Elliott reached out and stroked one of Buba's dangling legs. "Aw, it's O.K., Buba," he said. With Buba pressed against her, Vienna started for home, ignoring Mr. Aimes's offers to carry him. Sister put her hand down heavily on Elliott's head, using it like a walking stick to balance herself, complaining wearily about the "fuss and bother of it all," while

Vienna strode ahead, leaving Sister's voice to be muffled by the indifferent dark and the thick new growth against which she railed.

After Elliott was put to bed and Buba had been fed and bathed and inspected for cuts and bruises and tucked into the metal cot Vienna set up in Elliott's room, Vienna sent word of Buba's safety to Etta through Mr. Aimes, who was driving Hegemony home anyway, and said it didn't bother him to go a few doors down the lane to Etta's.

Dr. Barstow stopped by the next morning, ostensibly to listen to Elliott's chest, which seemed none the worse for his late-night heroics, and while Dr. Barstow was there, Vienna asked him to check Buba before she sent him home with Etta. Dr. Barstow spent half an hour secluded with Buba, only to emerge and pronounce him healthy, but host to infectious ringworm. He wrote a prescription for an ointment that would clear it up and left, with his familiar farewell to Sister and a quick nod to Etta, who waited on the porch to take Buba home.

Though Etta left with a purse full of dollar bills folded around the prescription and Vienna's most eloquent apologies, Buba never returned to The Heights. Sister was glad to be rid of any reminders of the messy business; Vienna took a detached philosophical view that at least now Buba would be cured of ringworm and Elliott had taught him the alphabet, so the ordeal had been improving in a concrete and abstract sense, and that was something. Willa was grateful that the immediacy of Buba's plight had delayed her punishment long enough for it to have been reduced by general weariness to a long lecture from Sister, and that in Buba's absence Elliott had been more willing to accept an apology and resume their routine games.

Only Elliott mourned the loss of his assistant and first friend from outside the sanctuary of The Heights; for him, Saturdays were now lonely days, as bereft of shape and as cutting as the wind sharpening itself at his window, whistling with wild abandon like Buba's ambitious but failed attempts to imitate a bird Elliott had named for him.

18

ADDISON AIMES ASKED questions and kept his ears open, and within his first month in Winsville he had collected enough Daniels trivia that if his tidbits had been stamps or baseball cards or Cracker Jack prizes he would have been a major contender in the schoolyard competitions.

Certain grown-ups, he had discovered, could be counted on to deliver considerably more than expected, like a broken gumball machine—a single question would reap an effusive spill of unsolicited additional information. It didn't matter to him that there were jarring contradictions, variations, superstitions, and obvious inventions all jumbled together. It only made the task of interpreting the tales more challenging, and Addison enjoyed teasing and twisting the truth out of the accumulated lore. He finally understood the pleasure his mother and uncles had taken from their Bible studies, once described to him by his mother as an effort akin to wringing from a wet mop the one drop of pure, clean water.

Everyone, it seemed, had private reasons for the shaping and shadings that differentiated their version, and Addison came to learn as much about the tellers of the tale as about the tale's subject just by noticing where the emphasis was placed, which details were altered, or even when the narrator chose to smile. Addison inferred, for example, that Hegemony felt competitive with Fayette from the vigor with which she discounted her rival's household. Hegemony had tried to scare him off his fascination with the neighbor children by recounting the incident with Buba: "Jus' a few weeks before you come here, and what a tizzy it turned into, a light-minded colored boy, dudn't have enough tongue in his mouth to rightly tell what happen, traipsin' alone in the woods at night waitin' to be et by some nasty varmint or other, on account of those kids, up to a dangersome prank as best as we cud figger. Boy's family dudn't want Mrs. Daniels meddlin' or agitatin' up no trouble more than they already had with a lost little boy not right in the head and the town in spasmotics over Dee's makin' good in Philadelphia and bringin' it on home so as his kin wasn't possum-poor no longer, no sir, goed from whitewash to paint, and broke-down putterin' to head-high proud but that woman has gracious plenty contrary in her when it comes to doin' what she thinks she ought no matter what or who says otherwise. She won't do the least thing on someone else's say so. You count your mercies those chillun don't take a shine to you like they done to Buba, or you might could end with something unfittin' befallin' you and the very least, a case of the mulligrubs spang in the center of your young heart. No sir, you stay clear of them Daniels and their bookish razzmatazz."

Addison promised heartily that he would, knowing full well that he wouldn't, but Hegemony was pleased by his compliance and gave him an extra helping of blueberry cake. He ate well and went to bed early, having already planned his next move. In the morning, after a big bowl of oatmeal and a laconic exchange with his father, in which the interrogative "Hungry?" had been met with "Very," he set out for Long

Lane, the unpaved washboard road that ran by the entrance to The Heights and connected Winsville with the highway. He had intended to stake out The Heights in the manner of a penny-dreadful detective, but he didn't have long to wait. No sooner did he settle himself comfortably in a shallow ditch by the side of the road when he heard his name being called. Swiveling his head like an owl, he scanned the empty road.

"Addison Aimes," he heard again. "That is who you are, isn't it? I've been expecting we'd meet sooner or later."

Addison stood up warily, and still not seeing the voice that addressed him, felt somewhat foolish as he answered, "That'd be me, all right," and then, putting his hand to his forehead to shield the sun, he gazed out at the field that ran parallel to the crumbling stone wall, looking for his interlocutor.

"Up here." The voice laughed, and, craning his neck, Addison saw a booted leg and a swirl of gray fabric. "Just one minute and I'll be done," she said, adding, "better stand back from the tree now, a branch is coming down."

There was a commotion in the leaves and a sound like birds being flushed from a thicket as the cracked branch fell to the ground, followed by a pair of clippers, two paring knives, a short-handled trowel, and a small handsaw.

The metal tools glinted in the grass, catching the sun, and from behind the tree Vienna Daniels emerged, smiling, holding in one hand the narrowest ladder Addison had ever seen, and extending the other for a handshake. Addison helped Mrs. Daniels gather her tools and carried her canvas satchel back to the barn for her as she chatted amiably, asking him about his impressions of the town and offering her sympathies for the circumstances which brought him there.

When the last implement had been hung in its place on the pegboard, Mrs. Daniels picked through a heap of discarded gardening utensils rusting in an old footlocker until at last she extracted a pocketknife with a dark cherrywood handle. "Would this be of any use to you?" she asked casually, holding out the knife for his inspection.

"You betcha," Addison answered, grabbing the folded knife from her hand in a quick greedy snap he realized with a little shame was the same way his dog had lunged for treats of hard cheese. "I didn't intend to be rude, ma'am, it's just so beautiful is why I couldn't help myself," he tried awkwardly to explain. Vienna watched his large ears turn carmine and the flush in his cheeks obscure the liberal shake of freckles that, it occurred to her, spanned across his wide face like a map of the Andaman Islands.

She shook her head. "Don't give it another thought; it's waited there a long time for someone to care enough to clean it."

Vienna was almost beyond the horse pasture when Addison shouted, "Ma'am?" She stopped and waited for him to catch up to her. "I was wondering, what's that music I hear?" he asked, standing a few feet away from her, his voice modulating with unexpected urgency.

Vienna smiled again at him and looked back toward the house.

"It depends on what time of day you hear it. In the morning, Fayette likes to work to the Jelly Roll Morton record her husband, Grant, gave her. In the afternoon, I sometimes listen to Puccini or Mozart operas. And evenings, Elliott practices the piano. Right now he's working on Chopin and Scarlatti."

Addison looked blank. "I'm not talking about New Orleans jazz or ragtime tunes, and I know there's no voices to the music I'm thinking of." Vienna put her hand on his shoulder tenderly. "I don't know for certain what music it is that you heard, but if you like, you come around one afternoon and we'll go through the possibilities until you recognize it."

"Thank you, I'll do that, I will," Addison said eagerly, clutching the pocketknife to his chest and as she walked up the rise to the house, he shouted, "and thanks again for the pocketblade. I'll smarten it up good." Vienna waved at him and then vanished inside the house.

That she had divined his most pressing desire and accommodated it was pure proof that she was indeed a witch, and that she had invited him into the house could only signify dangers he would be no better able to resist than the folded knife he fingered in his pocket.

On his way home to work on the dearly coveted knife, which would need to be honed and polished, Addison kept his eyes sharp for a chance sighting of Willa or Elliott. He was mulling over a significant piece of new information he had about the Daniels, wondering why so important a fact had been omitted: Mrs. Daniels was beautiful—not in the pretty dimpled way of Miss Jeannie Duffield, whose daddy owned the bakery and who sometimes helped out behind the counter, but striking nonetheless, and more aristocratic-looking, like a film star or a person in a painting, the kind of beautiful you usually didn't see up close, maybe just glimpsed through the window of a passing fancy car or in a magazine advertising something French.

His own mother's charms had not been visual ones, and she had cautioned him earnestly and often not to be taken in by the Devil's mirror, by which she meant anyone less fortunate than herself in deflecting the satanic devices that imparted attraction. She looked vaguely like the less-flattering portraits of Queen Elizabeth Addison had seen by flipping ahead in his history text during a boring discussion of the Battle of Hastings and the Domesday Book; like the queen, his mother had kinky red hair and her skin was badly pitted—from childhood smallpox, she claimed, but her sister Gilly confirmed in confidence that it was the result of adolescent acne. The sheen on her nose and cheeks indicated oily skin, so Addison had accepted his aunt's diagnosis, but out of loyalty to his mother he had tried to look on beauty as a taint in Christian rectitude. It wasn't one of his most successful efforts, but her words worked their way back into his thoughts to add perversely to the delight and danger of his recent encounter.

Now that he had the knife, he could cut down the remaining string traps he had set in the woods that marked the end of his father's land. Addison wondered if Mrs. Daniels had known about the traps and whether the gift had been intended as a foil to his plans for poaching. He began to indulge the notion that she did know—that her powers extended to encompass a kind of godlike surveillance, but on a local level.

He found it oddly comforting to think of her watching him. It made him feel less lonely, for one thing, and it incorporated the Daniels into his life in way that was no longer unrequited: his attentive fascination was being reciprocated by constant observation. She was actually squandering some of her mythic powers on him, which elevated his sense of self-esteem. Mr. Aimes was hunched over a bowl of summer soup when his son entered the house, and he raised his eyes for only a second to see Addison take the seat at the end of the table, but that glance was enough for him to notice the confident set of his son's shoulders and the new thrust to his chin.

"What have you been about? You're looking mighty pleased with yourself this morning. D'ya find a pot of gold in the fields there, son?" Mr. Aimes chortled over his soup.

Addison knew better than to mention the knife because he couldn't trust his father not to take it away from him in exchange for some homespun wisdom for which he would be expected to feel grateful.

"I met Mrs. Daniels," Addison said, withholding his excitement, though it filled him near to bursting and left little room for the midday meal.

"Where was that?" his father questioned, attentive now.

"Out by Long Lane."

"I don't want you bothering her none. She has better things to do than babysit my boy," Mr. Aimes said.

"It wasn't like that. She invited me over to listen to the gramophone," Addison said defensively, his throat constricting around his Adam's apple as if his body was already acknowledging guilt. Mr. Aimes's eyebrows shot up, becoming romanesque arches above the dark hollows of his eyes. In over a decade as her nearest neighbor, he had never once been invited in on a social call for no reason but to pass the time. He was disturbed by this news because it made him jealous, and being jealous of the gangly boy who sat before him was something unworthy of the way Mr. Aimes liked to think of himself. So he nodded and resumed his soup-sucking.

After that, Addison noticed that his stock was going up in his father's eyes in subtle ways. He could have credited this to the accretion of goodwill incumbent on those who spend large amounts of time together in small quarters, or the emerging bond of blood strengthening as the two grew more accustomed to each other, but he didn't. He accorded his inflating worth solely to Vienna and her magic.

She had been the reason he had been begrudgingly accepted by Bobby Maddox's gang, which included a handful of Overby boys, types Addison normally would have avoided until pressed into the obligatory fistfight. But when they called to him jeeringly from in front of the Coca-Cola freezer at the filling station, saying "Hey, Kentucky, what do you know?" he had stunned them with his reply.

"I know why Vienna Daniels wears gray, and you don't." It had been a piece of the riddle he had worked on since his meeting with her and he was feeling pretty proud of the Sherlock Holmesian deduction he'd used to arrive at his elegantly simple solution.

"Oh yeah? Well then let's hear it, Kentucky."

Addison knew enough about fishing to know he had something important tugging at the line and he took his time reeling it in.

"My name is Addison, and I don't know as I'm obliged to tell what I know," Addison said, as he swaggered over to the soda machine.

"Aw, you can tell us just that one thing—how come she wears gray," Froggy Overby said impatiently.

Addison took a long pull on the bottle of cola he had shaken before jacking up the metal crown and the pale fizz filled his throat and rushed into his nose, stinging in one of those confusing kinds of pain that borders on pleasure. He wiped his mouth on his sleeve and said, "Maybe."

"He don't know a damn thing about it. He's only been here a month. I don't put any store in his bragging," Bobby Maddox said before he spat authoritatively on the subject.

"Maybe he don't and maybe he do," Biddy Markham's pint-size nephew put in, unwilling to let the possibility go so easily.

"You're free to think what you like, if it dudn't strain your head too much. Don't get a headache on my account," Addison said as he started to walk off; he was afraid he might have pushed a little too hard and was eager to put more distance between himself and the motley pack which could leave off loitering and thrash him if he wasn't careful.

They started following him down the road and he finished the soda in fast gulps that were liable to upset his stomach, but he wanted the bottle empty in case things got ugly. In Alford, two boys had ambushed him on his way to church and cracked his front tooth before the upscuddle was interrupted by his uncle. He didn't want it to happen again, because he knew that by the Darwinian laws that governed the schoolyard, once a victim, always a victim.

"Hey you, Addison," Bobby Maddox called out, "wait up."

Addison stopped and perched on the split-rail fence that ran beside the road. He smiled to himself because he knew from their using his name he was safe, and now he was sorry he had rushed his refreshment. "No need to light off like that," Bobby said, chugging up to him at the head of the group. "Maybe we can swap you for it. Wanta know where Gilliam Deet keeps his still?" Addison shook his head no.

One of the smaller Overbys shouted from behind his brother, "How about taking a slingshot and a squirrel's tail for it?" but Addison shook his head again, and taking out the pocketknife he had momentarily forgotten, he rotated the newly honed blade in the sunlight and said, "I guess I don't need your slingshot. I can get my own squirrel if I want, and skin it with this old thing."

"Lemme see that," one of the boys said admiringly, and the pocketknife was duly passed through the descending hierarchy of dirty hands. "Say what you want, then," Bobby pressed.

"First you tell me your names, since you already know mine and it wouldn't be right to spill my secrets to people I'm not acquainted with." Addison was stalling. He wanted to make them wait as long as possible, not only so that they would value the revelation more for it having been harder to earn, but because he wanted to cement the developing camaraderie to the point where it would be firm enough to rely on when school started. Bobby Maddox allowed Addison was right to want to know who he was jawing with and made the introductions, providing a cursory biographical sketch for every name.

It was in this way that Addison learned Froggy Overby had survived snakebite and could skip a stone more times than he could count. His older brother, Joe, knew how to steal wild honey and could imitate any number of barnyard animals, and Stan Lee, the eldest, called Lee for short, was the one their daddy beat on. Little Jack Markham hadn't grown in two years but was stronger than he looked, and fast-fisted too, and Wilbur Washaw, the tallest boy and maybe the slowest in the bunch, only had fifteen teeth in his head, a fact immediately verified by a wide grin. The littlest fellow was Jackson, who didn't have a last name because his mother was a whore, but he could read and write and had his own .22 rifle, and if you cared to flip a can in the air he'd plug it with a hole before it landed.

"O.K.," Addison said gravely, "there are two conditions: first, this secret I am about to share with you goes no farther than the ears here now. And second, you all owe me for this, each one of you on his own and once as a group and I can call in my dues at any time during the next year. Is that agreed?"

The boys nodded soberly and spat through their index and middle finger to seal the deal. Then, closing around Addison, they waited in an expectant hush. "The reason Mrs. Daniels wears gray—" he began, reveling in the attention his audience was giving his oration. It was a drop-jawed concentration he had never seen his mother and uncle attain in their years of preaching from a wagon, and it revealed to Addison the dominion subject had over style, forcing him to conclude that salvation was less compelling than curiosity. After a dramatic pause he continued—"is because Mrs. Daniels is a Confederate."

"How'd you mean?" Froggy hollered. He didn't seem capable of controlling the decibels at which his voice erupted.

"Shut up," Wilbur snapped at Froggy. "We'll never hear anything if you're going to interrupt with such stone-stupid questions." Wilbur's family on his father's side came from

Georgia, and his grandfather had been a captain in the War of Northern Aggression, he told Addison, politely asking him to go on.

"Well, Mrs. Daniels is a Northerner, everyone knows that, and West Virginia went with the North, but what you saps don't know, 'cause you never studied hard on a map, is there's a town called Vienna not too terrifically far from here in Virginia and it's no coincidence neither. Her way of doing things to the botheration of this town is more proof that she is waging her own war, not between the States, but *within* them, right here, in protest because she is a Confederate, and that is why she wears rebel gray. Simple as that."

As he said it out loud it sounded more tenuous than when he was mulling it over in his head, but any doubts he harbored vanished when Bobby Maddox whistled and Joe Overby exclaimed a long wheezy "Jeez." Their admiration for Addison was unbounded: they clapped him on the back and gave him Indian handshakes and Jackson tossed one stone in the air and hit it with another just to expel his nervous excitement.

"You're sworn to silence on this," Addison reminded them, because they were already working up scenarios to express their approval to Mrs. Daniels, who had, in the turn of a sentence, became a folk hero and symbol of the spunk that was conspicuously lacking in their more downtrodden parents. They still considered Mrs. Daniels crazy, but her madness had now been framed by a cause they could understand and respect, not because they knew enough about the underpinnings or implications of the war to have weighed its political, ethical, or economic aspects, but because it exerted a force in their parents' lives. Invisible as an undertow influencing the shape of the crags on a shoreline, it represented their kin's last or only glory, no matter how brief or bloody, and the grand tragedy they returned to to add meaning to the poignancy of their meager lot and a lingering trace of dignity to the demeaning drop in crop prices and demoralizing erosion of land value. In fact, the degree to which Mrs. Daniels got under the skin of the town now seemed a call to solidarity rather than a source of amusement or contempt.

"We're not gonna tell anyone, we just want to let Miss Vienna know that we know," Lee said.

"How can we do that?" Little Jake Markham asked. "It's too risky to go up to her. Who knows what she's liable to do?"

Bobby Maddox and Joe Overby lifted their heads from a sibilant exchange of whispers. "If Addison takes to the notion, we thought we could leave her a message in one of the trees."

Froggy shouted an objection. "A note's liable to blow away afor she ever finds it." But Joe hushed his younger brother sharply and explained that they would carve their message in the tree.

"I don't want to do that," Jackson whined. "She's funny about those trees and now that I like her some I don't want to cross her anymore."

"That's just it," Bobby said smoothly, "this would be the last time."

"Cain't be," Wilbur piped up, "my sister don't yet have her initials in a tree and she'll be plain livid if I tell her no."

At that there was a unanimous response of prepubescent male outrage.

"Hell, if you're gonna let your sister boss you about you can resign right now," Bobby Maddox said. The Overby boys chanted, "Tell her no, tell her no," until Wilbur agreed, somewhat uncomfortably, to the new code of behavior. There remained the question of what the message should be, who would be entrusted to deliver it, and which tree was the best candidate for the job. Argument ensued and a scuffle between Froggy and Jackson required all of the others to separate them.

Finally the project sorted itself out. They decided against the old maple in front of the post office and the chestnut behind the Baptist church because they were already too marked up. Moreover, they wanted a tree that only she would have access to, so the message would be private, but, as Bobby pointed out, that would mean going onto her land, and then there was too wide a choice. How could they be sure she ever saw it?

Addison spoke up. "There's a tree she'll see for sure. My father says it's the only one of its kind in these parts. And she fusses with it. I could take you there. If we go at night it's not likely we'd be seen. It's a good piece aways from the house and not too far from my father's place."

"Do you want to carve it?" Lee Overby asked deferentially, but his voice betrayed his concern.

"Nope. It wuddn't my idea, so the privilege should go to someone else," Addison demurred, with a Solomon-like air of fairness. Actually, it was an easy offering; he had never much enjoyed the sport and he didn't relish dulling the blade or breaking the tip of his newly restored knife.

More clamoring followed until Bobby assigned Lee Overby to the task. "The way I figger it, Overbys have always been first and last to leave their mark, and since this is the last, we should let the oldest Overby have the honor." Once this was settled, the message was easy and obvious and the group began to disperse in a buoyant mood, chucking stones at roadside crows, spitting, with Jackson going so far as to write the message in the dust of the road with his pee "just to see how it would look." Addison got a satisfying laugh from his comment, "I sure hope it will be easier to read than that!" and after arranging to regroup after dinner, meeting behind Mr. Aimes's spring-house at nine and demonstrating for Addison the two-fingered whistle by which they would identify themselves in the dark (nearly identical, Addison noted with disappointment, to the call his cousins had used for the same purpose), they parted.

Addison had no way of knowing the bafflement with which Vienna would regard the crudely shaped, jagged motto that appeared with the suddenness of a stigmata and the wonderment of an annunciation, going straight to the heart of her secret with the directness of the painted words forming a golden shaft in a Fra Angelico painting, equally mysterious and divined: GraY 4 eveR, shining in the exposed yellow wood of the weeping beech.

She stood in the chill damp of mist rising from the ground like the manufactured magic of dry ice, remembering the painting that had moved her father to extend their stay in Italy. With the eidetic power of an image burned into the retina, she saw Mary's answer to the angel written from right to left across the panel: "Be it unto me according to Thy word." Picking up the handles of her canvas satchel, Vienna walked back to the house, her head bowed in bewildered reflection.

19

$\mathcal{T}$HE WEEKS PASSED rapidly with the competing distractions of Bobby Maddox's gang and Addison's diligent monitoring of the Daniels family movements. He had become familiar with Fayette's morning routines, knew when she would step out onto the porch and lean on her broom briefly, then shake her head and go back inside, as if disappointed by the unvarying view.

Addison befriended Murphy, and found that a small comestible bribe went a long way toward securing his silence, but generally his guttural warnings were disregarded by Elliott anyway, probably because, like a faulty alarm bell that the slightest vibration sets off, Murphy could be triggered by the sight of a squirrel or groundhog, both of which were abundant. He knew that Mackie was stealing half the wood he cut, and doing a cursory job of tending the one horse the Daniels kept—its coat was often thick with dust, its mane matted with burdock and its hoofs clotted with dried mud. Addison had added to the chores he did for his father a few he voluntarily undertook for the Daniels, barn work mostly, which kept him out of sight but close at hand.

He found the graveyard, the almost inevitable end for most

of the gaping baby birds Elliott rescued; it consisted of a small plot of land enclosed by stones alternately painted blue and green. Inside the plot, seven crosses made of ice-cream sticks had been planted to mark the remains of the birds buried below in biscuit tins.

Addison had already called in two of the debts owed him for his disclosure. Froggy had relinquished to him the tortoiseshell hairpin he found near the base of the weeping beech the night they left their message. From Joe Overby, Addison had taken a downy nestling Joe would otherwise have used to train his bird dog. The nestling had been left carefully positioned in the barn so that it would stay safe and warm until Elliott found it the next morning. From Little Jack Markham, Addison had a month's loan of a pair of field glasses that were Jack's father's, whose permission had not been solicited in the discharge of the debt.

Addison had used the borrowed binoculars to watch from an outcropping in the field while Elliott discovered the nestling. Elliott's pale hair and delicate frame were slightly unnerving to Addison; he worried that the least bump or fall might cause Elliott to snap like a quail bone and somehow the blanched color of his hair contributed to the appearance of frailty, as if it didn't even have the yellow strength of straw. But Elliott's behavior betrayed no indication of infirmity. He sashayed briskly across the stubble of the hayed field slapping his thigh, absorbed in a solitary game, shouting out commands to an invisible cavalry as he loped ahead. A minute or two later he craned his neck out of the wide barn door and yelled, "Willa!"

Addison swept the binoculars over the field and back to the house, but couldn't find Willa anywhere. When Elliott emerged from the barn, Addison refocused the field glasses on him and began to edge closer, snaking through the tall grass on his belly.

"Willa, over here. I've got something to show you," Elliott shouted. Willa came into view, descending from the roof of the barn by way of the copper drainpipe.

"Let's see," she said, flicking a tangle of hair out of her eyes. Elliott ducked back into the barn and brought out the tiny catbird, cupped in his hands.

"Oh Elliott, you know you're not supposed to get your smell on them; that's why they die, I reckon," Willa said, taking the bird from Elliott and cradling it against her chest.

"It's a squirmy one; you can have it back," she said a moment later.

"That means it's healthy. I can tell this one will make it. You'll see," Elliott said confidently.

"Miss Margayt says you're just supposed to leave them for the mother to find."

"What if she can't find it?"

"Of course she can. She can smell it, silly."

"But what if she can't? What if she's funny—like Vienna?"

Willa looked thoughtfully at Elliott. One leg of his knickers rode up above the knob of his knee and his face had the swollen look it got before he cried.

"Vienna can smell us better than anyone, you know that," Willa said, lacing her hands behind her head. "Sister says it's because we don't bathe enough."

At this Elliott laughed, and Addison laughed too. The children looked around suddenly, but, seeing nothing, returned to their discussion.

"Anyhow, most of the time you don't want Vienna to find us, which she could in a jiff, if she set her mind to it, or else she'd find out about your keeping Murphy."

"You're right," Elliott admitted, pushing his glasses up with his upper arm because he needed both hands to hold the chick. Then he held it up to within an inch or two of his eyes.

"What are you doing?" Willa asked, bending over like a hairpin and looking up at him through her ankles.

"Just looking."

Willa straightened up and flung back her hair, which remained momentarily puffed like a lion's mane. "It's got human smell on it now so the mother won't take it back," she said.

"I don't care," Elliott said, "I'll look after it."

"Yeah?" Willa said, folding her arms behind her back, making her shoulder blades protrude like wings from beneath the faded straps of her bib overalls. "How are you gonna teach it to fly, huh?"

Elliott squinted in thought for a moment and bit his lip.

"He'll have to learn that part from another bird, I guess," and then he added, turning to the barn to find a nest for the chick, "Daddy knew how to fly. He could have showed him."

Willa whirled around and snapped, "Don't talk about Daddy, you hear?" but Elliott continued to walk toward the barn, and without turning his head replied sulkily, "I'll talk about who I want and I dare you to stop me."

Willa turned and skipped a few yards away from the barn and then broke into a full run down toward the woods, faster than Addison had ever seen anyone move barefoot before.

Addison set down the field glasses and took a soiled piece of paper and a pencil out of his pocket. After flattening the paper out on his thigh, he sharpened the pencil with his knife and then put down the word *father* followed by a large question mark. He had already heard enough to put Willa's remark in context, but realized now that he had been careless about following up on certain of the leads he had been given, and besides, making notes made him feel like a detective.

THE LAST DAYS of August were cruel: the heat seemed to have its own density, muting sounds, absorbing them into its blinding brightness, blurring the edges of things in wavering shimmery warps, in the drone and drowsiness of saturating summer sun.

The paved roads swam in the distance through witch-water mirages rising from the melting tar. Encouraged by the compliments he had received from Vienna on his boy's manners, Mr. Aimes chose this time, when Addison would have rather reclined beneath a tree by the creek with one of the books Vienna had lent him, to tout the boy to the neighboring towns, where he had some chores to do.

Addison had longed for his father to claim him, to appreciate his company and include him in his day, especially on the trips to Bantanburg, but now that it had come, it came inopportunely, just when Addison was feeling the mounting dread of another year and a new school and the indolent sweetness of vacation days slipping away. He forgot the boredom that had wearied him when he first arrived and had nothing but time to fill. And now, in this heat, even the pranks of Bobby Maddox and the Overbys had been temporarily retired in favor of listlessness and shade. Houses were shuttered against the afternoon light and recumbent women filled darkened rooms all over Winsville, pressing handkerchiefs doused with rosewater or orange-blossom tonic to their temples, trying not to glow.

It was hard for Addison to summon the enthusiasm his father expected in return for the opportunity to squander a precious afternoon being shuffled through stores, his father's rough hand cupping the nape of his neck, greeting merchants, who sized him up like a prize cow at the state fair, and nodding knowingly to his father. They all asked him the same two or three requisite questions: "So, how do you like it here?" and "Getting mighty big, aren't you?" and "What about this weather?" after which Addison had to wait, awkwardly expendable, through the long conversations his father would have about fertilizers and tractor parts.

On the ride home, sitting next to his father on the bench

seat of the old hay cart his father drove on these expeditions to save wear on the automobile he'd bought new but only used for church or special occasions, like his black suit and wingtip shoes, Addison let the creak of the wood and the rhythmic clop of the Morgan lull him into a sleepy daze.

The cart stopped suddenly and Addison's eyes winked open. A woman built like his Aunt Gilly was cutting the tiger lilies that grew wild by the road. Dangling from the crook of one arm was a basket heavy with Queen Anne's lace and hellebore scavenged from the tangle of weeds that encroached on the asphalt; she waved a pair of clippers at them.

"Can we give you a ride?" Mr. Aimes asked Sister.

"No, sir, I have my eye on some blue chicory back in there," Sister answered, gesturing again with the clippers.

"This is my son, Addison."

Prompted by hearing his name on his father's lips, he responded by rote, "How do you do, ma'am."

Sister nodded, "Sister Daniels, pleased to meet you. How old are you, boy?"

"Eleven."

"Well, that's good," Sister said curtly, as if she had run out of pleasantries and wished to continue her clipping unimpeded by the distraction of observation.

"We'll be seeing you," Mr. Aimes said, and the Morgan's head jolted up at the touch of the reins, and the cart wobbled on, leaving Sister bent over the flowers, her large behind all that could be seen from the corner of Addison's eye as he looked back.

"That can't be Mrs. Daniels' sister," Addison said, hoping for confirmation.

"Sister-in-law."

"Thank God."

"For what?" Mr. Aimes asked, staring bleakly at the road

ahead as if it were the bathetic metaphor for his life, as in the weepy ballads his father used to pick out on a banjo at the end of harvest.

"Miss Vienna is too beautimous to have a sister looks like that."

Mr. Aimes turned to look at his son. Then he did a strange thing. He reached out his arm and set it on the boy's shoulder, and it was as spontaneous and comfortable as the smile that settled on his thin cracked lips.

20

―■―

$\mathcal{T}$HE LAST OF the morning's dew glinted on the scorched grass and Sister's footsteps out to the woodshed were still visible as creases in the sway of neglected lawn.

"Did the grass crackle?" Elliott asked Sister, as she unloaded the wood by the kitchen hearth. Sister stood in front of the fire, brushing the splinters of wood from her plain, shapeless clothes.

"I didn't notice," she said.

"How come? I would have. That's the only good part of a hot spell, the crunch when you walk, because the grass is dry."

"Elliott, how you go on," Sister said. She was not talkative in the morning and she moved around the large kitchen in a businesslike manner. Elliott sat at one end of the kitchen table, resting his head on the thin arm that lay stretched out before him, eyes fixed on an ant struggling with an oversized crumb. He stared until his eyes began to water, but would not turn to get the glasses which were neatly folded to the other side of his arm.

"Don't tire your eyes, Elliott," Sister said, without turning around to look at him. She was at the stove, rapidly peeling apples into a stewing pot. Elliott said nothing.

"Do you hear me?"

"I hear you. Nothing's wrong with my ears yet." Elliott closed his eyes, tucking his face into the crook of his arm where he could smell in the warmth of his skin the scent of the horse that had licked him there the night before, when he brought carrots to the barn. Though he wouldn't admit it, his eyes did feel strained. Sister turned to look at him without replying.

She was afraid he was going blind. He was only eight and a half. He should see a specialist, she thought, but Vienna wouldn't let him. Vienna was afraid of doctors, except Dr. Barstow, whom she disliked but trusted above all other men in Winsville, though not enough to heed. Vienna wandered into the kitchen, wearing the same nightgown she had worn for three days. She was humming a waltz, but stopped to listen to the exchange between her son and sister-in-law.

Vienna picked up Elliott's glasses and held them in her hand as if they were both fragile and repulsive, like the larger variety of insect that sometimes chose her hearth on which to leave the husk of a discarded, desiccated body. Then she put them back on the table and spoke to Elliott, though her gaze was fixed with unblinking purpose on Sister.

"You'll outgrow it," Vienna said, "my family has always had good eyes and clear skin," as if that resolved the problem in a way that doctors simply couldn't. She turned and looked at Elliott, so frail in the morning light; sometimes he seemed to her translucent, like the petals of certain flowers, like irises when they have dried. Not like Willa, her firstborn, with the firm flexible flesh of gardenias or apple blossoms, strength that is rooted in the earth, that flowers in trees and cannot be crushed by carelessness or neglect.

When Willa slammed into the kitchen, all angles and attitude, her clothing hanging on her like an argument, her mother looked at her with astonishment, as if, like Linnaeus, Vienna had discovered by accident the difference between two related species that renders them categorically distinct. Finishing the last spoonfuls of oatmeal Elliott had abandoned, Vienna mused on whether her diet or disposition had produced in her children examples of Nietzsche's dialectic between Apollonian and Dionysian character.

Willa, last to gather in the kitchen, sat backward in a chair, leaning her head into the space dividing her from her mother so that Vienna could comb out her rusty hair. Vienna understood that this was an offering, a gesture of capitulation proffered in a way that would not jeopardize Willa's pride. Therefore it was with love that she gathered the mess in her arms, a weedy bouquet of snarls, while her eyes scanned the shelves for a hairbrush among the toys, the books and boxes of dried goods, the loose odds and ends of clutter that had been tossed on the open shelving in a halfhearted semblance of order.

Sister looked over at Willa. "Looks like barn swallows have been nesting in your hair. If you can't take better care than that I'm going to have to cut it."

"No you ain't," Willa snapped back at her aunt, jerking her hair out of her mother's hands, the moment of pliant submission retracted.

"Don't you start up and don't say *ain't* as if you didn't know better, as if you were one of the Overby children or worse," Sister commanded imperiously. Vienna had found the hairbrush, full of Ulyssa's long black strands that she scraped away from her with a comb.

Sister's irritation now expanded to encompass the other two: she scolded Elliott for using a hairbrush on the horse. He knew where the currycombs were, after all, and besides, it was Mackie's job to groom that horse which was nothing but money out the window and should be sold off to the factory where it could be useful to someone for God knows it had no use here but to add to the filth Elliott wore into the house. And then, folding her arms across her heavy bosom, she leaned back against the stove and watched the first few strokes Vienna applied to Willa's hair before shaking her head and saying, "I wish you wouldn't do that in the kitchen, it's unsanitary."

"No it ain't," Willa shot back, testing.

"Hush now," Vienna said.

Keeping her eyes on Sister, Willa continued to intone softly "ain't, ain't, ain't," like a challenge, but with the gentleness of a lullaby, while Vienna set to work with the bristle brush. When the brush snagged, Willa stamped her foot, and Vienna said "hush" again.

Aunt Augusta's visits were, for Vienna, something to be endured, like a drought or an illness, something from which she retreated involuntarily, feeling herself contract like an eye exposed suddenly to a harsh light that penetrated her depths, scanned her days with the sterile criticism of a scalpel and left in its wake a numbing emptiness.

The kitchen filled with the sweet spices of Sister's cooking, ink-black jams and pastel jellies she would line their shelves with for the coming winter. Elliott put his glasses on and shifted the position of his head to follow the progress of the ant, whose herculean task seemed to Elliott filled with whatever epic nobility was possible for an ant. Perhaps that crumb, three times the poor fellow's size, would feed his family, or entire community, for a week. And how long was a week to an ant? Maybe like a year to a human, he mused.

"There. That's the last of them," Sister said, covering the pot with a lid. "Mmmm, cinnamon," Elliott commented, wiping his nose with his arm and looking up at Sister, his large eyes made larger now by his glasses. Sister extended a

wooden spoon, sticky with brown sugar and cinnamon, in
Elliott's direction. He steadied the handle of the spoon with
one hand and began to lick it.

"What about me?" Willa asked.

"When you've cleaned up and look like a lady."

"Forget it. I won't want it *then* cause it's never going to
happen if I can help it." Willa sulked, pulling herself up and
scuffing out of the kitchen.

"Now, why did you do that?" Vienna asked Sister, a thin,
querulous edge in her voice.

Sister moved toward the table and leaned over it. "Hand
me the paper, will you, Elliott?" she asked, ignoring Vienna,
as she wiped the ant and the crumb into the grain of the
wooden table with one sweep of her large capable hand. Taking
the paper, she sat down heavily. She pushed her hair back
and let out a wheezy sigh. She was not a woman to bother
about grace; she did not own a pair of pumps and scoffed at
the finery that filled storefront displays. Like the lawn, her
lassitude had grown wild, overtaking areas of her life that had
previously been cultivated by ambition or duty. But as always
she had her justifications, and held her plainness up as a proof
of substance.

Willa scuffed back into the kitchen from the pantry, holding
a jam jar to her chest and eating from it with a spoon, one
shoe on and the other stuffed under her armpit, once again
happy and defiant. Her hip bumped the edge of the table as
she passed, rattling the glasses and plates and setting a tiger's-
eye marble off in a precarious trajectory of vibrations.

"Mind the dishes, please. Hardly anything matches here as
it is," Sister snapped, reaching her hand out to steady a water
glass. Vienna followed Willa around the kitchen, trying to
brush her hair as her daughter assembled from all corners of
the room her daily necessities, a penny elongated by the wheels
of a train into a flat talisman of good luck, rubber bands she

wore as bracelets and the round stone she liked to keep in her overall pocket, though Sister said it made the fabric sag.

Sister glanced over at them and made a disparaging noise by sucking her lips together, then fluffed out her paper like a linen sheet she was about to fold and looked over at Elliott. Elliott had put his nose to within an inch of the table, looking for the ant.

"What is it, hon?" she asked, folding the paper and putting it down. "Tell me what you're looking for."

"Nothing."

For a moment the kitchen filled with the lulling sounds of boiling water, hissings and snappings from the hearth, and the rhythmic sigh of the brush repeating its long syllables over and over as it was pulled through Willa's hair down to her waist. Vienna began to hum again and Elliott scraped his chair around to be nearer to Sister, to sit in the crook of her arm as she held the paper out before her. She put her cheek down on his head, which balanced precariously on too slender a neck, and kissed his hair.

"You're a good boy," she said.

"C'mon. Read us the paper," Elliott said, uncomfortable with the affection, wanting it, but not at the price of Willa's scorn.

"All right then, I'll read the headlines but then we need to plan for school."

Willa snorted and narrowed her eyes at Elliott so that they looked like sharp green slits.

"Why are you making your snake-face?" Vienna asked, feeling tired from the competing heat of August and Sister's steaming projects, waiting for an opportunity to retreat.

"I still don't see why I have to go to school."

Vienna didn't either. It was a battle she had waged with the town for several years and had won, until now. At first no one in Winsville had noticed or cared whether her children had been among the assortment of bumbling bodies that pressed into the overcrowded and poorly ventilated elementary school on Redley Road. Then one day, in the bleak thaw of March, prompted by the repeated urging of Mrs. Stepple, who took exception to Willa's occasional matinal ramblings through the Rexall, where she "disrespectfully" fingered the rotating rack of dime romances and crime stories at an age when most children stumbled through primers, Johnson Trupp came to The Heights.

Vienna ushered him into the hall with no more greeting than "Ah, the *force majeure* of the law." He had come to investigate "some truancy" he said apologetically, holding his hat in his hand and rotating it compulsively, inching his fingers around the soiled brim. He was unpleasantly fat, his weight hung on him like a snowdrift and his face had the sweaty pallor of surprise as if he had moments before been enveloped and was afraid of drowning in the avalanching white folds of skin.

His hair, dark as boot blacking and certainly the work of artifice, contrasted stridently with the unhealthy white glare of his flesh, the color of skin that has sweated for months beneath a plaster cast, which had earned him the nickname "Snowman," though no one had dared to call him by it to his face. It was a cruel nickname, even for a cruel man, for in addition to the burden of the body he carried, Vienna realized he was an albino.

"There's no truancy here," she replied briskly, for she could see in his pale, searching eyes a meanness that yearned for victims to replace his own pain, and she was afraid of yielding to the smooth danger of his flaccid façade. She looked away quickly, to the window and beyond, to the rise of fields that still wore the shabby look of a discolored carpet, threadbare and worn, from which only the occasional burst of forsythia shouted against the mute colors of the melting winter.

"It's just that, ma'am, we have no record of your daughter being registered for school. Should be in the third grade by now."

"Willa doesn't need your school. I would think the county would be grateful to be spared the additional burden of her education."

"Well now, the law says every child needs some learning," Johnson said in his sticky sweet voice, punctuating his sure, smiling words with a wink.

It was the wink that did it. Vienna felt her disgust rising with bile and her determination to purge her house of the obsequious threat that stood damply before her, as if the effort to disguise his malice was actually melting him, overwhelmed any earlier intentions of civility or sympathy. Vienna called out for Willa with a sharpness to her voice that brought Willa to the edge of the door almost instantly.

"Mr. Trupp," Vienna said, holding her eyes on him, though she could feel Willa looking up at her for reassurance, "was just telling me about the *learning* you could get at school. Can you be more specific, Mr. Trupp?"

"The usual . . . reading, math . . . geography," Mr. Trupp responded, pausing as if searching his mind to be sure he had exhausted the litany of intellectual endeavor.

"Willa, I want you to do a math problem for Mr. Trupp since he has taken the time and trouble to come to The Heights. If Mr. Trupp weighs three hundred and forty-three pounds and then loses twenty-one pounds, what percent of his total weight has he lost?"

Johnson's eyes narrowed and he flushed a spreading pink that diffused along his neck and ears like watercolor traveling across wet paper, splotching at the borders.

"Now just a minute . . ." he protested, but Vienna cut him off.

"Yes, it will take her at least a minute to do the calculation. We can't expect her to do it too much faster, can we?" Vienna continued.

Willa paused, her face contracting with purpose.

"Um. He'd weigh, um, three hundred twenty-one, no, two, pounds and have lost about six percent. I need paper and a pencil to tell you exactly," Willa said.

"That won't be necessary. Now tell Mr. Trupp the mountain ranges you've studied."

"In order of height?"

"Fine."

"The Himalayas, the Andes, the Alaska range, the Elburzes, the Alps . . ." Willa recited nervously.

"Enough," Vienna cut her off. "Now tell Mr. Trupp, who is so interested in geography, about the river systems in—" but this time Mr. Trupp interrupted with a wave of his hand. "I don't really see—" he began, but Vienna continued speaking.

"But Mr. Trupp, you mentioned reading. I really think we should hear Willa read. Willa, pick up that book on my desk and read us a few sentences."

"From anywhere?" Willa asked, lifting the leatherbound book to the light filtering through the one unshuttered pane of the parlor window, like a spotlight into which she stepped with the earnestness of fear.

"Yes, anywhere," Vienna said tersely.

Willa began in a small voice, tracing the words with her index finger, slowly so she would not stumble.

"There is another species of false intelligence, given by those who profess to shew the way to the summit of knowledge, of equal tendency to depress the mind with false distrust of itself, and weaken it by needless solicitude and dejection."

Willa stopped and looked up quizzically. "Shall I go on?"

"Samuel Johnson, your namesake of sorts. Would you like to hear more, Mr. Johnson Trupp, or shall Willa define *solici-*

tude or *dejection* or any of the other multisyllabic words in the sentence?"

Trupp's eyes had squinted tighter into the swollen corpulence of his luminous face and he looked more than ever like the kind of parasite that is suddenly exposed by the overturning of a rotted log. His lips had tiny beads of spittle on them, like the foam of an anger that has not yet found words. It would not have been incongruous, Vienna thought, to discover that he secreted a transparent mucous smear, like the trail of a slug or snail. He pursed his moist lips to speak, but Vienna, who had taken the book from Willa, added, "Now here's a Latin epigram I'm sure you'll like: *Non ego mendosos ausim defendere mores.* Willa, translate it, please, for Mr. Trupp before he takes his leave of us."

"I won't never defend bad manners."

Vienna smiled unexpectedly, and turned for the first time to look upon her daughter.

"I've told you about double negatives canceling each other out, but in this case I think your translation is more apt than accurate!"

Mr. Trupp smashed his hat on with a vehemence he was unaccustomed to displaying in front of women.

"You've got her trained like a circus monkey," he spat out, "that ain't normal and you know it," his voice high and shrill as a petulant child's. "It's plain freakish, is what it is," he added, turning to the door and yanking the knob so roughly that the glass in the fanlight rattled above the door.

Vienna put her hand down on Willa's shoulder as if to hold her and, still smiling, said with quiet composure, "If you say so, Mr. Trupp, I'm sure you'd know."

WILLA HAD FOLLOWED her mother into the kitchen, where Vienna sank into an unraveling rush chair, her legs having turned spongy almost the moment Johnson Trupp left. Vienna's heart was pumping furiously in her throat.

"Was he here to take me to jail?" Willa asked.

"In a manner of speaking."

"I *didn't* know what *solicitude* meant, or the other word either."

Vienna smiled again. "That's all right, baby, neither did he. We were just bluffing."

Willa was silent. She pulled up the sock that had collapsed around her left ankle, wishing it were warm enough to be barefoot again and then examined for a moment the Sears catalogue, which lay on the table opened to the display of field glasses Elliott coveted. Then with an urgency that bordered on querulous, she looked at Vienna and asked, "Am I a freak?"

Vienna stood up abruptly. "What rubbish—John Stuart Mill wrote Greek at three. Of course, he was precocious, but your Latin, as you know, is hardly . . ."

Vienna stopped herself. There was something in Willa's face that dried the flow of words on her tongue. She pulled Willa to her and looked in her eyes. "No," Vienna said quietly, "you are not a freak. You are my own flame. Like a magnet, you're pulling light from the far stars and that's bound to blind weak eyes."

"Elliott's got weak eyes."

"Elliott has a pure heart: he can see more with that than an owl, an archer, two black leopards, and you and I all put together."

She could feel, through the thin challis of her dress, Willa's breath on her stomach as she hugged her daughter close, letting her own tears fall silently on Willa's head, which was tucked between her arms.

The door slammed and Fayette and Elliott burst in, hardly stopping to scrape the mud from their feet, Elliott pushing past Fayette and shouting, "We saw the car from the meadow and he ran over all the daffodil beds and now the stalks are mashed down and there's a big black slash in the grass from where his wheels went."

Elliott was prancing with excitement around Fayette's worn calico skirt, dodging between the women like a small dog nipping for attention.

"Hush," Fayette said, "I figgered it was the Snowman right away from the nasty way he druve that car, like he wanted to hurt the road, and we started running back faster n' we had breath, Elliott, stop your clamor, baby, but he didn't do nothing to you did he?"

"No, everyone's fine. We talked about school and Willa acquitted herself beautifully with an inspired translation of Ovid," Vienna answered calmly, extracting a pin from her chignon to reposition it more firmly.

Elliott rolled his eyes at his sister who was already beginning to thrill to the role of celebrity in an encounter which was important enough to have Fayette and Elliott breathless with running and panting for details with which she could tease them in the kitchen.

"You tell us all about it while I make us some juice and biscuits," Fayette said, pushing Elliott gently into a chair. "You look like you could use a lay down," Fayette said to Vienna, who was staring absently at the floor.

"Yes, I think I will," Vienna replied wearily, feeling the fatigue of released tension and spent emotion.

"I just hope he don't come back," Fayette went on, talking to no one in particular.

"He won't," Vienna assured them firmly, closing the kitchen door behind her.

BUT JOHNSON TRUPP had returned. The following fall, seven months after his first visit and a month into a new school year, he climbed the porch steps to where Fayette sat with Elliott and Willa, and asked to speak to Mrs. Daniels. Fayette directed him down to the lower field, to the stand of silver maples, where Vienna was arranging stones around the trunks of the trees like necklaces. She had a wheelbarrow beside her which was piled with some of the remains of a ruined stone wall.

From the barn, Fayette and the children could see them, tiny in the distance, talking. Elliott pointed his beloved field glasses toward the stand of maples, but had trouble focusing with his glasses on, so the three of them passed the binoculars back and forth, quibbling for control. Fayette thought she saw Vienna pointing up at the trees and worried about the craziness she might be saying. Willa thought she saw Johnson Trupp mop his brow with a white handkerchief and she was confident of victory. Elliott thought he saw an eastern phoebe, a brown thrasher, and a Carolina wren, but no one seemed to care.

A quarter of a hour later Johnson Trupp lumbered heavily back to his car and left, but Vienna didn't return to the house. She lay on the grass below the silver maples, amid the falling leaves, with her arms under her head, and when Fayette and the children surrounded her, peering down and asking her questions all at once, she said that everything was fine, that unless Johnson Trupp intended to round up all the Overby children and the Hokins and just about a fifth of Jackson County they wouldn't be hearing from him again. And then she said, "But we're wasting the moment. Hush now and listen to the trees." And the three heads tilted to look up into the dazzle and splendor of the branches, which seemed to gather the whole of the sky in their gusty sway, loosing with each breath of wind, a whirl of fluttering, sibilant leaves, drifting in the lazy air like the feathers of a firebird.

FIVE MONTHS LATER Johnson Trupp had shocked the county by dying from a heart attack that seized him in circumstances not fit to be discussed in polite company and that even made some of the men who spat their tobacco juice over the porch rail at Henshaw's Hardware squeamish about helping to carry his stiffened body out of the storage shed behind the jail, where he had been discovered by Henshaw's yappy dog, Sam.

It was a discovery that no one was prepared for. Hane Corbitt, who was deputy and had seen about as much death as anyone, having grown up with his father being an undertaker and then putting in three months for the Balwin-Felts Detective Agency during the West Virginia Mine War, backed out of the shed and coughed a long cascade of vomit onto his shoes. It wasn't so much from the smell, which was already strong, or from the spectacle of Johnson Trupp's naked contortion. It was the pictures that did it, *official* pictures from police file drawers Hane later traced to Texas, to Johnson Trupp's last job, spread out on the floor like a mosaic of mutilation.

Mr. Stepple, who had, in fact, been afraid of Johnson Trupp, had as mayor refused to let him be buried in Winsville. He had paid the fare himself for the body to be sent back to Texas. He was so shaken by the incident that he had tried to resign from office, but no one would let him.

When Vienna heard the news, she made one of her rare appearances in Winsville, to watch the oversized coffin be loaded on the train and then wait for the train to pull out, as if she couldn't believe she was really free of Johnson Trupp.

But she wasn't: he returned, seven months after his death. "In spirit and in letter," Vienna said, fanning herself with the yellow envelope from the Board of Education, "this is Johnson Trupp." Vienna had fumed over the enclosed letter, reading and rereading the stiff prose requiring her to document an accredited program or enroll her children in school. Then she brightened. "This is only a paperwork problem," Vienna insisted. "Johnson Trupp must have written to them or put my name on a list, but I can straighten it out. It just means more bother." But to Sister, just arrived for an indefinite stay, it meant there was nothing to do but register the children, which was exactly what she did the very next day.

So WHEN WILLA asked again, this time petulantly, why she had to go to school, Vienna replied with defeat, "Ask your Aunt Augusta."

Sister shook the newspaper out as if to shake off the reproach she knew was intended for her, and said, in her infuriating, matter-of-fact way, "Because the time has come. And you'll see that it's for the best once you start to like it, as I'm sure you will."

"Ha!" said Willa.

"Hush," said Vienna.

"O.K. Now for the headlines—" Elliott urged, not wanting the squabbling to preclude his favorite part of breakfast. Sister rattled the gazette to signal that she was beginning, to acknowledge the temporary silence that could so easily be broken and to ensure the attention of her audience for the few moments of peace that filled the kitchen.

21

——■——

*S*CHOOL FOR THE Daniels children was an ordeal unmitigated by the solace available to the other children. For the younger McCrorys it was a temporary reprieve from the field; for Jane Markham, Little Jack's older sister by a year, it was an opportunity for adulation and preferment to her brother; for Addison it was a confirmation of his newfound popularity, and for the Pace boys it provided a source of maternal supervision desperately lacking in their motherless home.

For Willa and Elliott, it was a profoundly painful introduction to boredom. Moreover, Miss Eugenia Dobbs, who had replaced Miss Felix on short notice many years before, was very set in her ways. She had devised a system of dividing the children into three classes, which meant she could teach grades one through six simultaneously. Her system was predicated on the small numbers of students at each level, proportional to the number of repeaters, students who remained for years at a time on one level because of poor attendance for the months of the year devoted to the more pressing timetable of the crops. It was a system much applauded by Winsville's administration, such as it was, because it saved the town the additional burden of a second salary; there being no high school in Winsville, once Miss Dobbs was through with a pupil, it was up to Bantanburg to provide the next segment of education.

Miss Dobbs had arranged the schoolroom into thirds so that she could rotate her attention evenly, leaving one section to work on exercises of the material she had just taught while she proceeded to the next section, which would have by then completed an exercise or reading assignment designed to occupy them, or at least silence them while she was required in one of the other sections.

It was a design, like so many employed in the education of children, that worked better in theory than in practice. Rarely did the time it took for one group to be taught a lesson coincide with the time it took another to finish the set of problems they had been assigned, and the section that started the day with a chapter of text was usually the group that had the longest to wait until Miss Dobbs graced them again with her pedagogy. But heaven forfend, as Willa found out, one should read ahead, and unwittingly finish the day's work by the first bell. Miss Dobbs's starched bosom would rise to accompany the ascending pitch of her adenoidal voice as her annoyance expressed itself in the form of a public humiliation. Thus she maintained a level of mediocrity in which no one would dare grasp the material any faster than the cumbersome pace necessary for her to fulfill her heroic rounds. She expected to one day be recognized, like John Dewey, for the enormity of her contribution—namely, for her innovations in didactic dissemination, which enabled her to teach (however poorly) on a variety of levels at once, thereby multiplying the efficiency of the educational process while saving the township money.

Willa and Elliott tested her faith sorely; they were the classroom equivalent to the hemorrhoids or boils visited upon Job; for the first time in her teaching career, Miss Dobbs's system encountered sabotage, and caused her to question, albeit briefly, its integrity. No matter how she tried, she couldn't seem to fit these two children into her system. She was forced to conclude, and it was a great blow to her natural sentimental attachment to children, that the Daniels children were simply evil.

Elliott did not work out his arithmetic computations on the ruled paper provided expressly for that purpose, which infuriated Miss Dobbs because no matter how she tried to determine the manner by which he cheated, she could never catch him out. Repeating the questions to him in a varied order, he still answered her correctly without recourse to paper, forcing her to conclude that the answers were memorized and that the boy was endowed with the retention of a cardsharp, but that still did not explain where the answers came from.

She changed his seat repeatedly, surrounding him by students as singularly ungifted as two-footed creatures could be, although the thick glasses that rested precariously askew on his small nose should have been enough to ensure a limited view of his classmates' work. It baffled her almost as much as the odd vocabulary he brought to the classroom: asked to describe a shark's mouth, Elliott, perking up with excitement because at last he thought he recognized the kind of game they played with Vienna, had eagerly volunteered "a flash of fierce serration" when Miss Dobbs was looking for the spelling word "frightful," and when she shouted "No, no, no" at him and sent him to the corner, he had politely asked her how long he was to be sequestered.

Willa was worse. When Miss Dobbs copied a lengthy sentence on the board for her section to parse, Willa had asked if it was an example of anacoluthon and for a moment, before Miss Dobbs was able to recover herself and recognize plain impertinence, she had thought the child was speaking in tongues. Miss Dobbs was not one to be trifled with. She was slightly hard of hearing, and this affliction had led her to compensate by being impeccably correct in her attire and maintaining strict discipline as a way of fending off the paranoia that in her occupation would find so many opportunities for justification, with or without the hearing impairment.

"Explain yourself," she demanded and Willa, flustered by the silence that seized the classroom, arresting the scratch of pens and heads tormented by lice, the constant nose sniffling, page shuffling, and seat creaking that formed a comforting background for thought, had answered, "I was wondering if, you know, this was like Caliban's speech." When Willa would not apologize for interrupting the class with imaginary nonsense (by far the worst kind of nonsense, in Miss Dobbs' experience), Willa had been asked to find the word anacoluthon in the classroom dictionary, and when she failed, her hand was scalded with a sharp smack from Miss Dobbs's ruler. This had so appalled Elliott that from the corner in which he slumped on a low stool, he had shouted out, "It's because you left out some words on the chalkboard, and it's only fair to tell if it's ungrammatical on purpose."

Indeed, in her haste to adhere to her rigorous schedule, Miss Dobbs had omitted two words from the sentence on the board, an oversight she quickly rectified while the room enjoyed an unruly outburst of laughter. For this, the entire population subject to Miss Dobbs's supervision was punished, reestablishing Miss Dobbs's credibility as a scholar and creating immediate dissent among the ranks of Daniels supporters.

WILLA AND ELLIOTT always sat together during lunch, away from the noisy euphoria of their peers. They did not participate in the loosely organized games or ride the seesaw or swing sets or exchange more civilities than were demanded by expedience. It seemed incomprehensible to them that the others professed to like Miss Dobbs, to consider her evenhanded in her demonstrations of authority; what the other children hated and found difficult was the actual work she required.

This was as clearly inverted and mistaken an appreciation of the bare reality confronting the Daniels as any topsy-turvy world imagined by Rabelais or Swift, and, still more disturbing, it was one on which Vienna could shed no light. At her mother's suggestion, Willa had lugged to school a weighty tome of rhetorical terms and usage expressly to exonerate herself from the shame she had suffered at the hands of a deficient dictionary, only to have Miss Dobbs pronounce her "saucy."

While the schoolwork was depressingly unchallenging, their teacher remained a cipher they could not crack and their efforts to please her were as unrewarded as poor Tommy Pace's futile attempts to master fractions. Although the Daniels children had always been readers, now, in their misery, they were driven to a frantic level of literary consumption, smuggling in the contraband like prisoners preparing for an escape, not only to relieve the agony of the empty hours during which they were trapped on Redley Road, but because fiction seemed to offer the only safe diversion; they now devoted themselves to warding off the danger of unwittingly acquiring facts that produced such a volatile reaction from Miss Dobbs.

They shunned all forms of nonfiction. They made it a rule never to speak unless called on, and then to speak as colloquially as possible, as they did with each other, avoiding the Augustan multisyllabics they used with Vienna and had been taught was the diction preferred by adults. Even confining their vocabulary to Anglo-Saxon words was not enough. They developed an ear for slang and emulated the most impoverished speakers of the classroom in their campaign to win the elusive approval of Miss Dobbs.

Never did she pause by either of their desks to bestow a smiling nod. Her manicured hand was never laid tenderly on their shoulders, neither was a Daniels head patted, although they were among the very few that always had clean hair.

Elliott in particular suffered. For Willa, words were subtly shaded collectibles forming a glittering palette of variation and choice—like the tin paintbox with its forty-eight separate squares of color, which she had desperately coveted, though as Vienna had pointed out, she could mix all those colors herself with a set of twelve—her pleasure was derived not from applying the paints, but simply from *having* them, knowing that the precise shade, like the right word, was available, without the mess of slow approximation, the frustration of using ten words to arrive at the precision of one. For Elliott, however, language was a chiefly musical endeavor, the human link between the two areas in which he was prodigiously gifted, the piano and ornithology, and many of the words he loved he loved for their rhythm, the way the vowels combined or the alliterative lilt of repeated sound. Their meaning was considerably less significant, as evidenced by the two words he thought were among the most beautiful to say: diarrhea and cacophonous.

The problem with debased diction was that it was too dependent on short words that were fine for dialogue, but, as he complained to Willa, "In compositions this makes for staccato sentences that don't scan right. They sound choppy, like when you crenellate the piano keys instead of playing music."

"Yeah," Willa said, "and worse than that, it's having no effect on the vituperative old hellhound."

ADDISON WATCHED HELPLESSLY from his section, devoid of either of the Daniels, the evolution of their status as pariahs, and it seemed disturbingly ironic that in the face of his impressive popularity the only friends he had failed to gain were the two he most wanted, making his rejection all the more acute as the swell of resentment against them grew.

It is a familiar phenomenon, a basic law of nature absorbed by even the most unobservant, that a group will turn on the minority most despised by the powerful, indulging its primitive need for a scapegoat while enjoying the protection of an authority that condemns the expression of those same feelings it shares so ineffectually as to condone the behavior. Thus the class, acting in microcosm and rehearsing for the larger society into which they aspired to be released, began to extend, quite casually, an outstretched leg into the narrow aisle as one or the other Daniels tried to attain their desks.

Willa's long hair always seemed to find its way into the inkwell of the student sitting behind her, guaranteeing a large black stain on the back of her white shirt. Elliott's desk became the repository for snails or dead frogs or mice. Rubber bands launched from dirty fingernails had only two targets. Messages designed to antagonize Miss Dobbs mysteriously filled the chalkboard at night, signed by a Daniels. Willa and Elliott began arriving at school half an hour before the bell to wipe the board and clean their desks and take their seats in peace.

Addison, on their behalf, called in the debt owed to him by Bobby Maddox's gang, who agreed to wait behind the hydrangea bushes, until dawn if necessary, to find out who was behind the provocative messages and to deter them permanently from the prank. The Overbys were especially enthusiastic about the mission because never having attended school, it was gratifying for them to be able to exercise some mischief against the institution they feared and because Lee had borrowed for the occasion his father's clan hood, which served a dual purpose: it covered the unsightly black eye Stan Lee had recently received and it added powerfully to the terror they hoped to inspire.

Jackson showed up with his .22, and two bullets, making Addison and Wilbur uneasy, but Jackson assured them it was just for shock value, and the others said, "You never know," and "It's better to be safe than sorry," somberly echoing the phrases they heard at home. Bobby brought a pack of Lucky Strikes and two nudie pictures he wouldn't say how he had gotten. The pictures created quite a stir and engendered a lively conversation that filled the better part of an hour. After that, the waiting became boring, and Froggy fell asleep.

Finally, when morale was dangerously low and there was seditious talk of disbanding in favor of the comforts of a straw mattress and a patched quilt, they heard footsteps. A figure appeared at the far end of the playground, near the rope swing. "It's Becky McCrory," Little Jack said in horror, "she's my sister's best friend and I'll bet she's doing it for her, so as Jane can be Miss Dobbs' little star." Little Jack's disgust for his prim and supercilious sister was long-standing, as was his delight in thwarting her at the least opportunity. Impulsively, he grabbed the rifle from Jackson's loose grip and fired a shot in the air, reloaded and fired another, laughing with unrestrained mirth as the figure scrambled over the fence, tripping in terrified flight in the direction of the McCrory farm. "That'll show those girls a thing or two," Little Jack sneered, but Jackson was furious at having been upstaged and it took the promise of two replacement bullets, a pack of gum, and a tin of snuff to appease him.

Wilbur, who had never been in the schoolhouse either, wanted to have a look, so, single file, they climbed in the back window, stepping on Little Jack's knee as a perch. Little Jack stayed outside keeping watch, because he said he had seen more than enough of the room, but it was generally understood that he was serving an unspoken sentence for being in disgrace with the gang. Inside, Jackson was allowed to write a damning disclosure signed with the name Janie Markham, to give him a larger role in the night's adventure and as a means of making peace with Little Jack, who whistled a lonely air outside and seemed sufficiently contrite.

It was late when the group dispersed, but spirits were high. There was much back-slapping and self-congratulation amid competing imitations of the clumsy, terrified departure of the McCrory girl. Only Stan Lee, carrying the hood carefully folded under his arm, was disappointed and felt that, as usual, he had missed his moment.

The following morning, however, Little Jack and Addison were shocked to find, upon entering the classroom, the slate wiped clean and the Daniels children sitting quietly in their places, backs straight and eyes averted, the same posture with which they had withstood the slanderous attacks on themselves.

That was when Little Jack and Bobby Maddox yielded to the magnetic pull of the overwhelming indictment against the Daniels children. After that, Addison walked an impossible line between the two factions competing for his allegiance, and as a result felt that misery had taken residence in his lower intestine. He was too guilty and sickened to enjoy participating in the bullying into which Bobby Maddox poured his arrogance and ingenuity with an abandonment that was remarkable to behold and outstripped anything previously attempted, because by this time in the year the class was mostly composed of the students who actually hoped to graduate to another grade, a constraint that meant nothing to Bobby, who had already repeated the first grade twice, the third grade once, and had learned the advantage of being the biggest, if not the best, in a grade.

On the other hand, it gave Addison no pleasure to endure repeated rebuffs from the two for whom he had already made embarrassing sacrifices, risked disfavor, and was now verging dangerously on jeopardizing all that he had gained that mattered since he came to Winsville. Moreover, their attitude made it too awkward for him to return to their mother the books he had borrowed, which sat in a column by his desk, growing dusty and redolent of the remorse and anxiety associated with a trust he felt he had somehow betrayed.

That Willa and Elliott were miserable was obvious, but what was not as readily apparent was that they were also deeply ashamed. They were ashamed of the mysterious and mortifying stigma they bore that singled them out for abuse, but what made the situation most unbearable was that they feared it had something to do with Vienna. For this reason, they tried to protect her from any revelation that would disclose their pain.

Vienna was also miserable. She had known something was wrong from the first day they returned from Redley Road, pursing their lips the way they did when enduring the extraction of a splinter, their eyes dulled and evasive. They no longer filled the evenings with exuberant reenactments of great historical moments: the coronations or executions, knighthoods and druidic rituals that had previously delighted them. The antique saber had not once been removed from the wall, and the tiny spoons that were frequently missing from the silver saltcellars were undisturbed. Vienna found that Willa's dollhouse family, the Nostrils, had been massacred in a most unsettling way. Elliott's leaf fossil, a prized possession, was smashed, its shards heaped like rubble in a china bowl next to a nub of candle, like an offering to a malevolent god.

Before she left, Sister had pronounced a diagnosis— "Frankly, I think it's growing pains. Entirely natural for children their ages. I wouldn't fret over it unduly. If you ask me, you're liable to encourage sulking by doing anything other than ignoring what is clearly just a phase."

But now, with Sister's departure and the absence of the children during the day, Vienna found the house unbearable. Without the interruptions and squabbles, the bursts of song and banging doors and floorboards creaking beneath prancing feet and impromptu marches, Vienna found it hard to concentrate on her work. She followed Fayette through her chores or spent time beneath the silver maples, watching the day pass through a filter of leaves, feeling lonely and restless.

Fayette also knew something was wrong, though she couldn't put her finger on it. "All chil'un mind school, but that don't seem to be what this about." She tried to cheer Vienna by remarking that whatever else was ailing them, the children had never seemed closer. It was true: Willa and Elliott no longer disputed on whose bed Vienna sat while she read them the next chapter of their bedtime book, in fact, they had become fatigued by their studies to the preclusion of the ritual nighttime readings. The dinner-table conversation was devoid of the usual discussions of whose slice of pie was larger, or who hadn't finished the brussels sprouts. In response to almost fatuous queries about what they were learning in school, her children made stricken, queasy faces, and were oddly inarticulate.

22

---

*T*HEN IT HAPPENED, as it inevitably does, in the heat that breeds infection: the gangrenous swelling pushes to a head and opens to the innocent air its fetid poison. Willa had been detained by Miss Dobbs into the beginning of lunch hour, not being allowed her release until she had covered the board fifty times in script with the words, "I am an obstinate and willful girl for reading in school."

Miss Dobbs was busy beating the chalk dust out of the dishrags she used to wipe the board, swatting the limp cloth against the oak table on which the globe was situated, with the result that the multicolored planet was always encased in a delicate sheath of fine powder, a permanent snow that covered the world she offered to the children, adjusting the climate visually as well as emotionally to a colder norm.

From the stool on which she stood to reach the upper portion of the board, Willa could see, through the irregularities in the streaked windowpanes, the corner of the yard where Elliott stood waiting for her. There was a small circle gathering around him and Bobby Maddox and Tommy Veen were pointing at Elliott as they closed in on him. She glanced back at Miss Dobbs, whose attentions were now focused on the gold stars she was pressing neatly onto the progress chart which hung on the wall, a list so generously comprehensive as to guarantee even the Daniels could qualify for approbation, if only for attendance and hygiene.

Willa quietly replaced the chalk in its holder and tiptoed out of the room. When she reached the hall, where a tattered collection of summer jackets and bookbags slumped from metal hooks, she broke into a run. The noise of her classmates, as she reached the yard, concentrated into a single angry sound that hit her with the same stunning impact as Miss Dobbs's ruler.

They were mobbed around Elliott, a thick body of jeering taunts she tried to push into, shoving her way slowly to the center, where Elliott, his face quizzical without his glasses, which had been knocked off, was being pushed back and forth between the two boys, while the onlookers shouted rudimentary instructions of encouragement or derision.

Addison got to the center first, just as Bobby was drawing his arm back for a blow that Addison's tackle deflected, spinning Bobby off balance and hurtling the two to the ground in the long-delayed but ineluctable combat that splintered the spectators into two camps: those who now observed the evenly matched contest in which Addison and Bobby contended for a title only one could hold, and those who preferred the bear-baiting sport of Tommy's attack on Elliott, triply handicapped without his glasses, without the stature or breadth of his opponent, and without the inclination to fight.

Willa jumped on Tommy's back and pulled at his hair as if to scalp him; he bent over to shake her off and failing, used her additional weight to butt his head against Elliott, which knocked Elliott flat on the ground, landing a foot away from his glasses, one lens of which was shattered.

Miss Dobbs's shrill metal whistle pierced the air, parting all but the participants into neat rows, like soldiers falling in for inspection, allowing her brisk and dignified progress to the two boys who still rolled furiously in the dirt.

"Up, up, up this minute!" she shrieked, prodding Addison with the toe of her black shoe just as he finally pinned Bobby and was now attempting to kneel over from astride Bobby's chest onto his outstretched arms.

Addison and Bobby staggered to their feet and she held them disdainfully extended from her bulk with her hands firmly clamped on their shoulders, pushing them forward to examine the next piece of nastiness. Willa still clung to Tommy's back, her teeth embedded in his shoulder, while he, on all fours, tried simultaneously to clamber to his feet, strike Willa with a flailing arm, and shake her off him by gyrating his hips.

"Let go this instant, missy. You are an incorrigible child and I can't abide that. I shall see to it that you are severely punished for this." Tommy Veen rose up blubbering, examining the teethmarks in his flesh through the rip in his almost-new shirt.

"You too, on your feet," Miss Dobbs shouted at Elliott, but the boy didn't move. Willa knelt beside him, shaking him gently. "C'mon, Elliott, it's over now, we're going home," Willa said with shaky authority.

"Stand up at once," Miss Dobbs shouted impatiently and blasted her whistle again.

"Shut up, you old crow," Willa said, eliciting a gasp that ran through the ranks of students spontaneously reassembled in ascending order of height just as Miss Dobbs had taught them. "He can't get up, something's wrong."

Miss Dobbs's demeanor changed in an instant. She knelt beside Elliott, soiling her yellow wool skirt in the process, and lifting his limp head to her ample chest she felt the warm wet mat of the back of his head. When she withdrew her hand it was bright with blood.

"Is he dead?" someone asked and Miss Dobbs said sharply, "Silence. This is no time for foolery. I want every one of you at your desks with your hands folded quietly. Jack, you go call Dr. Barstow from the telephone in my quarters. The door is open and don't dawdle and don't touch anything. You understand?"

"Yes'm," Little Jack said, pleased to be entrusted with such an important duty and as he ran by his sister, he paused to catch her eye and extrude his tongue.

Miss Dobbs looked at Willa and said softly, with all the gentleness she had hitherto denied the Daniels, "I can feel his pulse fine, so don't fuss now. He's hit his head unconscious, but the doctor will fix him up in two winks. Why don't you go fetch a glass of cold water, and bring me one as well."

"I'll get it," Addison offered from his crouch behind them. Willa looked over at him, as if noticing him only now for the first time, and cringed. His face was bloody and misshapen, one eye was rapidly swelling closed and there was a trickle of blood working its way from the clot at his nose down to a split upper lip, which also dripped a slow stream of blood.

"Thank you, Addison," Miss Dobbs said, "that would be kindly of you," and without turning to look, she added, "and while you're about it, you tell those children to get away from peering out the window and go back to their seats."

By the time Dr. Barstow arrived, the entire grammar school was waiting for him by the road, and he looked in quick confusion at their assorted wounds and bruises, stopping momentarily to examine the bite on Tommy Veen's shoulder, before Addison, almost unrecognizable beneath dried smears and clots of coagulated blood bulging out from the rising planes of his bruised face, waved him on, frantically calling, "Up there, it's Elliott Daniels, sir."

"What in the name of sweet Jesus has gone on here?" Dr. Barstow snapped at Miss Dobbs, whose face was blotchy with tears.

"The Daniels boy has just had a seizure. Convulsions. I didn't know what to do: his legs were jumping like the needle on a sewing machine and he vomited."

"If he was vomiting and unconscious why is he still on his back? Move away, Miss Dobbs, to where I will not be tempted to slap you," Dr. Barstow said in his genteel bedside tone, and then he lifted Elliott and carried him to the car, laying him carefully on the back seat the way he would a freshly pressed suit, instructing Willa to sit beside him and hold him still. He advised Bobby Maddox, in parting, to clean his face, and put an icepack on his nose and a steak on his eye. "The same goes for you," he said to Addison, "and tell that boy with the bite to have Miss Dobbs disinfect it immediately." Then Dr. Barstow nervously lit a cigarette and drove to the Bantanburg Hospital, pushing the car to the upper register of the speedometer.

TWO DAYS LATER, Elliott was still unconscious. His fever had broken, but Dr. Barstow was being conservative with his optimism. X rays implied a swelling of the soft tissue in the brain resulting from the trauma of the skull fracture, so there was nothing to do but wait, and waiting was the hardest thing to do.

Dr. Barstow had never seen Vienna so humble: she had taken his hand and filled it with her tears; she had implored him to save her son. He didn't dare tell her that in all probability that was not what she wanted.

Dr. Barstow knew that the child she loved was already gone.

The small body lying between the stiff white sheets with a slow pulse, high blood pressure, and an enlarged pupil in the left eye had already sustained enough damage to make him unrecognizable to his family even if, *mirabile dictu*, he were to regain not only consciousness, but speech. Looking down at the boy from the foot of the metal bed, Dr. Barstow sighed, and tested Elliott's reflexes again, running the edge of a speculum down the small unresponding foot, not because he expected to see a change, but because there was so little to do it comforted him to run through the routines over and over again.

Dr. Barstow was trying to work himself up to telling Vienna the truth: the fracture had caused internal bleeding. That was one way of putting it. Even if Elliott survived transfer to a city hospital, at this point there was not much use in operating to drain the blood and relieve the pressure: it was doubtful that he could survive the operation. And even if he did, chances were even slimmer that he would regain consciousness. Elliott was hemorrhaging to death. That was another way of putting it. Looking at his peaceful face, pale and smooth with sleep, it was hard to fathom; except for the underside of his head, now buried in the depths of a goosedown pillow, he was unscathed by any sign of trauma. Half the children Dr. Barstow had seen standing on Redley Road two days earlier had looked more imperiled than Elliott did now, a slight coral blush gently illuminating his cheeks like the glow that emanates from a lampshade lined in pink silk, or the glossy interior of conch shells.

Vienna entered the room quietly, as if the slightest noise might cause her sleeping child to stir. "Well?" she asked. Her eyes were rimmed with the dark bruised purples of sleeplessness and worry, but the effect was strangely flattering, dramatic as a dancer's makeup, and, like a dancer, Vienna's body seemed poised on the verge of some sweeping movement, as if her energy was tightly contained, ready to be released when the proper cue came.

Dr. Barstow hesitated, hating his slight and pathetic role in the tragedy she now faced with composed and unflinching grandeur, her rumpled gray dress and tumbled hair stuffed beneath a shapeless hat, commanding him by her posture to say his lines and exit.

"The x rays show a multiple fracture of the lower—"

Vienna interrupted. "James Barstow, don't," she said almost tenderly, as if her vast love for Elliott was now sweeping over everyone in its path, like a tidal wave rushing beyond familiar shores to the dry plains that have only known the sea by the lingering hint of salt the air carries at dusk.

"Don't tell me about the contusion or the fracture, concussions or x rays. I need to know one thing only. Is my boy dying?"

The question was delivered with control, but Vienna's voice was pinched and Dr. Barstow guessed how costly her words had been. His body betrayed him: his throat closed with a dry ache around his swelling Adam's apple, his eyes watered, his nose became moist, and he was suffused with shame that the wasted years should culminate thus, in the damning futility of a practice in which he must answer like an American Bovary, impotent before the randomness of his profession, when he would gladly have traded his remaining breath to be able to seize one gloriously transcendent moment, speaking the mythic words of a hero, the role for which he had been auditioning in grimy examining rooms and at badly lit bedsides for three full decades.

"I need to know, Dr. Barstow" Vienna continued slowly, "because this hospital won't let me have but three hours a day with him. Regulations don't permit Willa to visit because she is a child under twelve and Fayette cannot be admitted into the building because she is a Negro. I need to know, Dr. Barstow, because we three are all he has; we have been with him since the day you delivered him, and he is not going to die alone in this ugly unfamiliar barren little room with the acrid smell of loneliness and cheap disinfectant the last of this earth he has."

Dr. Barstow cleared his throat and looked at her, nodding.

"I can't release him. It would be illegal," he said weakly.

"Dr. Barstow, if you can't help him live, please let me help him die. It is so little. I can have at least this." Her lips were twitching. She put a hand up to hide behind, and he saw that the cuticles on three fingers had been gnawed raw, like an animal trying to work its way out of a trap.

"Give me an hour. The next rounds aren't until twelve. Come back with Fayette and Mr. Aimes, and tell him to bring . . . never mind, I'll tell him myself. I'll try to be in the front hall near reception with as many doctors as I can detain. Have Fayette insist on a visit and tell her to stand her ground for as long as possible. That should be distraction enough for you and Mr. Aimes to get Elliott, but take him out the back exit, through the door marked 'orderlies only' and don't stop for anything. I'll come to The Heights as soon as I can, but it won't be for a while."

"Thank you," Vienna whispered, looking at him with such candid gratitude and warmth that he felt more acutely the meagerness of his offering. He looked away and caught his reflection in the glass porthole of the door, hollow and substanceless like his gesture, he thought, seeing through his features to the hallway beyond.

"I wish I could have earned it," he replied flatly, twisting a stethoscope in his large fingers, refusing the comfort of unwon glory.

As THEY LEFT the hospital with Elliott swaddled in a horse blanket, Vienna and Mr. Aimes emerged into the alley that contained a row of metal waste bins. They surprised an orderly leaning idly against the brick wall of the hospital, enjoying a cigarette in solitude. Vienna froze momentarily on the steps, but Mr. Aimes gave her a nudge in the small of her back as he raised his shotgun in the startled face of the young man, whose cigarette dropped to the ground.

"Say a word about this, son, and I'll put so much buckshot between your legs you'll think it's pepper steak," Mr. Aimes said from behind the barrel of the gun. The fellow's hands automatically flew up in the air, and he licked his fledgling mustache in a reflex of panic, "No sir, I've seen nuthin', just had myself a smoke, sir."

"Well, that's O.K.," Mr. Aimes answered, recovering from his loquacious outburst, but he kept the gun trained on the young man's stained white uniform until he heard Vienna start the car. Then Aimes lowered the gun and, backing out of the alley, said apologetically, "Mighty sorry to have intruded on your smoke. I'll be obliged, though, if you remember what I said."

After stowing the gun under the seat of his car, he went around to the front entrance, where there was still a commotion surrounding Fayette. Taking her by the arm, he said, "Let's get. We don't need to bother these folks any longer," and he smiled as a few doctors called out their thanks for his help.

At The Heights, Willa had been opening the door to well-wishers. Sophronius Moody had stopped by with a small brown sack of fireballs for Elliott, and Mrs. Stepple had sent a tepid chicken casserole care of her husband, who had closed school until the end of the week while he searched for someone to replace Miss Dobbs, whose resignation had been tendered with the alacrity of one who fears dismissal. Mr. Veen had come by twice asking to speak to Vienna, and the second time, he left a barely legible note threatening to sue the family for the bite his son had received, but suggesting that compensation, represented by three dollar signs, would be accepted.

Addison had come too, delivering to Willa the items he had gone back to Redley Road to retrieve: Elliott's broken glasses, a shirt button, and the spade that had been buried for God knows how long in the earth, working its slow way to the surface, the metal tip of which had only just broken through the dirt, waiting under a scuff of topsoil for Elliott's head, to find with improbable accuracy its exposed lip and kiss it with the softest part of his cranium, the unheard crack no louder than a perfectly executed billiards shot. The spade was still clumped with the tenacious dirt Addison had dug it from.

It was meaningless now, the answer to the riddle that had perplexed so many two days earlier. Willa took the spade from Addison and put it on the sideboard and then she went to the kitchen and found a cucumber that was chilling in the icebox.

"Here," she said, as if making a trade, "put this on your eye."

Addison held the cool vegetable skin to his eye and Willa laughed. "Not like that. You have to slice it. Give me it, I'll show you," she said, taking the cucumber back to the kitchen and returning with a handful of thin pale rings pushed on her finger through the soft seeded centers.

Shortly after Addison left, Biddy Markham knocked. She held a huge bouquet of her famous star-eye chrysanthemums. "Tell your mother if she needs anything she has only to call." Willa took the flowers and thanked her, but once the door was closed she let them fall into a jumbled heap behind the umbrella stand.

VIENNA TUCKED ELLIOTT into his bed and then called Willa into his room. "Do me a favor, baby, go get his dog as fast as you can." Willa stared in disbelief. Fearing disapproval, they had never acknowledged Murphy to the grown-ups, much less brought him inside the house. "He's probably down behind the barn," Vienna said. "Fayette fed him there this morning."

When Willa came back with Murphy, she was further shocked to see Vienna pat the foot of the bed, signaling Murphy to jump up and cover the counterpane with muddy paw prints. Then Vienna went downstairs and returned staggering precariously behind the gramophone she lugged in her arms, wishing it were the new electric Victrola Elliott had campaigned for so earnestly. She banged the weighty box down on Elliott's desk, replaced the needle, and put on a scratchy recording of a Schubert piece for four hands, the last duet the two of them had played together.

Dr. Barstow came by twice to change the dressing on Elliott's head and told Vienna before he left the second time that there was a chance Elliott would regain consciousness briefly, but that it would be a prelude to the end, not a miraculous new beginning.

Fayette had arranged with Grant to spend the night at The Heights and she dragged her favorite porch rocker up to Elliott's room, bumping it loudly behind her on each step of the staircase as Elliott would have, and then, with a breathy sigh, she planted herself in the deep sway of its seat. Willa curled up at the foot of the bed, sharing the space with Murphy, allowing his wagging tail to thump on her thigh and his carrion breath to foul the space in which she retracted like a snail, clinging to the mound Elliott's feet made beneath the covers. Vienna positioned herself at the headboard, holding Elliott's hand and stroking it gently, absentmindedly, as she half listened to the Chopin that had replaced Schubert in a methodical selection of Elliott's favorites, and to Willa's whining litany of callers.

Shortly after nine, the phone rang and reluctantly Vienna rose to answer it. It was only Mr. Aimes, inquiring about Elliott, and asking if there was anything she needed. She said no and replaced the receiver. On the third tread of the stair she heard Murphy barking and took the remaining steps in threes.

Elliott's eyes were open and he was smiling, but it was hard to say if, without his glasses, he was focused on anything in the room. She reached his bed as his eyelids fluttered shut, the delicate skin lined with fine blue veins puckering closed as his eyelashes interlaced. Vienna bent quickly to kiss his eyelids, muttering his name, but he was beyond the call of her voice.

"He spoke," Fayette said. "I couldn't quite make it out because the dog was barking—and his words sounded drunk, sort of like, 'He got us,' or something like that."

"I think he said 'Icarus,' " Willa piped up, "that's what I think he said." Vienna looked from one to the other. Icarus was the name Elliott had given his first bird, a starling with an injured wing he had nursed back to health and had had the honor of watching fly off into the camouflage of trees and beyond to the all-absorbing sky.

Vienna's hands were shaking with rage. Elliott had spoken and she had missed it, and for what? A useless exchange with Mr. Aimes. She leaned her head over Elliott's face and listened to the soft puff of breath on his dry lips; taking a wet cloth, she tremblingly moistened them.

Willa was the first to fall asleep, then Fayette, her head

dangling onto one shoulder and her mouth gaping and dark. The record had finished playing, but Vienna didn't want to get up to remove the heavy arm of the gramophone, which had stopped with the needle pressing down into the record. Finally, she heard the dog's nasal snore, and the excited snap of its jaws tracing the course of its reverie, and she was alone with Elliott.

The enormity of what remained unspoken occluded the thoughts she had been saving until now, the words she had winnowed down to a final farewell were lost, and tracing the bitten nails on Elliott's hand with her index finger, she found nothing came from her but the refrain "I'm sorry," repeated like a mantra in a comfortless meditation, until the words sounded dull and foreign. At four twenty-five in the morning, Elliott died.

Vienna held him until she could no longer feel warmth in his hands, and then she stood up. Feeling the ache that had settled in her lower back, she lifted Willa and carried her to her bed. Then she returned to Elliott's room and, tucking behind her head the terrycloth elephant he had loved into baldness, she slept for a few hours in the comb-back armchair Elliott had used at his desk.

23

━━━■━━━

$\mathcal{S}$ISTER, WITH HER usual uncanny timing, arrived the next morning, almost pleased to have had the sense of foreboding, the premonition which had prompted her to take the night train, confirmed by disaster. Within the hour, she had argued with everyone in the house, had slapped Willa and threatened to slap Fayette, and when Willa said, "Don't mind her, Fayette, she's a fat old churl," Sister had burst into tears at the "unnatural ill treatment" she was receiving at "a time like this."

Vienna dispatched Sister to Winsville with a list of unnecessary errands to give her something to do besides get underfoot and criticize, the only form of grieving she was allowing herself while the shock of the news was still barely credible. Brandishing the list, with her sense of importance restored, she lingered at the door to stuff her swollen fingers into a misshapen kid glove, taking the opportunity to impart one final caveat: "Willa, don't blow so hard; that snout has got to last you a lifetime and you'll wear it out by afternoon, honking like a lost goose. Besides, the sound is most unbecoming, and frankly, my nerves are dangerously frayed already."

In Sister's absence, Vienna called Dr. Barstow and then the lumber mill where Grant worked. Although it was irregular for a colored worker to be allowed to receive a call in the foreman's office, Vienna's weary yet imperative tone dissuaded the usually officious overseer from insisting on formalities. Once she heard Grant's gravelly hello, she handed the phone to Fayette and went upstairs, leaving Fayette to arrange with Grant the coffin he would select and deliver from the shed in which he did occasional woodwork in the evenings to supplement their income. Grant was nonplussed by the request. "Baby, you know I only got pine to work with. How come she don't want a fancy job from Bantanburg, with velvet quilting or sateen?" Grant had had few occasions to meet the Daniels, and his wife's allegiance to the family was something he indulged without comprehending.

"Honey, we'll talk later," was all the explanation Fayette offered, having found it formed an effective and economic basis for their relationship over the years. After she hung up, Grant looked at the foreman, who waited by the door with his arms folded across his chest expecting an explanation, but all Grant said was "Amen," and, shaking his head, he clicked his tongue against his teeth and clanked down the metal stairs back to work.

Fayette and Vienna washed Elliott, and then dressed him in his navy blue Sunday suit, only to have Willa petulantly, adamantly insist that he be redressed in his brown corduroy knickers, white cotton shirt, and faded blue vest with three pockets, into which she put a pencil, his shooter marble, his arrowhead and falcon's talon, his bird notebook and a handful of Sophronius's fireballs, even though Fayette didn't like the way it made his pockets bulge. Willa was equally unrelenting about shoes, and in the end Elliott was buried barefoot. Vienna spent more than half an hour combing his hair with the silent preoccupation of a child pampering a favorite doll, while Fayette ironed with a compulsive rigor the white shirt Willa had chosen.

When Grant finally arrived with the plain casket, it was clear he had been delayed by some last-minute refinements. He was more than a little vain about how finely sanded the wood was, and not until everyone had touched and commented on its silken finish was he content to busy himself with a shovel at the grave site, which had been the only easy choice of the difficult decisions: Elliott was to be buried with his birds, in the plot he had laboriously and lovingly made himself. Before the coffin was closed, Fayette burrowed through the large fabric bag she always carried to work and pulled out a small parcel neatly bound up in brown paper, which she painstakingly unwrapped so that the paper could be used again. "I always meant to give him this," she mumbled, extracting the blue cloth sash Grayson Saunder had given her. It was faded and only a few gold stars remained, but Vienna took it from her with a gasp of gratitude. "I know he would have treasured this."

Vienna carefully fitted it over Elliott's head, smoothing it flat over his vest, taking care that it was not wrinkled beneath him. Then she went over to the piano and brought back the sheet music Elliott had been memorizing. "I think he should have this too," she said, and placed it under Elliott's arm. Fayette agreed cautiously. "I suppose so, I just hope it's not too crowded in there," but Willa put her arm around Fayette and said, "This isn't so much; you should see what the pharaohs got." Then Vienna smoothed Elliott's hair one final time and signaled for Grant to close the coffin.

"Wait," Willa shouted. She ran out of the room and came skidding back with Elliott's broken glasses; she had glued the shattered lens together and the dark seams of mucilage made the one lens look like a miniature leaded window, the makeshift mullion emphasizing the irregular geometry of the break. One of the temples was held in place by a safety pin. "He needs these," she said hoarsely, handing them to Vienna and then turning away.

Sister, when she returned to The Heights to discover Elliott laid out barefoot in worn play clothes, had thrown a royal fit that, when she learned he was to be buried in a plain pine coffin on the property without benefit of a minister, had rapidly escalated to hysterics. Fortunately, this had coincided with Dr. Barstow's arrival to sign the death certificate, and while Sister had continued to shout, "I'll pay for it myself. No matter what it costs I want to see *something* done right around here," she had been given a morphine-based sedative that had prompted her to nap while the rest of the house hastened their efforts to bury Elliott before she reawoke and resumed her well-meant interference.

The heat wave of late October had broken during the two days of Elliott's unconsciousness, but no one had paid much attention to the dropping temperature until now, watching Grant dig open a wound in the earth. He paused to wipe his brow and he said to no one in particular, "I is right thankful cold's come. Day befo', this shovelin'd be twice as hot, and by day after tomorrow ground'll already be gettin hard to dig with temperatures keepin' on fallin' this way."

Fayette pulled a few wool pills from her sweater and said, "That's so." Turning to Vienna, she asked with maternal solicitude if she could fetch her anything. Vienna took a long while to answer, as if it were a complex question that required careful consideration, and after staring into the widening hole in which Grant stood up to his waist, she finally said, "No," and shifting her eyes away from the grave, looked at Willa as she continued to untangle slowly the difficult knot of her response, "but I'm sure we can oblige your husband with a beverage and a plate of whatever he likes, though. Your cheese biscuits, maybe."

Grant looked up at Fayette and smiled broadly. "Almost there," he said, but seeing only blank faces, he returned to his work without further effort at conversation.

The service was short; Vienna read I Corinthians 13, and part of Mozart's Requiem played from the porch until it was curtailed by a series of skips, the musical hiccups everyone except Grant understood as the result of grief like those that impeded Willa's selections from Genesis, "And out of the ground the Lord God formed every beast of the field, and every fowl of the air; . . . for out of it wast thou taken: for dust thou art, and unto dust shalt thou return." Then Fayette sang a spiritual, one that Elliott had loved for the huskiness it brought out in her voice. "It's so warm and chilling at the same time," Elliott had once said, in a complimentary effusion that had included a hug. Then it was over. Grant refilled the grave with the dark mound of earth and tamped it down with the flat side of the shovel. Willa hung from a branch that reached out toward Elliott the mobile Grayson had made for her, so that Elliott would always have a flight of birds encircling him, and then Fayette and Grant headed up to the circular drive, where Grant's wagon waited to take them home, the mules hungry and restless to be barned.

Willa trailed behind, feeling uncomfortable and awkward in the pink dress Sister had given her and she had outgrown while it hung in pristine condition in the dark of her armoire. The dress pinched in the arms and at the waist, and Willa irritably inserted her fingers under the smocking of one of the sleeves until the fabric gave and the seam ripped, freeing her puny biceps in such a satisfying way that she repeated the exercise immediately on the other sleeve.

"Fayette, are you coming tomorrow?" Willa called out. Grant was helping Fayette onto the cracked leather seat beside him. "No, honey, now you have Sister for a stay," Fayette said, looking back at The Heights. There had never seemed to be enough room in the large house for the both of them, and gradually a routine had been established whereby Fayette mostly kept away during Sister's visits, coming in only occasionally for the heavy cleaning, and to take laundry and mending home with her.

"Maybe she won't stay," Willa said, feeling tears well up.

"I don't know about that," Fayette replied, "but Vienna will send for me when it's time," and then, noticing the sprung sleeves of Willa's dress, she added, "Willa, baby, you change your clothes before Sister catches you shredding her finery."

Willa watched Fayette and Grant's slow departure; it was generally agreed that Grant's two mules were the slowest beasts a man had ever fed, but that, Fayette said, was a testament to the man's amazing patience, as if it were an honor he accepted every time he took up the reins.

When Fayette and Grant disappeared in the bend of the road, Willa went upstairs and without bothering to undress, got into Elliott's bed, between the sheets that had held his human heat, and there she fell asleep for almost sixteen hours.

On the way home, Grant asked Fayette if it was a legal funeral. "What'd you mean, legal?" she asked.

"Well it was just about the strangest ceremony I ever seen. I didn't know you could get to heaven like that."

"Get to heaven? Grant, that boy *was* heaven, and if the Good Lord won't take the likes of him, then it's not a place you or I want to be," Fayette said sharply, but she laid her head on his shoulder restfully and he let the subject drop. It wasn't worth mentioning that he had just assumed heaven, like earth, was segregated.

THAT NIGHT IT snowed. Unseasonably early, the light dusting set a precedent for mistrust that sent faithful farmers back to their almanacs two and three times, incredulous and unaccepting of the betrayal that was conspicuously omitted from the bleary print.

Sister was so hurt and angry about missing the funeral that she refused to visit the grave while Vienna was there, and Vienna was there through the night, sitting in Elliott's desk chair, a coat, two blankets, and a quilt wrapped around her, with Murphy at her feet, catching the falling flakes on his nose and tongue when he wasn't trying to exhume Elliott or cadge a sympathetic pat from his distracted companion.

Alone in the falling snow and gathering darkness, Vienna's carapace cracked like an ornamental veneer buckling from extremes of the weather. Her composure gave way to frightening wails and ululations of grief that set dogs howling in their kennels, straining on the chains that tethered them in backyards the way the scent of bear was supposed to do. Even with the thin cover of snow thickening the night and hampering the circulation of sound, there were few houses that were not awakened by the disturbing cries, thin with distance and haunting with pain. Lights flickered on and off in Winsville like the flashing signals of fireflies; a few sleepy curses were tossed out of windows and one or two confused queries remained unanswered.

Addison lay in the suffocating dark of his sleeping loft, rigid with sadness and sickened by guilt, ashamed of the harsh animal sounds that a beautiful woman could make. Only Willa, it seemed, slept through Vienna's disquieting lament.

Sister, who had fully intended to stay, found the night so excruciatingly difficult to witness that she repacked her large leather valise three times and systematically picked at the chicken casserole and the odd assortment of aging leftovers until the pantry was as bereft of sustenance as the raw sounds of Vienna's soul echoing in the emptiness of the interminable night.

24

$\mathcal{T}$RAGEDY IS A great leveler, and after what the town heard that night it was prepared to forgive Vienna, to let go its differences with her and welcome her to its core, accepting the death of Elliott as more of a comeuppance than they had ever intended in their desire to see her humbled. Condolences poured in, and with them, shy invitations and offerings.

Mr. Stepple, in his capacity as mayor of Winsville, had personally attended to quieting the fuss at the Bantanburg hospital, suggesting that, since Vienna was not pressing charges against them for the breach of security that had resulted in the abduction of her dying child, they would be best off letting the matter drop rather than disturbing the hornet's nest of legal inquiry by which they themselves might be stung.

Miss Margayt and Biddy Markham collected donations for a small brass plaque to be put up in the Episcopal church as a memorial to Elliott, and the Snead sisters had made a rare foray from their rooms to deliver their note to The Heights by hand. Mrs. Stepple wanted the post-office flag lowered to half-mast, but her husband, again in his capacity as mayor, had asked her to get a grip on herself, reminding her that the flag was official government property. Instead, Margaret Stepple had contented herself with a gesture she felt, with a certain competitive pride, outshone any other in originality and pathos: she tied all the dogwood trees in the town square with black grosgrain ribbon, so that the trees, now bare of all but their last leaves, looked like mournful wraiths wearing armbands.

But when Vienna at last appeared in town, it was clearly too late. She was far too distracted to notice or appreciate the considerations being made for her. Like a shellshocked soldier, she had retreated into a private damnation from which the concern of her neighbors was diminished to a frequency she could not register; urgent and earnest as the communication of crickets or bees, the language of the tiny complex tribes of insects that had fascinated her son, it was remote and inaudible, as vacuous as static. Elliott's absence, like a severed limb that continues to throb, preoccupied her, pushing out the animate world to the extreme and nebulous periphery of her attention.

Her pain was as consuming as a cancer. The sharp edge of her wit, the fierce demanding intelligence that had seemed so formidable, had been dulled, and her face had a strange softness about it that was hard to place, since the skin over the fine bones remained as taut as cellophane, and her thin frame was possibly thinner now. Biddy Markham, after the briefest encounter with Vienna on the sidewalk, had been shudderingly reminded of the vacant, gentle look the infamous Tim Bolling had returned with after a sojourn in the state mental hospital, where it was rumored unspeakable things had happened to produce his much-applauded transformation.

In Sadie's Notions, Vienna had asked to buy buttons. The girl behind the counter had asked her what size and color she was interested in, and when Vienna said, "All of them," the girl had gone to get Sadie from the back room, where she was going over the accounting ledgers.

"I'd like them all," Vienna repeated to Sadie, who was no

less perplexed than her salesgirl. "But Mrs. Daniels," Sadie had said, clearing her throat nervously, "there are over thirty-five boxes of buttons in stock."

"Yes please," Vienna said, and she opened her hand to reveal a thick wad of five-dollar bills. Sadie was conflicted by the dilemma this presented. While it would be an unanticipated boon to sell out her button inventory in one transaction, it would mean frustrating her other customers in the interim it took her to restock; moreover, she didn't want it to be said that she had taken advantage of Vienna Daniels' lapse in judgment while she was still clearly discombobulated by grief.

"Are you sure you need so many?" Sadie tried again. "That's an awful lot of buttons," she said kindly.

"Oh yes," Vienna replied. "They're for Elliott," she said with a wistful smile.

Sadie turned from the counter and discreetly brushed a tear from her eyelash, taking the salesgirl with her into the back room.

"Give Mrs. Daniels the buttons at cost. We'll make up for it somehow, maybe on the French ribbon that just came in, or the new zippers. And wrap the boxes up nicely." And then, resuming her mercantile professionalism, she added, "Do it now, before other customers come in and think I've become a Mennonite, and for mercy sake stop staring like a cow that swallowed a horsefly."

IT WAS BEAUTIFUL, Addison thought, fit for a monarch or magician, when Willa showed him the grave. Hanging from the maple trees by invisible threads, covering them with twirling spots of color, thousands of buttons decorated the old limbs, turning brightly in the numbing breeze. "It's a kind of mobile," Willa said simply, and then to fill the silence that followed, she added: "It's a thing they do a lot in France."

"It sort of looks French," Addison agreed, not sure what he meant but confident that French was synonymous with a special rarefied beauty.

"Which ones do you like best?" she asked, taking his hand and pulling him over to examine the lowest danglers twisting within reach.

"I don't know. Maybe the copper ones or silver ones, or no, this one. What is it, ivory?"

"Yeah, probably. Some kind of bone. Look at these, though. I like the pearly ones best, and then the satin-covered ones. That fuchsia up there with the black rim, you see it? That's a beautiful color. Doesn't it make you want to put it right in your mouth? And look next to it: that's shot silk, iridescent blue and purple, just like a peacock feather. The metal ones are too obvious, the way they shine and flash the light."

Addison, chastened by Willa's unthinking criticism of his taste, was only briefly hurt. She was right, of course, and looking at the tree again he saw it less as a gorgeous ornament—like the town Christmas tree swathed in dime-store tinsel—and more like an imagined wonderment, and it occurred to him, for the first time in his eleven-some years, that this, right before him, was art, and he, Addison Aimes, understood its subtle thrill, the ineffable frisson that made his neck tingle, unlike his reaction to the postcard reproductions of famous paintings he had thumbed through again and again at the bookstall in Kentucky, always disappointed to find he had soiled his fingers for nothing. The postcards had never prompted him to him feel anything but inadequate for feeling nothing; their elusive charms were lost on him. His sweaty pennies would buy him no sophistication or improvement there, and were better spent on candied apples and plastic whistles.

"You gave Vienna the idea," Willa said casually, nibbling the brown curl of a leaf. "Somewhere up there is the button you returned, but now it has a lot of company: the whole tree is blooming. All these little bursts of color, they're like tiny trumpets. Can you hear them?" she asked.

Addison nodded. "Your mother is *amazing*," he said, with a suddenness and force that embarrassed him, especially since Willa did not reply and Addison was left with the queasy sensation that he had said the wrong thing. As he walked beside her through the trees he comforted himself that at least he hadn't said *Willa* was amazing. Addison was learning to be grateful for small favors, and that his impetuous and candid mouth had not revealed him utterly was tantamount to a blessing.

"Let's run," Willa said and broke into flight like a spooked horse, kicking up leaves and tearing through the piles Mackie had only just finished raking the day before, with Addison gaining on her as she sprinted ahead, laughing, spending her energy in meaningless showy bursts, like a new millionaire taking the high road back to bankruptcy.

If Willa was spendthrift with her time as well, it did not seem to concern Vienna. There had been no suggestion of Willa's returning to school, and by her eleventh birthday Willa's curriculum of study was, with few exceptions, left to her own discretion. Addison, whom Mr. Aimes was compelling to stay in school through tenth grade in the great tradition of bettering the preceding generation, had mentioned that his new teacher, a Mr. Cavell, was "not a bad fellow at all."

But Willa wouldn't discuss school or anything relating to Redley Road. She spent her days lying on the camelback sofa in the living room, reading and listening to the radio, cutting up magazines and filling notebooks with encoded messages, collages, painstaking watercolors (for she no longer cared about preserving the perfect untouched integrity of her forty-eight-color paintbox), and most important of all, working on the project into which she concentrated her greatest effort, *The Encyclopedia of Lists,* a work which in her naïveté she put on a par with Johnson's dictionary.

Vienna applauded the direction and scope of her daughter's pursuits, offering editorial assistance and recommending texts, oblivious to the fact that the living room was littered with glasses of pastel-tinged water Willa had used to clean her brushes, as well as flecks of newsprint and shiny paper from magazines, the detritus of her endless clippings, slivers no larger than nail cuttings scattered everywhere, like confetti but without the festive association. Books Willa had abandoned lay open on the furniture like great broken-winged birds, their spines cracked and their pages crushed against a pillow or upright, fluttering helplessly on a footstool when the wind gushed through the double-height windows, billowing the curtains and dandling the corded silk fringe of the tassel pulls.

Now that Fayette was gone with Grant to Detroit, where relatives had lured them with grand promises of opportunities that would never be equaled in Winsville, The Heights had begun a slow degeneration from the ordered coziness it had known under Fayette's august housekeeping, the legerdemain by which she maintained consummate cleanliness without the imposition of any signs of effort. The idea of replacing Fayette had been unimaginable; her postcards were pinned to curtains, taped to mirrors, and propped on fireplace mantels, occupying the most prominent positions of honor Willa could find, and certainly the most eye-catching.

"It's a good thing Vienna taught her how to write," Willa had said casually, showing Addison the latest arrival, a scene of the towering Fisher building with its green roof lit up against the darkening night, but he could tell from the way she cradled the card how important it was to her.

Except for when she felt plain cabin crazy, Willa tried to save her roaming for the afternoons, when Addison would come to her directly from school and they would ramble through the fields, Murphy snapping at their heels and weaving excited circles around them until the light faded; then in the living room, despoiled of its former aspirations to formality, she would sweep clear a space on the sofa and help him with his homework.

After Elliott's death, Sister's visits became increasingly rare, brief and fraught with tensions that could no longer be contained under the ominously smooth surface of civility; now her stays were punctuated by open confrontations with Willa that left Sister sobbing in her bedroom, and occasioned long incoherent protestations of misdirected love and worry that followed from the safe retreat of Morgana, in small plump envelopes the same tallow color of her hands.

Willa delighted in shocking Winsville, as if the gasps of disapproval, the raised eyebrows, and expressions of consternation and disgust were a more palatable replacement for the pity Winsville longed to bestow. Toward this end, she cropped her waist-length hair with garden clippers, painted herself blue right down to her tennis shoes and walked into the Blue Star Luncheonette announcing, "Here I am, your long-lost star, and I'll have a cherry Coke please." When Amos refused to serve her, saying the fountain was closed, demanding that she leave at once before she left paint on the new counter stools, she laughed, and turning to Addison, said, "Let's go, buddy. Seems they discriminate against druids here. If they don't want colored customers, what can we do?"

LIKE A SELF-ASSIGNED town crier, Willa ran through Winsville shouting out the news she deemed important. She especially delighted in disasters, for then she would carry a strip of torn veiling she had found in one of the cedar chests in the attic and attached to a bamboo fishing rod, letting its black length furl behind her like a medieval banner of doom. In this rude way, Winsville citizens who did not own a radio, or listened only at night, first learned about the *Hindenburg* tragedy, Amelia Earhart's disappearance over the Pacific, the earthquake in Anatolia, and the death of a poet named Yeats.

When Willa announced that England had gone to war, Mrs. Stepple complained to Everett that "the little human radio" was going too far—she had no respect for the news she disseminated like a circus hawker, and there was no good reason Winsville had to be subjected to her political commentaries, no matter how brief and breathless. That, Mrs. Stepple felt, was exclusively the rightful domain of Will Rogers. But Everett, applying the skills he had so carefully honed in his many years in office, did nothing.

However, Willa's last bulletin, which she dispatched on an early December morning wearing nothing more than her slippers and a winter coat, brought the town out of their houses to gather incredulously around the weeping girl, who like a lachrymose Cassandra repeated over and again the unacceptable news that had Henshaw shaking her by the shoulders as if she alone could take back the blasphemous lie, the impending horror embedded in the words *Pearl Harbor*.

THE TREES IN Winsville's modest square began to languish, almost spitefully, in response to Vienna's neglect, for after Elliott's death she confined her care only to those trees on her own acres, avoiding the town even to the extent of having Hegemony do the grocery shopping for The Heights at the same time she bought Mr. Aimes's provisions. It was almost a year before anyone noticed that the leaves were withering and stunted, and it wasn't until two of the dogwoods died that anyone cared to discover what disease was blighting the formerly exuberant plantings.

An expert was brought in from Bantanburg to make a diagnosis, and after several months and an exorbitant fee it became clear to those following the demise of the dogwoods that nothing had been gained by hiring Heck's Tree Service. The following spring, three more dogwoods died, and a rumor began to circulate among the more fanatical followers of Reverend Will that, as per standard biblical practice, the trees were dying for the unrepented sins of the town; the stark winter silhouettes were pointed reminders, amidst the shouting lushness of lawns, the promiscuous groping of honeysuckle and clematis, the rowdy imposition of Virginia creeper and gangling weeds, of the foreboding disfavor into which the town had fallen. The dead trees, it was said, harbinged as certainly as hailstones in July the drought, pestilence, and eclipse of locusts that would follow if sufficient atonement was not made.

Although Reverend Will's followers comprised a fringe minority, the aspersions of guilt cast a shadow wide enough to make most of Winsville uneasy, anxious to denounce Reverend Will and at the same time exonerate themselves as among the few excluded from the sweep of his pointing finger.

"It's because we all have a child's blood on our hands," Biddy Markham said, but Henshaw, weighing out some furniture nails, had dismissed this with unusual asperity: "Superstitious twaddle," he said, "just to make us feel bad at a time when we have more than enough to make us miserable. And another thing too: I didn't have anything to do with that boy's death. I was right here stacking sacks of grain and no one can say otherwise, so you can count me out of the Apocalypse."

Miss Margayt, who was waiting patiently for a quarter's

worth of birdseed, spoke out from the small line that was forming during Henshaw's peroration, her dry voice overloud and nervous, "No one will be counted out of the Apocalypse, Mr. Henshaw, but the righteous."

Mr. McCrory, tilting back a dirty felt hat, said, "Well there goes Winsville, I guess," and the small crowd laughed, Henshaw heartiest of all, slapping the counter and snorting, "You got that right," but as she took her dollar's worth of brass upholstery nails, Biddy Markham had said, "Don't be so literal. Everything is a metaphor, or there wouldn't be any poetry in the world around us." When this was recounted to Sophronius Moody, he choked down the chocolate he was sampling and stroked his hair—the only thinning part of him, it received a good deal of affection—and, reflecting on Miss Markham's words, said somberly, "Maybe that's why I have never had much use for poetry."

Sophronius had long ago stopped conjuring with large perplexing questions. He had adopted a secret philosophy, akin to his belief that only foul-tasting medicines or cures that were painful had any restorative value, which enabled him to navigate his world with confidence because he understood his position in the mysterious hierarchy of the heavens: he was simply, irrefutably and irrationally, guilty. When a car stalled on Center Street or someone dropped a package in the mud, Sophronius felt a twinge of responsibility devolve to him; if the driver had not slowed to return his wave or if he had seen to it that the customer had counted his change before leaving, nothing untoward would have happened. Since the rumors about the trees started, Sophronius had not had a good night's rest or a satisfying bowel movement, and even sugar, his faithful anodyne, was failing to provide the requisite comfort he counted on.

Mr. Overby, on a drunk, declared that it was the Daniels

woman working her black arts, adding that his tomato plants had suffered because of her too, and that one day he'd get even, but no one ever took Mr. Overby seriously. It was taxing enough just to tolerate the way he mistreated his mules and children.

Mrs. Stepple had worried her husband late one night with the notion that perhaps he should have had charges brought for the incident at Redley Road, as it was euphemistically referred to. Everett Stepple had turned away from his wife and crushed the pillow into a tight wad under his head and his words in the dark room were impatient and bitter.

"Just who do you suppose I should have charged? A twelve-year-old boy who pushed a playmate to the ground? We could have every boy under twenty in the clink for that. Or maybe we should have arrested his bankrupt father, barely keeping those Veens fed, for having produced such an unlucky sullen son. Or how about Miss Dobbs, the most devoted teacher this town has ever lost? Margaret, please, let me sleep. It is the least a man can expect in his own bed."

25

---

*A*DDISON, HABITUATED BY years of accompanying Willa so inseparably that they had been dubbed "the sweet-and-sour twins," had little trouble dodging the glances for which they were a moving target when they walked together down Center Street. He had readily exchanged Winsville's acceptance for membership in the exclusive world the Daniels women inhabited, though Vienna had warned him, with what he felt was an especially winning smile, that it was a Faustian bargain at best.

After five years of close association with the Daniels, Addison had grown six inches, measuring just over six feet in darned wool socks on the morning of his sixteenth birthday. He could play a miserable rendition of "Für Elise" on the piano, identify anaphora and pleonasm in the speeches of Churchill, and had read fifteen Dickens novels, the only noteworthy omission being *David Copperfield*, seven Shakespearean tragedies, and could recite a line or two of Tennyson. For all of this his father was, in his restrained way, proud and grateful. The inclusion his son had experienced had been balanced by even greater remoteness toward himself dating from the night Elliott died. While he had hoped that his bold display of valiance at the hospital would have endeared him to Vienna, it seemed to have estranged her beyond recall.

When he was feeling more benevolent, and refraining from the seductive pleasures of self-laceration and doubt, Mr. Aimes posited that grief had interposed itself between him and Vienna. He took solace in the vicarious intimacy afforded by his son's proximity to her love, and conceded in odd moments of reflection that it was through them that he had learned to love and need Addison, and it was for this reason that Mr. Aimes indulgently excused him from chores on weekends, that Addison could better devote himself to the whimsical delights offered by the Daniels.

Willa had grown too, but it was easier for Winsville to measure the change in wildness rather than inches. At fifteen, her hair had grown back and darkened to a deep rust that even henna could not match, though Marlene Overby had tried twice, unsuccessfully, to imitate the color, before settling on the peroxide treatments that eventually caused portions of her hair to fall out. If local preachers ever needed to illustrate the dichotomy between appearance and reality, no more vivid example came to mind than the wide-eyed, willowy Daniels girl, whose fragile features and Christmas-card smile belied a temperament keen on trouble and who had already learned to use her looks as an effective foil in the creation of mischief to which she attended so dutifully.

Most Saturdays, Willa and Addison thumbed their way to Bantanburg for the pleasure of escaping the confines of Winsville, and once their tour through the five-and-dime, McCray's Department Store, and Parker's Used Books and Music had been completed, they often found themselves at the movie palace, studying the lobby posters and arguing about whether or not to invest in the show.

They had seen *The Lady Vanishes* three times, *49th Parallel* and *Citizen Kane* twice, and *The Wizard of Oz*, two Chaplin, and one Marx Brothers film once, because Willa had decided that with the exception of Carol Lombard movies, she didn't like comedies and she was not apologetic about imposing her tastes on Addison. That same year she had decided that she would read only the works of dead authors, beginning with a memorial retrospective of Fitzgerald's oeuvre, to be followed by Thomas Wolfe; Addison's refusal to abandon Raymond Chandler just because he still breathed was felt to be something of a defection.

They had also argued viciously over which death was more devastating to the country's morale, Lou Gehrig's or Carole Lombard's. Addison had learned, however, that the impassioned discussions in front of the glittering marquees were merely formal debating challenges, for after the newsreels of Allied accomplishments, Willa often fell asleep on his shoulder. The relaxed weight of her head was an exquisite distraction few directors could compete with and when she awoke in the second or third reel of the feature, whispering episodes from her dreams to him, he later found them fused with the movie in his memory.

Early in their friendship he had impulsively kissed her following her first disclosure about Elliott. They had been gathering their towels after a swim in the creek, and, seeing the roller-coaster undulations of a common monarch butterfly, Willa had recalled that Elliott, in his infancy, had called them "flutterbys." That revelation had prompted the unpracticed peck that landed a little too hard on Willa's unreceptive lips. Willa had wiped her mouth with her arm, made an expression of disgust, and kicked him swiftly in the shin. He had not repeated the experiment in the intervening years, but he had appropriated in his mind's eye isolated body parts, in an unsatisfying compromise between stoking the feverish fantasies with which he put himself to sleep and according Willa the respect she deserved as the object of his devotion—and, more important, mollifying her mother, whom Addison still believed, in a visceral way he could not banish with reasoning intellect, knew everything.

The situation was, in Addison's heightened perception, verging on crisis. Recently, Willa had taken his hand to examine a fingernail blackened by a hasty hammer stroke inflicted while mending the door on his father's chicken coop. As she held his hand in her own, her feathery touch had, in its delicate effort to avoid paining him, made him so acutely uncomfortable that when she had lifted his thumb to her mouth to lick the dried blood from under the nail he had jerked his hand away as if she had held it in fire. He had ached for hours afterward, entirely unmindful of his thumb. Their Sunday explorations of the no-trespassing areas of Winsville's environs were becoming a torturous minefield of accidental contact, and, feeling that he could no longer endure the tantalizing burn of her grazing skin, and having found the remains of Old Duda's shack, Addison had begun to formulate a plan to advance their friendship in a more carnal direction.

It was imperative that the plan be implemented swiftly, not only because of the urgency of Addison's desire, but because of the increasingly troubling attention Addison was receiving from Marlene Overby when he ventured into Winsville without Willa. Marlene's reputation had only descended from the low it had reached when she gave birth at twelve and a half to a sickly baby that had immediately died of influenza. It had been hoped that, while it would be impossible to regain her childhood, Marlene would at least retrieve some dignity after the baby's death, and make reparations to the disadvantages her honor had suffered by being an Overby, which she couldn't help, and by having

disgraced herself, which presumably she could have prevented. The childless Trayfords had taken Marlene into their
home in a generous attempt to improve her, an arrangement
Mr. Overby had welcomed as it relieved him of an open
mouth at the oversubscribed kitchen table, but Marlene had
proved impervious to the Trayfords' morality.

Her wantonness was legend, and made for any number of
lascivious jokes best enjoyed by adolescents. Addison had heard
that a pack of chewing gum and a lipstick, or a pair of nylons
or a two-dollar bill was enough to secure an option on her
natural resources. Hitherto, Addison had felt sorry for Marlene;
she had no friends and was the subject of childish pranks:
bruised bananas and dried corncobs with wax-candy lips
shoved on the tapered tip would be left at the Trayfords' door
and condoms swollen with water had been thrown at her from
a moving car. The sight of her bleached hair tied up in a
ferociously loud bow and the ridiculous high heels she wobbled
around in made her look cartoonish, but the tight set of her
lips and the expression prematurely graven on her seventeen-
year-old face had disgusted Addison, until now. It was not that
she was offering her services for free that tempted him—the
pecuniary nature of the transaction had not been what had
deterred Addison in the past. It was the unrelenting way in
which she played on his desperation for Willa that was proving
increasingly hard to resist.

The last time he had seen Marlene she was sitting behind
Mr. Bisbee's corncrib, eating candied popcorn. "Hey Addison," she called out.

"Hey Marlene," he called back.

"Ain't you gonna stop and be friendly?" she said, dropping
the rhinestone-studded sunglasses from her forehead to the
bridge of her nose.

"I guess," Addison said irritably. Her perch was visible to

the road and it annoyed him to think he might be seen lingering beside her.

"What do you think of my sunglasses?" she asked flirtatiously.

"I think they're nice."

The answer disappointed Marlene and she removed the sparkling frames to study them herself. "They are genuine movie-star glasses. I know because I paid for them myself."

"They're nice" Addison repeated.

"You ever read this book?" Marlene continued, trying another tack and pointing to a copy of *Gone with the Wind* that lay closed at her feet.

"Can't say I have, Marlene. Is it like *Ben Hur*? I read that."

"Uh-huh, sort of, but it's got more female fashions in it."

"Oh," Addison replied, looking anxiously at the road, "I'll keep that in mind." Addison was fairly oblivious of fashion— he didn't know the difference between a peplum and a pocket, but he *had* noticed that Willa was beginning to wear dresses.

Marlene, sensing his impatience, stood up abruptly, letting her bag of sweets spill on the ground. "You don't have to be a virgin, you know," she said, hoping to sound seductive but her delivery was freighted with desperation.

"That's none of your business, and who says I am anyhow?"

Marlene laughed and reached her shellacked fingers down to the bottom of his fly. "He says so," she answered, applying a slight pressure to his groin.

"Cut it out," Addison said, flicking her hand off him, but she repositioned it on his shoulder, pushing her fingertips up behind his ear.

"You don't have to be afraid, I won't tell anyone if you go with me once. Besides, don't you want some experience for your sweetheart? Girls appreciate that, lemme tell you."

Addison pulled away from her and hurried back to the road,

but with his loins still tingling against the friction of his denim trousers, it was hard not to feel the persuasive sway of her logic, which seemed almost to justify a solitary betrayal of Willa in the name of his long-standing love for her.

THERE WAS ANOTHER reason too, for the urgency of his conquest. Willa's restlessness and contempt for Winsville were increasing dangerously; like a talent that grows bored with the amateur opportunities for displaying gifts that have outgrown their circumstance, Willa's ambitions exceeded the boundaries of Winsville. Having none of her mother's hard-earned loyalty to their land, she viewed Vienna as the last link that held her in town.

More and more, Willa's confidences returned to elaborately detailed plans of escape. They always included Addison, and, if it came down to it, he was prepared to leave with her on a moment's notice, but he maintained the hope that the awesome and perhaps infinite powers of sex would reconcile Willa to a few more stationary years, keeping her home at least until he was drafted.

Summer was upon them and with it the humid heat that drove them like lemmings to the back of Duffield's bakery, where they would immerse their arms and faces in the open flour barrels and then repair to the quarry to rinse off the absorbent powder that made them look like miners in reverse, photographic negatives.

"Why don't we swim naked anymore?" Addison asked Willa at the quarry. "We used to."

"That's right, but I was flatter than you then," Willa said, pulling her wet dress away from her chest and peering down into its hold. "I'm working on a pair of breasts now that no one's going to see until they're finished."

"Come on, Willa," Addison urged, "I'll tell you if they're done yet."

"Nope," she said. "Just stay there for a minute. I'll be right back." Releasing her wet shift to suck back against her flesh, insinuating her contours in the darkened cloth, she scrambled into a thicket. Addison listened to the stream of her urine splattering on the dry ground, and when she returned, combing out her hair with her fingers, he excused himself and followed her trail back into the woods. He found the damp stain she had left in the dust and studied its shape as if it hid the potent archetypal meaning of a Rorschach blot. Then he unzipped his trousers and carefully covered her pee with his own, like a dog marking territory, superstitiously believing that gestures like this would guarantee them a life together as surely as an accepted proposal of marriage.

In the restlessness of summer, Saturdays were no longer the only times Willa turned to Addison saying, "Let's go covet," and when he returned to the water's edge she linked her arm in his, tugging on him for a trip to Bantanburg to stare greedily at the window displays and storefronts. Their clothes had dried stiffly on their bodies before they got a ride in the back of a pickup, but Willa's excitement was undiminished, and she pulled two sticks of chalk from her pocket, smiling wickedly.

Willa's most recent obsession had been to cover the sides of barns, the weather-torn façades of billboards, and the black canvas of paved roads with the graffiti, "Ducky Lives." Addison had assisted in a number of such guerrilla forays before he learned that "Ducky" was not a deliberately meaningless word chosen to frustrate the county's human inclination to yearn for meaning, but the nickname Willa had given Elliott when he was learning to walk and had used thereafter in moments of uncompromised affection. It had also become the basis for the private joke she and Elliott shared; though the humor was lost on Addison, Willa had laughed herself red in the face repeating, "Ducky had animal magnetism, get it?"

It hadn't mattered to Addison that, in fact, he didn't. Because Willa rarely indulged the giddy simplicity of silliness, it made him happy just to watch her blink away the tears of childish hilarity. When he first befriended Willa, he had told her a dirty limerick that had seemed at the time the apex of daring wit; the culminating rhyme was "whore ass." Willa's response had been to squint suspiciously at him and inquire who he was referring to, Horace the Roman poet or Horus the Egyptian god; remembering this, Addison smiled to himself, recalling the fear he had let germinate that they would never share a laugh. Looking back, it seemed incredible that he should ever have worried about the laughter that came so easily to them and which he took for granted now that he was desirous of sharing more forbidden pleasures.

He caught the chalk nub she tossed him across the truck and put it in his pocket for later. Megaphoning his hands around his mouth, he shouted over the noise of the engine and the metallic vibration of the flatbed, "I forgot to tell you: Jack Markham's studying French."

"Jesus H. Christ," Willa shouted back, "isn't English grammar enough of a second language for him?" and then the truck quivered to a stop and they jumped off the back and thanked the driver as he turned onto the highway that ran behind Bantanburg.

Staring at the jewelry display on the second floor of McCray's, Willa picked up the conversation they had abandoned as she tried on a selection of rings to the pouty annoyance of the salesgirl.

"Who'd you hear that from, about Little Jack?"

"Biddy Markham. She's fearsome proud of her nephew, which just proves how blind love is."

"Or bored," Willa said, plucking the rings from her fingers and dropping them like spare change in the cup of the salesgirl's hands.

"Are you ready?" she asked Addison.

"I'm waiting on you. Want to check to see if the map's been sold?"

"Genius idea."

"We had better hurry because it's going to close any minute," Addison said as he stepped around a mannequin, extending his hand behind him for Willa to catch hold of. K.C.'s Collectibles, two blocks away, was full of musty attic refuse, but it was one of their favorite browsing places. K.C. had a cigar box full of old war medals that Addison liked to poke through, and Willa was taken with an old map in a baroque gilt frame. The mat surrounding the map was speckled with brown age freckles, which had only endeared it to Willa. "Just like an old lady," she had said, seeing it for the first time. They had visited it regularly since then; each time Willa noticed something else about its allegorical depiction.

In the upper right, there was a forest labeled V*anity* and the center of the composition was divided by a rushing river, A*mbition*, in which fantastical sea monsters raised their heads appealingly. A range of mountains appropriately labeled *Hope* rose just beyond the chasm labeled *Despair*, and smaller details scattered throughout the scenery depicted false love, misplaced trust, and the Seven Deadly Sins. From the upper-right and lower-left corners two tiny lovers in medieval costume embarked on the treacherous journey to the center heart, an area labeled *Happiness*, but no larger than a fingernail.

Willa wanted the map desperately, but it cost over a hundred dollars; K.C. said it was *the* really good thing in his store. K.C. was a tiny man who had been to France, claimed to know Mrs. Wally Simpson *personally* and talked pompously about decor, ending sentences with ellipses. He swaddled his neck in cravats, smoked Lucky Strikes through a jeweled holder, and wore a Japanese wedding kimono in place of a smoking jacket when he presided over his establishment. He was fond of Willa, called her "darling" and "my Botticelli baby," but his indifference to Addison was marked. Addison was jealous of the unctuous compliments and insignificant gifts K.C. pressed on Willa. When Willa had first pronounced K.C. "a character," Addison was quick to disagree.

"He's a phony and a queer."

"So what? That just makes him more interesting."

Addison conceded, in the interest of reconciliation, that K.C. was unusual, and since he liked Willa he was O.K., but secretly the way K.C. wiggled his itty-bitty beringed fingers made Addison want to mash them with a heavy book.

The map was still there, and after a few minutes of breathing on its protective glass, Willa and Addison were shooed out by K.C., who wanted to lock up.

"I don't want much, but what I want, I want so hard it's like to give me apoplexy," Willa said, as they walked down an alley looking for an inviting surface on which to scratch their obscure message.

"I have a gift for you," Addison answered, pausing to pull out of his pocket a silver charm on a thin link chain. "I wish it could have been the map."

Willa took the tiny angel, not much larger than a mosquito, and rotated it gently in her fingers.

"It's really beautiful, Addison," she said, "I love it; it's so damn delicate it's making my veins hum."

"I swiped it for you from McCray's."

"Thank you," she said, "that makes it extra special. But you can never steal again now or it will diminish its importance."

"I won't," Addison said sheepishly, avoiding her eyes. "I don't even know why I did it this time."

"I do, because it made the present that much more extravagant and daring. Sort of like the map, in a way, full of Spenserian courtliness and grandeur. Help me put it on."

Willa flipped her hair forward and pulled it up in a loose knot to clear her neck while Addison fumbled with the necklace's clasp. He stood behind her and secured the chain, feeling dizzied by the prospect of her slender neck bowed within inches of his lips, white as the skin in daguerreotypes, the autumn bouquet of her hair gathered in her arms, and he suddenly wanted her so much that it made him angry. He fleetingly imagined pulling the chain sharply against her neck the way you would check a horse with a harsh jerk of the reins.

"I love you, Addison," she said, turning to face him, and he was so shocked by the moment he had spent so long preparing for that he was rendered dumb; by the time he had recovered himself, she was busy scrawling large letters on a brick wall, and he hadn't had a chance to say the words he had been choking back for years.

26

$\mathcal{O}$NE NIGHT IN September, as the Germans entered Stalingrad, Addison kissed Willa twice, and the second time she parted her lips slightly. That winter was characterized by hardship, unusual cold, and rationing: shoes, then meat, cheese, fats, and canned goods, none of which was as difficult for Addison to bear as the frugal way Willa, with a stringency that far surpassed any measures taken by Roosevelt, rationed her kisses, which had blossomed in the bleak months of scattered snow and bluish-white desolation into deep, open feverish cabbage roses of lips and tongues and breathlessness.

By the Allied landing in Sicily, the days were scorching and the cornstalks were tall enough to hide a grown man. Willa had turned sixteen, and Addison had persuaded her to sleep with him. The remains of Duda's shack had been chosen for the location, and Willa arrived late, full of complaints. *The Encyclopedia of Lists* was proving a frustrating and endless task: her entry under *translucence*, for example, included aspic, mosquito wings, stained glass, and silk chiffon, but twenty items was the minimum she insisted on for each entry. Moreover, she was the only girl in the world who didn't know how to jitterbug or Lindy Hop, even the Lambeth Walk had passed her by; John Donne's clever conceits were getting on her nerves; Walter Lippmann had not responded to her letter, and Murphy, in a rare demonstration of incontinence, had soaked the three maps on which she was charting the course of the war, filling her bedroom with the permeating stink of ammonia.

Addison had the temerity to suggest that perhaps she was feeling nervous and Willa had asked irritably, "What exactly is that supposed to mean? Maybe I should go home and read a few chapters of *The Psychopathology of Everyday Life*, or do you think Boethius's *Consolation of Philosophy* would be more to the point?" They stared angrily at each other as Willa sat on the floor and smoked a cigarette self-consciously, blowing smoke rings through a spider's web that hung between the legs of an overturned table.

Finally, Addison spoke. "What do you want, Willa?" Letting the tears trickle down her face she said, "I don't know. I want to be happy. I want to leave Winsville, I want Fayette to come back. She's the only friend Vienna ever had, and I want Vienna to finish her damn epic. I want you to love me forever and I want to stop missing Elliott. I want to stop feeling hollow and useless, like an echo no one can hear."

Willa paused to blow her nose on her fingers and wipe them on the wall behind her. She smiled and added, "I wouldn't mind a typewriter and a pair of satin pumps and unspeakable wealth either."

Crouching over her like an ambulance medic ministering to the injured, Addison whispered, "I can hear you. You echo inside me, Willa. You always have, and it's the best, most beautiful sound I've ever heard."

"No bullshit, Addison?" Willa hiccuped.

"No bullshit."

"Well in that case, let's kiss. I think we could steam up these broken windows if we really try."

Undressed and lying on the cool dirt floor with a scattered

pallet of straw beneath him, Addison failed to get an erection. "I don't get it," he apologized, "I've been practicing for years and this has never happened."

"Well, goddamnit, you're making me feel ugly," Willa said, standing up. "This wouldn't happen if you were with that diseased skank, Marlene Overby." She flung back the ill-fitting door and stood glowing in the warp of the doorjamb, a rush of light pouring around her into the dark room.

"Come away from the door. Someone could happen by and see you naked."

Willa didn't move. The afternoon sun felt almost as good on her skin as the warm water of the quarry. "You sound like Sister now, and no one is going to happen by. That's why we chose this place, remember?" Then she twirled on her toes in an improvised ballet step and said, "I'm hungry."

"I'm miserable," Addison answered from the ground, one arm flung over his eyes, "but if you want to eat, there are some boiled eggs and buttered rolls in my rucksack."

"Don't be miserable," Willa said, sitting cross-legged beside him with the rucksack next to her. "Have an egg."

Addison shook his head, but he sat up to watch Willa eat two rolls in quick succession.

"Willa, I can't stand for you to feel anything less than gorgeous. Even with butter smeared on your nose you're prettier than half the starlets in Hollywood."

Willa put down the remaining half of her roll and walked her fingers over the freckles on Addison's chest asking, "Yeah, but what about Marlene Overby?"

"She's a skank. She can't hold a candle to a dog's vomit," Addison answered, trying to catch her hand, but she pulled it away, grinning. He had said just the right thing and her satisfaction was intense. She curled her toes to diffuse the shrill delight of his words and leaning her face over his, said, "Why don't you lick the butter off my nose, sailor?"

ADDISON FELL ASLEEP with his leg over Willa, exhausted by the triumph of consummation, while Willa sang softly to herself a half-remembered Scottish lullaby. Feeling her bladder uncomfortably swollen under Addison's hip, she wriggled out from beneath him and went outside to squat in front of a stalk of Queen Anne's lace that grew incongruously amid the abandoned decay of the yard.

Returning to Addison, she shook him awake, her eyes wide with apprehension.

"Addison, I'm bleeding and you're broken."

Addison yawned and pulled her against him for another kiss, but she pushed away. "Baby, I'm serious. Look down before you decide if you'll ever kiss me again."

Addison rose up on an elbow and surveyed his loins. There was a thin smear of diluted blood on his penis and inner thigh, but he had expected that. "What are you talking about?" he asked her, looking not at her face but at the small breasts that seemed "done" just right.

"Look at the way your thing is shriveled at the end. We must have done something wrong. It's disfigured." Realizing she was in earnest, Addison sat up and examined his penis. "Did you ever see Elliott's dickie?" he asked.

"Sure thing, about a hundred thousand times. He used to write my name in the snow when he pee-peed because his name had too many letters."

Addison pulled the foreskin back on his flaccid penis and asked, "Did it look like this?"

"Uh-huh. It did," Willa said. "Something like that."

"Well, that just means he was circumcised and I'm not. Mine is *supposed* to look like this. Hell, Willa, we used to swim together in the buff once upon a time."

"I guess I didn't pay much mind to your body back then, I was so stuck on your personality. Say, would you do that again?"

"This?" Addison said, indulgently repeating the retraction of his foreskin.

"I never realized how much they look like turtles' heads, with those wrinkly collars."

Addison laughed. "Willa darling, you sure know how to say the most romantic things."

Willa laughed too, rolling over on her back, enjoying the relief of being childish together until she got a stitch in her side and sat up, feeling restless again. "We had better get back. I don't want Vienna to worry."

"You're sitting on my shirt."

Willa leapt up, pulling her dress over her head and quickly buttoning the side of it. "I think I got blood on your shirt. What are you going to tell your father if he asks about it?"

"He won't," Addison answered, bending over his rucksack in his workpants and one sock. Straightening up, he reached out to pick a straw from her hair. "I can't find my other sock."

"What will you give me for it?" Willa asked impishly.

"A sack of gold," Addison said, putting his arms into the bloodstained shirt.

"What if that's not enough?"

"Pearls from the Orient. A diamond tiara and that volume of Colette you've been hankering for."

"You found it? When?" Willa said, clapping her hands with acquisitive excitement.

"Couple days ago. It's in French just like you wanted."

Willa's rule about dead authors did not extend to works in other languages and lately she had been burning through the Claudine series, working her vocabulary up to take on Proust.

"Addison, you are heroic and handsome to boot," Willa cooed, and Addison, pulling on the sock she handed him, just scratched his ankle and beamed at her.

"You want to get married?" he asked her when they reached the road.

"What do you mean," she said, skipping ahead of him.

"You know perfectly well what I mean. Have a family with a couple of kids, like the Nostrils," he said seriously, walking in long strides.

"It's pronounced Nöse-trill, and the O has an umlaut," Willa said, circling back to him, like Murphy did. "Anyway, they came to a bad end."

"I know, you told me when you showed me the dollhouse, but that doesn't mean we would."

"You're plumb crazy, boy. You're only seventeen and a half. You won't be legal for another six months. And I have even longer."

"I didn't mean we'd get married now. We could just be engaged."

"I thought we already were."

"All right then, it's a deal. Hey, did I tell you that I love you?"

"I don't believe you did, or not enough at any rate," Willa answered, darting off again.

Walking behind her pirouettes in the gathering dusk, hearing the sliding notes of a veery, Addison thought he had gotten all he ever wanted. He felt expansive, as if his soul were spreading out like pollen on the warm evening air.

WHEN WILLA RETURNED to The Heights she found Vienna on the porch shucking corn, the blind horse standing beside her nosing at the husks.

"What's Ulyssa doing up here on the porch?" Willa asked.

"She must have gotten out of her pasture—that fence is rotted and I know I should have had it replaced, but it always seemed such a joyless way to spend money, when I thought of the books it could buy, or clothes for you. Anyway, I guess Ulyssa just wanted some companionship or smelled the sweetness of these cobs Mr. Moody brought by while you were out. She came shambling up the steps as if she expected to be invited to dine with us."

"And you just let her stay? She's pooped on the top step, for Christsake!"

"Of course I let her stay. I couldn't turn her away after she made such a perilous journey, sightless as Lear or Milton, but with a much more winning disposition than either. You'll never hear a gloomy diatribe from Ulyssa. I gave her the rest of the oatmeal teacakes that you thought were getting stale and she was most appreciative. I also read her the final couplet of my epic."

"You finished? Really? You're not pulling my leg, are you?"

The news made Willa slightly queasy, because even more than the loss of her virginity it marked a turning point, a separation between then and now that had an unpleasant finality to it, the irrevocable closure she had wished for when it seemed an impossible abstraction. She cursed her own culpability for having spoken aloud the wish she had been granted, which now cut loose the moorings of all the dependable assumptions that had provided a sense of security to the precarious lives they improvised together. The completion of the work that had occupied her mother for as long as Willa had been sentient was a horrible blow, staggering as a sudden death.

"Congratulations," she said without spirit. "How are we going to get her down the steps without a lead?"

"I haven't thought about it yet," Vienna answered, putting the last cob in the metal bowl at her feet. "She likes candy. You could always bribe her."

Willa pushed the horse's flank out of her way and went into the house. Inside, she lurched into the bathroom and vomited watery brown bile into the toilet bowl, watching it swirl slowly down the porcelain neck. She flushed the toilet two more times and then washed her face and hands and went into her room and flung open the window with more violence than was necessary.

In one of her desk drawers she found half a roll of Life Savers, which she took downstairs and fed to the horse two at a time, coaxing it step by step, bracing herself against its front shoulder so that it wouldn't stumble down the stairs. Then she put her arm over Ulyssa's neck, and holding the stiff, graying mane loosely in her hand, she walked the horse back to the barn and put it in an empty stall. She refilled the feed bucket, though the horse was tending to plumpness from lack of exercise and frequent meals; she freshened the water in the trough and then brushed out the forelock, mane, and tail. She didn't bother going over Ulyssa's coat with the currycomb, because it looked as if Addison had done it that morning. The huge cloudy eyes turned to her gratefully. Willa nuzzled briefly against Ulyssa's slobbering jaws and then left the barn, kicking over a tin pail that was in her way.

"We have to do something about the rats," she said to Vienna, who was moving around the kitchen in a disorganized fashion, leaving unfinished piles of culinary endeavor scattered everywhere in her attempts to make their evening meal.

"Of course we will, just as soon as we finish celebrating," Vienna said, distracted by the three pots boiling on the stove at once, as if she couldn't remember which one it was she wanted at that moment.

"What are you thinking of for a celebration?" Willa asked, tipping her chair back on its hind legs.

"Something truly dazzling. I thought I'd give Hegemony some money to buy us champagne. I don't think I've had liquor since it became legal, so it must be over a decade. Hand me the peppermill? I'm not sure where to go from there. Do you have any ideas?"

"You could have a party," Willa offered, summoning a spark of enthusiasm.

"Brilliant suggestion. We could string the porch with Japanese lanterns—there are dozens in a box in the blue barn. I think there are a few bolts of chintz, too; we could wrap up the pillars and loop garlands from the eaves. Willa honey, it sounds heavenly. I'm feeling the giddy swoon of dance music in my temples already."

Willa imagined the glorious mythical pageantry of her mother's patrician childhood with the fashionable families of New York, names she knew first from her mother's stories and later from their occasional appearances in the newspapers, conjuring up a splendor no less remote than the lyrical descriptions of the Round Table in Tennyson's *Idylls of the King*.

It had always seemed to her improbably fitting that Vienna had, by twenty, experienced the glamor touted by magazines and movie stars as the essence of romance, slept in hilltop castles in Italy, chatted with European nobility across banquet tables, and waltzed in the gilded ballrooms of ocean liners. It was as if her mother had squandered the quota of excitement allotted to her life early on, and for that reason accepted with such equanimity the dreariness of Winsville, without availing herself of any of the familiar comforts other women took in mundane luxuries like trips to the beauty parlor or milliner's, dress shops or matinees. Though she was not yet forty, Vienna's austere presentation aged her. The blond hair she braided around her head, like, Willa said, Miss Havisham, was streaked with white, and though Willa had tried to share a newfound interest in lipstick and night cream, Vienna had no use for cosmetics.

"So who are you going to invite?" Willa asked, admiring nonetheless her mother's stark beauty.

"What's that?" Vienna said, putting down a paring knife.

"The guests."

"What guests?"

"Friends, for your party," Willa prompted.

Vienna stared at her for a moment in uncomprehending silence and then she drew in her breath and said simply, "I don't have any friends."

The thrill of burgeoning hope fizzed out of Willa like the air released from a balloon in the withering spiral throes of deflation, and the parade of Christmases and birthdays commemorated *à deux* rushed to mind, filling Willa with unspeakable depression.

"It's not important. We'll do fine ourselves. We always have," Willa said without emotion, the tips of her ears burning, defeat and dread stiffening the hair on the back of her head.

"We always have," Vienna echoed cheerfully.

27

THE DAY OF Vienna's party a stranger came to town. Henshaw gave her directions to The Heights himself. He assumed, because of the way she was dressed, and the thick Spanish accent in which she spoke, that she was looking for work, and he would have told her that Mrs. Daniels hadn't hired any household help for a handful of years, to spare her the walk there and back, since "she seemed wore out already," but he kept his tongue. The square, with all of the dogwoods dead, had the grim look of a cemetery—even the pots of lobelia, added for color and to distract from the deadwoods were reminiscent of the floral offerings that decorated tombstones. It seemed prudent not to interfere with anything relating to the Daniels.

Vienna was on a wooden stepladder draping the paper lanterns in graceful swags between the posts when the woman came up the drive, covered in a thin film of dust from the road, looking parched as a dry riverbed, as if her appearance reflected the wide, exposed landscape she came from.

"Where do I find Mrs. Daniels?" she asked impatiently, clicking off her words like the wooden beads of a rosary.

"You have found her. I am she," Vienna said briskly, descending the ladder and coming forward.

The woman looked disappointed, but pulling her fringed shawl tightly around her shoulders as if gathering in the strength that was escaping like heat, she said, "I am going to marry your husband."

Vienna opened the screen door and motioned for the woman to enter.

"If you have come all this way for my blessings, that was needlessly sentimental," Vienna responded, dropping herself carefully into an armchair with a broken spring.

The woman sat on the absolute edge of the sofa, too proud to accept more hospitality than the rim she balanced on and too tired to eschew it altogether.

"I have come to kill you."

Only Vienna's eyes registered surprise. Her posture remained placid as she leaned back.

"If you really think that's necessary, but it strikes me as melodramatic and in rather poor taste as a prelude to your impending nuptials," she said in the same wry tone she had used to respond to the threats her children had brought to her of refusing to eat or never talking to the other again.

But her guest was in no mood for irony. Her lip curled up as she spat out her angry response. "Don't try smart words on me. I have heard them all; for thirteen years I have heard excuses and shit." She said the last word, pronouncing it "*chit*," with such vehemence a bead of spittle flew from her lips.

Vienna's eyebrows arched. "I'm not following. From whom have you heard these smart words? Surely not from me."

"From Willard Daniels, who got them from you."

"I would like to think he had been improving himself lo these many years, but I'm afraid I can't claim any credit. You see, I haven't heard from him since September sixth, 1928. Not directly, at any rate, for fifteen years."

"No," the woman shouted, her accent thickening with rage,

"that is lies. He has asked you for a divorce to marry me a thousand times and now I take actions myself."

Vienna laughed. "I am terribly sorry about this, but I repeat, I haven't heard from Willard since the day I shot at him and grazed his shoulder."

"Stop or I cut you now," the woman said furiously. "The shoulder was from the war."

"Willard was nineteen when World War One ended without him. As far as I know he never had any regrets about the way it worked out."

The woman looked around desperately, her face such a battlefield of competing emotion that Vienna was moved.

"As for divorce," she continued, "at one time I thought of initiating proceedings myself, but I didn't and don't know where Willard is, and the issue became moot before I had a chance to pursue it. I, however, have stayed rooted here, my toes in the ground and an easy mark for any attempt of Willard's to alter the status quo. I assure you the only emotion that binds us together at this point is inertia. I'll sign him away to you gladly, if that is what you want."

The woman looked confused and hurt, her eyes had the cringing look of a threatened animal torn between flight or fight. She chose the truculence of injured pride.

"Your house is worn out and shitty. In Texas we have a gold clock and new furniture and a modern kitchen," she bragged in a childish lilt.

"How lovely for you. Congratulations."

"This rug," the woman said, contemptuously eyeing the threadbare Persian carpet at her feet, "should be throwed in the garbage. I would not let my dog sleep on something as old and ugly."

Vienna was growing annoyed and impatient. She stood up and clasped her hands with an air of dismissal.

"I am actually quite fond of that Harisse rug, and I don't

think I could bring myself to part with it. On the other hand, my husband, and that is the matter you come about, is more than expendable. I have already offered to sign a divorce agreement. You can speak to Mr. Woodruff in Winsville about drawing up the appropriate papers if you like. Other than that, I'm not sure how I can help you and I am a little busy this afternoon."

The woman stayed seated on the rim of the couch. She kept her eyes on the disreputable rug and showed no inclination to move. Trying another tack, Vienna said, "If you would like to rest for a while, please do. You have come a long way and you are welcome to help yourself to whatever appeals to you in the kitchen. It is not modern, but I'm sure you can overlook its antiquated decor and lack of linoleum in favor of its proximity. If you are thirsty, there is a variety of refreshments in the icebox, and you'll find fresh mint in a glass on the table. I will be out on the porch."

The woman raised her sullen eyes to watch Vienna leave and then she slowly unpinned her heavy coil of hair, blue-black as a crow's plumage, swung her legs up on the couch and stretched out prone, not bothering to take off her scuffed patent-leather shoes, noticing with a smile as she tipped back her head the large crack that ran like a scar across the ceiling. She fell asleep almost instantly and never heard Willa's sobs from the landing of the stairs, where she had crouched behind the bars of the rail like a prisoner, overhearing the entire conversation.

ADDISON WAS LEANING back against a piece of machinery, talking to three of the hands his father hired to help with the orchard, his body liquid with confidence and sunned relaxation. The men's shirts had dark oily stains under their armpits and their hair was slick with sweat, and they were laughing at something Addison had said when Willa appeared like a dervish.

Her face, distorted by the swelling of a prolonged cry, had lost some of its fragility, and she pulled his arm roughly as she took him out of earshot of the men.

"What's up with you, being so rude to the boys? You didn't even say hello."

"I've had a huge fight with Vienna," she said hoarsely, her voice uneven and ragged. "Everything I knew has been a lie. My father's still alive somewhere in Texas. He's been living all these years with some tarty Mexican woman and he never even saw Elliott once. I'm going to get his address from Mr. Woodruff and then I'm leaving on the 7:08 freight train. Are you coming with me?"

"Yes, of course I am, but why so sudden? Why don't we plan it out? You aim to find your father, is that it?"

"I don't relish the notion of spending another night at The Heights, that's why. That Mexican woman was still hanging around like a stray dog, eating peaches from a can out back of the house last I saw, and she took a nap on our couch. And even if she goes this minute I can't stay. Don't you understand? All those years, the stories and letters, it was all false. My whole life. Everything Elliott and I shared, the way he worried about sandstorms and frostbite and amnesia keeping our daddy somewhere far away. I don't know exactly where we should go. I'm not sure I want to see him at all, but I'm getting the address anyway. Meet me up at the tunnel where the tracks cross at seven. We can hop the boxcars and see where we get. And bring as much money as you've got. And Addison, if you're not there, I'm going without you. I'll understand that you turned yellow and all those lovely words were just that."

Addison pulled his pants up and tucked in his shirt, feeling a combination of fear and manliness stir him, making his chest lift to accommodate the excited beat of his heart. He wondered if this was the feeling boys had going into battle. It almost seemed sexy and he wanted to touch her breasts, but her face warned him not to.

"Willa, sweetheart, you know I'll be there. Let me pack a few things and write my father a letter. I don't want him to feel bad about my leaving so suddenly and there are things I've never told him." Addison thought of how his father's eyes crinkled kindly, giving his craggy face an unexpected warmth. "I don't want to go without saying a real good-bye but you know how long it takes me to write anything decent."

Willa kept looking at him in a penetrating way he had never seen before and Addison was scared, but, as he had hoped, it only improved the kiss he gave her before she ran back into the woods shouting, "Seven o'clock. Don't be late."

28

■

ATER THERE WERE a lot of versions of how the fire started. Some said the Mexican woman started it out of green liver jealousy before she left. Some said Willa did it for spite in adolescent anger gone awry. Some even suggested that Vienna did it herself, in despair. And of course, there were a few who said it was an accident—with the wind and the paper lanterns and the old cloth wrapped around the columns, a tipped candle was all it took.

Addison was on page three of his letter, going slowly in an effort to write legibly, when he heard the shouts of his father and the hired hands, as they ran with pails toward The Heights. From the west window in his father's room he could see the sky filling with smoke and birds, hundreds of birds, taking flight in a dark swarm across the twilight. He pulled his shoes on without lacing them, grabbed his rucksack, and ran too. By the time he got to The Heights the porch was ablaze, throwing off a chafing heat that had the volunteer firemen moving the truck into position working without their shirts, their faces red and glowing in the satanic light, their bodies oiled and glistening in the miasma of heat that swam in the night's flickering brightness like a visible roar, louder than an open forge.

Cars were pulling up on the lawn as if it were the fair-grounds, discharging people who came to help or just to watch the blue tendrils of flames tongue the windowframes where the glass had burst, or to hear the bellowing of the fire compete with the continuous clang of church bells. Clem Morgan had gone inside with two firemen and found the dog in an upstairs bedroom, hysterical, white foam spattered on his fur and dripping from his jaws, shaking and whimpering. When Clem carried out the dog in his arms, the spectators cheered and whistled and banged empty pails with the heels of their hands. Addison stood in front of Henshaw in the line of men his father headed, passing buckets from a slow spigot at the barn; by the time the porch caved in, he had worked up blood blisters on all the fingers of his right hand.

Two more fire trucks arrived from Bantanburg and the volunteers from Walker's Junction were said to be on their way. Vienna had been brought out when the fire had first been sighted, and she lay covered with a blanket, someone's jacket folded for a pillow beneath her head, while the ambulance made its way from Bantanburg. But whoever had been left to watch her, and there was argument about that later, was paying less attention to the fainted woman than to the spectacle of the splintering showers of falling beams, the explosion of panes, the black smoke pouring from windowframes in dense columns, covering the men and lawn and cars in thick silky soot when the currents shifted to a downdraft, and, most mes-merizing of all, the vicious feathery tentacles of flame claiming increasing possession of The Heights in a wide, greedy embrace, climbing upward with the sprawling reach of twisted ropes of wisteria, spraying dark bunched sparks more brilliant than any blossoms.

No one saw Vienna go back into the house from the kitchen entrance. Sophronius Moody, who was taking a rest from the water line, mopping the sweat from his neck and hands with a soiled hankie, was the first to spot her through an upstairs window. Pointing out the ghostly figure to the nearest fireman, he stood paralyzed, unable to move out of the way of men dragging a mattress from the back of a truck toward the house. He was wailing loudly and several men rebuked him to act like an adult and to get out of the goddamn way.

Voices joined together to yell "jump" when she appeared on the sloping roof, her duster flaming on her back like furious wings, a fiery angel clutching a sheaf of papers to her breast, frozen for a moment high above them so that all who looked would remember it, and then she threw the bundle of papers out toward the safety of the lawn, but they lifted on the hot currents of air and took flight like a flock of swallows beating upward, singed wings fluttering wildly into their cremation.

The crowd clamored for her to jump like an eager audience at a carnival stomping for the next acrobat to dive, the voices urgent and strained, and for a blink of an eye it seemed she flew.

There was a thud as she hit a corner of the mattress, a dull sound like a bag of feed dropped from a storage loft. A man ran up and threw himself and his rain slicker over her burning clothes, rolling her like a log into the center of the mattress; Dr. Barstow fell on his knees beside her and John Aimes helped lift the arm twisted unnaturally behind her. As the ambulance officers slid Vienna onto their stretcher, she looked up at the men crowding over her, as if searching in panic for a particular face. Her voice was a broken croak with an interrogative lift that could be interpreted in many ways. Mr. Aimes heard her say, "John Aimes." Dr. Barstow was confident she had said "James," and both men were gratified by the belief that her last words were the call for which they had been waiting for so many years.

As Vienna was being loaded into the ambulance, Addison heard a husky voice ask where the daughter was, and as he wiped the soot from the face of his watch, his shoulders heaved in the first of a series of wrenching silent convulsions, ripping soul from marrow, gutting and eviscerating, twisting his mouth in a contortion of excruciating, empty martyrdom. He had seen the iconography of hell, more beautiful and brutal and fearsome even than the infinitesimal visions illuminated by the Limbourg brothers and the Master of Catherine of Cleves, copied laboriously from glossy facsimiles by Willa's painstaking untrembling hand, and he knew that Vienna had been right. He had forfeited to the Daniels a spirit he could feel dying inside him, exiting through pores wide and blackened from the night's feverish work.

Clem Morgan sat out on the hood of his automobile all night, guarding the charred rubble and half-standing shell from adventurous souvenir-seekers and disaster opportunists. John Aimes sent his last anonymous telegram to Sister, and Addison, on receiving confirmation that Vienna was dead, took five sacks of lime from his father's shed and using the rickety wheelbarrow in which Vienna had carted her instruments from tree to tree, he wrote across the crackled, heat-withered field, dry as parchment and dark as a blanket of locusts, his giant cry like the S.O.S. of downed pilots, in letters too large to be understood from the ground, the fertile white words composing an eerie graffiti for the gods in the incandescence of calcium oxide: DUCKY LIVES.

Pacing out the ruined remains beside Mr. Aimes, Sister had begun to say, "Frankly . . ." when Mr. Aimes cut her off with machete swiftness, "No, Sister, I swear for all these years you've prefaced every niggling swipe at your family with that word, as if it were your God-given obligation to unburden yourself to the world, no matter how unkind or expensive the cost of your candor, and I'm plain sick and tired of it. It was her house all along, ask Mr. Woodruff. You had as much right as a hobo to take up residence when it pleased you, but she wouldn't ever have told you that, because she wouldn't. I'd say you've been frank enough. Now just be quiet."

And so she was, all through the service that buried Vienna beside Elliott, under the faded and windtorn paper birds, beneath the storm-tangled buttons that tattered the trees, half shed with time, beside the unprecedented turnout of Winsville's township from both sides of Solomon's Road, black and white, who maintained an awed silence, the hush of disbelief and devastation, as if they had received the punishment Reverend Will had foretold. Like chastened children they would have to reckon thereafter with a diminishment in their life, impoverished by the loss of what they had astigmatically refused to acknowledge was the foil by which they defined themselves, the peripheral ends of the spectrum that combined to create the complex landscape inhabited by the Daniels in the vicissitudes of The Heights, making Winsville's dreams, as they floated up into the night air like wisps of evaporating steam, more intricate and artful.

THAT WAS HOW the story was told, over and over, as if repetition would purge it of its sting. In the autumn, Mr. Aimes put down the horse and adopted the dog, sole survivor of the last days of the Daniels' careless reign. Addison, receiving no reply to the telegrams he sent to Texas and Detroit, waited patiently for Willa to return, as the Daniels always had, to Winsville.

It wasn't hard, actually, for they had invested Addison with their shadows, which he bore faithfully within him. In the wind, rushing down the rows of corn or stirring the wheat and ripe alfalfa, he heard Vienna's comforting "hush now, hush";

the shivering aspens were full of Willa's whispery confessions, and turning a bend on a narrow lane, the light pooling around him through a green clot of trees infused him with Elliott's promise of angelic possibilities, the divine calculus of invisible music he could hear with his eyes closed. Their presence was continually revealed in momentary magic: a flash of wings, the spark of dust or trace of scent, returning him to the lost landscape of his heart, buried beneath the foliage of revision and regret. In the infallible alchemy of metaphor and imagination, sometimes the smell of rain is enough.

ACKNOWLEDGMENTS

My thanks to the following people: Susanna Porter, Lisa Bankoff, Thomas Guinzburg, Kate Guinzburg, Eden Collinsworth, Howard and William Adams, Ken Skalski, and Geraldine and Joseph Mindell.

ABOUT THE AUTHOR

KATHERINE MOSBY, a poet, teaches writing courses at Co-
lumbia and N.Y.U., and conducts poetry workshops in New
York public schools. She lives in New York City.

ABOUT THE TYPE

This book was set in Electra, a typeface designed for Lino-
type by W. A. Dwiggins, the renowned type designer
(1880–1956). Electra is a fluid typeface, avoiding the con-
trasts of thick and thin strokes that are prevalent in most
modern typefaces.